ab initio

Page intentionally left blank

ab initio

a novel

by Jacob Terracina

Book Cover by Jason Gurley (jgbookdesign.com)

Illustrations by Jacob Terracina

Published by Arnerld Books

1st edition 2025

This book is dedicated. Way to be, book.

Page unintentionally left blank

Contents

THE CITIZENS TECHNOLOGY REFORMATION
ORGANIZATION

v.

JINHWA

CHAPTER 1
TRIAL DAY 1.0 - JIVANTA

"... Let's get the exposition out of the way."

Jivanta Puri pivoted to face the panel of Intercontinental High Court Justices. The world's tribunal, all robed in black. It took a nontrivial amount of effort on her part *not* to see them as a fleet of geriatric grim reapers. Who better than this troupe of nonagenarians wheeled in from hospice to decide the fate of what *could* be considered (if you took the defendant's absurd claims at face value) the biggest technological marvel since the nuclear bomb? 'Nuclear bomb' certainly wasn't the right comparison, she thought to herself. Too leading.

"As many of you may recall from your primary school chemistry classes, atomic and molecular interactions follow well-defined mathematical rules. These rules are simple enough that even non-PhDs like you and me can follow along. At least, until you get to the quantum level."

Some of the less-restrained talking heads in the media were already calling this the trial of the century. A phrase that got thrown around every three years or so, sure, but the truth was that this one felt different. Bigger than any case she had represented in her illustrious career. Illustrious? Someone's feeling themselves today, she mused.

Eight months earlier, the unlikable CEO of a no-name tech company had stood stiffly behind a podium and announced to the world the creation of an artificial intelligence so impossibly advanced that it deserved all the protections typically reserved for living, breathing humans.

Even by tech executive standards, it was a whopper of a claim. Such a whopper, in fact, that the governing bodies across the Greater UN tied themselves into knots deciding which committee of which branch of which division of which agency from which country would be responsible for exposing the obvious lie. Then, to Jivanta's surprise, a challenge issued against the tech company by a fringe anti-science group was rushed up the steps of the High Court. Even more surprisingly, her name was on the docket to represent the prosecution.

In the weeks leading up to trial, Jivanta rebuilt the plaintiff's challenge from the ground up. What began as an amateurish and scattershot rebuke of technology (and progress at large) with far more Bible quotes than legalese, she reconstituted into a nuanced and precedentially sound demand for evidence. Her client's instructions were clear: convince the judicial panel that a piece of machinery—no matter how complex—could not be considered *human*.

"The most basic, fundamental blueprints that describe an atom's activity are known as 'first principles'. First principles deal in the strange world of quantum mechanics. There are many ways to dumb down these first-principles rules, using a variety of assumptions and approximations to simplify the math. These assumptions drag the equations from the quantum world to the more familiar, ball-and-spring, meat-and-potatoes, Newtonian world in which we live. These assumptions make the math more manageable, but that simplification comes with a great cost: *accuracy.*"

She knew the defendants would have to dive deep into the quantum mechanical and mathematical theory of their invention. It was the wobbly pillar on which their entire argument stood. They wouldn't go there willingly, but she'd give them little choice. And she was counting on the panel being glassy-eyed and full-bladdered by the time the defense called their first technical witness.

Still, she needed to set the context. "When computers burst onto the scene in the middle of the last century, first-principles calculations could be employed to simulate only the simplest of interactions. Models of a few atoms here interacting with a few atoms there, over a simulated timescale of tiny fractions of a second. The mathematical load, and therefore the computational processing time required for first-principles simulations, does not scale linearly, but rather *exponentially* with the number of particles in the system. Doubling the atoms in the model doesn't double the computational time. It increases it by roughly a factor of ten." She eyed each judge in turn to keep their minds from straying too far outside the courtroom. "So. Going from two atoms to a measly one thousand would require *10 billion* times more processing power. Now, keep in mind that a single strand of DNA contains over 200 billion atoms. The human body contains about 8 octillion atoms. That's an eight with *twenty-seven zeros.*"

She paused a moment for emphasis.

"Computational power grew year over year. Those of you of a certain age may remember hearing of Moore's Law in your computer history lessons. Moore's Law stated that transistor density, which roughly translates to processing speed, would double every two years or so. This was certainly more of an astute observation than a 'law'." She hesitated, hoping for the subtext—*engineers don't make laws*—to filter through the hearing aids of her audience. "Misnomers aside, it held true for decades."

She had played out every argument in her head, organizing immense thought webs tracing potential avenues to victory. Of course, there was no way to know with certainty which direction the defense would take, but she could narrow down the possible paths and assign a probability to the arguments using what she knew about the parties involved. A semi-empirical approach to the inherent uncertainty of the courtroom, she joked to herself at the time.

"At that rate, doubling every twenty-four months, surely processors were soon catching up with the mathematical load required to run first-principles simulations of meaningfully complex chemical systems, right?" She took a long, slow breath to give the slower minds of the panel a chance to catch up. "Well, of course not. Not even close.

"Drug discovery, the *one* field in which computational chemistry had managed to make any industry headway, was still heavily utilizing all manner of assumptions and approximations in order to simulate biologically relevant components. Every molecular sim was built with a real murderer's row of hacks, shortcuts, and guesstimations."

A man in the back row yawned and Jivanta bristled. Fucking hell. If the attention of the public onlookers was waning, the panel was already lost. Fuck her for trying to summarize the entire history of the field and to provide the necessary context for the entire *fucking* argument... She took a long breath in and let it out through her nose, picturing the yawning man's head on a spike, then one more breath (and one more imagined spike) for good measure. Time to score a few easy points.

"The thing is, just because you can approximate an American football with a six-sided featureless cube—or, while we're at it, why not a volumeless point mass—doesn't mean your approximated model will *behave* like a football. Once you strip away the bumps and the stitches, does it still act like a football? How about when you change the shape? Or replace the air inside and outside with something less... mathematically complex? You get the idea. These simplifications don't just make the simulation less computationally demanding. They fundamentally change the essence of the problem, and with it, change the outcome. Chopping Schrodinger's equations into classical mechanics will help you predict drug configurations, in the same way that heaving a perfectly featureless cube in a vacuum will teach you how to throw a tight spiral. *Poorly.*"

Two birds, one stone. Justice Zhang was a sucker for easily digestible analogies, and Jivanta had heard through her vast grapevine of clerks and associates that Chebychev spent several hours a week reviewing game footage from his collegiate football days (presumably through the base of a whiskey tumbler). In her periphery, she saw them both sit up taller behind the bench, tuning in for perhaps the first time since their aides helped them get dressed this morning.

"Over time, computational chemistry industrial groups grew smaller and smaller as their predictive models were consistently outpaced by laboratory rapid assays. Then came the University of Colorado debacle. In the 40s, all eyes were pointed just down the road, at UC-Boulder, as they announced the most ambitious first-principles simulation to date. Using the most state-of-the-art classical computers, they sought to model the interaction of a single protein with a small-molecule agglomeration inhibitor over a simulated timescale of just under two minutes. It was touted as the key to finally zeroing in on a preventative Alzheimer's therapeutic. Skeptics saw this as a Hail Mary to re-establish relevance for the dying field, and perhaps it would work. The simulation took three and a half years to crunch. Five million dollars' worth of graphical processing units, plus another million in energy costs, running at full capacity for 43 months. In those three years, public interest grew to a fever pitch. Then, on the day the simulation was completed..."

Another weighty pause.

"Nothing."

The panel members would have been in their seventies at the time of the non-announcement, bright-eyed and bushy-tailed compared to their current selves, and surely at least one of them had gotten their hopes up for a senility-free future. Jivanta stole a glance at Justice Hoffer. There were whispers that Hoffer's hereditary analysis found her to be at risk for cognitive decline, and that she'd buried the analysis (and the physician who'd conducted the test) under the steps of the courthouse. Ridiculous, to be sure, but most rumors contain nuggets of truth.

"We later learned, through leaked intranet messages, that a misplaced minus sign positioned the protein facing away from the inhibitor instead of toward it, and during those three years of calculations, while the world waited with bated breath, the protein never reoriented itself. It was stuck, like a turtle on its back, in what is known as a local minimum energy state. That is to say, it was comfortable right where it was, and the protein-inhibitor interaction was so dependent on the starting conditions, so dependent on the two components facing each other in just such a way, that nothing ever *happened*. Public enthusiasm and funding plummeted. Research ground to a halt as grants were pulled. Pharmaceutical conglomerates went as far as to sue their academic collaborators for overpromising the capabilities of their comp chem. In fact, some of those cases made it all the way *here*, where the panel overwhelmingly sided with the prosecution. This appeared to nail the coffin shut for the long-overhyped field of computational chemistry."

Looking over at the bench to her left, she saw the defendants whispering to one another and she knew she was getting under their skin. Each minor 'error' she made in her representation of quantum theory and the history of the field would drive them further into the losing corner. "Long-overhyped" was a fairly transparent barb, but one that would hopefully slip by unnoticed by all but the opposing team. Frustrating the technical witnesses into correcting the particulars of her opening statement would only serve to waste their valuable time and paint them as rigid pedants in the eyes of the panel, dehumanizing them and humanizing herself in the process.

"Twelve years passed. Comp chem was still dead and buried. The Moore's Law curve, which had been gradually flattening and stagnating since the turn of century, had finally plateaued. For the first time, new computers weren't measurably better than last season's model. Then SenZero unveiled QuNet—the world's first commercial quantum computing system. QuNet didn't just introduce a new inflection point in the curve of Moore's Law. It broke the curve entirely. Overnight, life was breathed back into all manner of industry efforts that had been butting up against the limitations of classical computers. Encryption advanced by leaps and bounds. Traditional AI, whose strength lies in the volumes of data consumed and the speed with which the dataset is categorized, made notable strides. With the sudden windfall of QuNet's processing advancements, academics reexamined the potential of first-principles chemical simulations. And you know what they found?"

Jivanta found the yawning man in the back of the room and stared right through him. She waited for him to break eye contact before she continued. It didn't take long. "Dead ends. Walls. The same walls met by classical computers were still there. Just as tall and just as strong. Remember, the processing load scales *exponentially* with the size of the simulation. Even with the thousand-fold increase in processing power offered by quantum computers, first-principles simulations of systems containing anything more than a few proteins still were a complete nonstarter."

She was going on longer than she'd originally planned, but that was all part of the game. She kept her tone and her content flexible to navigate the plethora of unknowns that invariably influenced the High Court's most important indicator: The Mood of the Room. Rigidity could sink even the sturdiest of cases. An argument, and those responsible for making the argument, needed a certain degree of elasticity. It was a hard-earned skill, and one in which she took a measure of pride.

"Keeping in mind the claims of the defendant, which I won't waste time repeating now, consider this: Trying to create a truly first-principles simulation of a single bacterium—the smallest, simplest life-form known to man—using the most advanced classical computer network, has been compared to standing on Earth, holding a shovel, looking at Mars, and attempting to move it." She shared Zhang's enthusiasm for analogies. She imagined all the journos frantically searching for the origins of the comparison, and they'd find nothing because Jivanta had made it up about twenty minutes earlier. "QuNet leaves classical systems in the dust. Really, it's no contest. It'll take your shovel and replace it with a bulldozer and a whole team of excavators. But the result is the same. The red planet doesn't move a centimeter."

The table was set—set in a way that dared them to reach over and straighten out the silverware. And no one at the table would ever notice that her napkin concealed a carving knife.

CHAPTER 2
8 YEARS EARLIER - RAZA

It wasn't uncommon to interview for a tech job without knowing too much about the position, or the company as a whole for that matter. Everything in the sector was hyper-proprietary. Even the most mundane of company secrets would be squirreled away in the paranoid minds of C-level executives, and underlings would be so siloed into their discrete tasks that they often wouldn't even know what the company ultimately *did*. Discretion by discretization. Raza had signed half a dozen non-disclosure agreements just to get in the door of his last job. There, he'd coded with his three-person team 60 hours a week for 6 months before he learned that the company was just a contract upward-conversion firm; other companies would hire them to take their dusty old software, ancient code that had been optimized decades ago to operate on classical comp systems, and they'd modify the underlying algorithms to be better suited for QuNet. Cool? At least it wasn't shady military shit.

A few gigs back he'd learned that his code was bound for AI in a next-gen ballistic missile program. He left that day and never looked back. It marked him as Unreliable with a capital "U" in the tech workforce database, a black mark on his permanent record, but... a man's gotta have a code, right? That's what Aunt Roo always said, anyway. His big walkout was ages ago, but that scarlet letter was an evergreen target on his back, marking him as easy prey every time a company needed to cut costs. Man. That metaphor was a hot mess. Even the colors were inconsistent, he thought. Where was he? Oh right, the evergreen/scarlet/black mark. The colors of the pan-African flag, like his mom's earrings. Jesus, his new meds were making him even more scatterbrained than usual. Forget it.

He caught the train into the city to grab some dinner before heading home. Aunt Roo told him to come back with either dim sum or a job, or not to come home at all. He didn't have the job, at least not yet, so dim sum it was. On the ride in, he began to replay that morning's interview in his head. It was a standard cattle call interview at a stealth mode startup called *jinhwa*. That lower-case 'j' sure was pretentious. As far as interviews go, it wasn't so bad, though they spent more time than he was comfortable with discussing his graduate work in evolutionary biology. What was there to say? He spent five years chasing his passion, only to find that a doctorate in ev bio was, in the eyes of employers, slightly less valuable than the paper on which the degree was printed. At least a blank sheet of paper had the potential to become something else. He'd learned the hard way that just because he found a subject interesting didn't mean he could expect that anyone would pay him to study it. So, he enrolled in government Codeforce training and resigned himself to the tried-and-true career path of a worker bee.

He hadn't said all that out loud, obviously. He had painted his graduate work as a quirky but perfectly innocuous bit of character detail, something that would help him stand out (but not so far out as to be considered a liability). After that, they moved on to standard code competency talk. Plenty of gotchas and riddles and on-the-spot puzzles, as he had come to expect for all these "change the world" tech company contract gigs, but at this point he was familiar with the tricks of the trade. He said all the right stuff, played up his desire to leave a lasting impact on humanity, played down his desire to maintain a life outside of the office, and looked Dr. Whatshername in the eye when the situation called for eye contact.

Dammit, what *was* her name? He swore he had a hole in the "people's names" voxel of his brain. He could slap on the veneer of an eager and competent worker for the three hours of interview time required to land the occasional gig, but it was the ol' name hole that kept him from climbing the ladder. You had to see a coworker's face and be able to say,

"Hey Melvin, how's Gormpo?" at the drop of a hat if you ever wanted a management position. Christ, *Gormpo?* How can you be so bad with names you can't come up with *two* examples, he thought. Gormpo. Sounds like a racist cartoon character from the 1920s. For a time, he had kept a visual rolodex open on his AR-Lens, but it was difficult to effectively navigate without the other party noticing. And the Lens tended to dry out his eyes. He blinked in response to the memory of the dryness. What was he thinking about? Right, the job.

It was time to play the waiting game. These tech companies tended to take their sweet ass time when it came to filling positions. Ass time. He'd once gone 11 months between first and second round interviews. The second-round interviewer was the same person as the first-round interviewer. She didn't remember him.

The train was even more crowded than usual, and he was getting pressed on all sides by sweaty strangers. Sweaty strangers with their own sweaty stories and sweaty lives. His ex had once called him a "solipsistic shit-for-brains". Ever since, he'd made a point of internally acknowledging other people's distinct existences. He noted the distinctly unkempt and smelly existence of the old woman to his right, the distinctly youthful and obnoxious existence of the tween to his left gabbing loudly into their Lens, the distinctly enormous existence of the giant man in the giant suit looming over him. It was a bizarre mental exercise, but it'd become part of his routine. He thought he felt one of the sweaty strangers' sweaty hands fishing for his pocket, so he reached his hand back to slap it away and make sure his belongings were still in place. It wasn't like he had anything worth taking. QuNet encryption and biometrics had advanced so much in the last decade that phone theft was exceedingly rare. No one on the dark market would shell out for a piece of virtually inaccessible hardware. Regardless, he pulled his SenZ out to move it to his front pocket just in case. Better safe than sorry, Aunt Roo would say.

As he moved the device, he noticed a new message waiting and pulled it up. From Stephanie Seong-Cooper, VP of Operations at *jinhwa* with a lower-case j. Whatshername? *That's* her name, he thought. That particular thought may have come out of his mouth, judging by the looks people were giving him. He skimmed the formalities and got to the meaty bit.

"We're excited to extend an offer letter for this position..."

Was this happening? He must've done something right in that interview. What could the job entail that hiring moved so quickly?

"... starting this Sunday."

Sunday? THIS Sunday? Could he have misread that? He started over and read the whole thing more carefully. The words didn't change. Then, at the bottom, "Start date is non-negotiable". Okay, damn, sorry for questioning you, Steph. Was this real? He had a million questions but set them aside so he could text Aunt Roo. "Dim sum is on me tonight."

~ ~ ~

A month passed without incident. For all the rush to get him in the door, Raza wasn't being asked to do anything that any other semi-competent coder couldn't handle. If there were pressing deadlines or looming targets, they weren't reflected in the work he was given. He was part of a two-person team running generic efficacy tests on a flow of growth models being passed down the pipeline from the second floor. Or the *Second Floor*, capitalized, as it was referred to with reverence by his fellow First Floorers. There must be spare capital letters to throw around, what with all the capitalization they're saving with *jinhwa*, he mused. His partner, Mei, was quiet, terse, and a frustratingly sharp coder. That sharpness was reflected in her appearance. Her cheekbones, chin, and nose were razor edges between the crystalline facets that shaped her face. She usually wore a suit jacket with shoulders that formed perfect right angles and her jet-black hair appeared to have been cropped by a high-precision laser cutter. Four weeks together and that was all he knew about her. She'd flag his mistakes as quickly as he could turn them out, and she rarely spoke except to tell him to check his workchat. Workchat was for communication. Speaking was apparently just an audio alert signal for the chat.

The First Floor / Second Floor model was standard practice these days; a physical barrier delineating those *in the know* (ITK) from those *in the dark* (ITD). jinhwa (which was spelled with a lowercase 'j' even if it was the start of a sentence; he had double-checked with Mei—through the workchat, naturally) seemed to take that separation of powers very seriously. Security at the front door wasn't light by any means, but security at the elevator made the front door barriers look like an afterthought.

It was usually around this time, after onboarding and settling in for a bit, that his curiosity would get the best of him and he'd begin poking around for clues pointing to the company's purpose. He eyed the comings and goings at the elevator. From what he could tell, that's where all the urgency lie. Wait. Is it lie or lay? Are they both wrong? No way to know. Nobody knows. It's a known unknown. Mei probably knows. He'd ask but she might defenestrate him through that Johari Window. Johari with a capital 'J'. Dammit, *focus*. Whatever was happening upstairs must have led to the immediacy of his hiring. Why that immediacy evaporated once he arrived to work that first non-negotiable Sunday, he could only guess. Maybe they solved whatever problem they rush-hired him to fix and were only keeping him around for... other reasons? That didn't check out. Market churn was brutal, and companies didn't keep employees around if they weren't obviously and transparently adding more value than they cost to employ. So. Maybe the immediacy didn't evaporate after all. It was still there, impatiently tapping its foot and waiting for him on the Second Floor.

~ ~ ~

Three months into his tenure, Raza's curiosity grew into restlessness. Couldn't he just ask? Surely he could find at least a vague set of company aims. Even just a boilerplate mission statement. His workchat pinged. New message from Mei. *raz - stop fidgeting - it's distracting.*

~ ~ ~

Six months in and his restlessness transmuted into suspicion. He'd come to believe that at least some portion of the work being passed to him was dummy code, purposely designed to misdirect the engineering pawns and keep them removed from the goings-on upstairs. Though the models varied wildly, there were subtle but distinct signatures separating what he came to think of as "true code" from the chaff. Subtle as the 'b' in 'subtle'. Has 'subtle' always been spelled that way? That couldn't possibly be right. He shook his head to dislodge the distracting thought. Time to test the hypothesis. He stayed late, waiting for Mei to log out for the evening. She workchatted him a warning not to make any messes for her to clean up. He closed the message and immediately dropped a bug into the dummy code.

~ ~ ~

Eight months in, suspicion evolved into paranoia. For all he knew, Raza was back coding for military weaponry all over again. Or worse. What could be worse than smart missiles? He thought about it, and didn't like the possibilities. What were the odds that jinhwa was worse than the AI ICBM company? If you histogrammed all of the tech gigs with some metric for moral bankruptcy on the x-axis, surely the weapon-mongers were to the extreme right of the bell curve, right? But what's a good metric for a company's shittiness? It can't just be a count of lives *taken*, or even *potentially* taken, because a product can be plenty damaging without a clear body count. Maybe it's a summation of individual lives *worsened* (N^i_{LW}) multiplied by the degree to which it was worsened (W^i), where W is a 0 to 1 score of how much worse things got for the individual in question thanks to the company in question.

W=0, no impact.

W=0.5, heavy physical and/or psychological damage.

W=1, they'd be alive if not for said company.

Now, the company would argue that *improved* lives should be factored into the equation, with, say, a *negative* W value. But at that point, aren't they admitting to playing God?

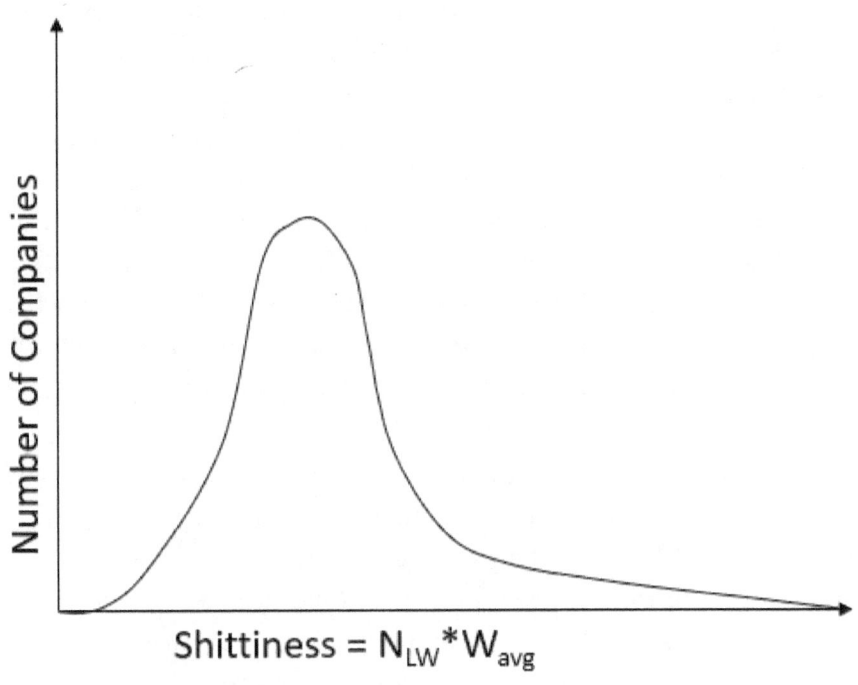

$$\text{Shittiness} = N_{LW}{}^{*}W_{avg}$$

~ ~ ~

Nine months in, a breakthrough came in the form of a pair of revelations. Revelations always come in twos. Celebrity deaths come in threes, revelations come in twos, and binary comes in ones and zeros. Some referred to binary as a dead language, but he rather liked the rigidity and certainty locked into those two discrete figures. And, as his thesis advisor once said, *nihil umquam vere moritur.* "Nothing ever truly dies," spoken in a dead language. She'd been known to slip into Latin after a few drinks. She was... how did she describe it? Grandiloquent. Pompous, but authentically and charmingly pompous. He made a mental note to message her, and promptly lost the note under a stack of other unwritten to-dos.

Back to the revelations.

Revelation Zero: The Connection. He'd been quality controlling and optimizing the Second Floor algorithms for the better part of a year.

Floor Two went to great lengths to generalize and obfuscate the code on its way down the elevator, so as to keep Floor One firmly *ITD*. Despite the care being taken to keep the wool over their eyes, patterns began to emerge and resonate in the back of his mind. The growth models were peculiar, unlike any he'd worked with since beginning his coding career, but there was a nagging familiarity to them. Sometimes inspiration strikes in an instant. In this case, inspiration must've been tapping his shoulder for the last two hundred days, and he finally decided to listen to what she had to say. The growth models looked familiar because they were a shade from his past. They were models of life. Models of biological evolution. Nothing ever truly dies.

Revelation One: The Encounter. He ran into Mei outside of work. It was disorienting, like seeing water flowing uphill. He was juggling some errands for Aunt Roo and saw her sitting alone in the food court. She was on her SenZ and didn't notice him. He could just slip by and avoid the awkward pleasantries. His own phone pinged. New workchat message from Mei. *i ordered too much chow fun - quit leering and help me finish my lunch.*

Food Court Mei certainly *looked* like Coworker Mei, a familiar rigid assembly of perfectly stacked polygons, but was otherwise unrecognizable. She made eye contact. The hard, practiced eye contact of someone for whom socialization was a learned behavior, but eye contact nonetheless. She spoke unprompted. She asked questions and actively listened. They chatted about trivial things. She razzed him about a bug he'd let slip into the codestream a few months back. He tensed. She noticed, and changed the subject. "It's bizarre," she said, "working shoulder-to-shoulder with someone for nearly a year before asking them about themselves, but, well..." She gave a non-committal 'what-are-ya-gonna-do' shrug. "Anyway, what's your story? Are you a native Texan, or are you just another techie moving here to jack up my rent?"

"I've been in Dallas long enough to be able to complain about the influx of techies."

"I'll be the judge of that."

16

A joke? A threat? Too early to tell. Food Court Mei (FCM) was something new. New wasn't always bad, but he had his guard up. Better safe than sorry.

"You still in there? I asked where you moved *from*, but you were lost on one of your brain rides."

"Sorry, I was... my what?"

"Brain rides. You know, when your eyes go out of focus and you're a bona fide space-cadet for 3 to 10 seconds."

"Oh, right. I've got a bit of an attention issue, and I've been on these meds that crank it up to eleven."

"Eleven what?"

"Uh, hmmm. Good question. I don't actually know. It's something my aunt says, and I never thought to ask her."

"I'm just messing with you. So, you were about to tell me your life story."

"Right," he thought. "Well, buckle up." He was starting to get the feel of FCM. She treated conversations like a competition. Normally he hated diving into his history, but Mei had him on his heels and an emotional counterpunch might establish a more level playing field. He took aim. "I was born in San Francisco."

"Wait," she said, doing some quick mental math, "how old are you?"

"Thirty-one." He put on his most pitiable expression.

"Did your family...."

"Hold Outs." Pause for effect. "Both of them."

"Shiiiiiiiiiit". FCM sat back in her chair. "That's.... Shit."

"Couldn't've said it better myself."

Hold Outs. That's how they came to be known. Those who stayed behind and welcomed the inevitable. It'd been a generation since The Aattoq. Rising tides forced mass migrations inland around the world, but the former Silicon Valley, with water encroaching from the west and wildfires pressing in from every other direction, had perhaps the most catastrophic fall of all the Old Coast metropolises. His parents were civil engineers working on the levee project. That's how they met, as just two of seven hundred thousand people contracted to save the city. As tidal rise projections worsened, as wildfire season stretched to touch both ends of the calendar, the tech monopolies that had been congregating in the valley for decades fled inland and took the economy with them. Most of the general population packed their bags and followed suit. Levee funding left with the billionaires, but his parents, along with over twenty thousand of the levee crew, *Held Out.* They continued building up the embankment, working around the clock on a plan that Sisyphus would've generously described as a lost cause. They moved earth and piled sandbags. They routed the Bay through the valley as a stopgap against the marching fires.

As the outlook grew dimmer and smoke choked out the sun, his parents grew closer and closer. Then they had the gall to bring a child into that world.

There'd been countless thinkpieces and half a dozen big budget productions about the Hold Outs. In most iterations, it was a tragic ballad of duty and heroism in the face of impossible odds. In others, it was a tale of the helpless victims of failed government action. In some, it was a story of a brainwashed fatalist cult. As a rule, he avoided all media on the subject. Not because they were too personal for him. Kind of the opposite, really. They were too *im*personal. Each telling, whether through the lens of duty or victimhood or a death cult, robbed his parents of their agency and individuality. He never knew them. Aunt Roo had arranged for him to be taken out of the city. She didn't like to talk about it, but he'd pieced it together over the years. The fact was, his parents didn't give him up willingly. He was their beacon of hope, their promise of a tomorrow. He may have editorialized a bit, but why the hell else would you keep an infant in that environment? He was the product of hubris. A lack of foresight. A mistake. Aunt Roo and a team of social workers had to forcibly pry him from his mother's arms. They broke all contact with Roo after that. She'd taken their bright future away from them. Fourteen months later they were dead.

There was a picture of him as a baby with his parents, taken a few weeks before Aunt Roo came. He found it when he was twelve and copied it to his CloudSafe. He'd only looked at it a few times since, but every detail was hard-coded into his memory. Raza was a living stack of Punnett squares, a testimony of the genetic dominance of his mother's bright, almond-shaped eyes and skin so dark it glowed, and his dad's square head and broad shoulders. In the picture, his mom was wearing her black, red, and green earrings, and his dad was in a beige boonie hat. Baby Raza wore a filter mask playfully disguised as an orange duckbill. His parents' masks were drab and dirty. There were bags under their eyes and ash on their cheeks. Though their mouths were hidden, he could see that they were smiling.

He grinned. Why was he grinning? Mei absorbed the information and processed it, glancing away for only a moment before recovering her target-lock eye contact. "Well," she said conciliatorily, "my parents hate each other but they're very much alive, so I guess you win this round."

With that, the walls came down. They talked freely about their childhoods. Previous jobs. Favorite pasta shapes. He felt, for the first time in ages, present. Fully and truly present, without his mind leaving him to explore elsewhere. An hour passed in the blink of an eye and his thoughts only wandered once, ironically, to note how long Mei had been holding his attention. It was at exactly that moment that he would've made his second revelation, had he not gotten distracted congratulating himself for not getting distracted. Fortunately, Mei noticed the brain ride and circled back. "Is that too boring for you?"

"Huh? Oh, dammit, sorry, I'm here. I'm back. You were telling me about your academic background?"

"Lucky guess. Yeah, I was just saying that it was a strange set of stepping stones that led to me being where I am. In undergrad I studied quantum comp sci. I never felt like I had much of a calling toward or passion for it, but when QuNet launched during my last year of secondary school, it seemed like a career choice with staying power and growth potential, you know? Plus, I was good at it. Then I stumbled into a niche corner of the academic world called computational cognitive neurobiology."

19

His mouth went dry.

"It's kind of embarrassing how much I enjoyed it. It's basically the study of—"

"Algorithms and modeling of neural networks and... consciousness?"

"Hmmm. I'll ignore the 'interrupt you to finish your sentence' thing once, and only once. But that's not far off. It started as a coding project to help a friend with her neuro class, and it evolved into my graduate thesis."

His mind was reeling. Revelation Zero had convinced him that jinhwa was somehow connected to the field of evolutionary biology, though he had no good guesses as to *why*. This time inspiration struck him with a shovel.

CHAPTER 3
TRIAL DAY 1.1 - SOHVI

The opening arguments from the prosecution were thorough. Incredibly thorough. Exhaustive. Exhausting, at least. At first, the prosecutor seemed to be like any other non-scientific scoffer, thumbing her nose at the hubris of the lab coats. But every detail that was stretched, every failing that was exaggerated, every misgiving that was inflated was done so with such meticulous precision that it soon became clear what they were dealing with: a woman who knew her shit. She was never blatantly wrong; she was wrong within a margin of error that strengthened her case without being worthwhile to correct. They knew that now, because they tried, repeatedly, embarrassing themselves in the process. One of her clients swore that he saw Justice Hoffer, famous for her unflappable stoicism, bring her hand to her face to conceal an eye-roll. They retreated to recess, anxious to collect their thoughts and lick their wounds.

Vilho, the lead defense attorney, was staring into the gray early afternoon sky. Sohvi, his long-time assistant, couldn't read him, which was itself a concern. She had a growing unease that had begun long before the prosecution started sniping their legs out from under them; though now, given the morning they'd all suffered, that unease had been "turned up to eleven," as one of the jinhwa representatives would say. The leader of the defense team, her boss, mentor, and friend, had been... slipping. She first noticed his declining condition eight months ago, around the time they were hired to represent jinhwa, and she couldn't shake the feeling that the two were somehow linked.

The changes were subtle, at least at first. Even now, nobody *else* seemed to think there was cause for concern. For Sohvi, who'd been brought up in the shadow of Vilho's legendary charisma and monumental intellect, the effect was undeniable. She never minded living in the shadow. It was a protective and comforting presence. He was still a master of his craft and sharper than most, but each day his umbra grew a bit smaller, and she could feel the light inching closer to her heels. It came in waves. One moment he would be the astoundingly wise and exceedingly quick man she'd known most of her life, and the next he would just dissolve into a quiet haze.

The jinhwa crew was visibly shaken. This wasn't going as they'd hoped or planned. Sohvi cleared her throat. "Before we go back inside, remember to keep your chins up. The panel responds well to confidence. And, for the love of God, don't let Ms. Puri bait you into correcting her. She's making asses out of each and every one of you."

"You don't get to talk to us like that." Dr. Zametti, naturally. Sohvi wasn't the type to play favorites with her clients, but she did play *least* favorites and Arden Zametti was the clear frontrunner. "We're paying you, remember? Isn't it your job to keep exactly *that* from happening? What even was the strategy back there?"

She felt her pulse thumping in the back of her eyes. Strategy? How could she have formed a coherent strategy for clients who refused to let her investigate their claims? She'd warned Vilho over and over about jinhwa's troubling lack of transparency, not to mention all the baggage surrounding the death of a co-founder a few years prior, but he insisted time and time again that "all will be well". It was wildly out of character for him, generally such a data-driven decision maker, but she trusted him to the ends of the earth. She did at the time, at least. Now, she couldn't say. She darted a glance at Vilho, who was still lost in thought. Over his shoulder, she saw a familiar-looking vehicle drive slowly by. Vantablack, two-door... She shook the thought away, took a deep breath, and turned to face Arden.

"Look. That woman in there, she's not what you expected. I get it. To be honest, she's not what we expected either. We've dealt with these ultra-conservative anti-science groups plenty of times. They've all been, without fail, rigid zealots without a leg to stand on. Regressive extremists and neo-luddites armed with little more than baseless fear mongering and broad slippery slopes, for which this court has precious little patience. Clearly, we're dealing with a higher class of prosecution here." All true, but she was leaving a great deal unsaid so as not to send her clients into a frenzy. Should they be worried? Certainly. Would they perform well under additional pressure? If this morning was any indication, absolutely not.

"We'll be expected back in a few minutes," she continued. "It's going to be a tough afternoon, but we're *not* going to make it easy for her. Keep your answers brief and remember who your audience is. We are going to make it through the next few hours, and tonight we're going to talk about what I, your *lawyer*, need from you, my *clients*, in order to get you what you want. Consider what you're willing to sacrifice in order to keep your tech hidden from us, your *legally bound confidants*." Arden clenched his jaw and suddenly seemed very interested in his own shoelaces. "Consider once more what you gain by keeping the world in the dark, and ask yourselves who you're trying to protect. If you're not willing to cooperate, we're dead in the water. But if you're willing to answer these questions for us, well, this whole thing is just getting started."

CHAPTER 4
7 YEARS EARLIER - RAZA

The day after Raza was introduced to her food court alter ego, Mei wasn't at the office. Two more days slipped by and there was still no sign of her. She hadn't taken a day off since he started and now she was missing, immediately after their run-in? His grad school advisor had once called him an apopheniac, which she was quick to define before giving him the opportunity to pretend he understood. "One prone to drawing correlations where none exist." Sure, in that particular instance, he'd been chasing a meaningful connection between two variables that ultimately proved to be utterly independent. But *this* wasn't *that*. *This* and *that* were independent. Mei had disappeared and it had something to do with their conversation, he was sure of it. He pinged her workchat again with no reply. He went as far as to stake out the mall where he'd run into her a few days prior, to no avail. Each day his worry grew exponentially, and by the fourth day he'd convinced himself of the worst. He'd gotten her killed. At least fired and blacklisted from all the major databases, but probably dead. "Unidentifiable corpse" dead. "Erased from existence" dead. Sleeping with the fishes. Disappeared.

It was the morning of the fifth day. He was picturing all of the ways in which *They* (with a capital 'T' (and a silent lower-case 'j'?)) would've had her eliminated when his workchat pingpinged. Two pings? That was new. He opened the app to see an urgent-flagged message from his manager. In his nearly ten months of employment, he'd never been directly messaged by the management; all communication had passed through Mei. Now that he thought about it, he hadn't even seen his manager since his onboarding.

Not that he needed more evidence of her demise, but there it was. Mei was fish food. He shook the image out of his head for long enough to read the text. *Meeting in conference room 2C at 12:15. (Lunch provided!).* That exclamation mark was a threat, surely. 2C? Where even was 2C? 2C or not 2C. 2C is 2 Believe. He shook his head again. Focus. Wait a minute, all the conference rooms were labeled 1A through 1G. Was 1 the floor number? That would mean 2C was... oh. Oh God. *Capital Two.*

~ ~ ~

The next few hours ticked by at one quarter speed. He kept glancing at the clock and suspected that someone must've slipped a reducer in the gearbox. He wrote a variety of timer scripts (not trusting just one) and confirmed that it was reality itself and not just the hands on the clock that had slowed to a crawl. At exactly noon, he stood up too fast from his desk and had to sit back down to wait for the blood to pump its way back into his skull. He sat for another six minutes by his internal chronometer and looked back to the clock, which read 12:01. Huh. Time was slowing further as his appointment in 2C grew nearer. Maybe reality was approaching 12:15 asymptotically and his meeting would take place sometime after the universe died. He took a deep breath and stood up more slowly this time.

Walking toward the elevator, he questioned and doubted every movement he made. Was his stride too long? Were his hands swinging in sync with his legs? Christ on a cracker, had he never walked before? He watched his feet to check if his steps were at least somewhat symmetrical and was startled half to death when his painstakingly overprocessed gait carried him right into the broad chest of a security guard in front of the elevator. "Shit! Sorry, I'm, uhhh... looking for 2C?" The guard's face did nothing to betray whatever emotions were behind it, but after a lengthy stare-down he let out an exasperated sigh and held out the biomet scanner. Raza pressed his thumbs into the ports and looked into the eye of the sensor.

"First time Upstairs?"

Raza clocked the Capital 'U'. "How can you tell?" he asked, not at all casually.

"You're sweating through your shirt. And it says so on the calendar."

"Right. That makes sense."

Another security officer walked over to investigate the scene.

"This guy new?" she asked Broad Chest.

"Yes, ma'am, how could you tell?" he responded, without taking his eyes off Raza.

"Calendar notification. And the flop sweat. You okay there, kid?"

"Yes. Yes, ma'am."

"You know," she said, looking back at Broad Chest, "The last new guy who got called up to the Second Floor came back down in a body bag."

"What?" Raza squeaked.

"Exactly." Broad Chest, tapping back in. " *What.* That's the billion-dollar question. Unfortunately, we're paid *not* to ask questions."

"When you've been in the game as long as we have, you pick up on things. All I can say is... watch your back up there."

Raza felt the color drain from his skin.

Broad Chest cracked first, letting out a snort. Ma'am wasn't far behind. Soon they were both doubled over, wheezing.

"Ahhhhh, shoot fire," Ma'am said, seeing that Raza had gone rigid and pallid as a fossil. "We're sorry, sweetie. It's been a slow day."

"Make that a slow... ten months?" chimed BC.

"Look, you're a bit early." She had softened significantly, and Raza noticed the person behind the uniform and gun for the first time. She was younger than Aunt Roo, but not by much. She had graying hair that may have once been bright red, kind green eyes, and a deep pink scar running perpendicular to the deeper laugh lines around her mouth. "Clearance doesn't activate until five minutes before your meeting. Why don't you go splash some water on your face and meet us back here in a few, okay, hon? Get some air in your lungs. You're gonna be fine."

"Yes, Ma'am."

In the restroom, dabbing his face with a towel, he felt his heart rate begin to settle. The temporal anomaly appeared to be self-correcting as well; time was returning to its standard pace; now his clock was only 30% faster than the universe's clock and the variation was collapsing. He suspected the clocks would reconverge at 12:15, Universal Standard Time. Regression to the Universal Mean.

He made his way back to the security desk, where he was subjected to a rapid-fire round of milliwave scanning, prodding, patting, and light ribbing from Broad Chest and Ma'am. "One last thing and you're free to head to the elevator," she said with an impish grin.

"Yes, Ma'am?" he said, fearing the worst and hoping she didn't hear the capital 'M'.

"If your meeting goes well, you and I are gonna be seeing a lot more of each other. We'll need a secret handshake. That way if you get body-snatched or face-offed or cyborged, I'll know. Don't you come down without a handshake, okay, hon?"

"I won't let you down, Ma'am," he said, more earnestly than he intended, as he stepped into the elevator. With the doors closing, Raza exhaled and pressed '2'.

~ ~ ~

For all the mystery, the Second Floor looked remarkably unremarkable. Like any other lowercase second floor, really. Same stain-masking patterned carpet, same not-quite-white walls, same laminated bamboo desks as the First Floor. Same view out of the darkened one-way windows, once you accounted for the five-meter change in vantage point. He fumbled his way to conference room 2C, passing a pair of older men who switched seamlessly from arguing with each other about some high-minded, navel-gazey philosophical conundrum to eying him suspiciously and then back to arguing. He opened the door to the conference room to find an old school drawing board, a screen of code projected onto a wall, and a group of people staring at him. He knew he was in the right room (he'd checked three times before turning the door handle), and he knew he had the right time (he'd checked his watch, his SenZ, and his watch again before stepping in), but the collective force of the glares pushed him back out through the door to check the time and room number a fourth time. No change to the room ID. The time on his watch had changed slightly, but no more than expected. His workchat pinged as he stepped back into the room.

"There he is! Don't worry, you're not late. These vultures just like to swoop in early to take all the goodies for themselves. We're doing fajitas this week." This svelte guy with the strong jaw flanking his too-white teeth was vaguely familiar. Perhaps his manager? "Everyone, this is Dr. Raza Mugabi. He's been working closely under me downstairs for nearly a year and we're excited to finally bring him up." Must be the manager. What was his name? 'R' something? It definitely started with an 'R'.

He looked around at the other faces, most of which were unfamiliar, or familiar in a 'maybe she helped me with onboarding' kind of way. But off to the side, one face was shockingly familiar. That face spoke up when she saw his eyes go wide.

"I'm sure you have lots of questions." Mei? But he was certain she was—

"Fish food?"

She looked at him quizzically and made the executive decision not to ask. Instead, she said, "This is our biweekly hardware/software sync and progress update meeting. We'll all try to include additional context to catch you up, and we'll keep the homegrown acronyms to a minimum. After the meeting, Arden and I will sit with you to fill in the gaps and to discuss your new role." She nodded toward the manager when she said 'Arden'. See, he knew it started with an 'R'. "Grab a plate and a seat and we'll get started."

He made a sad looking fajita with what remained of the catering platter. The tray really did look like it had been picked over by scavengers. That was fine, he was too mentally taxed to even register if he was hungry.

First up was the hardware group. The discussion was led by a wiry, wild-eyed man with a shock of gray hair and a beard that was smuggling at least half a fajita's worth of bell peppers. He and his team were proudly but hurriedly presenting the latest results in the most dry and monotoned manner imaginable. Qubit concomitancy was approaching 90%, which was apparently laudable. Something called Fredkin-Ivanovic-CNOT Shells (mercifully abbreviated to FICNOTSs, or "Fick Knots") were responsible for these latest and greatest results. He'd never paid much mind to the hardware behind his screen, and the import of the update was fully lost on him. The hardware was the engine under the hood, but his chief concerns were the destination and route. He thought back on Revelations Zero and One, feeling strongly that they were tied to the route and destination, respectively. He then felt Mei side-eyeing him, willing him to rain-check any impromptu brain rides.

Managing to stay alert for the hour-long hardware report was a testament to the lingering adrenaline in his bloodstream. After forty-plus slides of statistical analysis and statistics of the statistical methods and meta-statistical breakdowns of the statistics' stats, the presentation concluded, seemingly in the middle of a sentence. There was a nervous shuffling of seats as the meeting transitioned into the software update. Or maybe he was just projecting his internal turmoil onto the mood of the room. Solipsistic shit-for-brains that he was.

Arden waited for everyone to settle before transitioning to the software portion of the meeting. "As I'm sure you've all heard, we made the decision to terminate Eighty-Six last week." More shuffling. "It was a long time coming. We've been butting up against a developmental roadblock for a while now, and while we have many avenues yet to explore, we... agreed to expand our team to help us get over that hump as quickly and efficiently as possible." He looked around the room, pausing briefly at Raza before moving on. "This will be less of a progress update and more of a postmortem." Arden motioned and a projection was cast onto the wall behind him. It was a revolving image of what appeared to be a flatworm. For Raza, it was like seeing a childhood friend on the train; he recognized the image but couldn't immediately place it. The visualization included a scale bar, indicating that the worm was around 10mm in length. The scale bar grew as the image zoomed toward the head. Ah! He suddenly recognized the old friend sitting across from him in the train car. This was—

"*Pikaia.* Brain structure at the time of her execution had a 9-log congruency with *Pikaia gracilens. P. gracilens* is a known vertebrate progenitor, and has always been a target node on The Tree." Raza could hear that the 'T's were capitalized and scribbled a mental note. "This is our fifteenth test in a row with clear cephalization." He motioned and the head region was highlighted, with labels appearing to identify the miniscule cluster of nerves that was described, somewhat generously, as the brain. "Eighty-six possessed left-right symmetry, segmented musculature, and a frustrating penchant for producing genetically identical offspring."

Everything was beginning to make sense. His Revelations were nodes of information and now he was interpolating and extrapolating between them and beyond them to map out the secrets of the Second Floor.

For the next half-hour, Arden guided the room through this virtual dissection of an ancient species, focusing on the features that made *Pikaia* evolutionarily important. The concentration of sensory organs and swelling of the nerve cord near the head, the branching of the spinal column, the expanded proto-tailfin. Clearly the *Pikaia* was destined to become something greater, given a few billion years. Raza imagined the smell of formaldehyde and triggered a sense-memory of his past life in a biology lab, sifting through gristle with a scalpel and tweezer.

Once the simulated creature had been thoroughly picked apart, Arden pulled up a large and extraordinarily busy 3D plot. Well, make that 4D; this thing was dynamic. It was a windswept tumbleweed of lines snaking from one corner of the conference room to another with branches breaking off and reconnecting all over. Most of the tangle was grayed-out, with a surplus of color concentrated near what he assumed was the origin of the plot. There were dozens of large spheres dispersed in the matrix. Or... these must be the aforementioned target nodes and this is—

"The Tree." Arden looked to Raza, seeming to gauge his level of comprehension. Fortunately for Raza, he'd just untangled the web and grasped its meaning. The origin near the colored region had a label, partially hidden except when The Tree's rotation oriented itself properly toward him. It read "Abiogenesis". The origin of life. The Tree was an evolutionary map. On the other extreme, hidden behind the bulk of the grayed-out volume, was another label. After a quarter spin, the far corner label was just coming into view, like a rising star on a pollution-heavy night. It was barely legible, but he'd known what was written there since his conversation with Food Court Mei. Simulated Evolution was the route. The destination: "Human-Level Consciousness."

Arden looked back toward the screen and paused. When the grayed-out mass rotated to fill the entire screen, his jaw clenched and his nose flared. More shuffling from the seats surrounding Raza. Finally, Arden exhaled, with a noticeable slackening of his neck and shoulders, and said, "Let's retrace our steps up to the *Pikaia* node."

The visualization magnified toward the colorful origin. He could now make more sense of the jumble. Near the corner there were traces labeled one through eighty-six. Many originated at the Abiogenesis corner and branched outward toward one of the nearby nodes, labeled "Prokaryota". From there, new colors emerged from the Prokaryota node to connect with a Eukaryota node, passing several smaller nodes en route. Further from the origin, nodes were labeled with species names of increasingly complex organisms. Monocellular and colonial choanoflagellates, urmetazoans, deuterostomes, all the way out to the highlighted *Pikaia gracilens* node, beyond which lay the gray abyss.

A looping time lapse showed progression over the last four years. Each colored ribbon represented an attempt to chart a path from abiogenesis to the far corner of The Tree. An effort to simulate evolution. Each ribbon halted, Raza presumed, when the evolutionary path stagnated or diverged from the historical record. After each termination, a new ribbon would emerge from the node where the previous ribbon finished, or occasionally from a few nodes prior. The time lapse showed that these were subsequent experiments, utilizing and building from the outcomes of what came before. "Each of the last dozen iterations has outperformed its predecessor. However, the degree of improvement has been successively reduced. We're bringing Eighty-Seven online next week, though ISCs have not yet been finalized."

ISCs? "Initial starting conditions". Mei, who could apparently read him like an open book out of the corner of her eye, leaned over to explain. "Environmental inputs, nutrient make-up, mutagen density... it's a long list. I'll fill you in."

Here, the floor opened to discussion. Everyone had an idea about which parameters to tweak in order to get over the roadblock. Then an argument broke out regarding the starting node. Some considered *Pikaia* to be a Key Node. From context, Raza gathered that Key Nodes were those through which you had to pass on the way from the Abiogenesis corner to the Human Level Consciousness corner. The paths regularly forked, which made sense given the non-linearity of evolution and the high degree of unknowns regarding our ancestry, but the paths converged around Key Nodes. A growing faction believed that *Pikaia* was not, in fact, a Key Node, and that they should be going around rather than over the wall. This would require them to dial the simulation back to give it the room to do so. Raza had a few ideas of his own, but wasn't itching to make them known without learning more about the model. Eventually the meeting time ran out and the group agreed to table the ISC discussion for another day.

Everyone filed out of the room, leaving Raza, Mei, and Arden. Arden was still standing in front of the room of now empty chairs, suddenly looking very tired. Mei was leaning on the buffet table and picking at some scraps. The full, zoomed out version of The Tree had returned to the screen and was rotating lazily behind Arden.

"So". Mei decided to break the ice. "Did security give you any guff?"

~ ~ ~

They spoke for another twenty minutes about the ISCs. Raza couldn't believe how variable-dense this model must be. His most burning questions were less about jinhwa and more along the lines of "What the hell, Mei?" but he swallowed them for now. Arden didn't seem the type

33

who would indulge that line of inquiry. So, they focused on the mysteries hiding in the gray mass of The Tree. After a while, Raza took a step back to make room for a bigger question. "I understand *what* you're doing. Erm, what *we're* doing. Simulating the evolutionary process in an effort to model some sort of higher intelligence. Can you help me understand the *how* and *why?*"

Arden rubbed his hands over his eyes, swallowed his frustrations, and said, "Mei can help fill in the missing gaps. I had intended to assist her in that endeavor, but I have another meeting across the hall." He looked at his watch. "You two have 2C."

"Have to see what?"

Arden arched a thick black eyebrow. "You have 2C. This room. For another half hour. Remember to keep the door shut, and do not continue your discussion once you leave the room." With that, he peeled himself from the front of the room, not looking back toward The Tree before turning off the projection. On his way out the door, he stopped, turned, and said, "We're happy to have you aboard." If he was happy, that emotion was hidden behind a decidedly unhappy face. The door shut behind him, not hard enough to be considered a slam, but hard enough to rattle Raza's already brittle nerves.

"You'll have to forgive him. Exterminations are always tough. It's not easy to admit fail—"

"I thought you were dead!" He was surprised at the tension in his voice.

Mei blinked.

"Look, Raz. There are certain ways we have to do things here. You'll understand in time." He was unconvinced. "I would've messaged you sooner, but there's a wired connection for Second Floor to First Floor communication that's heavily monitored, and there's only so far I can stick my neck out for you. Thanks for not mentioning the food court, by the way."

Raza remembered the ping in his pocket from when he first walked into the meeting. He pulled his phone out to check the message. *you've never had chow fun, right? p.s. don't embarrass me.* Of course he'd had chow fun. That's what they shared the other day at the mall. Ohhhh. It was a coded message. Roughly translated: *our meeting never happened.*

"Wait, did you not see my message until now?" Mei asked.

"Well yeah, I've had a lot going on."

"How did you know not to mention the meeting?"

"Dumb luck? And Arden seemed a bit impatient for questions about company protocol."

Mei slapped her forehead and muttered something obscene. "Well, thanks nonetheless." She looked toward the door. "We don't have too much time here. Let's try to address your big *why* question." She pulled up a chair and sat across from him. There was that hard-earned eye contact he recognized from the mall. "Five years ago, a small team of extremely dorky grad students challenged themselves with the extremely dorky task of simulating abiogenesis. Using a coarse-grained chemical model, they coded a system comprised of naturally occurring organic compounds, and they fed it the environmental conditions of Earth 4.3 billion years ago. After a lot of trial and error, the compounds were urged into a state of higher complexity and, eventually, self-replicability. Boom. The origin of life (OOL), reproduced on a simple quant comp processor." She nodded toward the door. "Arden Zametti was one of those students."

Mei paused, looking back toward the door, then continued. "Meanwhile, a group of quant hardware hackers were developing new ways to utilize SenZero tech. That's the beginning of the answer to your *how* question, which we'll put a pin in for now. Just know that Arden saw these new methods as a way to... significantly reduce the coarseness of his abiogenesis model. He replicated the OOL simulation over and over, each time with decreasing assumptions and increasing resolution. It was around this time that he had his 'apple on the head' moment."

"Like William Tell?"

"What? No, Isaac Newton's apple on the head moment. Not... Man. You really broke my rhythm. Why would you assume I was talking about William Tell?"

"He'd shoot apples off people's heads with a bow and—"

"I know, I get it, just... You're an odd duck, Raza."

"I prefer 'orthogonal thinker'." He smirked.

"Right. Back to the apple," she said, frowning as if to cancel out his smirk. "SenZero had been around for a while at this point, and it had breathed new life into artificial intelligence research. But AI was (and still is) *lousy* when tasked with anything requiring creativity. Human ingenuity needs a human mind. Despite all the advancements in medical science in recent decades, we're nowhere close to mapping the brain with the atomic-level, or even cellular-level precision necessary to understand it, let alone emulate it for AI." Raza was beginning to get the picture, but didn't want to interrupt.

"Arden proposed a creative solution. Some might call it an orthogonal approach, and they'd be correct, if a bit obnoxious. Where dissecting a brain with impossibly fine precision to map each and every neuron, connection, and transmitter, would be thought of as a 'top-down' approach, he considered a 'bottom-up' approach." She paused, waiting for Raza to finish the thought.

He did. "What if we could start with a model of simpler lifeforms, those that we *could* potentially map well enough to simulate a meaningful reproduction, and *evolve* them into simulations with human-like complexity."

"Exactly. So, you've reframed your original *why* into a *what if*. You're smart enough to consider those possibilities for yourself."

"Well..." Raza pondered, "for starters, we'd then have that fully mapped human brain. I'm no neuroscientist but I imagine that would help us understand and treat neurological disorders. Alzheimer's and the like."

"Sure," she shrugged. "What else?"

"Hmm. Psychology would certainly benefit from that brain model. If we can understand the physical and chemical nature of thought, maybe we could develop new means of filtering undesirable ideas or unwanted behaviors."

"You're on the right track but you're thinking too small. Put that orthogonal noggin in gear."

Raza furrowed his brow. What else could you learn from a model of the brain? He thought of the apple. He thought of Mei's description of

AI. He thought about thinking, briefly getting trapped in a metacognitive loop before shaking himself loose. He thought of the label on the extremity of The Tree: Human-Level Consciousness. His eyes went wide as he made the connection. "It wouldn't be just a model. It would be... functional. It could *think*. It could problem-solve. It could... hell, it could do anything that a human could do."

"Without distractions." Mei's hard eyes were glowing. "Without time constraints. Without other responsibilities or needs. Without limitations."

"Well," Raza jumped back in, trying to keep his distracted, constrained, limited mind in check, "even with this bottom-up approach, there's no way to get to human-brain levels of complexity without sacrificing a huge amount of resolution, right? We're still bound by processing capabilities. I mean, there's gotta be, what, a billion neurons up here?" He pointed at his head.

"Ten billion neurons. Each with several thousand connections," Mei answered, utterly unfazed by his skepticism. What was he missing?

"Right. And each of those cells is a hugely complex system." His heart was beginning to race, and he could feel his personal clock slipping out of sync with Universal Time again. "This isn't exactly in my wheelhouse, but has anyone ever simulated even a *single cell* without severely dumbing down the model?" Was this all a sham? Did everyone know they were working toward an impossible goal? If he figured it out on day one, surely the whole Second Floor was aware. Or brainwashed?

Mei's smile didn't break. Her confidence settled Raza's pulse and pulled his clock back into sync with hers. "Now you're getting into the *how*. I'd hoped the hardware update would have given you something to go on, but those guys... well, we didn't hire them for their presentation skills." She stood up, indicating that their meeting time was drawing to a close. "Meet me by the Second Floor elevator at 7 tomorrow morning. You're in for a treat."

Out in the hallway he nodded goodbye and walked toward the elevator. "Oh yeah, Raz", Mei poked her head around the corner at the end of the hall. "Don't forget, you owe the chief of security a secret handshake. Make it a good one."

CHAPTER 5
TRIAL DAY 1.2 - JIVANTA

Jivanta was already set up in the courtroom and raring to go when the defense team dragged themselves in from the recess. She was a hunter in a deer stand watching the herd tiptoe its way into the open field. To be honest, she was a little disappointed with their performance this morning. She had been expecting much, much more out of Vilho. She had to admit that she'd been, in a way, looking forward to the challenge. Of course, she'd heard of him long before the trial was put into motion. He was famous within the world of law, and his celebrity extended well outside of the courtroom. Vilho Ragnarsson. The People's Viking.

The UN News goons had branded him with that moniker when he defended the sovereignty of Nytt Reykjavik against foreign interests in the early days of The Aattoq. With his tiny, ruined nation under immense pressures to sell off to the highest bidder in exchange for aid, Vilho emerged from the brackish backwater with a wallop of a counterproposal; he filed a monstrous suit against the very nations trying to purchase his homeland, citing their abuse of the Rights of Nature. Pulling from the various municipal precedents established by indigenous tribal courts, he represented Iceland not just as a people, not just as a government, but as an *environment.*

It was a foolish gambit, Jivanta remembered thinking to herself as an early career corporate lawyer while watching the case play out between increasingly devastating news reports. But the foolish gambit paid off, ultimately ratifying the concept of environmental personhood across the greater UN collective.

While most UN decisions fall on deaf ears, this time the people were very much listening. The victory for Vilho largely defined the legal framework through which those most ravaged by the anthropogenic global disaster (i.e., poor nations) could demand restitution from those most responsible (i.e., rich nations) by anchoring their case to the land (even if that land was now under water). The People's Viking became a living folk hero, the handsome face of The Reconstruction.

He never cared for his nickname and tried to distance himself from it. But we don't always get to choose how we're presented to the public, now do we, Mr. Ragnarsson? She looked over at him with a calculated fury in her eyes, imploring him to meet her gaze, but he just looked... lost? Defeated? Certainly not like the lion for which she'd been preparing. She felt her gaze pulled one chair over, however, and found someone more than willing to lock eyes. The assistant, Sohvi. For a moment, she was taken aback. Sohvi was staring daggers right through her. Damn, what did she ever do to *her*? Against her character, Jivanta decided to break the stare first, telling herself she needed to review the list of follow-ups she'd prepared during the recess.

Hmm. Sohvi Egilsdottir. It was unusual to see someone so young in this court. Lawyers, at least in the typical role they'd held for centuries, were a dying breed. With the universality of surveillance and recording systems, not to mention the homogenization of laws across the greater UN, it seemed that very little was up for debate. As the rule of law grew more and more well defined and backed up with a colossal bibliography of precedent, mundane issues were settled before they reached the steps of the courthouse. The Hall of Justice had become a place to bring increasingly niche and abstract matters to the table. Speaking of which:

"Welcome back, all." Justice Hoffer spoke in a quiet monotone and waited for the din of the room to settle before continuing. "After a... contentious morning, I feel the need to remind all parties present, and those watching at home, of the claims and the challenge to the claims that bring us here today. We are not arguing the merit of various fields of study. We are not weighing the importance of one theory vs. another. At the risk of oversimplifying, the defendants, a private research and technology agency named jinhwa, in August of last year, publicly announced the development of an artificial form of high intelligence through a proprietary process known as 'Simulated Evolution'. Further, the defendants allege that this artificial form possesses a, quote 'human-level sentience and consciousness, deserving of all legal recognitions and protections that come with personhood,' end quote."

Justice Hoffer. Of all the High Court Justices, Hoffer was the one she had the hardest time reading. Hoffer was a statue. Her speech was soft, and prone to lengthy pauses. Meaningful silences that added density to the inflectionless words between them.

"These assertions have been challenged by The Citizens Technology Reformation Organization, a UN registered civil advocacy group." Jivanta, aware that the cameras were pointed in her direction, made an effort to soften her features. "Given the... particular enormity and potential implications of the claims, the case bypassed the lower courts and was escalated to the High Court without being subjected to the traditional route of prior trials and appeals. Consequently, the arguments before us are less... practiced than what we are accustomed to hearing in this room. As such, we have made certain allowances thus far, but we expect this afternoon to proceed with more tact and consideration for the House... the Law... and each *other*." The "*other*" was inflected as much as a soft monotone would allow. Jivanta leered toward the opposite bench, hoping to see the sting of Hoffer's words reflected in their faces. When she looked back to the stand, however, she found Hoffer's eyes pointed in her direction. What exactly was the old bag implying? "Let us begin."

CHAPTER 6
TRIAL DAY 1.3 - SOHVI

Sohvi looked to her left, waiting for Vilho to kick off the afternoon defense strategy. She found him staring blankly at his hands which sat limply on the table, one on top of the other, and making no motion to initiate the proceedings. She could feel the eyes of the court, and a fair portion of the world at large, on him. She closed her eyes, took a breath, and stepped out of the shadow.

"Thank you, Justice Hoffer." As she spoke, she shuffled around the desk and up to the front of the room, centering herself below the elevated bench of the judicial panel. She swept her eyes across the hall to take it all in, though she couldn't bring herself to look at Vilho. "The defense would like to call Dr. Arden Zametti to the stand."

She didn't care for Arden. He played the part of a slick executive well, for the most part, but his clenched jaw could only hide his short fuse for so long. In the wild, he would find excuses to extricate himself from conversations in order to release his anger elsewhere. In the courtroom, without an escape hatch, he was a problem. That morning, Jivanta had zeroed in on his fragile temperament and used it against them. Now the defense needed to rehabilitate his character in the eyes of the panel by the end of the day, before the old robes would reflect on their first impressions, etching them in stone.

"Just to quickly refresh everyone's memory, can you remind us of your job title?"

"Founder and CEO of jinhwa"

"Thank you. As a chief officer, is it fair to say that you have a thorough understanding of the technology behind jinhwa's invention?"

"Creation." Uh oh. There was that clenched jaw. "We prefer the term creation." Dammit. She knew that. As unhelpful as jinhwa had been throughout this process, they'd been very consistent and unified in their insistence on the term "creation". He took a breath and Sohvi held hers. "But yes, that is a fair statement. I have been heavily involved with both hardware and software development since day zero."

"Now, this morning, the prosecution repeatedly alluded to the case of The Corvis Group v. Turing Labs. Are you familiar with Corvis v. TL?"

"Of course."

"Could you briefly, in your own words, describe the case to the court?"

"Corvis v. TL was broadly about the assignment of responsibility for decisions made by artificial intelligence algorithms. The case grew out of a fatal accident involving two autonomous vehicles. TL argued that their AI platform had given driverless cars the ability to learn from the environment and make their own decisions. Which was true, in a sense. They said that blaming their engineers for the decisions of the car would be like prosecuting a parent for the crimes of their offspring."

"And how did that work out for them?" Sohvi was relieved to see that Arden was less tense now that he'd been given the chance to speak freely for a moment. As hesitant as he was to discuss any of jinhwa's technology, here was a man who clearly liked the sound of his own voice. She'd keep that in mind for the next time he went rigid.

"They lost. Unanimously. The court set a blanket precedent establishing all machine learning and artificial intelligence algorithms as non-entities, tying all algorithmic decisions and responsibilities back to the engineers."

"And do you agree with that ruling?"

"I do. Absolutely."

"Many people in your field dissented. Can you explain why you agree?"

"Traditional artificial intelligences are... tools. That is all. There's no reasonable argument for assigning moral agency to a tool. There's no essence of humanity in the code, and it shouldn't be treated as such."

"So, you full-throatedly agree with the outcome of Corvis v. Turing. And you claim that jinhwa's creation *does* deserve recognition as a legal entity. Is it safe to say then, that, with your extremely thorough understanding of jinhwa's technology, the creation does *not* fall under the umbrella of statutes set by Corvis v. Turing?"

Arden flashed his executive smile. "That is correct."

That morning, Jivanta's attack had been dynamic and multipronged. She had been probing the defense for weaknesses, laying traps, and, most importantly, reading the panel's reactions throughout; they responded most strongly when the prosecution brought up the Turing ruling. Judicial panels, even at the highest level, shied away from birthing new laws whole cloth. They much preferred to utilize existing rulings, expanding or merging them to envelop the conditions of a case. Given their reactions this morning, Sohvi expected Jivanta to pursue that line of attack further, painting the defense into a corner of established precedent. By addressing it head on and forcing the panel to acknowledge the novelty of jinhwa's claims, the defense would, for the first time that day, be one step ahead of the prosecution. Or at least on an even footing. It was a move right out of the Vilho playbook.

Out of habit, Sohvi looked toward her mentor. She was surprised to find him watching attentively, his eyes glowing with pride. For a moment, she wished he still looked vacant, and she hated herself for the notion. Goddammit, she thought, what's happening to you, Vilho? She shut her eyes. Stay on track, Sohvi.

"Now, it may be useful for us to address the specifics of that landmark case so we can better understand why it bears no relevance—"

"Objection, she's clearly leading the witness."

"Sustained. Ms. Egilsdottir, this is your first warning."

"Apologies, Your Honor." Sohvi smiled. Jivanta's frustration was confirmation that she'd correctly predicted the prosecutor's next move. She turned her attention back to Arden. "I will recite specific conditions of the unanimous opinion for Corvis v. Turing. Would you then explain to the court to what degree those conditions relate to the matter at hand?"

"Of course."

"Excellent. So, article 1.a of the opinion cites a 'fundamental lack of self-sufficiency in the machine learning process as a disqualifying characteristic in the assignment of moral agency'. Quite a mouthful, but the gist is this: AI systems can learn, but *how* they learn is hard-coded by the engineers, which ultimately directs responsibility for the AI's decisions back to the programmers. How would you say that applies to jinhwa's creation?"

"It does not apply."

"Could you please elaborate? Without divulging any proprietary information, of course," she said, giving him her best "work with me here, you ass" look.

"Our creation is completely divorced from the restrictive and hard-coded learning methods of AI algorithms. We have none of the limitations of the old so-called 'neural networks'."

"'So-called'?"

Arden was stiffening up again. "Traditional machine learning utilizes computation schemes known as neural networks. They're called that because they are very loosely modeled on small groups of neurons, but are not remotely as complex as their biological counterparts. It's just a data processing method, and a poorly named one at that."

"Thanks for clearing that up for us." Hell, judging by his reaction you'd think a rogue neural net bullied him as a kid. Defending Arden was like steering a ship in a storm and she *needed* to get him back on message and in the good graces of the panel. "The opinion goes on to cite the 'absence of intuition' in AI. Could you share your thoughts on that particular clause?"

"Sure. In a vacuum, a human mind still possesses some innate understanding of the world around it. With almost no data of life experience, infants display surprising levels of intuitive physics and intuitive psychology. They know up from down, friend from foe. Even the most sophisticated machine learning programs must be fed mountains of data to even come close to a newborn, in that respect."

"And jinhwa's creation?"

"Our creation possesses human-level intuition."

"Excellent. Finally, the opinion describes an 'unbridgeable gulf between the processes by which humans make decisions and those by which the algorithms make decisions'. Does that apply to jinhwa's creation?"

Arden thought for a moment. "It does not apply."

"Please elaborate."

He thought for another, longer moment. He was choosing his words very carefully. "With our creation, the unbridgeable gulf... Let's just say that it is irrelevant."

"Irrelevant?"

"Yes." He wanted to stop there, but Sohvi stared back at him until he capitulated. "In the case of Turing Labs, the court saw the enormous gap between the mathematical constructs of machine learning models and the biological constructs of human thought. The 'unbridgeable gulf'... On the left side, there's code, on the right side, a human mind." Arden used his hands to mime the positioning, with the railing of the witness stand serving as a makeshift axis. "On the left, discrete blocks of directions for ranking and linking data types, all according to the programmer's design. There's no *real* understanding of the data, it's all just statistical categorization of huge volumes of input." He held up his other hand and waved it to draw attention.

"On the right side, an immensely complex biological system of overlapping and dynamic components, constantly building and breaking and recombining unique experiential data in ways that no AI algorithm can remotely approximate. The mind doesn't just statistically rank data. It conceptualizes and understands the underlying meaning. In the years since that ruling, AI has advanced, but the gulf is just as wide and deep now as it was then. When I say that the gulf is irrelevant, it's not because our creation bridged or shrunk that gap. It's because our creation is not on the left side of the chasm at all. It's on the right."

Vilho had once told her that convincing a judge was like tending a flower bed. Overwatering can be as dangerous as underwatering. Judicial panels, he would say, were like ferns and lilies and succulents and a sunflower, each with their own unique and often conflicting needs, crowded together in the same pot. Sohvi looked to the garden of judges and felt that she had struck a strong balance. Some could benefit from more information, some from a bit less, but all were in better condition than they were before she turned on the tap. She thanked Arden and the panel before returning to her seat behind the bench as the adrenaline slowly filtered from her bloodstream.

CHAPTER 7
TRIAL DAY 1.4 - JIVANTA

Jivanta was impressed. She hadn't by any means overlooked Sohvi in her preparation for the hearing, but perhaps she'd put too much focus on the legendary lead attorney and undervalued the dutiful sidekick. She made a note to review and reassess her intel on Ms. Egilsdottir after the session closed for the evening. For now, she turned her attention to the witness stand. Cross-examinations were her bread and butter; few things were more enjoyable than pinning the witness to the wall with their own testimony.

The defense had used their time with the primary defendant, jinhwa CEO and smarmy powder keg Arden Zametti, to preemptively parry Jivanta's call to squash the case under the existing statutes. It was a hiccup, but any lawyer worth her salt, not to mention her exorbitant retention fee, came prepared with other angles of attack.

"Mr. Zametti." She knew he insisted on 'Dr.' Zametti, but why not have a little fun tossing sparks at this firecracker. "You've made it clear that you're at least passingly familiar with the statutes set by Corvis v. Turing Labs. Is that fair to say?"

"...Yes." He was already grinding his teeth. This shouldn't take long.

"You're aware, then, of the matter of 'transparency of ideation'? It was quite a sticking point for the case, after all."

"I am familiar."

"And how about AI interpretability?"

"...Yes, I'm aware of the concept."

"Great. I only bring these terms up to make sure the court has the *full* picture of that unanimous ruling. As a matter of record, the opinion cited a, quote, 'disturbing lack of transparency into the algorithmic decision making and ideation processes'." She paused a moment, allowing the panel to chew over the verbiage themselves before spoon feeding them the rest of the message. "Disturbing indeed. You see, though the programmers designed the learning algorithms, they could never fully log and explain the decisions made by the trained AI. I can't speak for everyone, but I know I wouldn't put my nephew in an auton if the software engineers couldn't even tell me *how* it would know to stop at a crosswalk."

"That's not—"

"Mr. Zametti, let us, for a moment, try to take your word for it that this... invention is so utterly unlike the Turing Labs algorithm that was ruled a non-entity. Unlike it in terms of self-sufficiency, in terms of intuition, and in terms of comparability to human thought processes. That's a large pill to blindly swallow, but let's go along with that hypothetical for just a moment. In all your discussion of the Turing Labs ruling, it's what you and Ms. Egilsdottir did *not* bring up that speaks the loudest." She glanced back toward the bench, expecting to see Sohvi's dagger stare. Instead, the young lawyer was furiously scribbling notes. Good, at least she was working on a plan. Vilho still had a fog around him, though he was looking up from his hands and right through Jivanta with a question in his eyes. She turned back to Arden and the panel behind him. "I'm talking, of course, about the 'disturbing' concessions of artificial intelligences: transparency of ideation and decision interpretability. Mr. Zam—"

"Doctor. I have a PhD and deserve—"

"My apologies." Her tone was somehow perfectly malleable to the ear of the individual. The panel, with the exception of maybe Hoffer, would hear sincerity. Arden and the defendants would hear quite the opposite. "How would you say jinhwa's system holds up to the standards of thorough interpretability, Dr. Zametti? Can every decision be fully traced? Fully explained?" she asked, already knowing the answer.

"Well, it's not that—"

"Yes or no, Dr. Zametti. It either can or cannot."

"It... if you consider—"

"Yes or no, Dr. Zametti."

"...No."

"Thank you. And if decisions cannot be fully explained, is it fair to say that the decision-making process is not transparent?"

"I... No... I mean, yes, it's fair, but—"

"Thank you. Now that that's cleared up, I must pull back from the hypothetical and turn a critical eye to the fact that *all* of these claims are apparently to just be taken on faith. I understand your unwillingness to divulge company secrets. Really, I do. But jinhwa's continued silence regarding what kind and what level of assumptions are employed in this 'human brain model' is the most disturbing part of this whole conversation. The Turing Labs case was predicated on the sharing of all the code in question. In its *entirety*. The decision was made after nonpartisan experts combed through it line by line for *months*. And yet, here we are, without even a redacted summary. I'm left to wonder, does jinhwa even have anything worth defending? Are we wasting our time here? That's an honest question for the witness. Are you wasting our time?"

"How dare you—"

"That'll be all, thank you, Mr. Zametti."

"Goddammit, you—"

"The defense requests a thirty-minute recess!" Sohvi was on her feet, waving Arden down from the stand.

"Granted. We'll take a recess. Half an hour." Hoffer slowly raked her gaze over both benches. "Everyone, I will advise you to use that time to collect yourselves. This is not a request. Come back with an attitude befitting the House, or do not come back. Dismissed."

CHAPTER 8
TRIAL DAY 1.5 - SOHVI

"Don't forget to put twenty dollars into the curse purse."

"Not now, Raza," Arden snapped as he fished his SenZ from his jacket pocket. "Wait, twenty? What did I say up there?" Mei cocked an eyebrow in response and Arden grimaced before keying something into his device.

Sohvi had no idea what they were talking about. She didn't care. All she wanted right then was for the earth to open up and swallow them whole, but the ground refused to comply with her wishes. Typical. She dug her fingernails into her palm and cleared her throat. "We have a lot of—"

"How are you letting this happen to us?" Arden interjected. "I'm being humiliated up there and you're just, what, waiting for her to tire herself out? We need—"

She unclenched her fist and held up her palm, incidentally exposing the four sharp crescent indentations she had just pressed into her flesh, in a gesture that was half *I hear you* and half *shut the hell up.* "As I was saying, we have a *lot of ground* to cover and twenty minutes to do it." She paused, daring him to interrupt her again. To her relief, he held his tongue. "I'd hoped it could wait until this evening, but at this rate the panel will set a decision in time to make dinner reservations downtown."

"...Fine." Arden's jaw was flexing in lock step with the throbbing behind Sohvi's eyes.

"No more hand-waving. No more philosophizing. I need you to tell me right here and now what you want out of this case." She studied the team. Arden had turned ninety degrees, a compromise between showing his back in contempt and facing Sohvi head-on. Mei had a look that suggested she had a lot to say, but was deferring to Arden. Raza was lost in thought, which was par for the course. She wasn't giving up that easily. "Eight months ago, you hired us to provide jinhwa with blanket protection in preparation for the announcement you had planned for that following week. Against my better judgment," she cast her eyes toward Vilho, who was reviewing notes a few steps away, "we accepted, without doing our due diligence. That was a mistake, but one that may yet be salvageable if you would just cooperate—"

"It wasn't protection for ourselves," Mei, apparently the only one here with any sense, interjected. "At least not *only* for ourselves. It was protection for what we created."

"Mei, you know we can't—"

"She's our lawyer, Ard. For... flip's sake. Actually, this is worth five bucks." She took out her SenZ and thumbed at it for a few seconds. "There. For *fuck*'s sake. I know how careful we have to be, but if our paranoia keeps us from winning this, then none of it will have mattered." Mei stepped closer to Sohvi while she spoke and didn't wait for Dr. Zametti to respond before continuing. "We made something amazing, Sohvi. It's... she's incredible."

"She? Your artificial intelligence?"

"She's so much more than that! We created *life*. *Human* life. Artificial only in that she doesn't have a physical body, at least not in the way that we do, but otherwise perfectly, wonderfully human."

"Please continue." Sohvi needed Mei to get to the point, and fast, but didn't want to push her luck.

"We set out to create a model of the mind, so complex and complete that it could process information with human-like intelligence. We thought we could enrich the world with a virtually unlimited supply of brain power. We could run these models at high speeds, day and night, to help us solve problems. They would be boundless think tanks, tasked with addressing all of the immense messes plaguing the human race, from overpopulation to corruption to the shortage of rare earth minerals... anything, really. But then... we succeeded. We created a model that could function with all the power and intricacies of the human mind. We started introducing her to the first problem we wanted our creation to address. Climate change. Why not start with the big one, right?" Mei smirked to herself, but seemed overcome with darkness.

"That seems sensible..." Sohvi glanced at her watch and nodded for Mei to continue.

"We fed her enormous volumes of information on the subject. History, data, projections, etc. We were just so excited to get started." Mei blinked away a tear and put her hand on her belly. "Then she spoke. Her first words. 'I'm scared'."

"What?"

Arden had turned back toward the conversation and put his hand on Mei's shoulder. He relaxed his jaw long enough to help Mei tell the story. "She was a child. Her brain had been hot-box developed to peak adult targets, but she... her first cognizant interaction with the world was a flood of tragedy. It's shameful that it took us up to that point to realize what we'd done. She wasn't a tool to solve problems. She was a person. *Is* a person. A human-level brain has human-level emotions. She could feel, and her first feeling was... terror."

Mei had shaken off her regret and continued. "We've since seen her experience joy, and anger, and hope, and love, and all the myriad of emotions that make up the human palette. We realized what we had made, and we knew what could... what *would* happen if the technology behind her fell into the wrong hands. Some of us wanted to keep her a secret forever. Some of us feared internal leaks, or corporate espionage, and wanted to seek a more concrete level of legal protection. Ultimately, though, it was her decision."

"You're telling me that the announcement was..."

Mei smiled. "It was her idea. She said she was ready for the world to know she exists."

Sohvi's mind was reeling, and she didn't know what to believe. Even if they were being honest, the news didn't provide her with any real insight into a winning strategy. Suddenly, Vilho cleared his throat.

"If this case is not won, if personhood is withheld, your creation and all her descendants will be in grave danger." He was present, fully present. Whatever was plaguing his mind ebbed and flowed like the tides, albeit with a frustrating lack of predictability. "You may cling to your proprietary technology with the jaws of life, but private knowledge has the nasty habit of becoming not-so-private in due time. The safe will open. By means of a clever lock-pick, or through time-rotted hinges, but make no mistake, it will open. That leaves us with a choice, though it is no choice at all."

"We sacrifice our secrets," Mei said, catching his meaning.

"Mei, no, we can't just—"

"Have you been listening, Ard? If we keep withholding information, we're going to lose *everything*, eventually. Our one shot is to convince the court to grant her legal personhood. This ends with her recognized as a human, to be protected, or as a... as a commodity. To be used." Mei was visibly shaking with a combination of fear, rage, desperation, and a host of other deep, uniquely human emotions. Sohvi watched and didn't see a scientist protecting her intellectual property. She saw a mother protecting her child. Her intensity sent a shiver up Sohvi's spine, returning to the atmosphere through the hairs on the back of her neck.

Arden rubbed his eyes with the heels of his hands. "I know, I know, but legal protection will only go so far, you have to see that." He pulled his hands away from his face. His eyes were red and raw. He no longer looked angry. Just exhausted. "Do you really think the whole world will just abide by the ruling? Do you trust mankind to just accept SimEv minds as their equals and treat them with respect? People can't even treat other humans with dignity. It'll just be a matter of time before they're subjected to the worst tendencies of our sadistic, cowardly... miserable species."

Sohvi knew he was right. And judging by the quiet that settled over the group, so did everyone else. The law can only define an action as wrong. After that, it was up to the individual to decide whether the risk of that action was worth the ramifications. Humans have rights and protections that aren't up for debate in the court, and people are still assaulted. Enslaved. Murdered.

Vilho broke the silence. "What you say is true. In the light, people will treat each other like people. In the dark, that is not always the case. With each degree of 'otherness', be it other race, other religion, other age, other sexuality, other gender identity, the human bond that weaves our moral fiber grows weaker, and the tendency towards evil grows stronger. To an entity as 'other' as your creation, I fear humanity will present its ugliest face."

"I have an idea," Raza said, pulling his head out of the clouds. "I don't think we need to release our source code, like the prosecution is pushing for. They're acting like it's either one or the other; we hoard our secrets or we open the door to everyone. I say we use that binary reasoning against them."

~ ~ ~

As time wound down, Raza relayed his plan. Sohvi was unconvinced, but didn't see any better options. When the jinhwa group headed back inside, she heard Vilho step up behind her. She turned to see him, somehow smaller than he had been just that morning. Was she taller than him? She'd never noticed before. He opened his mouth first. "You did wonderfully in there." Someone had to say something while you were gazing into the damn void, she screamed internally. "Sohvi, I have asked you to trust me far too many times of late."

She broke his gaze. He was in his late seventies, but until recently he'd carried such an air of vitality that she thought of him as ageless. Now he wore his years like an ill-fitting suit. "Do go on", she said, sounding more impatient than she intended. He didn't blink.

"I have been blindfolded, walking a path I know by heart, and asking others to follow. But now I lift the veil and find myself on unfamiliar terrain with a foot ensnared in a bear trap. Ég kem alveg af fjöllum."

She checked her watch again, relieved to see that they were out of time. Was he finally acknowledging that something was wrong? This was not a conversation she was ready to have. Not now, of all times. "We should get back inside. You know how those old robes feel about tardiness."

"Sohvi." He drew her gaze up to meet his and she saw a fire in his pale blue eyes. "I did not want to alarm the clients. The prosecutor... the entire prosecution is not what it seems."

CHAPTER 9
TRIAL DAY 1.6 - JIVANTA

Curious. She had been on the offensive all day, and, after *Dr.* Zametti's latest outburst, Jivanta felt that she was within reach of victory. That being said, it was always prudent to tread more gingerly when the opposition rebounds from a recess. They will have undoubtedly used that time to plot and scheme and rehearse their counterattacks. So, why hadn't they adjusted their strategy? The defense returned from their half-hour huddle and did not appear to have even slightly tweaked their approach. Very curious.

Sohvi had called Raza Mugabi, jinhwa's resident evolutionary biology and flop sweat specialist, to the witness stand. Once there, he reiterated the same claims they had made months ago and doubled-down on the need to maintain secrecy regarding their methods. 'Yes, we divined a sci-fi creature out of thin air. No, we can't tell you how.' On and on in that fashion. She saw Justice Chebychev pinch his wrist in an effort to stay awake. Zhang didn't even bother making the effort and audibly snored before being elbowed back to life by Hoffer.

Even Jivanta let her mind wander during the back and forth. She felt somehow cheated. The People's Viking didn't have his heart or head in the case, that much was evident, but Ms. Egilsdottir had shown a surprising amount of clout earlier that afternoon. Where was that clout now? Jivanta hated to lose, but winning without a challenge was almost as bad. Well, now somebody's just being a bit melodramatic, aren't they? A win's a win, she conceded. She just enjoyed the taste of victory more when the other side seasoned it with a fight.

Finally, it came time for the cross-examination of Raza. He was certainly less predictable than the CEO, which made him more difficult to trap, but he was by no means a star witness for the defense. He was squirrelly, easily distracted, and prone to rambling. And don't get her started on that suit. It appeared to be expensive, but he looked as uncomfortable in it as it looked on him. She would use his lack of discipline against him, and pick up his questioning where Sohvi had left off.

"Dr. Mugabi."

"Yes... uhhh, ma'am."

"I'd like to continue the discussion you and Ms. Egilsdottir were just having, if you don't mind."

"Yes. Of course." He looked anxiously toward his team. They gave no sign, other than a general look of dismay. Arden's jaw was flexing, presumably in pace with the meter as he read the writing on the wall.

"Wonderful. So, let's talk about 'assumptions', shall we?" Dr. Mugabi pulled an already-saturated sweat rag from his pocket and dabbed his forehead. Jivanta continued, "jinhwa is hardly the first to attempt to simulate lifeforms. Is that correct?"

"Well, yes, there have been some academic efforts to—"

"You are aware of the Lund University publications?"

"I am." He seemed to be trapped in a loop of reminding himself to make eye contact only to immediately forget and return his gaze downward to his fidgeting hands.

"Could you summarize them for us? Briefly."

"I'll do my best. The principal investigator, whose name is... shoot. It starts with a B, I think. Borkin?"

"Bergkvist."

"Yes, that's the one. His group explored the use of simulated cells as an alternative to living cell cultures—"

"Simulated cells... as an alternative to *living* cells. I want to hold onto that choice of words for the court." Sometimes the old robes needed it spelled out for them. Hopefully they were still alert enough to spot the contrast between the words 'simulated' and 'living'. "Please continue."

Again with the forehead sweat wipe. "Yes, the simulated cells were intended to be used as a substitute for cell cultures, particularly for pharmaceutical assays."

"What benefit would that offer? Using these simulated cells, instead of, as you put it, *living* cells."

"Well, if you could make a model that responded to an input the same way that a cell culture would respond to a dose of chemicals, you could hot box hundreds of variations to screen for reactions without the time or equipment or personnel required to run the cell assays manually."

"Hot box?" This should be a fun detour.

"Umm... yes, that's when you, umm. A simulation doesn't have to run in real time. You can control the timescale and rate. So, you can effectively slow down or fast-forward the model. A hot box is when you run through the timescale as quickly as your processors will permit. In the case of the Lund research group, they were hoping to take, for example, a month-long cellular response assay and hot box it."

"So, by 'hot-boxing', they could compress the month-long experiment into a, say ten minute simulation?"

"Well, maybe. Like I mentioned, how far you can compress the time depends on the processing power. And the complexity of the model, obviously."

Ah, now we're back on track. She filed the hot-boxing subject away to pick apart at a later date. "Of course. It all comes back to the complexity of the model. In other words, how many assumptions and approximations were made in order to manage the computational load. Is that right, Dr. Mugabi?"

"Yes, that's accurate."

"And, how has that work been received?" Jivanta looked to the panel to make sure they were all ready to receive her next message.

"Well... in academia there's always a certain hesitancy—"

"Industrially, then. It's been years since they first published. Has any of their work been employed in the pharmaceutical sector? Or any other sector, for that matter?"

"Not to my knowledge, no." He was looking quite pitiful.

"I can confirm, it has not. I recall one particularly salient quote from NanoPharma after their failed attempt to integrate the Lund tech. Their CTO, in describing the poor correlation between the model results and experimental results, said," Jivanta cleared her throat for emphasis—a perfect distillation of her thesis, cemented in the industry trades by a pharmaceutical giant years prior—"*Every assumption, every approximation, every simplified, decoupled, or bound variable, strips the essence of life from the model. Intangibles are ignored, error is propagated, and the simulation bears only a superficial, non-practical resemblance to the experimental product.*"

Jivanta let the quote marinate in the minds of the panel for a long moment. Then another moment. Tough old meat needed extra time for the flavor to penetrate. "Every assumption strips the essence of life from the model. Every approximation strips the essence of life from the model. This was with respect to a model of a cluster of single-celled organisms, and the results diverged so far from the experiments they were designed to mimic, that the models were completely discarded."

She rotated slowly back to face Raza. "Mr. Mugabi, do you agree with the statements made by NanoPharma's chief technology officer?"

"I think... well, it depends. Not absolutely." Damn scientists. Law lived in the binary classification of things. Yes or no. Legal or illegal. Innocent or guilty. Freedom or punishment. It was about looking through the gray middle ground and carving a line to separate black and white. Scientists were polar opposites, never content to confirm or deny anything absolutely. There were always exceptions, always alternative explanations, unknowns of the known and unknown varietals. They drove her crazy.

"Please elaborate, Dr. Mugabi."

"It's just, I don't believe you can say that a single approximation *strips the life away* from something. I mean, if we just start with a hypothetical, perfect-in-every-way, first-principles simulation of one of these cell assays, and throw in one tiny assumption... say we limit the randomness of a single electron in the big huge cell. I wouldn't think that would strip life from the model, right?"

Jivanta wasn't sure where this was going, which unnerved her slightly. Then again, Raza was a sweaty buffoon who may just ramble his way into a trap or an admission of their methods. She decided to play along. "Sure, I suppose that fixing a single electron may not change the behavior of the model. So, where do you draw the line, Dr. Mugabi? What percentage of the simulation can be simplified and rounded off before that essence of life is stripped away?" There's the bait. If jinhwa's model is 5% first-principles and 95% junk assumptions, that's where he'd draw the line. He'd have to, otherwise he would be debunking their own claims. She looked back to the defense, who were all in various states of distress. Sohvi was sharply shaking her head at Raza, signaling him to shut his mouth. Arden was trying to break his own teeth. All good signs.

"It's an oversimplification." Of course. No easy answers with this guy. "Models aren't just a mix of perfectly simulated components and uniformly fudged, dumbed-down components. There are many kinds and degrees of, um, fudginess. Assumptions with different accuracies depending on different conditions and—"

"I understand, I understand, but going back to *your* hypothetical, first-principles perfect simulation of a cell. Let's get a rough estimate. What percentage of those particles could you drop from quantum-level accuracy into, say, molecular mechanics level accuracy before you'd say life was stripped away?" Just give a number, you goon. Something to work with.

"I'd say, I don't know... 99%?"

Jivanta laughed out loud. Was he joking? "99% molecular mechanics? 1% quant chem, and 99%... fudge, and you've got *life*. Is that what you're saying?"

"Maybe. Like I said, it's an oversimplification. What would you say the answer is?"

"That's not how this works, Dr. Mugabi."

"Please answer the question, Ms. Puri." Justice Hoffer spoke quietly but assertively. "I realize this is atypical... but I myself am curious what you have to say on the matter."

A fleeting panic crept up Jivanta's throat but she swallowed it. This was nothing to worry about. Raza had just shown his cards and revealed a handful of nothing. Had they really made those claims with a model boasting only 1% quant chem resolution? 1% was greater than theoretically possible for a human brain model, but 99% assumptions was still an embarrassing number to present to the panel. All she really had to do was draw her line at a value below his. No point taking chances, though. "I suppose, if the cellular model were, on the far opposite side of the scale, say, 0.1% assumptions and 99.9% perfectly simulated down to the quantum level, the model would likely behave indistinguishably from the real-world counterpart."

"So, you think it would take a 99.9% accurate model to retain that essence of life?" Jivanta looked to Hoffer, whose nod indicated that Jivanta was still expected to answer questions coming from the witness stand of all places.

"Yes, I suppose that's what I'm saying."

Raza suddenly sat up higher in his chair and smiled. What the hell did he have to be grinning about? She turned to the defense bench, who were almost unrecognizable against the sad pity party that had been behind her moments ago. Arden looked relieved. Sohvi... did she just give a sly wink? With that, Jivanta realized she'd been led directly into a web. But that's impossible. How could they be modeling with a quantum-level accuracy of over 99.9%? There's just no way—

Raza interrupted her racing thoughts to drive the knife in. "That's great news. I'm so glad to hear that you agree with our claims."

CHAPTER 10
7 YEARS EARLIER, PART 2 - RAZA

The night after his first trip up to the Second Floor, he couldn't sleep. He'd never been particularly *good* at sleeping. Some people just had a knack for it. Aunt Roo swore she never counted more than twenty sheep in her entire life. His ex could—and *did*—sleep through a tornado. For Raza, trying to fall asleep was like fishing for brim. Lots of waiting, and waiting, and waiting, and then when the cork bobbed and he felt the grip of slumber closing, he'd get so excited at the prospect that he'd jerk the line and scare away the fish. In this analogy, the fish was... the sandman? These were the sort of thoughts that plagued his mind on the best of nights.

Nighttime was when his mind wandered the fastest and farthest, and this night was no exception. At least this time he could excuse the hyperactivity in his imagination. That afternoon he had been presented with an overwhelming swell of information, and his brain was still parsing the data. His head held a powerful but occasionally slow computer. More ROM than RAM. Rarely any REM. He sipped from the rim of the rum that he hid in his nightstand for special occasions and buried his face back into the cushion. What a day. What a damn day. He sighed into his favorite pillow and smelled the sugary ethanol vapors filtered through the polyester and shredded foam. He tried to guide his wandering thoughts toward more comfortable subject matter. His aunt. His ex. His friends. Hell, even his parents would be welcome, but not even they couldn't hold his attention.

What had he gotten himself into?

In times of distress, his mind would often unearth long-buried sticky notes. This time, the note was a reminder from a former therapist to try a new meditation exercise. It was one in a long line of suggestions that tended to pass through him like nitrogen. Might as well, he thought. Maybe it would lure the sandman back into his room. What did he have to lose? The meditation went as follows.

Inhale, slowly and deeply. Concentrate on the sounds coming from your left. He focused, shutting his eyes tighter. Sounds of the street drifted up into the sky and through his window. Wheels on pavement. Muffled shouts. Bassy music.

Exhale, deeply and slowly. Focus on the sounds coming from your right. He heard the hum from the electronics in his room. The ticking of his watch.

Inhale, slowly and deeply. Isolate the sounds in the direction of your crown. Through the wall, behind the headboard, he heard his neighbors having some sort of argument. Or... no, the noise was too rhythmic. Oh. Quick, what's the next step?

Exhale, deeply and slowly. Zero in on the sound in the direction of your feet. Aunt Roo's room. A box fan older than Raza and a heavy snore.

Inhale, slowly and deeply. Recognize the sound coming from in front of your face. The ceiling fan was on full-tilt with some asymmetry causing it to squeak every three cycles.

Exhale, deeply and slowly. Name the sound behind your head. The bulk of the high-rise was behind the base of his skull. Somewhere, a toilet flushed.

Inhale. Slower. Deeper. Hear the sound within your own body. A wavering breath and a rising, uncomfortable heartbeat.

Exhale. Deeper. Slower. Listen to everything and nothing. The sounds all around him mixed with the sound of his own voice cursing the exercise. "Shit." He started over.

~ ~ ~

Raza awoke with a start five minutes before his alarm, taking the fact that he woke as the only shred of evidence that he had actually slept, though he felt no better for it. He cleaned himself up, set the coffee timer for Aunt Roo, and was out the door in time to catch the early train. The ride was quieter and less crowded than his usual train. He caught the sunrise through the window before another passenger made a point to tint all the east-facing windows so they could go back to sleep. Since he wasn't in his bed actively trying to sleep, the sandman reared his head, the cork bobbed, and Raza dozed the rest of the way to his stop.

~ ~ ~

"Well, well, well, if it isn't my new boyfriend, looking like a million bucks."

"Are you trying to make me jealous? Jeez, new guy, do you live in a trash heap? And did you wake up on the wrong side of that trash heap? No offense if you really do live in a trash heap."

"Good morning. Is it that bad?"

"I've seen worse. Just yesterday there was this nervous kid, sweat dripping down his face, and—"

Ma'am elbowed Broad Chest in the shoulder and looked at Raza like he was a limping puppy. "Oh, hon. I'm not a morning person either. Now, you know the rules." She held out the biomet scanner, which dutifully reported that Raza Mugabi was still Raza Mugabi. "Now, one last test and we'll send you up," she said, with a half-smile creasing the scar on her cheek.

Raza had improvised a handshake for Ma'am when he returned from the Second Floor yesterday. It was largely ripped from his junior high soccer team's secret handshake, but he threw in some flair. Normal shaking hands grip to the 'arm-wrestle' grip, back and forth twice. Then a quick pivot to the 'thumb-wrestle' grip, pull back, fist bump into a palm-to-palm into an elbow slap into a back-of-the-hand five. Ma'am loved it, and had clearly practiced since yesterday. He imagined her going over the steps in front of her mirror, and it put a smile on his face.

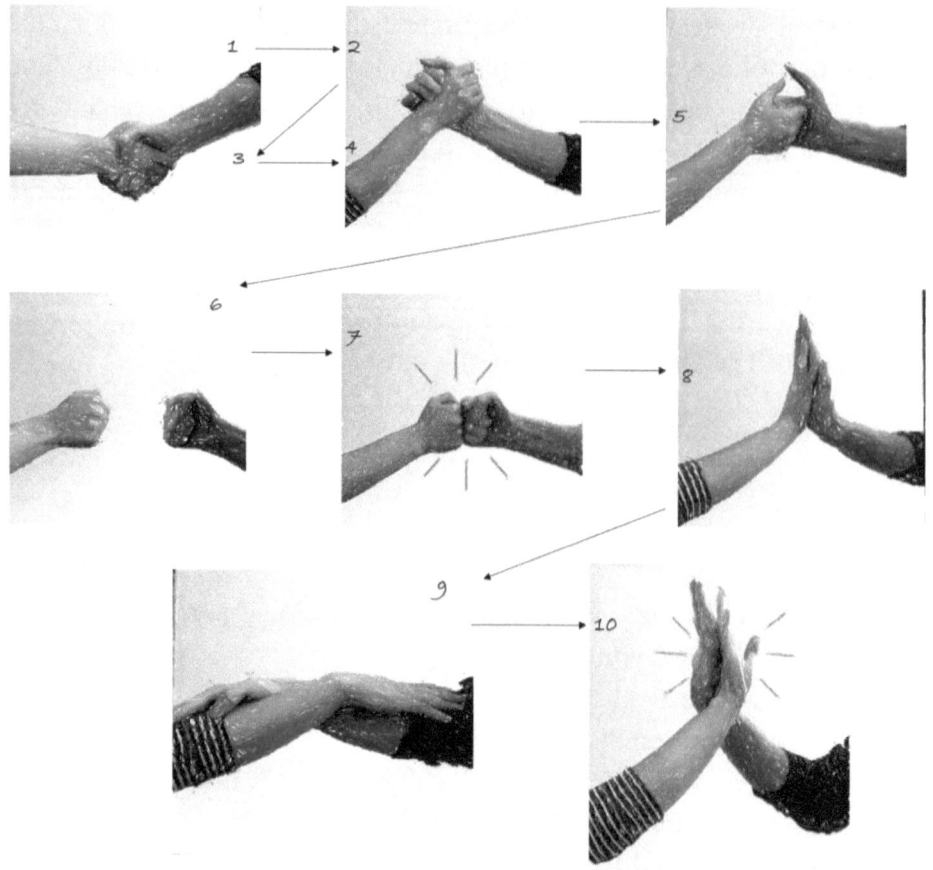

"What are you grinning at?" Broad Chest was feeling left out.

"Nothing. Uhh... sir. Thank you."

"You're all clear." Ma'am stepped aside to let him onto the elevator. As the door was closing, she said, "Ms. Kunihara will be waiting for you. She's wearing earrings today."

To which Raza responded, "Huh?" as the door shut.

~ ~ ~

"There you are. I was beginning to think you'd disappeared and that we were going to have to track you down."

"Good earring. I mean, morning. Good morning."

"Mmmmmmmkay." Mei was apparently a morning person. He could see that with his eyes. Her clothes were ironed, her hair was asymmetric by design rather than by accident. Everything he couldn't see, everything he'd learned about her since he joined, had been called into question after yesterday's events. He hoped to get some answers in time, but for now he'd just have to take their history together with a grain of salt. A cloud of doubt. A cloudy grain of salty doubt. A salty cloud of grainy—

"You ready to see the engine room?" Mei turned on a dime and walked toward the opposite end of the office. Raza followed at a safe distance. His eyes were drawn to her earrings. They were flat, iridescent slivers with some intricate pattern etched into them. Was it some sort of writing? He thought of his mother's earrings in his one family photo, and then his mind ping ponged, free associating from thought to thought until it landed back on Mei. They came to an elevator door.

"Wait, where are we?" In his distracted mind, he wondered if they'd somehow made a loop and returned to where they started. "There isn't an elevator on this side of the First Floor. Is there?"

Mei pressed her thumb to the mounted biomet and the doors parted in recognition. "This is the old freight elevator. We had to wall off the First Floor entrance to keep out the riffraff." She pressed a button and suddenly—

"We're going down?"

"Where did you think we were going, to the roof?"

"There's... Oh. Basement."

"Yep," Mei confirmed. "Basement. It's Second Floor material, so it's only accessible from here. Gotta go up to go down."

The ride was slow, partially because Raza's internal clock had picked up speed, but mostly, Raza would eventually learn, because the freight elevator was designed for moving fragile, acceleration-sensitive equipment.

Without looking over, Mei said, "They're silicon. The earrings."

"Oh, I wasn't—"

"I wear them for good luck."

"What's the story there?"

69

"I'll tell you some other time. We're here."

He didn't feel any change in the elevator's speed and direction, but they must've stopped because the doors began to open and the scene outside was different than it had been when they closed half-a-minute-or-so earlier. At first he couldn't see much beyond them. The basement was dim, with a track of overhead and floor lighting like a commercial airliner on a redeye flight. Before his eyes could adjust, his ears, nose, and skin were assaulted with a buzzing din, acrid scent, and oppressive heat, respectively.

Mei, seeing Raza blink and take a step back, reassured him, "You get used to it. And it's not so bad once we get away from the support server stack." She took a step out of the elevator. "Mikus should be in the lab. His office is over there, but he treats it more like a storage closet with some highly abstract rules of organization." She indicated where 'there' was with a slight nod of her head. Her lucky earrings swung in concert with her nod to add emphasis. She hadn't broken her stride or turned around since she left the elevator. Would she have noticed if Raza had stayed behind? *Should* he have stayed behind? "You remember Mikus from the meeting yesterday."

"I... to be honest with you, I do not."

"He stood in front of you and directed the hardware update for half an hour. How do you not remember him?"

"Ohhh, yes. Mikus."

"You remember the meeting yesterday, right? You're not a walking amnesiac, are you? If so, please speak up now and it'll save us both a lot of trouble."

"No, I'm just not great with names. Or good with them. I'm bad with names." After wiping the slate clean, here are the things he could confirm about Mei: 1) She was a morning person. 2) Her combative manner of communicating wasn't just a Food Court Mei (FCM) affectation.

They had arrived at a gowning chamber outside a darkly lit cleanroom. Inside, through the tinted plexiglass walls, he could see white-

70

suited figures moving from instrument to instrument. Ghosts puttering around a graveyard on a moonless night.

"I'll head into the changing room first. Remember to lint-roll yourself head to toe before grabbing a gown. The booties have an ESD tab; tuck those into your socks or you'll get zapped. And the bouffants have a liner that seals it to your skin, so pat the sweat off your forehead before putting them on. Oh, and the goggles... you know what, just come with me. It'll be cramped but I'd rather you not walk into the lab with your suit on backwards."

"Where would I be without you?" he asked, jokingly.

She turned, without a hint of laughter in her voice, and said, "You'd be one floor up. You'd be working on that meaningless busy work code for another couple months, and then you'd be fired on a Friday."

"Huh." Raza let that sink in for a moment. "Thanks, I guess?"

"Shit, that's not... I'm sorry. It's been a rough couple of days. I'll explain later, I promise." Mei softened, the same way she had when he'd told her about his parents.

He followed her into the gowning room. She was right, it was cramped. They had to coordinate their movements so as not to constantly bump into each other. Raza followed Mei's instructions, step-by-step, careful not to make an ass out of himself. It was an awkward dance. Suddenly he was back in the ballroom movement class he had signed up for with his ex. Well, before they were his ex. *Immediately* before. They were leading. Raza wasn't a bad dancer. He'd even been known to cut a rug, at least according to Aunt Roo's gaggle of doting old lady friends. Then again, they all thought he could lasso the moon. Regardless, in that class, he just couldn't keep his focus on the steps. His mind was elsewhere. He couldn't remember where, but it sure wasn't there. Somewhere between the waltz and the rumba, his ex, without losing their place in the 6-count, said, "We should break up." Raza didn't process the information at the time. He actually finished the class relatively unfazed. It wasn't until the drive home that the words made it to the front of the queue from his ears to his brain.

"Are you listening to me?" Mei pulled him from the dance floor back into the gowning room. The answer to her question was 'no'.

"Yes, of course," he lied, trying to catch up to her step of the robing process.

"You're a bad liar. You have a tell."

"Sorry. What's my tell?"

"I'll never tell. As much as I *love* the sound of my own voice, please don't make me repeat myself again. I was saying, just a heads-up, Mikus can be a bit... eccentric. I'll help keep him on track. If we don't nip his tangents in the bud, we'll be down here all day and you won't learn anything except how weird of a dude Mikus is. Don't be afraid to ask questions if they're relevant, but do not, I repeat, do *not* ask him about his pinky finger."

"What's up with his pinky—"

"Meiflower! How's my favorite software sell-out!" The door from the gowning room to the cleanroom had been flung open from the other side. In the frame stood a person whom Raza assumed must be Mikus. His eyes, which were the only part of his body that weren't fully hidden behind a layer of formless single-use protective outerwear, were both very tired and wide alert, like those of a man who was three days into an amphetamine bender. Raza tried not to notice anything about the man's little fingers, and did so by focusing on his wild eyes.

"Did you go home last night, Mikey?" asked Mei.

Mikus put on a cartoonish 'ya caught me' face, which was mostly lost behind the respirator mask, bouffant, and goggles. He turned to usher them into the lab. "Sorry for the noise," he shouted to Raza over the whir of the filters and hum of the instruments. "We used to use earpieces so we could chat over the din, but it was considered an 'at risk practice', so here we are now, screaming over the cacophony of our own machinations!" Mei rolled her eyes.

Raza could tell he was supposed to ask, so he did. "At risk from what?" Mei rolled her eyes even more deeply.

"Gremlins. Goblins. Ghoulies."

"Mikey."

"Yeah, yeah, yeah. The communication devices were found to be 'potentially hackable'. Sure, that potentiality relied on a bit of sci-fi, and a lot of hand-waving when I brought up the Faraday cage protecting the lab, not to mention the 4 feet of concrete surrounding the rest of the basement, but—"

"That's enough. Now's not the time. Let's get back on track." This was obviously a tender issue with Mei.

"Of course. Where were we? Yes, we were here, and, would you look at that, we still are!" He made a grand gesture with his arm to direct their attention to the rest of the lab. "Welcome to my engine room."

" *Your* engine room?"

"Yep. *Mine.* It's also *my* art studio. *My* candy factory. *My* crucible."

"Your *bedroom*?" Mei indicated with her head and Raza turned in that direction to see a cot folded up in the corner.

"When it needs to be. Why not?"

Raza could tell he wasn't supposed to answer, so he did not.

~ ~ ~

There was a short tour, which consisted of Mikus pointing vaguely at a cluster of devices, shouting about where they came from, what they used to do, who used to own them, what that person was up to now, whether that person's barbecue was as good as they seemed to think, anything but what the devices actually *did.* Then on to the next cluster, and so forth until they reached a door in the backside of the lab. The plexiglass in the rear was fully darkened so Raza hadn't the slightest idea what was on the other side. Mikus pulled his goggles up above his brow and peeled his gloves partially off to reveal his thumbs. Here was another biomet. A second layer of security? Or were only certain Second Floor credentials accepted? Mikus turned the handle and pulled. The door seemed surprisingly heavy for plexiglass; then Raza saw why. The plexiglass was mounted on what looked like the door of an old bank safe. Or a submarine. When opened, he could see the various locking mechanisms that activated when shut. Whatever was behind the door, jinhwa intended for it to stay there. "Here we are. This is The Vault." Capitalized, by the sound of it. "Step right up."

"*The* Vault? Not *your* vault?" Mei ribbed.

"The Vault belongs to nobody. None of *us*, anyway." Mikus smiled slightly behind the mask, but he clearly held a profound reverence for this place. Was it reverence? Or was it fear?

The three stepped over the threshold and into the room. It wasn't large, perhaps three-by-three meters. It was bright and Raza's eyes hadn't yet adjusted when the door shut behind him. The bombinating drone of the engine room blinked out in an instant. In the sudden quiet, Raza became intensely aware of the sound of his own breath. Once his eyes had made peace with the lighting, he looked around the room to take it all in. Three of the walls, including the one with the door, were featureless with a matte gray coat of what Raza guessed to be EM-blocking Faraday paint. The fourth wall, the one opposite the door, was anything but featureless. Featureful? Raza instinctively reached toward his pocket to look up whether 'featureful' was a real word before remembering that his SenZ was in a lockbox in the gowning chamber.

His attention snapped back to the data filtering in through his pupils. A mosaic of mechanical switches, snaking coils of wires and coolant, and dozens of status dials that wouldn't have looked out of place on the dashboard of a WWII bomber, all surrounding a box, maybe fifty centimeters to a side, protruding from the center of the featureful wall. The box was smooth, black, beautiful, and acutely anachronistic amongst the obsolete hardware surrounding it. He remembered a cartoon on his academic advisor's office door, a *Homo habilis* holding a stick and poking at a SenZero Qu-I. She thought it was hysterical. It must've been an inside joke between her and nobody else.

"So!" Mikus hadn't adjusted his volume to account for the quiet of The Vault and seemed surprised by the noise that came out of his mouth. He took a moment to recalibrate. "So. Raza. Can I call you Raza?"

"Yes, absolute—"

"Raz-matazz. *Tabula* Raza. Razzle-dazzle." Mikus continued, pulling down his mask.

"Get it out of your system, Mikey." Mei peeled the mask from her face, causing her earrings to swing pendulously, which Raza failed not to notice.

Mikus was quick to break the spell. "Razin the Bow?"

"What's happening?"

"He's bad with names," Mei offered, "but in an even more annoying way than you are."

"One more! Hmmmm. Razberry Beret."

Mei smirked and then washed it away with a performative scowl. "Are you done? We do have a lot to cover."

"I'm done. So, Razberry. Tell me what you know, and I'll pick up where you leave off."

"Erm... Sure thing." Seeing their bare faces, Raza pulled his own mask down to his chin as he racked his brain for a starting point. He pictured the enormously complex graphic from yesterday's meeting. Jesus, was that just yesterday? Considering all the time dilation he'd been experiencing, he couldn't be certain. He reflexively reached for his pocket to double-check the date and re-sync his clock with Universal Time and again found it empty.

"Pssst." Mei nudged him with sibilance.

"Right. Well, I've been introduced to The Tree. I understand, generally, the direction we're going. At least on the software side of the equation. Simulating small organic compounds, inputting the necessary environmental factors to promote abiogenesis, and then extrapolating the simulation toward the human end of the evolutionary spectrum. I know that, after five years of chasing that target, we're still stuck in the middle-Cambrian, pre-skeletal muck. Mei and I have talked a bit about what it could mean to actually reach that target, but, to be honest, I... have my doubts."

"Doubt is good! Doubt is great! You know where I'd be if not for doubt? Without it I'd be, without a doubt..."

"Without a doubt what?"

Mikus just grinned.

"Goddammit, Mikey." Mei tried to look impatient but let a tiny laugh escape through her nose, pursing her lips to suppress it further.

"Apologies, Meiflower. You know I'd turn it off if I could." Still grinning, he held up his gloved right hand and waggled his fingers. Raza tried not to notice the pinky, which twisted and curled in an impossible angle, and failed. "Yes, yes, you have doubts. What use is any of this if the end result is a coarse-grained model? It would be a rough approximation of a mind, heavily simplified to manage the computational load. Is this the source of your doubt?"

"That's exactly it." Raza was relieved to hear that his concerns weren't new.

"And I gather that your current level of understanding of our hardware is..."

"It's a complete unknown." Raza nodded toward the central feature distended from the wall. "It's a black box."

"Ahah! Very good, Razberry! Let's illuminate The Box, shall we?" Raza mentally noted The Box's evolution from a common noun to a proper noun as Mikus turned to face the featureful wall and began cycling through a complicated series of button presses, switch flips, and dial turns. "You should meet Helena."

"Mikey, don't call it—"

"Sorry, sorry, excuse my humanity. You should meet *Eighty-Six*."

"We don't name them," Mei said to Raza, though he wasn't following.

"*They* say it only makes things more difficult when it comes time to terminate," Mikus explained to Raza. "I don't disagree with that, but I for one think it's *good* to feel the loss. They aren't farm animals, raised for the slaughter. Our goal is for them *not* to be terminated."

"We don't name them." This time, Mei was speaking directly to Raza, knowing this argument with Mikus was a lost cause.

"*Eighty-Six*, whose Christian name will henceforth be redacted for the sensibilities of those present, was decoupled from the code last week, so what you're about to see isn't the true, active, *living* Eighty-Six. More of a ghost image. A replay of her last condition before the tether was cut."

A dim light emitted from the edges of the box. Looking directly at the surface that was parallel to the wall from which the box emerged, he saw a small blob appear against the black background. He took a step toward the blob to get a better look, moving around to see the box from all sides. The blob was not inside the box, but rather each surface appeared to be a viewscreen image of the same blob from each of the 2D cartesian perspectives. He took one more step to be within arm's reach of the device, and put his hands on his knees to get eye-level with the blob. There it was. Eighty-Six. *Pikaia gracilens* in all its wriggly, evolutionarily important glory. A slimy rung on the ladder that eventually pulled our ancestors out of the ocean and into the trees. "Well, it's a nice simulation. I did some work with flatworms in school and you really nailed the swimming motion." What was he supposed to get out of this?

"She sure loved swimming. Not a care in the world. I'll miss that about her."

Now it was Raza's patience that was beginning to wear thin. "So... I don't mean to be rude, this is a neat little aquarium and all, but how does this explain away the computational limitations of this... entire endeavor?"

"Very good, very good. I must apologize for all the posturing. I feel like a stage magician waving his wand around and around and around until the audience loses all interest. Let us skip to the damn reveal, shall we?"

Raza regretted his tone. Mikus clearly enjoyed this part of the job and he didn't mean to be a poor sport. Still, he felt that an apology would only delay things further.

"What you're looking at is *not* a rendering. Or, at least not one in the traditional sense. Your question is essentially one of resolution, right? Well, why don't you zoom in on our friend here. I'll slow her down so you don't get dizzy." Mikus rotated a dial and the wriggling blob stopped in a perfect S-shape. "Go on then."

Raza furrowed his brow and returned his attention to the small, simulated worm. He removed his gloves, brought his fingers to the screen, and gestured for the image to zoom. It magnified the frozen worm until it filled the viewscreen. It looked like any other worm he'd worked with in the lab, though less dead and chemically preserved. He could see the left/right symmetry, the directionality of its striated muscles, the 'head' that set it apart from its forebears. He wasn't sure what he was looking for, but he was impressed with the detail of the model. He motioned again and the image magnified further. A scale bar appeared to define the entire viewscreen as one square millimeter in area. He could discern the outlines of individual cells, which were about the size of his fingerprint on the screen. He birthed and ignored a thought about whether Mikus's pinky had a fingerprint and kept his attention on the box. It wouldn't stand out in a lineup of flatworm microscope slides. "Huh."

"Tell us what you're seeing, Razberry."

"Well, there are the cell membranes. This model has resolution down to the level of individual cells, and... hot damn, I'm seeing features within the cells, which is... fascinating. So, are you approximating each organelle as a point mass and assigning it different functions based on position, or—"

"Keep zooming," Mikus encouraged.

Raza magnified the image another 10X. Then another 10X. Then another 10X. The scale bar across the bottom of the screen now read one micrometer. He could see what appeared to be individual proteins, globs just a few millimeters wide on the screen, moving around a hazy matrix on the screen. Moving? "I thought you froze it?"

"I never said that. I just slowed it way down."

"I can see individual proteins. They have distinct shapes. This is incredible. So, are we working with a resolution on the scale of peptides? Or even... Are there point masses for each amino acid?"

"Keep zooming." Mikus turned to Mei. "And he thought *I* was dragging this out?"

Raza magnified again. And again. And again. He couldn't believe what he was seeing. Hazy globs, the size of his palm on the screen. "Individual atoms? How in the hell—"

"Don't make me say it again, Razberry."

78

Raza magnified again, and again, and again. He paused, looked back at Mikus, and continued. Again. The scale bar read 0.1 picometers. His sweaty fingers were leaving streaks on the screen. Again. Again. The scale bar read one femtometer. One quadrillionth of a meter. The screen depicted a cluster of particles, vibrating furiously. His legs were shaking nearly as furiously as the particles. He stepped back from the screen and took a moment to catch his breath. He was looking at subatomic particles. Neutrons and protons in a nucleus that was one hundred thousand times smaller than the whole atom.

Mikus cleared his throat as he stepped up beside Raza. "Abracadabra."

~ ~ ~

"Okay. Okay. Well... Okay."

"You think maybe we blew his fuse?"

"Give him time to process what he just saw. He'll get there."

"What makes you so sure, Meiflower?"

"Because he has to."

"Well... How could... Hmmm."

The three of them had made their way out of The Vault, back through the cleanroom, through the gowning room, down the hallway with the server stack, and into Mikus's office. Raza hadn't formulated a coherent thought since seeing an impossible display of an impossible simulation with an impossible resolution. He took a deep breath in an effort to reset his mind and found it wholly ineffective. You can't unscramble an egg. He turned toward the wall and closed eyes. "That was real, wasn't it?"

Mei and Mikus looked at each other, one worried and the other delighted. "How do you mean?"

"I mean... that was a functioning simulation? Not just some clever visualization? Those atoms... Those *subatomic particles*, they were actually contributing to the whole... the whole creature?"

"Well, like I said, it wasn't tethered to the code anymore, so it was more of a replay of a functioning simulation, but otherwise, yes."

Raza was a born skeptic. He wore his doubt the way an astronaut wears a spacesuit. It was uncomfortable and often restrictive, but it was a necessary protection against the daily bullshit barrage. He was finding, however, that this information was too large for him to hold in his mind without forcing a nugget of skepticism out through his ear canal. His brain wasn't big enough for the two of 'em. He had to make a decision to disregard what he had seen or accept it. He took another breath, picked a side, and was relieved to find that the egg had at least partially unscrambled.

"Okay." For the first time since this whole thing was set in motion, Raza felt excited. He turned back to the others, his eyes wide and his lips approximating a smile. "Mikus. Mikus The Magnificent. I'm sorry for rushing your magic back there."

"Don't mention it, Razberry."

"Now I'm ready to see how you did it. Show me what was up your sleeve."

Mikus was positively beaming. "Attaboy." Mikus proceeded to clear off a space to reveal a whiteboard that had been fully obscured behind a stack of unidentifiable electronic components, MSDS binders, and operator manuals surely too old to be relevant to anything in the lab. Mei and Raza tried to assist, but Mikus's indecipherable organizational language didn't allow for intervention by outsiders. "There, that oughta do it," he said, standing proudly (if a bit awkwardly stooped and slightly out of breath) between a pile of disassembled SenZero desktop chassis and an antique globe with the North Pole wired to a small DC motor and the South Pole wired to something hidden in another stack. Now that he was out of his cleanroom smock, Raza noticed that Mikus carried himself with the posture of someone who'd spent the last forty-plus years hunched over a workbench. The wiry man grabbed his marker, sniffed it, looked surprised at the smell, and began drawing a pair of perpendicular arrows emerging from what appeared to be an old wad of chewing gum stuck to the surface of the whiteboard. He labeled the x and y axes. The writing was hardly legible, but fortunately he spoke while he drew.

"Our independent axis here is in atom counts. The number of atoms in a simulation. It's a logarithmic scale, so," he ticked off marks on the horizontal line, "ten, a hundred, a thousand, etc., etc., etc., and way down here let's say, I don't know, ten to the twenty-sixth. By chance, that's about how many atoms are in your brain, Razberry. Give or take. I'll have more, because I've got a bigger head." He tapped his own head with the marker and left a blue blip on his temple. "The dependent axis, let's call it computational expense, which we can whittle down to 'time it takes to run the damn thing'." He wrote the label on the axis as "T.I.T.T.R.T.D.T."

Raza had seen this type of plot before, but he didn't want to interrupt. His exasperation and anxiety had been replaced with wonder, and he was enjoying the show.

Mikus drew a star just above the x-axis on the far right of the plot. "Here's the goal. A simulation with the particle volume and density of the human mind, with processing times as close to zero as possible. For what good is a model of a human brain if it takes ten thousand years to crunch through the sim?" He paused, seemingly considering his own rhetorical question before continuing.

"So, when you want to run a true *ab initio* simulation, where you're just defining your particles with the most basic mathematical laws of quantum mechanics and letting them run wild, making no approximations or simplifications..." He touched his marker to the gum-origin. He drew a line that started at a forty-five degree angle and quickly curled up, nearly parallel with the y-axis. "You run into trouble right out of the gate. The complexity of that math scales exponentially with particle count, and if you're asking your qubit transistors to crunch through a simulation as big as a normal brain, let alone a *big* one like mine," he gave the blue blip a neighbor, "you're looking at run times of... eons. Generations of universes would birth and live and expand into nothingness before you'd have a working model to poke at."

He returned his attention to the board. "Now, there are of course countless methods to *simplify* the calculations. We can start by keeping the quantum-level math but throwing in some restrictions, limiting the degrees of freedom, more rigidly defining electron mobility, etc. That'll still get you one of these." This second curve started out at a slightly more acute angle and proceeded a few centimeters further before curving sharply to the top of the board.

"So, what do you do? You say, 'to hell with all this quantum nonsense, what if we just treat atoms like point-masses and use some good old Newtonian physics?' It significantly simplifies the math, and isn't *too* outrageous of an idea. I mean, chemistry existed well before your Plancks and your Bohrs and your Heisenbergs and your Schrödingers dropped a heavy quantum turd on the party." He drew a third line, this one starting out at a low angle and curling up more gradually before hitting the top of the board well to the right of the first two. "Now we're looking at polynomial scaling rather than exponential, but it's a big fat polynomial. It gets you further, sure. Using these methods you can simulate proteins, organelles, even simple cells. However, the value loss attributed to the Newtonian assumptions renders the results less and less *meaningful*. Or... more and more meaningless?" Again he paused for a moment to consider the words that escaped from his own mouth. "And the loss only grows as the simulation gets bigger. So! Assuming you had the resources and the time—and we're still talking about millions of years here—to simulate a human brain with these simplified eighteenth-century chemical methods, the end product would be... perfectly useless. In our case, it's not *fear* that's the mind-killer. It's those pesky assumptions!"

Mei groaned at what, judging by Mikus's grin, must have been some sort of joke. He turned his head to Raza and tugged on his sleeve. "Here's the trick. All of these methods, all of these curves, are based on a computational crunch, using the qubit stackup to solve math problems. You have thousands of qubits working together to resolve the state of a single particle. Just like classical transistors in the dark ages before our lord and savior SenZero was born. What I realized—"

"*Ahem.*"

"Pardon me, Meiflower. What *we* realized is that we weren't properly using the tool that was right in front of us. We wanted to simulate a bead," he snuck a wink in Mei's direction, "and we were using an abacus to calculate its size, its weight, its position... why not just break the rung and grab the bead?"

"Oh... Oh wow..." Raza was finally piecing it together.

"Ah! You see it now, don't you! Instead of treating the transistors like transistors, we use each qubit to physically embody a particle in the simulation."

"But how—"

"How do we manage the error and prevent qubit decoherence from propagating throughout the system? Another great question, my friend!" Mikus smiled so wide that Raza spied his wisdom teeth. "You of course are familiar with error corrected logical qubits. You insulate an individual qubit with a thousand or so secondary qubits to keep the first one from going all wonky, like some sort of reverse-panopticon. Not very efficient if you need a thousand qubits to babysit each functional bit, right?"

"Errr, right?"

"Right! When you were nodding off in the meeting yesterday, you may have heard the phrase *Fick Knots* thrown around. I'll spare you the details because I don't want to put you to sleep again, but let me just say that, instead of insulating each individual qubit, we found a way to cage the entire system of qubits in an error-correcting mesh. Quite clever, if you'll allow me to toot my own snoot. We start with your standard ingot of ultra-dense crystalline neon, right?"

"I'm not sure he's still with us, Mikey."

She was right.

"No, I can tell by his waxy expression and dead eyes that he wants to learn more! Don't die on me yet, Dr. Berry, we're almost at the summit. So. We irradiate the neon ingot to high hell until it's maximally vacated, as one does. Then we let Mother Nature, in her infinite wisdom, populate those vacancies with qubits, and by blind coincidence we end up with a qubit density that's nearly identical to the subatomic particle density of your friend *Pikaia*! And of *Homo sapiens*! For that matter, of *all life*!"

"*Most* life, anyway. I always figured you were a little more dense than the average *sapiens*, Mikey."

"You jest, and brilliantly, but it's true. Even in salt water I sink like a stone. Anyway, back to the Fick Knots. Once the qubits are mapped and paired to the codebase, we wrap the vacated neon in a topological Majorana—"

"Wha..." Raza realized his jaw had gone slack and forced it back into place. His mouth was still bone dry. "So... it really is a one-to-one, qubit to particle simulation?"

"Ah, still stuck on that, are we? Well, more like one-to-one-point-zero-zero-zero-five, depending on the dimensions of the Fick Knot mesh, but close enough. The uncertainty of the simulated particle is the uncertainty of the qubit. The wave-function of the simulated particle is the wave-function of the qubit. There's no longer an exponential relationship between model density and processing time." He grabbed a red marker and drew a line from the gum-origin directly to the right along the x-axis until he reached the star. "Who's hungry?"

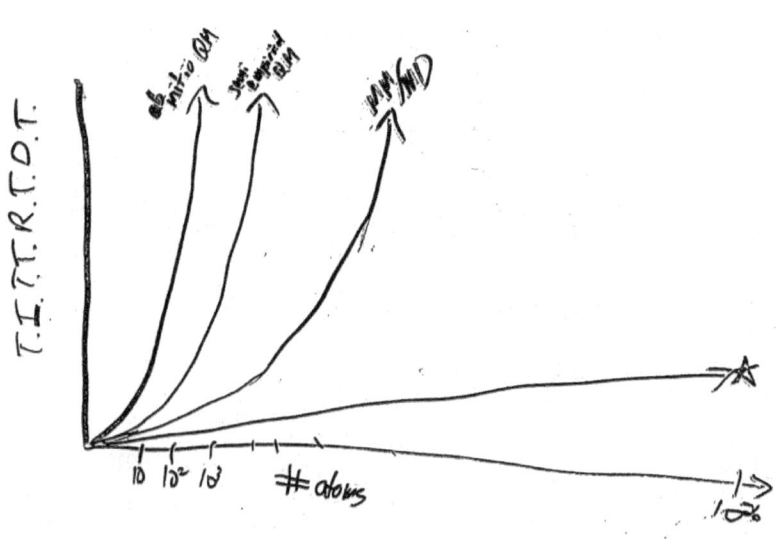

They took a break for lunch. Raza's churning mind was bubbling a new question to the surface every few seconds, but Mei reminded him that the matters surrounding his queries were not to be discussed outside of the designated areas. He had to admit, he was beginning to understand the secrecy. The security. The... whatever Mei's deal was. jinhwa had done something truly remarkable, and as far as he was concerned, they had earned the right to capitalize letters whenever and however they saw fit.

Mikus had elected to stay underground, leaving Mei and Raza to find food on their own. "Hey you, I said we couldn't chat about IP, not that we couldn't talk at all."

"Whuah?" Raza found himself seated across from Mei at the Mediterranean restaurant across the street. He had no recollection of the trek, or of ordering, or of taking the bite that was still in his mouth.

"I get it. I remember that feeling. It's hard to think about anything else right now, right?"

Raza started to answer in the affirmative but stopped himself when he remembered the mouthful of falafel. 'Mouthful of falafel' was itself a mouthful. He considered playing with the words but there was no room in his mouth. The string of dumb thoughts helped pull his mind back to the present. He nodded.

"I'd say it gets easier, but that's not exactly true. I've been here since almost the beginning, you know. I remember when I toured the engine room for the first time. I met Mikey. He called me Meiflower and I've tolerated it for... shit, four and half years? He used a different analogy then. The 'beads on an abacus' one was my suggestion."

Raza swallowed the food before remembering to taste it. "What was his first draft?"

"He said," Mei cleared her throat and imitated Mikus's spring-loaded eyebrows and exclamation mark-rich speech pattern, "'We've been trying to drive a nail into a plank using the flat side of toolbox, and we realized the toolbox was full of hammers!'"

Raza chuckled. "That analogy is about as clumsy as... a box of hammers?"

Mei let out a quick snort and retorted, "Now, which is clumsier, the original box of hammers or your meta box of hammers?"

"Hmmm... Pass me an abacus and I'll crunch the numbers for you."

Here are the things he knew about Mei. 1) Morning person. 2) Combative conversationalist. 3) Great laugh. He'd heard her stifled chortle before, but her deep, loud, unrestrained laugh was the type that he wanted to hear again and again. An aural addiction.

"Anyway," she said, looking suddenly wistful, "it's difficult, knowing what you now know. It's hard to make room for much else in your life. Seeing the potential, feeling just how big this could be, it can consume you if you're not careful. Trust me. Just... be aware of that. When your work is all you can think about, and you can't talk about it to anyone outside of work, your friends, your family... It can drive a wedge." She took a deep breath. "That's the last thing I'm going to say about work until we get back in there."

Raza racked his brain for any non-jinhwa content to discuss and came up empty. "One more work thing, if you'll allow it."

"Sustained."

"Downstairs, before we gowned up, you said something about me getting fired..."

Mei frowned. "I guess I promised I'd explain later, and technically now *is* later, so." She sipped her sparkling water with lemon. "Our Second Floor hiring process, as you may have noticed, is a bit... intensive. I don't think I need to tell you again that it's that way for a reason. You've seen what we're trying to create, and what we have to protect. Bringing the wrong person up doesn't just have the neutral effect of not helping the project. It puts the entire company at risk. That being said, our process is extremely, infuriatingly slow." She was idly running her fingers around the lip of the glass, creating a lovely tone. Raza found the combination of motion and sound to be oddly soothing. "I thought you were ready. Not everyone agreed. I knew that you were starting to catch on, purposefully dropping bugs in the false-code—clever move, by the way—and so I bent the rules."

"You met me at the food court?"

"Bingo. I knew you had made a connection between the growth algorithms and your experience in ev bio. That alone was pretty dangerous, enough for the Second Floor folks to get antsy and give you the boot. So, I figured I'd just make you too dangerous to release."

"By telling me *why* jinhwa was using ev bio."

"Well, I didn't '*tell* you' tell you. That would've gotten me thrown off the Second Floor." Raza stiffened and his eyelids shot up to meet his brows. Mei laughed through her nose. "Not literally. We're not the mob. I mean, I would've been out of the job and into a world of legal trouble, sure, but I wouldn't be wearing cement shoes at the bottom of Cedar Creek Reservoir. So, I repeat, I didn't '*tell* you' why we're using ev bio. I just told you about my background and you filled in the blanks."

"What happened to you? After that, I mean. You disappeared. I thought you were—"

"Fish food, yes, I gathered that. Well, they weren't happy, but I knew that would happen. They sidelined me for a few days while they figured out what to do with you. Ultimately, I didn't give them much of a choice."

"So, wait, they know about the food court meeting?"

"They know that you and I had a normal, healthy, non-work-related conversation, during which I slipped up, let my guard down, and mentioned my background in cognitive modeling, which allowed you to connect the dots on your own. I left out the part about where that meeting took place. I don't live anywhere near that mall, which might seem a bit suspicious to prying eyes. Still, Arden's none too pleased."

Raza was pushing his rice around his plate. "Why did you do it? Stick your neck out for me?"

Mei fished the lemon out of her glass with her index and middle fingers and took a bite out of it, rind and all. It was the second strangest thing Raza had seen all day. She swallowed, and said, "We're stuck. Everyone wants to deny it or downplay it, but the fact is that our progress has flatlined. My first year here, everything was moving *so* quickly." She smiled at the thought. "Each iteration moved further and further up The Tree and we thought we were well on our way to reaching the top. Then things stalled." Her smile faded. "It's been forty months since an iteration advanced notably further up The Tree than its predecessors. We're butting up against an asymptote and the same heads have been beating against the same walls the whole time. I thought it was time for a new head."

Raza suddenly felt a pressure in his chest. He was being brought in, against the wishes of at least some of his superiors, to solve a problem that had withstood nearly four years of hammering by greater and more experienced minds. He turned his new head toward his plate, and they finished their meals in silence.

~ ~ ~

They reconvened on the Second Floor and found Mikus and the man from yesterday (R... no, Ar... Arjen? Arden!) already in the room. There was a stench of conflict in the air. Raza wasn't what most would consider 'socially perceptive', and he'd been told so multiple times, but even he could tell that his and Mei's entrance had interrupted an argument. And a heated one at that, judging by Mikus's posture and the pulsing of Arden's jawline. Fortunately, Mikus was quick to table his emotions and change the subject from whatever it had been. "Welcome back, welcome back, Drs. Flower and Berry."

Arden, who was plainly less quick to compartmentalize, said nothing.

Mikus continued, "You've had a chance to chew it all over, I presume? The Vault, Helena." He side-eyed Arden who was practicing his bruxism in an effort not to take the bait. "And perhaps some baklava, judging by the sugary crumb on your lip?"

Raza's tongue darted to the corner of his mouth and found the offending bit of dessert. He felt a flush of embarrassment. Mei snickered, and the sound of her laugh reversed the flush. He smiled in response. "Sorry we didn't bring you any."

"Bah, I wouldn't accept it. I've been boycotting that place for years."

Mei turned to Raza to beg him not to ask, but it was too late. Raza had already committed. "Why the boyc—"

"WELL, I'LL TELL YOU!"

"I tried to warn you." Mei grabbed a seat and pulled out her SenZ.

"Three and a half years ago, I had a short fling with the head chef. Vadik. He's first generation, you know. The real deal. Our arrangement was... intense. I'll spare you the details, because they're not appropriate for work. Or anywhere, really."

"Get to the feta, Mikey."

"I'm getting there! One day, after a lot of hemming and hawing on my part, I cut to the chase. I told Vadik their salads had too much feta. That's all! I like feta. It's in my top five cheeses. Maybe top eight, depending on your definition of 'cheese'. But salads need *balance*. I told him all that. And you know what he did?"

"What did he do?"

"Nothing!"

"Umm... Nothing?"

"Next time I went in, he gave me the salad, and it was the same as it had always been. Very good. Best in the city even. But *too much feta*. He said, 'That's how we do it here. You can pick off some feta if it's too much for you.'" Mikus held up his spindly arms expressively, though it wasn't clear to anyone in the room what exactly he was expressing. Raza blinked, unsure of what to make of the story. "Haven't been back since."

"Thank you for being here, Raza. Mei." Arden walked right past the feta anecdote, which seemed to be the right move. "Between the update yesterday and your tour this morning, I expect you're getting a handle on what we do here, and why we decided to bring you up." Raza noticed, or imagined, a slight tick when he said the word 'we'. "I believe we were about to answer your latest questions."

"I... yes. Sir. I do have a few questions." Arden glanced toward his watch and didn't say anything, so Raza decided to surge ahead. "Yesterday in the hardware update, I heard that concomitancy is up to—"

"89.8%!" Mikus finished the sentence for him.

"Right, 89.8%. I take that to mean the level of agreement between the physical qubits and their, errr, simulated counterparts in the code?"

"That's the gist of it, yes."

"What's the target? What's considered *enough* agreement? If we reached the top of The Tree tomorrow, what differences could we expect to see between an 89.8% and, say, 99.9% concomitancy?"

"Hah! I thought you were a software guy? You're thinking like a hardware man." Mikus waved his hands to mime some nondescript hardware work. It was then that Raza noticed his ungloved hands for the first time. The pinky on his right hand was the shape and color of a copper spring with a bullet tip. Mikus saw Raza's eyes meet the pinky, but again Arden intercepted to keep the Q&A on track.

"That's a great question, and one we've been asking ourselves for years. Ultimately, we can't say until we reach the 'top of The Tree', as you put it. It's possible that we've already hit a sufficient target. A coarse analogy would be to consider a traumatized brain. You can remove problem areas without losing the core function of the mind, to *think*. Even hemispherectomies, in which an entire half of the brain is extracted, will leave a patient's essence intact. They can still comprehend and reason and solve problems in a way that no AI can. By that logic, 50% concomitancy may be enough. However," he finally let go of whatever anger he was still holding onto from his argument with Mikus and put on his managerial smile, "our goal is always to keep improving."

"The problem with that analogy," Mikus cut in, "is that with the maladies requiring a surgery, even one as significant as a hemispherectomy, the brain is still discretized into 'fully functioning' and 'not functioning', or at least 'not functioning in a way that benefits the body surrounding those 1.3 kilos of meat'. Or 1.4 kilos in my case." He winked at Raza and tapped his noggin next to the two blue blips that he'd given himself earlier. Raza tried not to imagine that if he'd had a marker in his hand he would've added a third dot. An ellipsis... He tried not to wonder whether 'ellipsis' was singular or plural, or whether there was a different name for two dots or four dots or five dots. Was 'ellipsis' a flexible descriptor for any number of dots greater than two, the way more than two people is a group? Was it context dependent, like how four people wouldn't be a crowd if they're all comfortable and separated, but the same count of people could undoubtedly become a crowd if said company consisted of two fighting geniuses, a third genius with a great laugh, and a fourth guy they were supposedly all counting on? Or was it just a measurement meaning 'exactly three dots', the way a dozen meant exactly twelve what-have-yous? Was a dozen dots equal to four ellipses? 'Ellipses'. That's the plural. These were the thoughts he narrowly avoided.

"Whereas with qubit concomitancy," Mikus continued, "whatever non-agreement you have, it's randomly distributed throughout your system. And it's not just random, it's untraceable, and *moving*. You see, the failed pairing can transfer to an adjacent particle. It's a free-floating question mark and there's no way to know what effect it would have on the brain if ten percent of all the trillions and trillions of particles are blinking in and out of cooperation."

Arden looked more tired than angry. It was a look he recognized from the meeting yesterday. "It's true, we don't know."

"Fortunately, concomitancy will only improve by the time we get to that point," Mei chimed in to hoist the mood of the room back up above sea-level. "Mikey here quite literally put the *i* in Fick Knots, and non-agreement has been plummeting since we started insulating the sim with Knots." She thumbed toward Mikus who took an elaborate bow. "And, for what it's worth, it's been ages since we've traced any evolutionary stagnation or erroneous mutation or... really *any* sim issues to insufficient pairing. Sixty-three was perfectly functional and reached early-Cambrian nodes with, what, 74% percent pairing?"

"Ah, Geraldine. A tube-footed goddess. Actually closer to 73%."

"So," Mei said to summarize the answer and give them all the chance to move on, "it's a known unknown. What else is on your mind?"

He thought for a moment. "I'm curious as to what y'all see as the ultimate benefit of all of this." Arden's jaw flexed and Raza padded his question reflexively. "I mean, my mind has been boiling over with the possibilities since things first started clicking into place. What potential outcome or application are you most excited by?" Arden's jaw relaxed, and Raza's nerves loosened with it.

"It's true what you say, the potential benefits are almost overwhelming to imagine." That's not exactly what Raza said, but he wasn't going to interrupt Arden and risk reigniting that man's jaw muscle. "I'll tell you what drives me." He broke eye contact with Raza, thank God. "Virtually unlimited sources of ingenuity and creativity: The commoditization of brain power." He spoke with passion, but even more so he spoke with precision; this was an answer he had given before. In his periphery, Raza saw Mikus bristle. Was this what they had been arguing about?

"Imagine today's think tanks," he continued. "A group of people committing their time and energy to solving a big problem. There are think tanks devoted to tackling various political, economic, and technological challenges. Not to mention environmental issues." With the last sentence, Arden turned to meet Raza's eye. "At the turn of the century, there were dozens of think tanks devoted specifically to addressing the matter of anthropogenic climate change. It's no stretch to say that they failed." Did he know about Raza's parents? Did Mei tell him? "Of course, looking back, we know what could have, and *should* have been done. What political and industrial and social factors could have prevented, or at least mitigated, so much devastation." Raza's heart was in his throat. "Now, imagine a think tank with boundless cognitive resources, able to process and collaborate and create without the limitations imposed by our fragile humanity." Arden took a deep breath and the rest of the room exhaled.

"A think tank of simulated minds could run continuously." Mei was picking up where Arden left off. "But, even more excitingly, it could run at warp speed."

"What do you mean?"

She smiled at him and his heart began to make its way back into his chest. "There's no reason the simulated brain has to operate on our time scale. Even with the processing power found in today's Q-clusters and using our pairing system, we could run the simulations at nearly 100X speed. Factor in the improvements we'll make to the hot-boxing algorithms and the growth in cluster density, in a few years we could conceivably run a simulated think tank of, say, twenty minds at 1000X speed."

"So, in one day of simulating, the think tank will have effectively experienced three years in which to... think?" Raza felt dizzy.

"Three years in which to *solve problems.*"

This new wrinkle was too much for Raza to handle. He and his *fragile humanity* just needed more time to process it, he supposed. Looking around the room, he saw that Arden and Mei were lost in the prospect of their imagined simulated brain trust, while Mikus chewed his lip in consternation.

"I guess that leaves me with one more." He set aside all the new questions begged by the answer to the last one and instead went with, "Downstairs, in The Vault, the wall... the, erm, featureful one." Mikus released his lip and looked up. "Was it built by a sci-fi set designer from the 1970s?"

Even Arden chuckled despite himself, and the tension in the room thinned.

"It's a security measure," Mikus said. "One I actually agree with."

Arden rolled his eyes but in a way that felt more playful than potentially violent, as had been the case just moments before. "The wall was originally outfitted with modern controlware. It was all third-party, and, we eventually realized, completely hackable. The smart sensors and smart user feedback systems and so-forth were all over-engineered to the point of being exposed, giving anyone with enough know-how a key to our most guarded room. Fortunately, our white hats identified the vulnerability before anything could be leaked."

"We didn't want entry points that would enable anyone to reach into our aquarium and grab our critters," Mikus added. "We've since retrofitted the wall with the dumbest dumb-tech controls we could get our hands on."

"It actually turned into a bit of a competition to see who could find the most obscure and obsolete component." Mei smiled, reminiscing. "There are hydraulic solenoids, a few vacuum tube logic gates... Anything was fair game, so long as it served an actual need, it was too simple to be hacked, and it didn't electrocute anybody."

"Meiflower! I will never stop apologizing for shocking your precious finger!" Mikus laughed, though it was clear to Raza that his remorse was genuine. "And yes, there were solenoids and vacuum gates aplenty, but we mustn't fail to mention the crème de la crème: a real beaut of a differential analyzer that Arden here installed himself." With that he turned and gave Arden a complicated expression that seemed to carry with it some hint of an olive branch.

Arden returned the look with faux exasperation. "Go on, get it over with."

"What do you mean?" Mikus's wide eyes and toothy grin suggested that he very much knew the answer to his own question.

"As much as I appreciate the complement, I can't help but assume you had ulterior motives for bringing that up."

"Well, if you twist my arm..." Mikus cracked his neck and bounced up and down as though readying himself for a boxing match. "Ok. Razberry."

"Me?" Raza gulped.

"You! So, all these years ago, we're working on the, as you called it, featureful wall. Every day there's some new bit of dumb-tech in the system. One fine morning, Arden comes to me and says, 'I've done it. I've successfully integrated the differential analyzer,' right? Real beaut by the way."

"I don't love that impression of me."

"Creative license. Anyway, I say to him, 'Oh no, don't you see what you've done?!' and he says, 'Huh?' and I say, 'My good man! You've integrated the differential analyzer? You've *integrated* the *differential* analyzer? Well, I suppose that's *one* way to turn it back into just a regular ol' analyzer.'"

The cadence and inflection communicated to Raza that there was a joke hidden in there somewhere, but he was having trouble locating it. After an eternity under the expectant, wild gaze of Mikus, Mei came to his rescue.

"He must've heard that one before."

Now Arden was outright laughing. They all were. Raza would later look back on this moment as the first time he really felt like part of the team.

~ ~ ~

He spent the rest of the afternoon reviewing the long and complicated history of jinhwa's efforts. It was surprisingly difficult to track down any source code for the first twenty or so simulations. Fortunately, something changed when Mei joined the company. Raza had grown familiar with the voice of her code during their time together on the First Floor. That voice could be heard in bits and pieces starting with iteration Twenty-One, and it grew louder through each generation. Mei was a fastidious code commenter (it wasn't uncommon for her final releases to contain more comment than code—and the comments were riddled with asides and the occasional joke to herself and future coders); and it was through those comments that he gained insight into the earlier trials. Evidently, Arden had the nasty habit of destroying the source code and starting over from scratch. Whether it was for security reasons or an extreme debugging-with-napalm exercise, he couldn't say. Mei was much more keen on building on prior successes, and she mapped, flagged, and color-coded legacy code every time it passed on from progenitor to progeny.

He was glad to see that his stint on the First Floor wasn't a total waste of time; he had garnered a strong understanding of the data structures and core algorithms, which meant he'd already hiked a fair portion up the slope of the learning curve. That being said, he had a *lot* of catching up to do. Catching up meant staying at work, because this was the type of code that wasn't allowed out of the building. He let Aunt Roo know he'd be home late, took his evening pill, and settled into his Second Floor desk. Gradually the floor emptied around him. Before long he was alone. He suspected Mikus was tinkering away ten meters below, and Broad Chest and Ma'am were likely guarding the mortal realm between, but otherwise he felt lightyears away from any living souls. He didn't notice when the lights turned off overhead. He was too busy. He didn't notice when his phone pinged. He was too busy. He didn't notice when the sun began to rise. He was too busy. He didn't notice when the office lights came back on, or when workers began to file in, or when Mei pulled her chair up next to his. He was—

"Good morning, Raz."

"AHHwherr?" Raza blinked furiously as his brain sought to retrace its steps to remind him who and where he was.

"I was about to say the same thing," Mei said with a wry smile. She turned her attention to his screen, which was smeared with code. Specifically, *her* code. "Oh, wow, it's like looking at an old yearbook photo."

Raza had finally placed himself in time and space. It was strange pulling out of his screen trance to find Mei, having spent the last twelve hours with her digital self in the form of her coding history. He was dealt a confusing barrage of feelings in rapid succession. First, he felt embarrassed, like he'd been caught reading someone else's diary. Then he felt the imbalanced emotional connection that often follows an intense dream about a person. Finally came the peripherals—exhaustion, self-consciousness, and, as a bonus, a twitchy eyelid that reminded him he'd missed his morning dose of medication. "I, umm." It came out deep and whispery. He cleared his throat. "I'm almost caught up."

Mei looked at him pityingly. "I take that you ignored the message I sent you last night?"

He remembered his phone pinging and unlocked his SenZ. He had several missed calls from Aunt Roo. Better call her back as soon as he made himself a cup of cold water and splashed some coffee on his face. He could already hear her yelling, "I thought you were face down in a ditch somewhere!" He gestured to open the workchat message from Mei. *hey raz, I heard you're the last one in the office. get some rest. nobody expects you to solve all of our problems overnight. arden will give you at least 48 hours.* There was a second message sent a few minutes later. *joking, by the way. go home.*

"I guess I missed that one." His eyes finally adjusted to focus on the world outside of his monitor. Raza looked at Mei and reaffirmed her status as a morning person. She was in a teal suit with white trim. The color matched her—

"Yes, I'm wearing the same earrings I wore yesterday." She brushed her lobe with the tip of her finger. "You're in no position to judge, given that you're wearing the same everything you wore yesterday."

"I wasn't judging, I swear." His eyelid twitch was quickening.

"I keep them on in the days leading up to initiations."

"I believe you were going to tell me what the story is with those. Why are they lucky?"

Mei checked her watch. "Your timing is terrible. Go clean yourself up. We have a meeting in six minutes."

Raza blinked. "What meeting?"

"The ISC meeting! We're finalizing the terms for Eighty-Seven, remember?" Mei looked exasperated. "Look, I meant what I said in the workchat. You're not going to be expected to work any miracles in the meeting, but it would make me look bad if you didn't show up. Room 2E. Don't be late." She got up to leave and then turned back. "Mikus keeps spare toiletries in his office. He'll trade you for a favor to be redeemed at a later date. Be warned, his interest rates are exorbitant."

CHAPTER 11
TRIAL DAY 1.7 - SOHVI

"Come out with us! We're grabbing drinks across the street to celebrate."

"You go ahead without me. Vilho and I have work to do." Sohvi knew her clients were putting the cart before the horse, but she bit her lip and kept that metaphor to herself. She had to admit, things were looking up. Raza's plan had played out beautifully. Baiting the prosecution into suggesting that the 'essence of life' would be retained in a cell model with sufficient accuracy had wounded their most persistent argument, that jinhwa's claims would collapse under the weight of the model's assumptions and approximations. That being said, there was quite a leap to be made between "the cell model is accurate enough to be clinically and industrially meaningful" and "the human mind model is alive and should have rights". Sohvi also knew that many of the prosecution's other arguments would still hold. The purported quantum-level accuracy of the model had taken Ms. Puri by surprise, but it made no attempt to address the matter of 'transparency and interpretability of ideation'. It was spelled out in the Corvis v. Turing opinion, and by virtue of precedent those five words would not be ignored.

Sohvi bid the trio farewell and set off to track down Vilho. She tried and failed to ignore the pit in her gut. Would she find the hero who saved her life and taught her how to fight the systems that had nearly killed her? Or would she find the shriveled husk of her mentor, an old man lost in the fog? She stepped back into the lobby and spotted him sitting on a marble bench near the elevator. He looked over to her and, to Sohvi's relief, smiled and patted the seat next to him. The lights were dim and the sun had set, but she could see that his eyes were clear and alert.

She sat next to him. Was now the time? Would he finally acknowledge that something was wrong? "Sohvi—"

"I need you to tell me more about your suspicions regarding the prosecution." She surprised herself. Maybe she wasn't ready to talk about his condition after all.

He smiled knowingly. He always knew. Maybe she was just projecting, but if history was any indication, he could read Sohvi's thoughts as well as she could. Perhaps better. "Of course."

"Before we broke from recess, you said that the prosecution was 'not what it seems'." She frowned. "When I asked for more details, you..." She wasn't sure how to phrase what she wanted to say. *You disappeared back into a mist?* "Vilho, I just don't know what to do with that information without more context."

He lowered his head and his knowing smile transformed into something that made Sohvi's heart ache. "I wish more than anything I could provide that context. All of my experience, all of my intuition is telling me so. But when I search my mind for the rationale behind my conclusions... I know the information is hidden somewhere up here," he pointed a tired finger to his crown, "but I cannot seem to find the damned keys. I am locked out of my own mind. It is a most dreadful place to find oneself. Believe me when I tell you that I have rapped on the door until my knuckles bled and calloused over."

Sohvi turned away. What could she possibly say to something like that? She looked out the window. Across the street, she could make out the figures of her clients sitting together at the bar. It was a slow night. Empty parking lot, and a lone Vantablack coupe parked on the end of the street.

"Huh," Vilho called her back to attention, "inspiration finds the oddest occasions to knock, knock, knock, does it not?"

"I'm sorry?" Sohvi's mind was still on the car.

"I may have a way to circumvent Ms. Puri's precedents."

CHAPTER 12
7 YEARS EARLIER, PART 3 - RAZA

Raza managed to make himself presentable just in time for the meeting. He washed his face and sold his soul to Mikus for a clean shirt and some mouthwash. He grabbed a seat in the back and was settling in when his eyelid twitched to remind him that he'd forgotten to take his medicine. *Shit.* He considered sneaking out to grab the pill from his desk, but before he could stand, Arden called the meeting to order. It had been a while since he'd missed a dose, but he knew what was in store. The fasciculating eyelid was just a minor annoyance but served as a bannerman for the cavalcade of withdrawal symptoms that were sure to follow if they weren't beaten back by his personalized cocktail of inhibitors and inducers.

"Good morning, everyone. Thank you all for being here. I'd also like to say thanks, especially, to those of you who submitted your ISC recommendations in advance through the workchat."

It was too bright by half, and it hurt his sore eyes to move them. Raza squinted and turned his head to see who else was in the room. No sign of Mikus's wild white mane. This must be strictly a software team decision. "We're all mostly aligned regarding the environmental conditions and initiation points, though there are a few finer details on which we'll need to come into agreement. I'll pull the contended conditions up on the viewscreen and we can open the discussion."

Each twitch of his eyelid was followed by a dull throb that began at the base of his optic nerve and shoved its way forcefully toward his brain stem, leaving a trail of ache in its wake. He imagined a drunk concert-goer bulldozing his way to the stage. He could feel the progression millimeter by millimeter. Micron by micron. The minutes ticked by and Raza shrank into his chair.

"There's no evidence to suggest nutrient concentration accounted for more than..."

The voice trailed off. Or, more accurately, it was drowned out by the ringing in Raza's ear that was amplifying in a staircase function, stepping louder and louder with each pulse behind his pupils.

"At this point, removing pre-Cambrian nodes from the discussion seems premature..."

Thirty minutes passed. Possibly an hour. He couldn't bear to look at the clock on the wall; its proximity to the overhead light rendered it completely out of reach for his hypersensitive eyes.

"I'm not convinced the atmospheric concentrations are sufficiently optimized, at least not so far as to take them off the table..."

Tension in the room was rising to meet the tension in Raza's skull.

"You know we can't pull too many levers at once. Do I need to remind everyone what happened with Sixty-One?"

In lock-step with the tension, the volume was climbing, as if in an effort to be heard over the ringing in his ear.

"We have to step back and look at the problem holistically."

The concert-goer had reached the front row.

"Do you know what Einstein said about insanity?"

The stage lights were blinding.

"GOD. DAMMIT!"

The room quieted. Raza looked around to triangulate the source of the outburst. Judging by all the startled faces pointed in his direction, it had come from someone sitting in his chair.

"Dr. Mugabi... do you need—"

"I'm... I'm sorry for my language, but... God. *Dammit*." He looked to the front of the room and saw Mei staring back worriedly. "You're nowhere close." Raza knew that his withdrawal was making him irrational, but knowing so didn't change it. Understanding the tides doesn't stop the ocean from rising.

"I beg your pardon?" Arden shouldn't have indulged him. He should have excused Raza from the room, where he could've taken his medicine and gone for a walk and come back in half an hour with his tail tucked between his legs, but Arden wasn't one to back down from a challenge.

"I said you're nowhere close."

Arden's jaw flexed. "With all due respect, Dr. Mugabi, we've gotten this far without you, and—"

"I'm sorry for Raza," Mei was trying to get between the two. "I gave him too much work and he was up all night."

"I mean what I said." He wasn't sure if that was true, but his throbbing skull was muddying his reasoning. "You're stuck, and if this is how these meetings tend to go, we're going to keep evolving flatworms until we die."

"Were you not impressed with what you saw yesterday?" Raza wasn't even sure where the comment came from. Arden? Mei? One of the lukewarm bodies next to him? It didn't matter.

"I..." Raza breathed. "What I saw was amazing. Honestly. I don't mean to downplay the truly incredible work that y'all have done. But I've been combing through all the legacy code... years of iterations. And I've seen how little of The Tree is illuminated."

Clearly he'd struck a nerve. Arden's nostrils flared as he took a long, audible breath through his nose. Everyone was glued to their seats, not knowing how he would react. Finally he exhaled. A quick transition from frustration to exhaustion, one Raza had now seen several times. "You know, life began 4.2 billion years ago. Of course you know that, but I want to put things in perspective. Abiogenesis. The origin of our Tree. It then took another 3.8 billion years for nature to evolve *Pikaia*. If The Tree were scaled by time, we'd already be 88% of the way to the finish line."

"But it's *not*. It's not scaled by time." Arden already knew it. Everyone in the room already knew it. Still, Raza felt compelled to keep talking lest his piercing headache cut him off mid-thought. "It's scaled by complexity. Evolutionary complexity has followed the same trajectory as technological complexity." A seed of an idea suddenly popped into Raza's cloudy mind. He couldn't quite discern it just yet through the murk. Better keep talking and see if it grows. "*H. sapiens* were using simple tools 300,000 years ago. Look at the timeline from then to now. If you go 99.9% of the way forward, humans are more advanced, sure, there's blacksmithery and guns and carriages, but would you say that 300 years ago we'd reached 99.9% of today's technical knowledge? Railroads, combustion engines, flight, space travel, telecommunications, computers, planetary colonization, a quantum computer in every pocket... All in the last 0.1% of that timeline. Backtracking 1.4 billion years, to our *Pikaia...*"

The seed took root. In an instant, it exploded outward, clearing the fog as it reached all the corners of his mind. Raza could envision the marvels of human innovation. Metalwork. The space race. AI-enhanced ballistic missiles, carrying code he'd written. He thought of Arden and Mikus at each other's throats. He thought of the *Pikaia* in The Vault, swimming freely. 'Not a care in the world', Mikus had said. That was the problem. That was the *answer.*

"Competition!" He saw the expressions of those around him, which ranged from bemused to worried to irritated, and realized that his idea hadn't fully spread out of his head and into the room, so he elaborated. "We're looking at Cambrian creatures, when biodiversity exploded, right?" He saw mostly blank stares, but Mei nodded slowly as if she was beginning to catch on. "More than any other time before it, evolution was driven not just by the conditions of the environment, but by competition... competition with *other species.*"

"What are you suggesting?" Arden's exhaustion and anger were nowhere to be seen. He looked... hopeful?

"I've seen the models and I understand how 'predator factors' were coarsely coded into variable matrices... but we need something much, umm... much more explicit." He was slowing and could feel the fog returning.

Fortunately, Mei picked up the relay stick. "He's right. We don't need qubit paired competitors, but we need to simulate competition at a level that the iteration *thinks* is real."

Finally the rest of the room started to trade in their discomfort and annoyance for excitement. "We already have a database of competitor species renderings." Raza hadn't met this woman. Or maybe he had. He was so, so tired. "We can use those as templates to supply the iteration with regular... competition events?"

"That's great!" Another face Raza couldn't name. "Applying concrete pressures to the model through regular competition events ought to light a fire under its tailfin."

Everyone suddenly had ideas to pitch in. How to make this work. How to put their stamp on it. The seed had flowered and was cross-pollinating around the room. Without saying a word, Raza stood and headed to the door. He didn't look back, but he imagined that if he had he would've seen Mei grinning.

~ ~ ~

The software team pushed back the launch of the next iteration in order to give themselves time to implement what became officially known as the "simulated competitive engagement events", and unofficially known as "Mugabi Brawls". In that time, Raza apologized to everyone individually and as a group for his behavior in the ISC meeting. Thankfully, everyone was quick to forgive, at least partially because he'd given the long-stalled project a boost of optimism. Even Arden was understanding. Most importantly to Raza, his idea had taken much of the heat off Mei. He had apparently proven his worth, which meant Mei could be forgiven for whatever breaches of protocol got Raza into the elevator in the first place.

The night before Eighty-Seven's initiation, Mei offered to take Raza out to dinner.

"Is it still dinner if it's after 23:00?"

"What else would it be?"

He thought for a moment. "I don't have *all* the answers."

Mei snorted. "You had one good idea a month ago and you've been riding that high ever since."

"To be fair, it's only been three weeks."

"Ah, my apologies, Doctor Calendar."

"...Doctor Calendar?"

"Shut up. I'm exhausted."

"What are my powers?"

"Do you want me to buy you dinner or not?"

"Hmmm, I might have an opening. Let me check my..." He put his fingers to his temples and closed his eyes. When he opened them, Mei was halfway down the hallway and he ran to catch up.

~ ~ ~

Thirty-five minutes later they walked into a late-night Vietnamese restaurant near the heart of Old Downtown.

"Mei's here!" A boy, maybe sixteen or seventeen years old, manning the front of the restaurant, dropped his book and shouted over his shoulder to no one in particular.

"Danny! I didn't expect to find you here. Aunt Van has you working the late shift?"

"Yes, ma'am." Danny looked guilty and cast his eyes downward.

"Daniel." Mei scowled and put her hands on her hips. "What did you do?"

"I caught him sneaking out. On a school night, no less. Can you believe that?" A tiny woman who Raza guessed to be somewhere between eighty and eight hundred years old was standing in the doorway to the kitchen. "Said he was going to *study*. Like I was born yesterday. I know what you were going to study. I play cards with her grandmother." Danny's skin flushed pink and he shuffled back to his post at the front desk.

"It's good to see you, Aunt Van."

"Who's this young fella? Is he the reason you haven't been around here in ages?"

"Ha, no man could keep me away from you. And it hasn't been *that* long. It's just been hectic at work. This is Raza, he can vouch for that." She patted his back. "We work together."

The woman turned to look up at him. Her eyes were sharp and Raza felt the urge to look away, but knew somehow that he shouldn't. "How long have you worked with my Mei?"

"Three weeks. Ummm, actually more like ten... eleven months?"

She stared at him blankly before turning back to Mei. "Grab a seat. I'll brew you two some tea."

Mei led Raza to a table by the window. He sat down across from her. "So," he said, "ever eaten here before?"

Mei smiled and looked out toward the street. "Aunt Van and my mom's mom go way back. They were the only two Asian children in their grade school, if you can believe it. This is back when Texas was even more white and racist than it is today. Some kids bullied nǎinai on her first day of school, Aunt Van splintered a two-by-four over one of their heads, and the two have been best friends ever since." She glanced toward the entrance. "I used to babysit Danny. I tutored his older sister, too."

The glow of the restaurant signs reflected off the puddles in the street. Had it rained recently? Raza had been so consumed by jinhwa since his meeting with Food Court Mei that he hadn't registered the weather. Speaking of FCM, "That's the most I've learned about you since you shared your chow fun with me. And to be honest, I'm not even sure how much of that was real."

Mei sighed. "I get chatty when I'm tired." Aunt Van approached with two glossy ceramic cups and a beautiful steaming teapot. Standing, she was only slightly taller than Raza in his seat. Judging by the look she gave him, he was relieved that she didn't have a plank of wood handy. After she retreated from their table, Mei continued, "I wasn't lying at the food court, if that's what's on your mind. I needed to pass a bit of information to you, but I wasn't, like, undercover or in character. I'm not a spy. I'm an engineer." She poured them both a cup of tea and then grinned. "You dork."

"That's good to know. I may have let my mind run a bit wild those few days. I was all out of sorts."

"You? Out of sorts? I'm not sure you ever had any sorts to begin with."

"Are you calling me sorts-less?"

"Hey, I get it. I..." She reached up and touched her ear. "Oh shit, what time is it?"

"Uhhh," Raza fumbled for his SenZ, "23:50."

"Phew, that was a close one."

"Why, are you gonna turn into a bumpkin?"

"No, I... what?" She unpinned her left earring and put it on the table. "Oh. Oh boy. I believe the word you're looking for is *pumpkin*. Do you think Cinderella turns into a *bumpkin* at midnight?" She repeated the process with her right earring. The same earrings she'd been wearing since the morning he was given the tour.

"But Cinderella doesn't turn into a pumpkin... Her carriage, which *was* a pumpkin, turns *back* into a pumpkin. Cinderella, who *was* a *bumpkin*, turns *back* into a *bumpkin*." Raza put his lips to his cup and let the steam fog up his glasses. He looked through the condensation on his lenses at a blurry Mei. The film of droplets evaporated as he inhaled and Mei was pulled back into focus. Her head tilted slightly as she studied him. His neck prickled under her gaze and he quickly redirected her attention to the jewelry she'd just removed. "So, as long as I've caught you in a chatty mood, what's the story with those?"

She looked back out the window. "They're silicon. I told you that, right? They're actually from an Old Coast wafer fab."

"Interesting..."

She looked guilty. "My family did a *bit* of disaster tourism when I was a kid, which sucks, I know. Don't judge me."

"I'm not judging. Just listening."

"Judgmentally."

"Mei..."

"Fine. Just, keep in mind that I was a child, with basically no moral agency and no say in the matter." She stalled with a sip of tea. "We visited a derelict wafer processing facility in Seoul. My dad had a thing for tech factories. Something about 'nature reclaiming dominance over the audacity of man'... don't ask me. Anyway, it was in quite a state. There was about three feet of water on the ground floor. We were in hazmat suits. I was on a little raft being pulled along by my parents. Everything was so... brown. Then, floating in the debris, we found a single wafer in a plastic FOUP, somehow still perfectly intact. It was beautiful. Just an ordinary wafer, but it shone like a beacon in that dingy, depressing facility. I remember, I couldn't take my eyes off it. I asked my folks if I could keep it, they said no, and I held my breath until they changed their minds. I was stubborn. Anyway, a decade or so later when I was in comp history, I dug up the wafer and analyzed it. It was nothing special. A memristor stack. Likely a misprint, on its way to a failure analysis lab when the Greenland Fault slipped and shit really hit the fan. I diced it up and made it into jewelry. They've been my lucky pair of earrings ever since."

"Huh. There's a lot to unpack there. Why do they have to come off before midnight?"

"Excellent question. They only provide good luck in the days leading up to a launch. They become bad luck once the iteration is actually initialized so I have to take them off the night before."

"Ah. That makes sense."

"I know, right?" Mei laughed and Raza felt it wash over him. "I know what you're thinking."

He wasn't thinking about anything but her laugh. The pitch, the timbre, the rhythm... the way it seemed to come out of nowhere, as if it originated outside of her body and worked its way back into the base of her lungs. "I doubt that very much."

"You're thinking, 'what's an engineer doing with superstitions?'"

"Well, now that you mention it, it's a bit of an odd character trait."

"Odd nothing. I ran the numbers and found a statistically significant correlation between the presence of the earrings and successful launches. Don't make that face! I'll show you the ANOVA."

"No, that's okay."

"Mmmmhmmmm." She narrowed her eyes.

"Is he bothering you, Mei?" Aunt Van had appeared out of thin air with a platter of miscellaneous delicious smelling foods.

"I can handle him just fine, but thanks, Aunt Van."

"I've got a clear shot from the kitchen. You say the word and I'll—"

"Aunt Van!"

"Okay, dearie, I'll leave you to it." She turned a sour eye on Raza before scuttling back behind the counter.

"Should I be concerned?" he asked. "For my life, I mean?"

"Always. You only get one, after all." She began distributing items from the platter onto their plates. "So, I'm not keeping score, but I do believe it's your turn to tell me something about yourself."

"What would you like to know?"

"Hmmmm." She took a bite of a crispy roll, closed her eyes, and smiled when the taste hit her tongue. "What's the last book you read? Ever been married? When was the last time you were upside-down? Would you rather be cremated or donated to science? Or are you one of those selfish 'stuff-me-with-sawdust and bury me whole' types?"

Raza liked tired-chatty Mei. "Is that not all covered in my company file?"

"It is, but I don't have your file in front of me."

"Fine. Let's see, I'm reading *The Illustrated Man*, but the last book I finished was some dry autobiography by one of SenZero's cofounders."

"Ooooh, was it *Quantum Method*, the one by Kevin Xiang?" Mei said with a mouthful of pickled cabbage.

"Bingo."

"It sucked major ass, right?"

"Yes! I'm so relieved to know someone else hated it." He took another bite.

"I've seen solo porn that was less self-indulgent and more informative than that damn book."

Raza choked on spiced greens and Mei laughed. At her own joke? At his gasping and sputtering? He didn't care. It was contagious and once his esophagus was cleared of roughage he joined her.

"Let's see, what was next. I've never been married. I was in a long-term relationship and, uh, now I'm not. It was actually my ex that recommended *Quantum Method*."

"That tells me all I need to know. You dodged a bullet."

"Yeah, well. That relationship was..." Raza shrugged. He didn't know what to say. It had been over a year since his ex left him behind with nothing but a battered ego and that annoyingly dog-eared slog of an e-book. He was slow to recover, but he had been so busy these last few weeks he hadn't taken time to probe the tenderness of those old wounds.

"Insightful."

"Thanks." He considered leaving it at that, but some combination of exhaustion and spices and company compelled him to continue. He breathed another protective layer of fog onto his glasses and continued. "Are you familiar with non-Newtonian fluid?"

"I did science fair projects as a kid, yes."

"Right, so you get the idea. The relationship was non-Newtonian."

"If that's a sex thing I'd rather not hear about it." She shoved the rest of the roll into her mouth. "At least not while I'm eating."

"No, no," he laughed. "Anyway, thinking back on it, the whole relationship was like trying to build a bridge out of non-Newtonian fluid. We had to constantly work on it, which is fine and all, relationships take work, but that work was the only thing providing structural integrity."

"And the moment you let up, the trusses all turn to gloopy soup and spill into the gorge?"

"Exactly."

She nodded knowingly. "Well, let's circle back to the items remaining in the queue."

He was pleased to find that talking about his ex didn't elicit the spiral of negative symptoms he'd expected. Still, he appreciated the off-ramp. "How upside-down do you mean?"

"Fully inverted. All or nothing."

"Huh. Wow." He pulled his mind away from his ex and back to the string of bizarre questions from the bizarre person across the table. "Maybe a decade?"

"Keg stands in grad school?"

"Close. Yoga."

"Even cooler." She grinned. "Now, answer the last question."

Raza balked. "Hmmm. Why? Do you need to know what to do with my corpse if Aunt Van decides I'm not leaving this place alive?"

"Nah. She'd just dissolve you in acid and pour you down the drain."

"Wouldn't that ruin the pipes?"

"You have to neutralize the solution first. Duh."

"Ah, of course. Just like titrations in chem lab."

"Precisely." Mei smiled and grabbed a shrimp roll from his plate. She had one on her own plate, and there were more on the platter in the middle of the table. This was purely a show of force.

Raza shuffled his weight in his chair. "Why this question?"

"I can't tell you until after you answer. Otherwise it will influence your response. Bad science. If it helps, I'm already learning so much. Let me guess, you're a 'donate my body to science' guy. Right?"

"Why would you assume that?"

"You're a scientist yourself, which means you're probably not too concerned about what Saint Peter will say to you at the Pearly Gates. You feel some sense of duty to science at large, the greater quest for knowledge and all that, and you want to pay your debts in the form of a handsome cadaver."

Did she say handsome? Well, she said handsome *cadaver*. Hard to know what to make of that phrase. "Actually, no. I mean, sure, I'm your stereotypical godless man of science. I used to think I'd donate my body, but... have you ever met any medical students? I don't want some hungover 22-year-old hacky-sacking my gallbladder around the anatomy lab to impress his classmates."

She snorted. "Fair enough. So, what's it gonna be? Where do you see yourself in a hundred years? Ashes on a mantle? Biodegradable burial pod? Crushed into a diamond and fired into orbit?"

"I... I guess I haven't given it much thought," he lied.

"You're lying."

"No, I'm not," he lied again.

"Fine, we can talk about something else if you're not ready to be honest with me."

"I'm not... oh, right. I have a *tell?*"

"HUGE tell."

Utterly outgunned, he capitulated. He looked over his shoulders to check for nothing in particular and returned his eyes to his plate. "I want to be buried at sea." He paused, waiting and hoping for Mei to interrupt him, but she was frustratingly patient for the first time tonight. "I want to be dumped—or sprinkled, I'm not too picky about my, umm, form factor at that point—into the ocean. Specifically, the Pacific Ocean. More specifically, the San Francisco Bay."

"Ah." Mei didn't elaborate, pushing him to continue with her silence.

"It's not about being reunited with my parents or anything like that. I mean, I didn't know them, and what little I know I'm not sure I like. It's not easy to reckon with. If they were better people, less hubristic and irrational, I wouldn't exist, because no decent human being would bring a life into that environment. What kind of person..." He was talking fast and felt his pulse quicken to match the staccato of his speech, which had taken him by surprise. "Sorry. That's all to say, I don't intend to be buried there for *them.*" Again, Mei just blinked. In the open space between them, Raza had no choice but to continue. "It's for me. I like the symmetry of it. Does that make sense?"

Mei smiled thoughtfully. "Like matching bookends. I understand."

"Exactly!" He pushed a cube of fried tofu into a ramekin of the most incredible sauce he'd ever tasted and left it there to marinate. "Well, that's the end of the quiz. Want to tell me how I did?"

She rolled her eyes. "I'm not grading you. I just wanted to know you better."

"By asking about my funeral plans?"

"Look, if you really want to understand someone, you need to know how they view and value life in general. I find it helpful to start with how they view their own life, specifically, and branch out from there."

"Huh. And asking about their death..."

"Is the most indirectly direct means of getting someone to open up about their personal relationship with *life*." She smiled. "If you *were* being graded, you would've passed."

Raza breathed a sigh of relief and reached for the marinated tofu. "What does a failing answer sound like?"

"In my opinion, and this is just one person's subjective experience—though that one person happens to be an incredible judge of character and what many would consider a genius—the *second* worst thing someone can say is 'I don't know' or 'I haven't thought about it'."

"Your humility is inspiring."

"Humility is a shield. Confidence is a weapon."

Raza didn't know what to say to that. Mei was many things, but 'easy to read' was not on her résumé. "So, what's the *first* worst thing someone can say?"

"I'm so glad you asked! I consider 'I haven't thought about it' to be the second worst because it indicates a sort of personal neutrality, not to mention a painful lack of long-term thinking. But, more importantly, it speaks to an absence of existential awareness. That void on an individual level causes humanity as a whole to stagnate."

Raza wasn't sure he was picking up everything Mei was putting down, but he didn't dare interrupt. He had to know what—

"The *first* worst—"

Or *forst* if you're into ineffective portmanteaus, he thought but didn't externalize.

"Did you just do some rhyming thing in your head?"

How did she do that? "I'd turn it off if I could."

"Leave it on. It's growing on me. Now, the *first* worst thing someone can say, worse than 'I don't *know*', is 'I don't *care*'. Not just 'I haven't thought about it', but 'I *have* thought about it and I'm completely apathetic.'"

"That kind of surprises me. That you consider not caring worse than not knowing, I mean."

"Because you're a scientist. That way of thinking has become normalized to you because everyone around you is of a similar mindset.

We're so committed to the concept of eternal oblivion that we refuse to *care* about what happens when we cease to exist, as if caring betrays our faith in nothingness."

"Did you minor in philosophy?"

"Music, and it was a double-major." She bared her teeth in some combination of a smile and a threat. "Look, with the work we're doing, a lot of high-minded questions are going to filter into that big head of yours. Don't fight them. But don't be an airfoil either."

"Airfoil?"

"It's something Mikus told me once. One of his better analogies. He said, 'Smooth brains are an airfoil, just redirecting ideas. Wrinkled brains add turbulence. Use those wrinkles. They were hard earned, evolutionarily speaking.'"

"I like it." He looked back out at the street. It was a quiet night. There was a single vehicle parked at the end of the block, a small car with one of those fancy blacker-than-black finishes. It was more of a coupe-shaped void; an absence of street and shop window in the shape of a car. In the void, his eyes refocused and he saw Mei looking at him through the reflection in the window. A thought sprung from the back left corner of his brain. "Do you ever ask anyone that question more than once?"

Mei cocked an eyebrow, broke the stare with his reflection to lock eyes with him across the table. "I can't say that I have. Why?"

"Well, I can understand your ranking; 'I haven't thought about it' is bad, 'I don't care' is worse. But what if you ask the 'I haven't thought about it' person again a week later?"

She saw where he was going and met him there. "Have they *still* not thought about it, after being asked directly? Huh."

"Exactly. Now it's not just a lack of... what did you call it? Existential awareness?"

"Being confronted with their mortality and just closing their eyes, plugging their ears, and ignoring it." She reached for a slice of pandan honeycomb cake that must have appeared between them when he wasn't looking. "That may take the cake."

"So," Raza grabbed a slice for himself. It was an otherworldly, almost fluorescent shade of green and smelled of fresh coconut and caramelized sugar. "What do you want done with your body after you, um, bite it?"

Mei looked Raza hard in the eyes, deadly serious. "Honestly?"

"Honestly."

Her lips crept back toward her ears. "Honestly, Raz, I couldn't give less of a shit."

CHAPTER 13
TRIAL DAY 2.0 - JIVANTA

Today was a new day, she thought, before admonishing herself for entertaining such trite platitudes. She wasn't especially nice to herself in the mornings, before the caffeine and joint pain medications had found their ways to the appropriate receptors. Facing the bathroom mirror of her luxury hotel room (a perk that made these international gigs more tolerable), she allowed her eyes to unfocus and look through her reflection. As her gaze passed over the aquiline nose and graying black hair—two features she'd trained herself to love through sheer strength of will, the first as a child and the second more recently—she recounted yesterday's events. The defense had landed one hell of a punch late in the round, a blow from which she hadn't yet fully recovered. That said, many... or rather *most* of her arguments were unaddressed and unaffected by Raza Mugabi's claim. His *impossible* claim, she reminded herself. A first-principles model of the brain, with greater than 99% quantum-level accuracy, was utter nonsense. It *had* to be. Right?

The implications were, frankly, overwhelming. She made a conscious effort to prevent her mind from wandering too far down that road, leashing it to her firm belief that Dr. Mugabi was mistaken. Or, more likely, outright lying. Was it even *partially* true? Even considering his statements to contain partial truths caused the knot in her leash to slacken, so she ignored the possibility. But, as with her efforts to ignore the ache in her left knee, the world sought to remind her. She dressed for the day, first reaching for more muted tones, which perhaps would soften her in the eyes of the panel and the court, and reflect a less purely offensive strategy.

She wrinkled her nose and reached for an altogether more striking ensemble.

~ ~ ~

Jivanta sat impatiently through the morning remarks by Justice Hoffer. There was no particular hierarchy to the panel, but it seemed that Hoffer had appointed herself as the primary voice for this case. The old judge hadn't historically shown much interest in tech law, typically taking more passive roles and deferring to other panel members in high profile matters of intellectual property, software monopolies, privacy, and other staples for the sector. Jivanta had been surprised by her apparent enthusiasm and presence behind the bench, and now recognized that Hoffer's opinions would carry more than their fair share of the weight behind closed doors. More than any of the others, she needed Hoffer on her side.

She eyed the defendants, several of whom looked as though they had stayed up late celebrating prematurely (and aggressively). None looked more bedraggled and bleary-eyed than her new least-favorite member of the jinhwa team, Dr. Mugabi. She smirked at his unironed suit and unkempt hair and briefly found it easier to scoff at what he had said yesterday. It was simply unacceptable. The leash tightened. Her knee felt fine.

What she *had* accepted was the notion that the trial may drag on for longer than she had hoped. The panel, which was largely primed to take jinhwa out to pasture for the majority of yesterday's session, was now settled in, alert (or at least awake), and signaling an openness to the defense that had been absent until Dr. Mugabi said... until Dr. Mugabi *lied* about the nature of their model. It wasn't an unfamiliar position; the defendants weren't being wholly honest, as is often the case, and she had no means of addressing the lies directly, so she sought to nullify their claims though other avenues. That's the life of a prosecutor, and there were few better than her.

She wasn't being totally honest with herself, and she knew that. This wasn't just any lie. It was extraordinary, and her unwillingness to entertain it, she had to admit, wasn't purely strategic. It was a matter of self-preservation. If she allowed herself even a moment of consideration... The leash slackened, her knee throbbed, and again she forcibly directed her thoughts elsewhere.

~ ~ ~

The first few hours of the morning session proceeded at about one tenth of the speed of yesterday's session. This wasn't going to be a drive-thru open and shut ruling and everyone in the courtroom adjusted their pace accordingly. She took the time to methodically construct a phalanx around what she considered to be the strongest arguments for discarding jinhwa's claims under the umbrella of Corvis v. Turing. Across the battlefield, Mr. Ragnarsson was still deferring to his first in command, Ms. Egilsdottir, who was nothing if not meticulous. Really, Jivanta? She woke up with toothless truisms and was now dabbling in war metaphors like some finance manager desperate to make himself feel masculine? She was off her game and she knew it. She blamed it on getting caught in Raza's snare yesterday, which wasn't the whole truth. Still, she was gradually pulling the panel back to her side.

Transparency. Interpretability. Precedent. Transparency. Interpretability. Precedent. Corvis. Turing. Corvis. Turing. Corvis. Turing. She was a broken record, but sometimes percussive repetition was exactly what the panel needed. That's what they would hear when they turned out the lights and closed their heavy eyelids tonight. And so far, the defense was making no moves to address those sticking points. At each turn, Ms. Egilsdottir would whisper to Mr. Ragnarsson, who gave no signal as to whether or not he heard her, and she would stand to proceed with their establishment of timelines, relationships, and other matters that held no particular sway over the panel.

And so it went, back and forth, through the morning and into the early afternoon. The good doctor Arden returned to the stand multiple times and did a passable job of not being an absolute asshat. Mr. Ragnarsson, the legal titan, blinked his watery eyes, and occasionally looked toward his open folder.

As the afternoon session ticked by, Ms. Egilsdottir was growing impatient, though with what, exactly, Jivanta couldn't say. Herself? Her prosecution? Her clients? Her wholly unhelpful leader? Smart money is on the latter, she thought. Mr. Ragnarsson had been borderline vegetative behind the defense bench and had begun to disappear from Jivanta's perception, the way you don't notice a tree you pass every day. At least not until it falls or flowers. And, as if in response to the thought, Vilho suddenly bloomed, snapping out of his reverie. He had been so still, so completely absent, that the sudden clarity in his eyes was enough to draw her attention before he even made a motion.

Jivanta was temporarily unmoored by the abrupt presence of Mr. Ragnarsson before shaking off her surprise. He rose and spoke with a surety that had been absent from the defense team up to that point, save for a few surprising bouts from Ms. Egilsdottir. "The defense calls Dr. Mei Kunihara to the stand." Ah, Mei. The witness touched her hand to her earring, rose from her seat, smoothed her blazer over her very pregnant belly, and walked to the front of the room, side-eyeing the bailiff when he made an after-the-fact "need any help up the step?" gesture. She had done extensive research on all members of the defense team and their list of witnesses. Dr. Kunihara's story was one of the more interesting ones. This should be good.

"Dr. Kunihara—"

"Call me Mei."

"Of course, my apologies. Mei, please explain your field of expertise and your role at jinhwa."

Mei took a breath. "I'm the Head of the Cognitive Development Team. It's a multidisciplinary group, but my particular specialty is in cognition modeling." She paused and looked toward Vilho, who gave a slight nod of encouragement to continue. "Human brains are extremely complex machines. Broadly speaking, our group is responsible for pushing our evolutionary models toward higher levels of complexity and pulling them toward consciousness."

Vilho paced slowly back and forth. He paused in front of Jivanta, then slowly walked back again. Was he stalling for time? Was it an act to build suspense for the casual viewer? The look on his assistant's face was one of worry, so perhaps this long silence wasn't part of the plan.

"Dr. Ku... Pardon me. Mei. You studied human cognitive modeling when you were a student, is that correct?"

"Ummm, yes, that's correct." Dr. Kunihara looked at Ms. Egilsdottir who only shrugged. Interesting. He must be going off script.

"Would you say that the human brain was fully understood? Completely and utterly unraveled? No mysteries left behind the skull?"

"I... No, not by a long shot."

"Ah. I see. What percentage of the human mind would you say is fully understood?"

"I couldn't possibly say... "

"Humor an old man."

"If I had to hazard a guess, maybe five percent?"

"Hmmm." Vilho paced again. Where was he going with this? "Ninety-five percent unknown. That is truly fascinating!" Again he stopped in front of the prosecution bench. "And would you, Mei, describe yourself as human?"

"I..." Mei smiled, undoubtedly relieved to sense what the old kook was prattling on about. "I would, yes. I am very much human."

"And your great-great-great-grandparents, who lived at a time when the mind was even less well understood, let's say 98% unknown, were *they* human?"

"Of course," Mei answered dutifully.

Vilho looked up toward the panel. Perhaps he was reading their faces, gauging their interest and patience. "You know, before I studied law, I studied history. A wonderful subject. Did you know that many of our ancestors believed that the center of thought was located not in the head, but in the gut? Nobody had the slightest idea how the human mind worked until three hundred years ago, and even today mysteries abound." He paused again, showing a furtive smile. "This is all to say that understanding *how* a person thinks is not a prerequisite for recognizing their humanity, nor has it ever been. There is no precedent for using our feeble understanding of the inner workings of the mind to qualify personhood. Without getting too philosophical, I think we can agree that what makes humans human is something more... external. More *abstract.* Our capabilities and behaviors. Our range and depth of emotions. Our shared individuality." He turned his back to the panel to face the benches.

"And on to a related matter, this 'transparency and interpretability of ideation'. Mei, it is no stretch to say that you are a brilliant scientist, I believe you told me as much when we first met."

Mei laughed. An ugly laugh. Sharp and bark-like. "Modesty is overrated. Yes, I'm very good at what I do." Jivanta found her confidence admirable and her laugh irritating.

"In your career, have you ever been struck with inspiration?"

Jivanta was growing impatient. "Objection, irrelevance—"

"Overruled." Hoffer peered down at Jivanta. "Please continue, Mr. Ragnarsson."

"Please, call me Vilho. Mei, you were saying?"

"I... yes, I've been struck with inspiration."

"How would you describe that feeling?"

"Well," Mei said, "it's difficult to explain. Sometimes solutions to problems I've been working on for months... sometimes *years*, will just pop into my head. I may not even be thinking about it, and then 'pow', there it is."

"As an expert in human cognition, can you explain the origination of these sudden solutions?"

"Nobody fully understands it. Subconscious thoughts and half-forgotten experiences suddenly mesh together, triggered by hidden stimuli and a bit of magic."

"A bit of magic, indeed. Untraceable thoughts, creativity, inspiration... all uniquely human qualities, would you say?"

"I couldn't agree more."

"I'm afraid the point I am making lacks such elegant subtleties, but I will summarize it, for my own benefit if not for anyone else's. Humanity is characterized, perhaps even *defined* by our ability to divine creative solutions out of thin air. We carry with us capabilities that are opaque even to ourselves. Interpretability and transparency hold *no bearing* on the recognition of personhood. Perhaps even the opposite is true. We are creatures of mystery and secrets." He turned his head and, for the first time since the hearing began, looked directly at Jivanta. "And who would any of us be should all our secrets be laid bare?"

Ah, there he is. The People's Viking lives after all.

CHAPTER 14
6.5 YEARS EARLIER - RAZA

12:35 [Private workchat thread - Mei] got sucked into a sw debate - go ahead without me

"Is that her?" Mikus's words were muffled by a mouthful of some bizarre off-menu item that looked as unappetizing as it smelled.

"Umm, yeah. Looks like she's not going to make it today. So, we can..." Raza tried to ignore the purple mush that Mikus was shoveling down his throat. "Get started."

Mikus smiled in acknowledgement of Raza's pregnant pause and then reached for Mei's carryout plate.

12:36 [Private workchat thread - Mei] if m touches my food i'm killing you both

"She said—"

"I'll order her a new one. The quality vs. time curve for this particular order drops like a stone kicked off a cliff after ten minutes."

"Fair enough." Raza considered Mikus a friend. They'd spent ample time together over the last six months. They had lunch together once a week. So why was he feeling so uncomfortable? The answer was in the empty seat next to him. Mei and Mikus had a natural, playful back-and-forth that was part brother-sister and part mentor-mentee (though they occasionally swapped roles). Mei allowed Raza to share her comfort with a profoundly odd man, and now her absence stood (or rather sat) firmly between them. Raza chewed on his food and wondered whether Mikus felt it too. "So," he managed between bites.

Mikus looked at him expectantly. "So?"

He queried his mind for a list of conversation topics and hit a runtime error. Mikus took another bite, furrowed his brow, and grinned. He was very much enjoying Raza's unease. Finally, Raza landed on a corker of a question. "You, uh, read any good books?"

Mikus's grin grew further until he was a Cheshire cat that had just enjoyed a bowl of pickled garbage mush. "Ever?"

"Lately, I mean."

"Hmmm, nobody has ever asked me that!"

"Really?"

"Apologies, Razberry. I'm having fun at your expense. As it so happens, I *have* been asked that before." His lips retreated from his ears and returned to a less maniacal resting state. "You know, I used to be a voracious reader. Poetry, mostly, but I took all comers."

"What happened?" Raza asked, relieved to be steering the conversation toward normalcy and literature, two worlds in which he felt reasonably secure. "Did you get too busy? I imagine it's tough to read for pleasure and also found a company."

"*Co*-found," he said with a slight wince. "And no, it's not the founding, or any of my other pursuits that keep my bookshelves dusty."

Raza could tell he was being baited, and he leapt for it. "Well, what is it that keeps—"

"I'll tell you!" Mikus spun in his chair and shot up toward the back of his office. "I have a running list of works that I've been ticking off since I was about your age. I follow the list in order." He paused and turned, expecting a question, but he caught Raza mid-bite. "Well, a few years back I got stuck. Simple as that. I haven't been able to get through it, so I can't move on to the next one."

"Sounds like—" Raza swallowed too early and coughed. "Like a node on The Tree."

"Quite right. My book list is an evolutionary pathway for me to become a more enlightened individual and I've reached an impasse."

Raza pondered for a moment as he massaged the lump of food in his throat down into his belly. "So, what's the work? What's your *Pikaia*?" Mikus cast an angry thumb toward a weighty tome on his desk that looked as though it had ridden a tumble dryer through hell. It was stabbed through with dozens of bookmarks of the sticky note, receipt, and takeout menu variety. *Et tu*, Raza imagined the book whimpering. He squinted but could only make out one word. "Borges? Is that a collection of his shorts?"

"Well it's not a collection of his pants, now is it?" Mikus shot back. "Pardon. Indeed it is, Razberry."

"Well, which—"

"Del rigor en la ciencia." He sighed and lowered his head before continuing, wearing a pained expression. "On. *Exactitude.* In. Science." With each word his voice rose in volume and exasperation.

"Ha!" Raza laughed at what he assumed was a punchline before Mikus's face communicated otherwise. "Oh, sorry. It's just... I'm familiar with it. Isn't that story, like, half a page long?"

"Depends. Borges only gave us one hundred and eighteen words in the original Spanish, the cruel ol' miser. Most English versions hover around one fifty. My latest translation is... substantially less economical."

Raza chewed his lip, wondering which of the many questions fluttering to the forefront of his mind to ask first, and how to phrase it delicately. After some consideration, he managed a thoughtful, "Huh?"

"You see, I first read the Hurley translation, which is widely accepted as a faithful interpretation for the English speakers of the world. Let's just say that I disagree, but I'm getting ahead of myself. I spent a year learning Spanish so that I could go to the source, as it were. Once I was comfortable with the language, I was able to see the text with fresh eyes, but there was still so much *unsaid.* There's the words, all one hundred and eighteen of them, and then there's the entire world of meaning hiding just behind the words. It's that world I've been trying to map out. It's my white whale. I think. Moby Dick is actually next on my list, but I fear I may never get to meet Ahab or fully appreciate the metaphor I just used."

Mikus was brilliant and often inscrutable, but he was obsessive and neurotic in ways that Raza recognized in himself. The sense of familiarity settled Raza's nerves and he was able to ease into the conversation. "That's... hmmm. Let me make sure I'm capturing the full irony of this situation." For a moment, Raza worried that he'd overstepped, but Mikus's self-effacing smile invited him to continue. "You read a one paragraph story about an empire so obsessed with the accuracy of their cartography that they collapsed under the weight of a map that was one-to-one, point-for-point the size of the empire."

"Correct."

"And your thought was to *expand* upon that story?"

"Precisely."

"To create a map *larger* than the material it's mapping."

"The irony is not lost on me."

"You're an interesting guy, you know that?"

"So I've been told, but hear me out!" Mikus took one awkward stride toward the whiteboard that had been unearthed during their first meeting. "Jorge Luis Borges." He popped the cap off the marker and wrote *JLB* on the board. "Jorgie Borgie, I call him. He gave us *Del Rigor*, on its surface a fun tale of hubris and ruin. But beneath the surface, a treasure map! Now, now, don't make that face. Not a *literal* treasure map. The treasure here is Jorgie's central philosophy. His commandments. His warning! They're unspoken, but they're *there*."

"So," Raza played along, "the text tells us of a collapsed empire. And you're saying the subtext tells us more about *why* it collapsed?"

"*Why* it collapsed, yes, and more importantly *why* the Cartographers Guild did what they did. What drove them to create the map in the first place?"

"Hubris, right? You said it yourself."

"Wrong! I mean, yes, I did just say 'hubris', but I don't believe that was their motivation. Hubris is on the surface and Jorgie saw deeper into the soul."

"Hmmm." Raza stepped next to Mikus at the whiteboard. "Is hubris an intentional misdirection? Some sort of philosophical red heron?"

"Exact..." Mikus froze mid-word and arched a bushy brow. "A red what?"

"A red heron. You know, a misleading clue."

Mikus scratched his beard thoughtfully. "Language evolves. Idioms evolve. Who am I to say that in the right circumstances, encouraged by the right accent, a fish can't become a bird?"

"I'm not sure I follow you," Raza admitted.

"Good! By sea or by air, forge your own path! But back to Borges and the matter at hand." Mikus spun on his heel and leaned over the heap that was his desk. "I've translated those words more times than I can count. Well, that's just a phrase. I know how many times I've done it and I'm withholding that information so you don't think less of me." He threw a quick wink over his shoulder. "I built an interpolative and extrapolative language engine trained on all of Jorgie's works, published and... otherwise."

"Otherwise?"

"I stole some material from an archive in Switzerland. A story for another time. Don't distract me, Razberry."

"Sorry."

"Don't be! Anyway, with a little borrowed power from jinhwa's processors during sim downtime, I used the language engine to fill in the blanks. I know more about the members of the Cartographers Guild than their own husbands and wives. I know their hopes and dreams. I know why they made the maps!"

Raza rubbed his chin, playing the role of the thoughtful audience awaiting Mikus's big reveal. "Well? Why'd they do it?!"

"Fear!" Mikus threw his hands into the air, accidentally launching the marker across the room and behind a teetering stack of coiled copper cables. "They were utterly terrified of the unknown. They drew maps to shine light into the shadows. They constructed a map of a province the size of a town and still couldn't sleep at night, for what mysteries lay in the space collapsed by their scaling? The only answer was a map of the land *as large as the land.* On it they drew themselves, as large as the selves they saw in the mirrors (which they also drew) and only then were they sated."

"Wow. So the pursuit of the Cartographers Guild was driven by... cowardice?"

"Sniveling milksops, the whole lot! A detestable bunch."

129

Raza fished the marker out from behind the dusty hardware pile and handed it back. "Sounds like you cracked it. What's keeping you from putting it down and moving on to Melville?"

"Surely you're joking, Dr. Mugabi! I've only scratched the surface! What becomes of the second empire? Will they fall prey to the same personal foibles as the first? Or, in this alternate reality, are people capable of learning from the mistakes of their forebears? Can society ever truly *change*?"

Raza was enjoying the ride. He sat back in the chair and pictured the text in his mind. "Huh. If I'm remembering it correctly, the story starts with an ellipsis, right?"

"That is correct, why?"

"That's an unusual way to start a story. If we're only being given one hundred and eighteen words, I have to assume the punctuation is purposeful. Maybe... Maybe the ellipsis tells us that the first empire wasn't really the *first* empire."

Mikus froze with his hand clutching the breast of his wrinkled, purple-goop-stained shirt. Only his eyes were moving, darting back and forth, reading and rereading a story burned into his pupils. *Oh shit*, Raza worried, *did I say something wrong?* Per the clock on the wall behind his head, a full minute passed before Mikus flinched. Raza instinctively tensed, half-expecting to be attacked, until his ears were filled with Mikus's laugh. "Razberry, you clever bastard!" He laughed, long and loud before the laughter grew softer and altogether more solemn. "Empires rise and empires fall and nothing breaks the cycle. Jorgie, you devastate me." As he spoke he grabbed the worn tome from his desk and walked it over to his bookshelf. He blew off the layer of dust that had accumulated in its spot (most of which curled back into his face, catching in his eyebrows, though he didn't seem to notice) and, with a satisfied sigh, tucked it back in. With his arm still extended, he finger-walked his hand to the next book over and pulled it down from the shelf. "Sorry to keep you waiting so long, Herman."

Seconds passed, then minutes, and Raza came to realize that Mikus was now miles away, lost at sea aboard the Pequod. Without saying a word, he gathered his things and slipped out the door, shaking his head and smiling to himself as he made his way back to the elevator.

CHAPTER 15
6 YEARS EARLIER - RAZA

Raza Mugabi was on a roll. He had been at jinhwa for about one year. Well, it was actually close to two years, but he and those around him marked his start date with his first steps onto the Second Floor. Those nine or ten months on the ground floor (Jesus on a jet plane, had it really been ten months?) were behind him. A necessary precaution, he had been told repeatedly until he believed it himself.

For the first time since graduating, he felt like part of something greater. There was the thrill of discovery, of tremendous, world-altering potential, sure. But, to his surprise, it wasn't the work itself that inspired him, at least not entirely. It was the team. They had become his... Huh. How many 'world-changing' tech startups had he interviewed for that described their team as a family? Skepticism was in his DNA (his academic advisor had once called him "a most prolific doubter") and every now and then, usually on the train with a strong coffee in his hand that was still too hot to consume (note: remember to ask for an ice cube next time), he would run a self-diagnostic to determine whether he had been brainwashed and welcomed into a cult. After all, some would say that cult susceptibility was *also* in his DNA, jockeying for dominance over the skeptical codons. Over and over the diagnostic scan came back negative. He was part of something real. But then again, that's exactly what a brainwashed person would think. Right?

His phone alarm buzzed and reminded him to take his medicine. The coffee in his hand was just about cool enough to drink. He could take the cap off to speed things up, but between his occasional tremors and the more-than-occasional jostling of the DHA train, well, better safe than sorry. Holding it to his mouth, lip to lip, he exhaled slowly into the lid and let the steam from the vent hole fog up his glasses. That oughta do it. He tossed the pill into the back of his throat and took a small sip of the oh-shit-still-way-too-hot liquid to wash it down. He closed his eyes and sensed the impact almost immediately, first from the placebo (for even his new ultra-fast-acting medicine took at least a few minutes to kick in—and knowing that didn't diminish the strength of his placebo response), and then (at least a few minutes later) the "real" effects. He felt the scattered vectors of thought in his brain begin to align, like iron filings on a magnet. He took a deep breath, grabbing a lungful of the heavily filtered and dehumidified cabin air, and passed it slowly through the lid of his coffee cup before opening his eyes again.

Raza stared out the window of the train car as the moisture slowly crept from his lenses into the hot scrubbed atmosphere around him. The early train had become his preferred choice, and this time of year that meant he would catch the sunrise in the last twenty minutes of the commute.

There's something to be said about a Texas sunrise. If you were to conduct a survey for "beautiful daybreak scenes", you would tend to see images of the sun appearing behind mountains or buildings, features natural and unnatural, through which the light of day first peers. The beauty is in the obscuring of the sun. It's a big solar strip tease. A Texas sunrise is another animal altogether. No mountains, not even so much as a hill, from wherever you stand all the way to the edge of the world. The sun doesn't slowly reveal itself, first with a loosening of a glove and then a sliding of strap. It springboards over the impossibly flat horizon, fully naked and blazing orange-yellow, cannonballing bare-assed onto the entire state at once. The warm dry air inside the cabin grew warmer and dryer as the rays flitted through the windows. Was it safe to stare at the sun this long? How long had he been staring? It was now fully above the horizon, seemingly perched on a flagpole somewhere in Louisiana.

A possibly-still-asleep passenger activated the window tint, breaking his staring contest with the glowing orb and giving Raza a fleeting sense of déjà vu. For a brief spell (Seconds? Minutes? His personal clock was particularly erratic in the first half-hour after his morning dose) a blue-black spot followed his gaze wherever it went. Raza wondered if perhaps it was permanent, but fortunately the spot gradually evaporated into the cabin air, where it was doomed to circulate and filter over and over again until nothing of it remained.

~ ~ ~

"There he is. Lookin' sharp today, hon."

"Yes, Ma'am."

In the last 12 months, Raza had developed a rapport with Ma'am and Broad Chest (whose names he did eventually learn but rarely ever used, so "Ma'am" and "Broad Chest" they remained).

"Whatcha think about this? It came to me in a dream about my ex-husband." She dug the toe of her left foot into the ground and did a quick heel-toe shuffle with her right foot. She looked different, somehow. He felt a tickle in the top left quadrant of his brain and knew that a seed of a thought had been planted but hadn't yet sprouted. He made a note to recheck later in the day. Back to the present.

Raza put his hand to his chin in mock deliberation. "Hmmm. I have to mull this one over." He closed his eyes, laying it on thick. "Aha! Like this?" He mirrored her footwork, throwing in a slight flourish because he was in a better-than-average mood, and Ma'am clapped her hands together in delight. Ma'am and Raza's handshake had become quite a spectacle. Every few weeks one of them would introduce a new element, and the tweaks and additions had compounded into a minute-long choreographed sequence that drew eyes (and eyerolls) from any First Floor employee unlucky enough to be in the office that early.

"Alright," she said. "From the top."

~ ~ ~

The elevator doors opened to reveal a still empty Second Floor. It wasn't rare for him to be the first one into the office (he'd managed to fool everyone, including himself, into believing that he was a morning person), though something felt a bit off today. Or rather, something was *on*, some of the motion-sensitive lighting toward the back of the office was activated, so there must be a few people hopping around. So why was it so eerily quiet? His mind rapidly cycled through half a dozen explanations, most of them quite harrowing, as he made his way toward the freight elevator to the engine room. The basement-dwelling hardware folks were mole people whose circadian rhythms followed no discernable patterns; day and night held no dominion over Mikus and his team. All of that was to say that there were always a few of them down there, and Raza needed to see someone in order to shake the unease he had built up in his gut.

The freight elevator's acceleration-sensitive travel still managed to play tricks on him. It was virtually impossible to sense when it started or stopped, so it was as if the enclosed space was static and it was the world around it that changed, like theater set pieces during an intermission. As the stage crew replaced the cubicles and meeting rooms with server stacks and a cleanroom, he decided that he was being silly. He had nothing to be concerned about. Of those half-dozen harrowing explanations he'd concocted upstairs, really only one of them was remotely feasible. Maybe three, if he was being generous. Still, knowing and acknowledging his irrationality didn't relieve his jitters.

He only knew he had reached his destination because the doors started to open. Raza stepped off the elevator as his eyes began to adjust to the dim light. Something was strange. He could sense a presence. Was somebody here? Hiding in the stacks? A tingle ran up his spine to meet a bead of sweat rolling in the other direction. His heart rate increased and his internal clock followed suit. Did he hear somebody breathe? No, that was his own breath. He heard a single footstep. Behind him? He whipped around, but his eyes hadn't fully adjusted. He balled up his fists, not knowing what else to do, and prepared to fight. Suddenly, lights. He saw someone. No, it was many people. He was surrounded!

"Happy jinhwaversary!"

"Awhathfuck!"

Raza heard Mei's deep laugh, and her face was the first to appear as his eyes adjusted. All around him were the smiling and laughing faces of those he'd spent the last year working with. Instinctively, he smiled and laughed in return as he processed awhathfuck was going on. He felt heavy as the adrenaline pooled in his tensed legs.

"I thought you were going to hit somebody."

Raza realized his fists were still clenched and loosened his fingers. "I... I think I almost did."

"Sorry. We couldn't resist. More specifically, *I* couldn't resist." Mei was still smiling and looking somewhat guilty. "What did you think was happening, exactly?"

Raza looked around at everyone. They were grouping off and chatting amongst themselves, apparently giving Mei and him a chance to talk before piping in with their own takes. "I'm not sure what I thought."

"Yes, you are."

"You got me." Mei could still read him like a book. Like she'd programmed every nuance of his personality herself and knew it character by character. "Honestly? My first thought was some sort of anti-tech terrorism, but the prevailing theory was more in line with corporate warfare."

"I'm so glad that came through!" She laughed, any hint of guilt melting away. "That's exactly what we were going for. I told the team, 'Let's throw Raza a paramilitary and espionage themed surprise party'. Just ask them."

Raza and Mei had, in the last year, developed their own form of communication. Their dialect was a heavy mix of semi-ironic one-upmanship, banter that outsiders perceived as combative, and impossibly dumb jokes that doubled as snare traps. Mikus, after joining them for lunch one day a few months back, had described their rapport as "alienating, insufferable, and exhausting, but not without its charms". Perhaps that's why the rest of the party was giving them their space. Or maybe they were perpetuating the office rumor that he and Mei were *more than just colleagues*, a notion that, fortunately, they both found to be absurd.

"I *will* ask them. I'll ask them right now." Raza entertained the idea of pulling a third-party into their sphere; an advanced move that, when successful, allowed them to join forces and direct their combined obnoxiousness at an unsuspecting coworker, though at the risk of popping the bubble. He turned and scoured the crowd for a victim. His eyes landed on Mikus and Arden, who were partially hidden behind a server stack, arguing.

Mei followed his gaze and sighed. "They've been at each other's throats since we terminated Ninety. That was months ago and they haven't let up."

"They're always like this though, right? I remember them arguing on my first full day." Being an anniversary, Raza felt that he could recall the circumstances of one year ago more clearly. He wondered whether memories were frozen at fixed points in space, left behind as the Earth orbited the sun only to come back into focus one full revolution later. He thought of Ma'am, and the seed of a thought that was planted earlier that morning began to germinate. Why did she seem different than she did when he last passed through this fixed point in space?

"It usually comes in waves that fairly strongly correlate to the initiation and termination cycles. And yes, before you ask, I have plotted their dynamic on a plethora of axes."

"That's the least surprising thing you've ever said."

Mei smiled, but Raza could see the worry in her eyes. "This is different. They've been arguing for longer, more intensely, and..." She tilted her head in their direction. "*Clearly* less discreetly than ever."

With the mention of discretion, Raza realized he never actually knew what they were arguing about. He supposed it was a typical hardware vs. software conflict. We need better hardware to reach the software goals, the software is limiting the hardware, the chicken needs a stronger egg to make a stronger chicken, et cetera. The respective heads of the hardware and software teams shared open disdain for each other, at least when Mei's plots called for it, but the subject of their disdain had been kept behind closed doors. "Any idea what's changed? I mean, by all accounts both teams have been on a hot streak."

"I don't know for certain, but I've heard bits and pieces."

"Raza! My man!" A hand patted him on the shoulder and he turned around to see a coworker. Someone he'd worked with for months. Shit. He cycled through the letters of the alphabet, hoping one would glow brighter than the others and trigger a memory of a name. A? B? C? D? E? F? **G**? H? Huh. Definitely **G**. G-something. Garth?

"Good morning, Gregg!" Mei winked slyly at Raza. "I'll fill you in later," she said quietly as she brushed past him on her way to the elevator.

~ ~ ~

After the morning festivities faded, Raza returned to his desk. He found a sticky note on his monitor. *praxis makes perfect. -mei.* He looked toward Mei's desk but saw that she was already deep into her coding cocoon, which is what she called her workspace when she donned her bulky headset and switched the electrochromic panels of her cubicle to the most opaque "don't you dare talk to me" setting. She would emerge from her casing hours later, having melted down a branch of code and reconstructed it into something entirely new. It was hypnotizing to watch, and more than once he'd caught himself staring over her shoulder as she reworked prior iterations into new creations, primed for initiation. She was the best programmer on the team by a country mile.

What the hell was a country mile? Is it more or less than a standard mile? Is a city mile longer? It must be another phrase he'd picked up from Aunt Roo, though he had no concrete memory of her ever saying it. Maybe he'd remember more clearly on the anniversary of the last time she said it (if in fact she ever did say it), when Earth carried him back to the fixed point in space that held the memory. The mind is a complicated mess, he thought as he slipped his own headphones over his ears.

Since the introduction of Mugabi Brawls, each iteration had both outpaced and outperformed its predecessor by leaps and bounds. Ninety-One was currently active, only the fifth iteration since he started, and had been running strong for seventeen weeks. It was the longest running SimEv to date, at least since Mei joined. (The finer details of the earlier runs were lost. Or, more accurately, burned.) Ninety-One had continued to climb from node to node; in terms of the human evolutionary timeline, Ninety-One had advanced approximately 220 million years beyond *Pikaia*. 220 million years beyond the wall Raza knocked down with one withdrawal-addled outburst. That outburst had made him something of a hero amongst his colleagues. He found it immensely embarrassing to have made his first impression with that uncharacteristic paroxysm, but almost everyone was quick to forgive (and the rest were won over once Eighty-Seven brought them to new heights).

The one exception, of course, was Arden. Though, to be fair, Raza was never sure exactly what Arden thought of him. He was never outwardly hostile toward Raza like he was with Mikus. On the contrary, Arden gave him ample credit and championed his contributions, but he couldn't help but worry about what the founder was thinking when his steely eyes were pointed in Raza's direction. A quick shiver crept up from his chair and shot into the back of his neck and Raza turned to see if any steely eyes were on him. They were not.

Focus, Raza. He imagined the negative, distracting thought as a rogue voxel of data in his head and corralled it toward his ear canal. From there, he could pluck it out and fling it into the waste bin under his desk. His therapist had recommended this "visualized discarding of unwanted and unproductive suppositions" a few months prior, and he was finding it to be surprisingly effective. He flicked his fingers toward the trash and then wiped them on his pants to remove any of the lingering negative residue. Time to get to work.

The team cheered when Eighty-Nine had first used its two pairs of fins to clumsily scoot from sea to land. Ninety picked up where its parent left off, trading its fins for pad-like feet and growing comfortably amphibious. Now Ninety-One was making land its permanent home. In the last few days, Ninety-One had come to a 3-log congruency with *Hylonomus lyelli*, arguably the first species of reptile, and a generally agreed upon Key Node on The Tree. It looked more or less like any lizard you would see scampering from shadow to shadow. Though it was similar in appearance to its proto-newt forebears, *H. lyelli* leapt two enormous biological hurdles to get where she was. (Mikus had named the sim Margerie, and though Raza made an effort to avoid using the name, he found himself occasionally slipping up and thinking of *it* as *her*).

The first hurdle was the ability to lay amniotic eggs, which cleanly severed the sea from its reproductive cycle. The second hurdle was the production of alpha keratin, the fibrous protein that gave her... that gave *it* scales and claws. In time, the same protein would become one of the primary structural building blocks for all of mammal-kind, forming horns, hair, hooves, and flesh. Ninety-One was capable of moving inland to keep herself and her offspring away from aquatic predators, and she was armed and armored for the trials she would face once she got there. *It*self. *It*s offspring. *It, it, it.*

With the keratinous scales and the newfound ability to lay shell-protected eggs came another boon: a more complex nervous system. *H. lyelli* possessed twelve cranial nerves that, in form and function, were remarkably similar to those found at the base of the human brain. Sitting at his desk and staring at his reflection in his dimmed monitor, Raza visualized where his cranial nerves sat in his head, somewhere back and above his throat. Reflexively, his tongue darted to the roof of his mouth and traced a line backwards, feeling where the bone under the skin gave way to pillowy tissue. The tip of his tongue pointed back toward his uvula. Just through that soft flesh, he imagined, were the same nerves driving the *Hylonomus.*

He knew that his mind was wandering, but his therapist had told him it could be fruitful to allow it the freedom to roam, on occasion, so long as the realms explored were "neutral to productive". Acknowledging it and *allowing* it to explore, she claimed, would help him retain control over it. She compared the process to letting a dog off the leash but keeping a close eye on it while it surveyed the yard. Trust would build, and the dog would no longer rush out at every opportunity. Raza had never had a dog, or a yard for that matter, but he got the gist of the analogy. He preferred to think of it as saying to himself, "Okay, let's open this door"; giving himself permission to open the door also gave him power over it. On good days, he could keep his hand on the knob and shut it willingly.

He had made several observations about his own mind in recent months. In no particular order:

1) His mind was more prone to wandering early in the morning, which he attributed to some combination of caffeine, his medication, and an inertial resistance to transitioning from the dream world to the real one.

2) The wandering often followed the plucking of negative voxels from his ear, as though the "neutral to productive" thoughts were expanding to fill the newly emptied space inside his head.

3) There was a strong relationship between his ability to control his thoughts (and keep the door shut (or keep the dog on a leash, if that's your analogy of choice)) and his physical proximity to Mei.

Raza's eyes unfocused as he pictured his tongue pushing through the flesh in the back of his throat and probing his cranial nerves. He imagined that he could determine which of the dozen nerves was which by pressing into them and gauging his body's response. Touch that one there and his balance may be thrown off. Must be the vestibulocochlear nerve. Graze this one over here and his heart rate may shoot up. That has to be the vagus nerve. Hmmm, what about the hypoglossal nerve, which itself controls the movement of the tongue? That may be trickier.

In imagining the cluster of nerves near his brainstem, he again spotted the germinated thought that had been growing in his head since he saw Ma'am that morning. As long as the door was open, he might as well explore the garden. Something was strange about her. But it wasn't that she looked any different than she had yesterday, or the day before. It must be that she looked different than she had one year ago, when they first met. Being back in that fixed point in space, he could better recall their first encounter. What changed? She had gotten a bit older (about a year older, if he had to guess), but what else? Her uniform was the same. Was it her voice? No, but he was getting closer. He thought of her mouth, the way it moved and creased when she spoke, and when she smiled at him.

Aha, there it is! The scar! She had a scar running down her cheek that must have disappeared in the last twelve months, gradually enough that he didn't notice. It took being back at this fixed point in Earth's orbit to be able to hold the two pictures of Ma'am side-by-side in his mind to spot the difference.

Now this was interesting. Was it? Yes, it was definitely interesting. Scars were a rare sight these days, which is why it stood out. Rejuve cream could be found in any standard first-aid kit, and it worked wonders. You just smear it on the affected tissue once a week and the scar would disappear. The process usually took between six to twenty-four months, depending on the size and age of the wound. However, being derived from stem-cells, there were still old-fashioned religious types who refused it (never mind that we're talking about induced pluripotent stem cells; not exactly the 'aborted baby slurry' described by some of the zealots' more colorful literature) so visible scars were often an indication of ultra-conservative values. Ma'am's dissipating scar meant one of two things. It meant she had, in the last few years, converted from a life of extreme fundamentalism (unlikely), or that the scar was from a recent injury (highly likely).

Highly likely was one of those phrases you could say without moving your lips. A great pair of words for a ventriloquist. Is it a tongue twister? *Highly likely highly likely highly likely highly likely highly likely.* Well, he could *think* it five times fast, but his internal voice wasn't beholden to the limitations of his tongue, which he now realized was still tightly folded in the back of his mouth.

Suddenly, another memory resolved into clarity as the Earth inched closer to the exact orbital position at which the memory was formed. That first day, when Ma'am and Broad Chest were teasing him and he was sweating through the seat of his pants, Ma'am mentioned that it had been a slow day. BC added that it had been a slow *ten months*. At the time, Raza had been on the First Floor for just shy of ten months. Had something happened right before he joined? Did that particular *something* have anything to do with his being hired? And had whatever happened resulted in Ma'am's scar?

He looked over his shoulder at Mei, who was still fully encased in her cocoon. She took a risk bringing him aboard a year ago. She broke the protocol and forced the hand of the Second Floor. In describing her reasoning, Mei had cited a general frustration with jinhwa's pace of hiring. The software team was stuck and needed a new perspective. Was that all there was to it? Raza's mouth tasted of syrupy filo and lemon rind. What did he have for breakfast? Focus. He decided he'd confront her about it, but it would have to wait until after she emerged from her chrysalis.

~ ~ ~

Four or twelve hours later, depending on whether you subscribe to Universal Time or Raza Time, respectively, Mei removed her headphones, rolled her neck sharply to the left, then to the right, and unfurled her wings. Raza started to get up, hoping to intercept her, but saw that she was already heading his way, and looking... angry? She was rapidly closing the gap between them. Why did she look—

"Well?"

"Huh?"

"You've been staring at me more than usual. *Way* more than usual. I counted 11 times. What is it?"

How did she do that? "How did you... uh, sorry. Yeah, I wanted to talk to you about something."

"Is it about *The Box*?"

"Definitely."

About The Box. It had become shorthand. More of a code, really. It translated to, 'what I want to talk to you about can only be discussed in the most secure of locations'. Mei led the way to the freight elevator. Down in the basement, they gowned up together in silence, nodded at the hardware engineers they passed in the cleanroom, and made their way toward The Vault. It was a busy room during times of active iterations, but fortunately they caught it just as a very frazzled (even by his standards) Mikus was exiting through the weighty door.

"Hey Mikey!" Mei tossed a friendly greeting his way and Raza considered ducking for cover; a wayward hello to Mikus was an open invitation into his tornado of eccentricity.

"What? Oh, hi, Mei." He hardly looked up and never broke his stride.

"What was that all about?" Raza asked her once Mikus had shuffled out of earshot. "I don't think I've ever heard him call you 'Mei'."

"Let alone pass up an opportunity to chit chat," she said, finishing his thought.

"Do you think it has something to do with the Mikus/Arden dynamic plot you were telling me about this morning?"

"Highly likely," she said.

Highly likely highly likely highly likely highly likely highly likely.

They stepped over the entryway and sealed the door behind them. "So. What's the deal?" Mei lowered her mask.

"I, umm." Shit. In the last four hours (or twelve, depending), he hadn't actually considered how he was going to ask her. He looked toward The Box. Not *The Box*, in italics, but the actual, physical box. The viewscreens were turned off and it was emanating a steady low-pitched hum. He turned back to Mei. Might as well go for it. Deep breath. "What happened before I joined?"

Mei looked at him quizzically. "I'm gonna need you to be a touch more specific there, my guy."

"I mean, *right* before I joined. Was there an... incident? An accident?"

"A green-and-yellow baskident?"

"What? I'm serious, Mei. I've just been putting pieces together and I think there's something nobody's telling me."

She relaxed her brow. "You're right. Sorry for saying baskident. That was... nothing."

"No, it was definitely something, and we can circle back later to figure out exactly what it was, but for now I need to get to the bottom of this."

"It's not that anyone's not telling *you* in particular. It's more that nobody wants to talk about it at all." Mei paused, hoping he'd let her off the hook that easily and knowing that he wouldn't. After a moment of silence, she continued, "Before you, there was a First Floor hire named Lochlan. He was onboarded with the hope of bringing him Upstairs after the First Floor screening time, which as you may recall is anywhere between six months and six eons. Big handsome Australian fella with an ev bio background. Like you."

"But I'm not Australian," he joked. Or at least, the intention was a joke. It came out raspy and stale, the words apparently flattened as they squeezed around the lump that had formed in his throat. He felt a deep uneasiness for the second time since he got to work that morning, though judging by Mei's demeanor this go-round wasn't going to have a surprise happy ending.

Mei mercifully ignored his comment. "After a short time here, just a few months, the security cam caught him trying to copy some of his work onto a non-encrypted drive. He wasn't working on anything particularly sensitive, it was all still screening material, but that's an obvious no-no, so I called him into a meeting to get to the bottom of it."

"You were—"

"I was his direct report, yes." She chewed her lip. "I wanted to talk to Lochlan one on one. I knew Arden would fire him on the spot, but he was away on one of his fundraising tours for a few days and I thought... I *hoped* it was just some sort of misunderstanding. So, I led him into a side office on the First Floor, I showed him the footage, and when I turned to ask for an explanation, he pulled a ceramic hunting knife out of his jacket and held it to my throat."

"Jesus f—"

"—ucking Christ, I know. He only made one demand. 'Take me to the Second Floor.'" She did an impression of his accent. Raza figured that she threw it in for a bit of levity, but it was clear that Lochlan's voice was seared into her brain. "What's nuts is that even when he was walking me toward the elevator, with a blade against my neck, I was thinking, 'I can turn this around; we can still use him; this hasn't been a waste of time.'"

"Mei, I don't know what to say... that's terrifying." Raza was suddenly keenly aware of the distance between them. He wanted to close it. He wanted to shield her. To protect her. Instead he took a step and awkwardly patted her on the shoulder.

"Thanks for the pat," she teased, but he knew it was appreciated. "Well, we made it to the elevator and the security team took care of him and that's that."

That's that? Raza had so many questions, but he was beginning to feel that dragging her into the basement and asking her to relive a traumatic experience to sate his curiosity wasn't in the best interest of their friendship. Fortunately, she had more to say.

"After the fact, we learned that Lochlan had actually figured out what was going on Upstairs. At least to some degree. He was extremely, *extremely* smart. Even smarter than we realized when we hired him. It turned out that the non-encrypted data transfer was just a trap to get my attention. He knew Arden was away. He knew I'd try to talk to him alone. And, according to the note he left behind, he knew he was going to die that day. He just thought he'd make it up the elevator first." Mei's voice was soft but clear and unwavering. She looked up at Raza, which reminded him to breathe. "I know that what happened with him wasn't my fault, but that doesn't mean it was unavoidable."

"There's no way anyone could've seen that coming," he heard himself say.

"Yeah... yeah." Mei sighed. "Anyway, that's why I kept such a close eye on you."

He probed his mind for something to say and found it to be empty.

CHAPTER 16
TRIAL DAY 2.1 - JIVANTA

In her professional opinion, this was a bunch of bullshit. Jivanta had spent the entire day gingerly fortifying her arguments for nullification on the basis of precedent. A lack of interpretability and transparency linked jinhwa's claims to those struck down in Corvis v. Turing, plain and simple. Then Old Man Ragnarsson had pulled his head out of the clouds just long enough to crack the foundation under her feet. So, where did that leave her?

The second day's session closed early, with Mr. Ragnarsson's haddock-soaked voice still echoing around the courtroom. It was never ideal for the opposing party to end the day on an upswing. It was even less ideal for it to happen two days in a row. Jivanta had been down plenty of times before mounting an eleventh-hour comeback. And, of course, she had, on occasion, *lost* cases (though her record was outstanding, if she did say so herself, and next to each loss she perceived an asterisk pointing to a footnote that explained exactly what went wrong and whom to blame). That being said, she was finding herself in a unique state of distress. Sure, this case was perhaps the largest, or at least the most publicized, of her career, but that wasn't what was eating at her. And sure, there were outside forces at play whose motivations were opaque, even to her, but that wasn't it either. If she were to be honest with herself, she knew exactly what was the matter, but honesty was in short supply these days. She needed a drink and a shower. Honestly.

~ ~ ~

The luxury auton was waiting for her when she exited the lobby (another hard-earned clause in her contract). On her way toward the pick-up area, she spied the defendants and their representation gabbing excitedly as they waited for their own sub-luxury autons. Should she say 'hi'? Chatting with the competition after hours was generally excruciating, but it served several tactical purposes. By humanizing herself in their eyes, they may let their guard down. "She's not really against us," they would say to themselves. "Maybe she even agrees with us! She's just doing her job." It also opened opportunities to identify weaknesses or catch whispers of their stratagems.

A few years back while working a land dispute case, after three weeks of rigid back-and-forth, the defense attorney had spilled his entire gameplan, along with a half-pint of beer, into her lap after a chance run-in at the local dive bar. Well, he perceived it as a chance run-in. Never one to leave it up to the gods, she'd had a colleague tail him for days in order to coordinate and calculate that particular bit of chance. The court ruled in her favor by noon the next day.

The chatter softened, which Jivanta took to mean that she'd been spotted. She put on her friendliest face and stepped toward the group, looking into their eyes and reading their body language. Dr. Zametti was stiff as a board. Ms. Egilsdottir was sneering like a rodeo bull. Dr. Kunihara looked more curious than anything. Perhaps she was the way in. The People's Viking was lost in thought. Had he not noticed her? Finally, she forced herself to look toward Dr. Mugabi. He was... happy? She felt her ears flush red hot. Her smile dissolved and she turned back to the car. Her knee throbbed every step of the way.

~ ~ ~

Twenty-five minutes later she pulled the auton off the freeway and toward the hotel drop-off zone. She traditionally used the cabs in passenger-mode, but tonight she opted for the distraction of being behind the wheel. Plus, after all of her grandstanding around Corvis v. Turing, turning off the self-driving AI felt like a matter of principle, if not of practicality. She scanned the parking lot for media vans and fortunately found none. Though, there was one vehicle that she thought she recognized. Goddammit.

She nodded curtly to the bellhop. He had been frustratingly friendly since she over-tipped him for carrying her luggage. She didn't consider it an over-tip at the time (it's always prudent to keep the staff on your side). But today, right now, looking at his big dumb smile and seeing her miserable week reflected in his excessively white teeth, she thought that perhaps she *was* too generous with the gratuity.

For the first time since she arrived, Jivanta noticed the redwood floors in the hotel lobby. She had the type of mother who forced her kids into a plane and then a train and then an RV to witness the splendor of America's national parks system; she was in the shrinking minority of people who had actually seen the great coastal redwoods in person before everything went to shit. On a hard drive in an attic somewhere in northern India, there was a video of her and her sister chasing each other around an impossibly massive trunk. Two tiny mortals and an ageless giant.

The hotel had certainly been built since the Sequoia blight, which had turned Earth's most magnificent evergreens into a sickly yellow pulp. Shadowy markets had since grown around the extraction and resale of extinct woods from Old Coast ruins. Each panel must've cost a small fortune, she thought, as she stared at the grain through a thick layer of protective lacquer polished to a mirror shine. It was like looking at a replica saber-toothed tiger through the display window at a natural history museum (another staple of her childhood).

"Is there anything I can do for you, Ms. Puri?"

"No. Thanks, Edward. I'm just procrastinating."

His high-beam smile grew wider. *She remembered my name*, he must be thinking. She thought again of the car parked outside and wondered if money had changed hands. Had Edward sold her out for his twenty pieces of silver? Before making the trek up to Golgotha, she decided to make a detour to the hotel bar. They could wait another half-hour.

She sat on a velvet-cushioned stool and signaled for the bartender. "What'll you be having this evening?"

Hmmm. "Surprise me." A minute later she was sipping on what seemed to be a bitter mix of licorice and detergent. Jivanta hated surprises.

As she sipped, and begrudgingly began to acquire a taste for the concoction, her mind was still dancing around the great megaflora with her sister. They had outlived the forest, a notion that was entirely unimaginable at the time. The trunk shot straight into the heavens where it presumably supported the cities of the gods in exchange for its immortality. How the mighty have fallen. Here lies King Sequoia, survived by two puny, squabbling humans, but not by their relationship, which also crumbled into a mound of parasite-digested sawdust.

She took another sip. Okay, it was a pretty good drink.

The gulf between her and her only sibling began with disagreements over the cases Jivanta took on, and only grew wider and deeper with time. She hadn't seen her sister or her nephew in... hell, over a decade now. She imagined what it may take to build a bridge across the chasm. A bridge made of apologies. And extensive family therapy. And black-market redwood, for good measure. With that thought, the ice cubes slid unceremoniously from the bottom of the glass into her lip and she knew it was time to make a move. She exhaled sharply through her nose to dispel the synthetic pine scent that perfused the ground floor of the hotel and she rose from her seat, making a point to land on her bad knee first.

In the elevator, her finger hovered over the floor button. Maybe she could head straight to the roof. And then what? Commandeer a skycab and disappear into the night? She continued to live in the fantasy well after she selected her floor. The tabloids would eat it up; a twist ending to this particular trial of the century, she thought as the elevator dinged and she stepped through the threshold into the hallway. She could make a new life for herself on a remote island somewhere in the Pacific, she imagined, as she pressed her palm to the biomet and stepped into her suite. Maybe she'd learn a trade and marry a local charter boat captain. She gestured for the lights to come on. "No need for the dramatics. I know you're in here."

He looked somewhat disappointed. "Did the bellboy tip you off?"

"It was the car."

"Ah, damn! The whole point of the paint job is for it *not* to be seen."

"You could've just parked around the side... Why am I helping you?"

"Because we're friends, Ms. Puri."

"Mmmhmmm." She stepped toward the to the minibar and considered attempting to brew herself another detergentini, but opted for water instead. She spied the open and picked-through welcome basket. "I see you've made yourself at home."

He shrugged his wide shoulders. "You kept us waiting. I got hungry."

"Us?" She looked around the room, redirecting her nerves into her grip on the glass.

He touched his earpiece.

"Ah. Well, I know you didn't come all this way just to eat my snacks. Let's get to it."

The bed creaked under his weight as he stood. Despite his size, Jivanta never thought of him as a physical threat. His enormity was what got him the job, she assumed, but he carried himself like a man who grew up apologizing for his dimensions, constantly sucking in and squeezing sideways and crouching in an effort to better fit into whatever overpopulated urban center he grew up (and up, and up) in. Of the goons that had been tailing her for the last eight months, he wasn't her least favorite. "Given the trajectory of the hearing thus far, we find it necessary to disclose certain... items of interest."

That was perfectly vague, though she was relieved to learn that this visitor had more to say than simply, 'We're firing you'. "Items of interest?"

Whenever someone on the other end of his earpiece spoke, his eyes shifted out of focus. Once he pulled them back to her, he relayed the message. "We first need to hear your assessment of the arguments in order to determine what you do and do not need to know."

"Okay, sure, what the hell." That cocktail must've been strong. She didn't intend to appear too cavalier around these people. Though the giant standing in front of her had shown himself to contain some semblance of a personality, the people he represented were generally quite severe and humorless. "As I'm sure you saw, I spent the day making the case for precedential dismissal. Corvis v. Turing argued that transparency and interpretability were key reasons for disconnecting AI from any moral responsibilities and shifting that agency and culpability back on the shoulders of its programmers. That logic *should* hold." His eyes unfocused and she took a sip of water, waiting for the earpiece to finish uploading its request to this man's mouth.

"Go on."

Worth the wait. "Vilho's little stunt earlier was an attempt to undercut that logic. As frustrating as it was to watch, some of the more influential members of the panel were clearly swayed, but I can pull them back."

"How do you plan to do that?"

So, this visit wasn't purely to relay information. Evidently some trust had been lost. "Ragnarsson's argument was built on the claim that Mugabi made yesterday, that the simulation was somehow a nearly perfect quantum-level, molecule-for-molecule, particle-for-particle construction of a human mind." The hulking man's eyes blurred but she didn't feel like slowing down. "I'm not a physicist, but I've done my research and I know that doesn't make any sense. So, I'll just need to put Mugabi back on the stand and break him. Get him to retract his lie and the rest of the claims will collapse. The only question is—"

"Dr. Mugabi's claims were accurate."

"What?" Jivanta's knee ached and her legs felt suddenly weak. "What does... how do you..." Her head was swimming with a new bitter cocktail, a one-to-one mix of absurdity and disgust. And, sure, a healthy splash of ethanol.

"We have told you what you need to know. Need we remind you of the conditions of your employment?"

"No... no, that's been very clear."

"Okay." Eyes unfocused. Messages relayed. "Just to reiterate, jinhwa's claim, that their simulation has a quantum-level accuracy of over ninety-nine percent, has been... verified."

"What do you mean, 'verified'? Who—"

He held up his enormous hand. It wasn't a threat, or, at least, it wasn't perceived as threatening, but the message was clear: that wasn't one of the things she needed to know. "Your job is to nullify their primary claims. Those regarding the *humanity* and *rights* of their simulation."

"Look, I understand that you don't want to tell me everything. I understand that you have your reasons, whatever those may be. But if the information you're withholding could cost you... could cost *us* the case, is it worth it?"

"We have told you what we can. If more is needed—"

"You'll break into my room and rummage through my things. Got it." She was tired, tipsy, and coming down from the adrenaline spike that's naturally induced by finding a well-dressed ogre in your hotel room.

He smiled in response. Not menacingly. Almost *sweetly*? Apologetically? Maybe she was just hoping to see some expression in contradiction to what was certainly a planned intimidation tactic. Another pause as someone whispered a final message into his ear. "And we encourage you not to allow the simulation into the courtroom. It would be detrimental to your case."

"What? If the panel wants to see the sim there's nothing I can do to—"

He stepped around her, surprisingly light on his feet, and toward the exit. "We do not expect jinhwa to volunteer it up as evidence. If you feel things heading in that direction... well, do what you do best. Control the conversation. Have a good night, Ms. Puri."

The sound of the door shutting shook her back to the present. "Well." She took a sip of water, frowned at glass, and turned her gaze to the minibar. "Fuck."

~ ~ ~

Jivanta Puri had many strengths. Among her plethora of talents was an ability to fall asleep quickly, on command, and to wake up, six hours and forty-five minutes later, with no perception of the time lost. Though she slept deeply and soundly, dreams were rare, and their absence left no roadmarkers by which to identify the continuation of the reality around her. Sleeping was much like blinking, with the added bonus of recharging her tired brain. She slept soundly the night before her international law exams. She slept soundly every night of her first trial. She slept soundly the night her father passed away. Hell, she slept soundly the night after a defendant tried to strangle her during a recess. (To be fair, that particular attempted murder had done her the favor of securing a quick victory in what had been an especially unsteady case.)

She readied herself for bed with her usual routine. A red-hot shower, teeth brushed a tad too forcefully (at least according to her dentist, but she'd always suspected that he was feeding her bad advice to create more work for himself), light stretching and massaging of her knees, and freshly dry-cleaned all-cotton pajamas. She looked at the clock, which read 11:22, slipped under the covers, wiggled her way into the center of the bed, and closed her eyes. In her mind, no time at all passed. She opened her eyes and was dismayed to learn that no time had passed outside of her mind either. "Fucking fuck."

~ ~ ~

Six hours and forty-five minutes later, Jivanta looked up from her notes. Despite having not slept, her finely tuned internal clock had sounded, informing her that it was time to get up. She hit snooze and returned to her document. It was fifty pages long and growing. Fifty pages of thoughts she had been avoiding since Dr. Mugabi had blindsided her with what was an impossible truth.

Jivanta was highly organized, and the document, though born of a ground-shaking revelation and a sleepless night, was no exception. It was written as a lengthy hierarchical outline, though, when the mood struck, she would reformat it into a thought web to be cast onto the augmented viewscreen above the desk in her suite. The web was broken into dozens of discrete notions, each with branching and linking sub-notions, all orbiting around the central prospect: *Simulated brain functionally indistinguishable from physical brain.* She had made an effort to weigh and color the notions by their respective relevance to the hearing.

Ever the pragmatist, she concentrated her time and energy on those items most immediately pertinent. *Imperfect Accuracy.* Could she focus the panel's attention on whatever fraction of a percent separated the simulation and a human brain from perfect quantum-level parity? She had a hard time convincing herself that the sliver of inaccuracy carried any import, but that didn't necessarily mean that she couldn't convince the panel. (She had built a career on persuading others of things she did not necessarily believe. In fact, she preferred it when she didn't fully agree with her own arguments; it allowed for her to maintain agility and fluidity. Taking a strong stance in the courtroom was like nailing your shoes to the dance floor.) She added a note on the time-stamped *sixth-pass* layer of the cloud: *Suggest an error cascading effect? Physical inaccuracy as a time function produces propagated error? May encourage Chebychev to push for declassification of source code.* She looked through the augmentation into her reflection on the screen. *Not a winning point on its own.*

She rotated the cloud toward a second brightly colored notion. *Blind Trust?* She now knew that the defendants had been truthful, as had been confirmed by certain earpiece-wearing forces who had no reason to lie about the matter (at least, no reason she could rationalize with her current level of understanding). The panel, however, lacked that key piece of evidence and would have to rely instead on the testimony of those who benefited from the claims. Nested under the notion were several notes she had written on passes one through five. *Weaken character (focus on Arden).* Underneath that branch, she wrote *Co-founder death. Bring up? (On the stand: Zametti or Mugabi? Not Kunihara.) How to justify relevance?* She flagged the sub-notion as *High Risk* and added the hover-text: *Likely discredit self with Hoffer, Zhang, and public.*

She was making this sixth pass sequentially, working her way from the most highly weighted items to those dimmed in the background, but she kept feeling her eyes dragged toward an item she had cast deep into the darkest ends of her thought cloud. Grimacing at the symbolism, she pulled it into focus. It read *Implications*. It was where she had been collecting her most fallacious projections. The slipperiest slopes. The reddest herrings. Surely not worth the panel's time, and hers even less so. Still, she magnified the two legs extending beneath the word. One read *If I Lose*. Underneath, she had short-handed a few possibilities. Wildly speculative projections of what could come if court-designated rights were ordained onto a simulation. Pessimistic sci-fi, that, if backed into a corner, she could use to shake things up.

The other leg read *If I Win*. She had introduced the sub-notion hours ago purely to maintain the symmetry of the thought, but as the hours ticked by, she imagined more and more items with which to populate the layer. Why couldn't she bring herself to write them down? Because they were too silly, she lied to herself. Because they weren't worth considering. Again, she saw her reflection in the mirror screen. She opened the sub-notion and typed three words. *Fuck. Fucking Fuck.*

CHAPTER 17
5 YEARS EARLIER - RAZA

"Alright Mikey. Why'd you drag us into The Vault? What's the emergency?" Mei and Raza were more impatient than curious. She checked the time. "We have a software sync upstairs in fifteen minutes, and it takes Raza nearly that long to get his bunny suit off."

"It's true, I am a bit rusty." Raza noticed that Mikus had wheeled the old whiteboard from his office into The Vault. Since being unearthed behind a pile of SenZero chassis in his office a few years prior, Mikus had become quite attached to it. Arden had to bar him from bringing it up the elevator and into the Second Floor conference rooms for hardware presentations, calling it "a silly distraction". There was still a wad of gum stuck to the third quadrant of the board, along with ghost images, hundreds of imperfectly erased equations and thought bubbles and sundry diagrams layered over each other.

"Okay, Meiflower, no time for pleasantries, I see... I didn't use the word 'emergency', did I?"

"That's precisely the word you used."

"Yeah," Raza added. "All caps, even."

"Well, maybe 'emergency' was a bit of a red heron." Mikus winked at Raza and Raza blinked back. "Or just a lure? No matter." He seemed more frenetic than usual. Though Raza had to admit to himself that he didn't have a great read on exactly how Mikus usually *was* these days. It had been a while since they had spent much time together.

Mikus pulled a green marker out of the hip pocket of the antistatic coat and wrote two names on the board. *Peter Shor + Lov Grover.* Judging by the ghost images, he had already done this several times.

"Peter Shor and Lov Grover. Fathers and founders of quantum algorithms." He paused to eye his audience. Mei gave Raza a glance that said *uh oh.* He responded with a shrug that said *let's see where this goes.* "So, Shor and Lov are working late one night, trying to crack P vs. NP, right? This is back before your time, when people were motivated by mystery rather than blind narcissism." A moment of anger flashed across his face. Or was it fear? It disappeared as quickly as it came. "So, they're burning the candle at both ends, trying to solve this thing that had plagued mathematicians and computer scientists for decades. And all of the sudden there's a knock on the door. Lov goes to answer it and it's none other than Euler's ghost."

"Mikey, is this a joke? I swear—"

"Now, now, hang on just a second or I'll have to start over. Where was I? Right. Shor and Lov are shocked, naturally. Or *un*naturally, I should say, because we're dealing with the paranormal! But they're happy to have an extra genius in the room to help them out. They tell him about the problem, front to back. Cryptographic hashing, quantum case exceptions, the works. Euler takes all this in, and smiles. 'Why are you smiling?' Shor asks. And he says to them, 'What you need—'"

"What on earth is that accent?"

"Do ghosts knock?"

"Swiss, and polite ones do. Don't interrupt. This is important."

"Sorry."

"Yeah, please get on with it, Mikey."

"You're forgiven. One of you is, anyway, but I'm not saying which... SO! Euler says to them, 'What you need is *my* number. The base for my natural logarithm: *e.*'" He paused for effect. "So, Dr. Euler slaps an *e* on the end of their names and the next thing you know..." Mikus pulled a new marker out of his breast pocket, blue this time, and wrote an "e" into the designated spots on the whiteboard. Shor + Lov → Shor*e* +

160

Lov*e*. Grinning from ear to ear, he announced, "Bing bang boom. You've got sex on the beach."

"Goddammit Mikey."

Mikus's grin stretched from wall to wall, and, despite himself, Raza felt it reach the corner of his lips as well. He turned to read Mei's expression. He'd grown to understand her emotions better than he understood his own. He saw Mei, in real time, compartmentalize her frustration with and concern for Mikus and allow the spreading grin to consume her. She laughed her deep, wonderful laugh and The Vault shook as Raza and Mikus's laughs rose to meet hers. It was a rich and filling sound that lingered like the smell of warm bread.

After a few false starts that devolved into razzing and giggling, Mikus apologized. "Sorry, that was not, umm. I wanted to share my very good joke, *and* I had another reason. For calling you down here, I mean. I was killing two birds with one stone, you see. Or wait, you two aren't the birds." He ran his hand through his wild hair, and it swirled to point upward like a greasy white flame. "Ah. I never cared for that expression. It's barbaric. I wanted to *help* two birds with one... err... birdbath?"

"Mikey!"

"Right. Look, I missed you two. I haven't seen you around. Ever since the observation and visualization suite was built upstairs, nobody comes down here anymore."

"Weren't you the architect behind the whole viz suite?" Mei nudged.

"Architect?" He smiled sadly to himself.

"Yeah, she's right, that whole thing was *your* idea. I seem to remember you pushing hard for it. You said—"

"Yes, yes, I know what I said. And I stand by it."

Mei frowned. "Even the part where you compared software folks using The Box to 'gnats swarming carrion'?"

"I... don't recall using those exact words." Raza and Mei shared another quick glance that Mikus tried to intercept with his own despairing expression. "But look, now you all have a window from the Second Floor, a direct line to run the observations without anyone needing to gown up

161

and march through the cleanroom and... It was the right move, or at least a necessary one, but I think I've been going a little stir crazy without a connection to the software side of this whole thing." The sentence was punctuated by a sharp gesticulation toward The Box.

Raza turned to face it. "It just keeps getting bigger, doesn't it?"

The Box, which was currently in its blackout unobserved state, had been upgraded several times over the last two years to make room for the inevitable step up in the size of simulated entities. The latest incarnation was approximately one cubic meter, jutting ominously from the featureful wall. "Sally's asleep in there, bless her. Biding her time. No doubt dreaming of quantum tunneling her way out of this cell like Andy Dufresne." Mikus sighed woefully and put a hand on The Box. "The road to *H. sapiens* was paved with good intentions."

Mei was eyeing him quizzically, not wanting to take the conversation out of Mikus's hands. He clearly needed this, whatever *this* was.

"I guess that's supposed to inspire us to fill it, you know?" The silence after Mikus's odd statement made Raza uncomfortable, inspiring him to fill it. "The size, I mean. Sort of like nesting. Setting up the nursery and all that."

"Ah!" Raza couldn't read him the way he could read Mei, not by a country mile, but he recognized in Mikus the same sort of compartmentalization and pivoting that he saw in Mei moments earlier. "Somebody has kids on the brain I see. You two have been spending a lot of time together, eh? Got plans to make a little Flowerberry?"

"What the hell, Mikey!"

"Are you two not, err..." Mikus started to make what Raza projected to be an obscene gesture, but wisely aborted the endeavor.

Mei rubbed the bridge of her nose. Raza could have fielded this one, but he was curious as to what she would say. "I don't suppose that's any of your business, now is it?"

Well handled. The truth was a bit messy at the moment and it was probably for the best that she didn't expound on the matter. Mei and Raza's friendship had only grown stronger in the last two years. They challenged and bettered each other as engineers, as well as as people. As well as as? That can't be right. He made a note to check his grammar, knowing that he would forget by the time he was back in front of a computer. Where was he? Right. He and Mei felt a kinship that was stronger than in any other relationship either of them had had. Had Had? Forget it. So, a few months prior, as if to somehow spite the office gossip that always assumed something more was going on between them, they decided to see if anything more *could* go on between them. They took each other on a few dates, tried holding hands a handful times (which is once—a single handhold technically counts as a handful, they both agreed), and the effort ultimately fizzled out. Or was actively fizzling out. Raza wasn't completely sure where Mei stood, which is why part of him hoped she would have said more to Mikus. Would she have said "fizzled" or "fizzling"? Did it matter? They were on the same page, right?

"Yes, yes, apologies. Manners fade in the absence of polite conversation."

Mei checked her watch again and decided to cut to the chase. "Alright, enough goofing around. You didn't really call us down here just because you missed our company, did you?"

Mikus furrowed his bushy brows. He had something weighing on him and was deciding if or how he should say it. "Sure, Meiflower." He fidgeted with the markers, pulling the caps off and swapping them. "The team sure has been making a lot of progress. You guys are really flying up The Tree."

Was he just feeling left out? "'You guys'? Last I checked you were still a huge part of all this, Mikus. If not for you we'd still be at the base of The Tree looking up."

Mikus winced at Raza's words. Maybe he was just bad at receiving compliments? No, that didn't really jive with the man he knew. "You know, when Arden and I started this project, all those years ago, I was so focused on getting a grip on the first few branches that I couldn't even begin to conceive what was at the top of The Tree. It was so distant. So *radical.* Arden, on the other hand, could see it as though it were right in front of him. Or at least he talked as though he could." He fumbled one of the marker caps and let it roll across the floor, its plasticky thud dampened by the low hum radiating from The Box. "After a while, once the hardware was in place and the goal seemed more achievable, I caught my own view of the top and... well, he and I have been arguing ever since."

"Mikey, we're not going to be pawns in whatever fight you're having with Arden."

"Only a fool would think to make a pawn of you, Meiflower."

"And you're not *only* a fool." She smiled gently toward Mikus. "You're a fool and so much more."

"Kinder or truer words have never been spoken. I know you have to run, I just want to say this. Until we get there, you have to form your own view of the top, alright? I don't want to tell you to listen to me. I'm half-mad. Maybe I'm just scared of heights. But... Promise me you'll form your *own* views."

"Mikey..." Mei chewed her lip and debated with herself before acquiescing. "I promise."

"I, uhh." Raza shifted his weight, eyeing the door. "I do too."

"Good. See you later, you two." He waved them along with his four-fingered hand. On his way through the doorway out of The Vault, Raza turned and saw Mikus staring at the whiteboard and then vigorously erasing the punchline with his palm.

CHAPTER 18
TRIAL DAY 3.0 - SOHVI

Sohvi didn't sleep well before the first day of the trial. How could she? She was terrified. And of course she couldn't sleep well before the second day of the trial. How could she? She was sticky with adrenaline and had all new arguments to prepare. On the morning of the third day, she opened her eyes after nine hours of the deep, dreamless sleep of the dead, and she smiled. She sprang from her bed, the sheets still tucked in around the corners (a rare morning sight; she was a fitful sleeper prone to kicking and spinning, fighting to stay asleep like a crocodile trying to drown a gazelle), and made her way to the shower without breaking her stride. The thick bathmat protected the soles of her feet from having their precious heat robbed by the stone tiles. She turned the knobs all the way to the right and waited.

Sohvi had grown up as the only daughter at the terminus of a generation-spanning string of farmers whose land was now anywhere from two to five meters underwater, depending on the time of day. Once the levees around the property finally gave way, Sohvi was shipped inland to be passed between family friends, whichever ones could afford to care for her at the time. For two years she was raised by the community and never slept in the same bed for more than a month at a time. That is, until she wound up on the doorstep of Vilho Ragnarsson.

If she had ever been settled anywhere long enough to pay attention to the world around her, she surely would have recognized him. He was a striking figure whose icy blue eyes, not-quite-white blonde mane, and charmingly weathered skin had been plastered on the news for the better part of a year. Vilho, Mr. Ragnarsson (or Frændi, as he insisted she call him) lived in a modest home his grandfather had built, "with his bare hands... and the hands of a bear", he used to say. Sohvi always laughed at that. She would imagine this funny man's afi stacking logs and bricks and sod alongside a grizzly dressed in jeans. In that home, erected by man and possibly beast, Vilho carved a room for her out of warmth and generosity. To hear him tell it, offering shelter was the least he could do; it was an obligation afforded to him by the privilege of having something that someone did not. But, even then, Sohvi knew there was more to it than just a sense of duty to his tiny, grubby, needy countryman. Frændi wanted a family. His partner had been a rescue worker who passed away during The Aattoq, and after that he lost himself in his legal work. Or, rather, he *found* himself in his legal work. Sohvi was the daughter the world never gave him the opportunity to have.

The very first tour of what would become her home for the next eleven years included one warning that Sohvi could still remember word for word. "Young Sohvi, when my afi (and his hairy friend) built this place, he made a pact with the Earth. He promised he would honor her, taking only what was needed, and in exchange she would offer her boundless energy to power his new life."

"What does that mean?"

"It means that if you are not careful, the shower will boil you to bits."

Years later she would learn that it was geothermal energy and not magic that powered the home. Which, Vilho contended, was a kind of magic in its own right. Regardless, the end result was the same. She had grown accustomed to blisteringly hot showers, with sulfurous water heated by magic in the earth's crust, and these western showers, heated by some unholy agreement between electricity and the sun, always left her unsatisfied.

After two minutes, Sohvi sighed, accepting that the shower had reached its paltry maximum temperature and that she'd better move quickly before it started to drop from the peak. She stepped from the mat onto the now warm(ish) porcelain tiles of the bath, watched the stream become steam as it slapped against her skin, and shivered. Still, she smiled. Things were going well.

~ ~ ~

Ninety minutes later, her auton rounded the corner and came to an abrupt stop. She depolarized the windows and saw that she was a block away from the courthouse. Between her and her destination, Sohvi counted a dozen emergency response vehicles, a handful of news vans, a small crowd of spectators, and one very tired looking lady in a navy blue uniform standing directly in front of the auton. For the first time today, Sohvi's smile faded.

"What's going on?" Sohvi cracked the window in order to hear and be heard. The officer shook her head and waved her away. "I work here. I'm Sohvi Egilsdottir, with the defense team for the jinhwa case?" Again, the officer acknowledged her with only a curt shake of her head and a somehow more dismissive point. She felt an ember of frustration ignite deep in her gut, her smile-turned-frown now inching into a full-blown scowl. As her downturned lips neared their nadir, a tap came from the opposite side of the vehicle. She recognized the midsection of the man on the other side of the door and motioned for the right-side door to open.

"I found a lovely tea shop around the corner." He handed her a warm cup as he stooped in and swung his way into the seat.

"What's all the fuss about?"

"The owner is a lovely woman. It takes a special type to make tea of this quality. "

"Vilho—"

"Her wife's family lives in Berufjordur! Can you believe that?" The ember in Sohvi's small intestine burned brighter. "I may have crossed paths with them. I may have stolen fruit from their garden as a boy." He reached the control panel and rerouted the auton to a public park five blocks away. "I am endlessly astounded by the smallness of this enormous planet. Invisible strings—"

"I need to know what the hell is going on!"

He looked up from his cup and frowned. "Of course, of course. My apologies, Sohvi. I have been trying to reach you."

"I don't have any messages from you." She winced at the sharpness in her voice.

"Yes, it seems technology is working against me today." He furrowed his brow, as though a thought was dancing on the edge of the fog of his mind before slipping back into obscurity. "There is a bomb. Or, rather, there *was* a bomb. Now there is a mess of debris and the remains of a delivery bot that must have activated the explosion. Few details are escaping the wall of uniformed personnel back there, and who can say whether the information that filters through has been modified for our consumption."

"Oh." Her voice squeaked through her suddenly saliva-less throat. She sipped her tea. "Wow."

"Delicious, right?"

"I didn't mean... actually, yes. This is the best tea I've had in ages."

"Certainly the best I've had in the States. I thought you may need something to warm you up. The showers here certainly leave something to be desired."

The auton came to a stop by a patch of unsullied forest, standing tall and proud amidst the much taller and prouder glass obelisks that carved the skyline. Sohvi felt the ember cool. Partially from the surprise of greenery. Partially from a truly amazing cup of tea. And partially from Vilho's calm in the face of... some sort of terrorism? A horrible prank gone wrong? She couldn't say.

They sat and sipped in silence. The tea slowly heated her blood from within.

"Who do you think did it? The bomb, I mean."

He nodded slowly, carefully, weighing his words. "My first thought was of anti-science activists."

"Right, that was my guess as well. Given the trajectory of the hearing, they may be feeling desperate." She felt a sense of relief. Putting a face on the enemy, stripping away the unknowns, added a sense of control over the situation. "And a motion-activated trigger? That sounds like the sort of rudimentary IED shit those hillbillies love. If anything, it tells us that we're doing a good job, right?" She smirked over to Vilho, but he didn't seem to hear her. Was he back in the fog? No, he was still present, but he wasn't telling her everything. "Vilho. What was your *second* thought?"

A small, knowing smile met his lips, though his eyes were heavy with worry. "Sohvi, who was the first to arrive at the courthouse yesterday?"

She didn't understand. "We were? Well, I got there first." Did he not remember? "We met to debrief in the defense chamber, and I went an hour early to get a head start. I don't understand what—"

"And the day before?"

"Umm." So much happened in the last two days. "I was the first to arrive. I had trouble getting in, so I called you and you had to call in a favor to get the door unlocked. What does that—"

"You established a pattern of being the first to the courthouse." The warmth was ripped from her bones as the tea in her chest turned to sour ice. "Given such a pattern, it would seem as if the bomb may have been for you."

The windows had fogged from the vapor swirling up from their cups. Through the haze, Sohvi could make out the silhouettes of the evergreens, looking more scared than proud in the shadows of the skyscrapers behind them.

"And I must apologize for interrupting you. My thoughts... I am finding that I must force them over my tongue before my mind starts taking them apart, piece by piece, at the expense of common courtesy." He took a final sip of tea and leaned his head back in the seat. "Berufjordur. Invisible strings, impossibly taut, pulling us together."

CHAPTER 19
3 YEARS EARLIER - RAZA

Raza Mugabi was in a rut.

"Has anything changed in your personal or work life in the last few months?"

The waste bin under his work desk was overflowing with his unwanted and unproductive suppositions. The discarded voxels had gotten smarter. First they found ways to leap from the trash can back into his ear, so he bought a new bin with a lid to trap them inside. That worked for a spell, but they must have found a way to open it from the inside because they kept flooding back. Perhaps they were all working together in an effort to get back inside his head. His negative ideations were teaming up to bring him down.

"Nothing major, I guess. I don't know."

He detailed the status of his waste bin to his therapist, and, to her credit, she didn't press the "forced lobotomy" button that Raza assumed was hidden under her desk for especially hopeless cases. Instead, she just wrote a few notes and asked a few questions.

"It doesn't need to be major. Any minor change is worth discussing, Raza. I just want to help you better understand any potential triggers so we're prepared to address problems at their root."

Raza knew how the conversation would end. She would recommend a new medication regimen. "It will get worse before it gets better," she would remind him matter-of-factly as he started his month-long transition from treatment plan N to treatment plan $N+1$. Not that he needed reminding.

"Well, a project at work has been stalled for a while. Everything was going so well, until... Until it just wasn't anymore. That has everyone a bit stressed." Despite the therapist-patient confidentiality, Raza kept any specifics of his work at jinhwa close to the vest. The secrecy of jinhwa's intellectual property was *sacrosanct*. That's the word Arden used. It was an ugly word. Bad on the tongue. Like a mealy apple. Sour spit collected in the back of his mouth.

"We've discussed how much time you spend at work. It's understandable that your moods could become attached to successes and failures at the office. Have you given any more thought to what we discussed during your last visit? Maybe cutting down your hours and carving out some space for your personal life?"

For nearly two decades, Raza's mental state had been wrangled by a constantly evolving medicinal load of various ocular, oral, nasal, and topical inhibitors, initiators, stabilizers, and enhancers. A previous therapist (Two therapists ago? No, three?) had once compared Raza's mind to a wild animal; each treatment was like a clever new trap that would pin it to the jungle floor, but over time it would adapt and chew through the netting or gnaw off its own leg in order to escape, and the process would start all over again. (It wasn't something he was intended to hear. He had come back to the office to pick up a book he had forgotten in the lobby when he overheard the therapist venting to his assistant.)

"I, um. Not really. I've been too busy. I mean, I still have friends at work, but... I don't know."

Therapists came and went, but the story was the same as it ever was. Every few years, spurred by personal crises or work stresses or the tides or the misalignments of unseen celestial bodies or a perfect storm of nothing at all, Raza's moods would untangle themselves from his pharmaceutical net and run wild.

"Hmmm, can you say more about that? How are things with your work friend? Mei, I believe?"

His sleep would become more erratic. His conversations, more strained. His thoughts, more stochastic. His metaphors, more mixed. His tangents grew tangents nested behind tangents and his mind left no trail of breadcrumbs for him to find his way back. This was familiar territory. Well, that wasn't entirely fair to say. The states of mind that brought him to these points were varied, but one thing they shared in common was a blindness to the familiarity of the feeling—an utter inability to recognize that he'd been here before. The mind, Raza's in particular, was great for recalling certain concrete aspects of lived experiences. He could remember conversations (except for the key bit where names were exchanged), he could remember food orders, he could remember lyrics and handshakes and dance steps. But recalling *emotions*, and especially *heightened* emotions, was like trying to remember a dream. Or the colors of a black and white movie. Or like trying to visualize higher dimensions.

"Things with Mei are fine." He had slipped up a few sessions back and mentioned her by name. "Well, she's actually been pretty distant. She started seeing Ar— uhh, a guy I work with. He's sort of my boss." Raza felt dizzy. He put his head back on the couch.

Approximations could be made using easier-to-remember context clues, sure. You could envision the setting, the sights and sounds and smells and goings-on that accompanied or even elicited the emotion, but you couldn't truly *recall* an emotion. These were the types of navel-gazey excuses Raza made to himself when, for the Nth time in a row, Aunt Roo recognized what was happening and helped cushion his fall long before he realized he was going down. It was Aunt Roo who moved up his appointment and briefed his therapist in advance.

"Ah. That sounds like a challenging new dynamic." She checked her watch.

Raza looked at the clock. In so many words, it told him why she didn't ask for more details about the 'challenging new dynamic'. His session was winding down. Which meant it was almost time for her to recommend a change of—

"Given the severity of your condition, I'd like to recommend a new prescription. If you're up for it, I suggest we start you on..."

~ ~ ~

"Call me if you start feeling too much of anything. Or too little of anything. Or—"

"I'll be fine."

"You'll be worse than fine if you interrupt me like that again." Aunt Roo had taken to waking up early so she could have coffee with her nephew before he caught the sunrise train. She was often in bed by the time he got home, and she missed having someone to chide. She was decidedly not a morning person.

"Sorry. You're right. I'll check in with you at lunchtime."

"It's your first day all in with the new meds. If you go all Billy Pilgrim on us, I want to be the first one to know, okay? I'll zip right over there to pick you up. I already told the clinic I'd need flexibility today and I have a sub on standby."

He rubbed his eyes with the heels of his hands until he saw spots. She was referencing an episode he'd had over a dozen years ago now in which he *briefly* got a tiny bit unstuck in time. He preferred not to think about it. "I appreciate that." He'd forced himself to become a morning person through sheer force of will over the last four years, but a recent restructuring of the biochemistry in his brain had pulled him strongly in the other direction. For the last two months, his peak alertness hours were typically between midnight and three in the morning, and he spent the rest of the day wishing he was in bed.

"Thanks, Aunt Roo. Remember not to panic if you can't reach me. Security has tightened up and phone access is limited."

"Yeah, yeah, yeah. Top secret. Be good, Raza Mugabi." She pushed herself up from her seat. As she passed behind him, he heard a pause in her step and he smiled to himself as she kissed the top of his head. Those kisses stayed on his scalp and emitted some sort of pulse that inhibited the propagation of negative thoughts across his brain. The effect was strong, but the pharmacokinetics were such that the half-life was brief in the best of times and snapped to zero in response to even the most minor of inconveniences.

"Yes, ma'am."

His feet carried him to the train, which in turn carried him to jinhwa. No active memory was logged during his trek to the office. He drifted through his handshake dance with Ma'am and made his way up the elevator. If anyone were to ask how his commute had been that morning, he would have been forced to extrapolate from prior experiences. Effectively, he would have had to retroactively predict the future, which is famously tricky business. Though, he did now have a few post-commute data points that could be used to narrow the bounds of the extrapolated data. For instance, he was alive, so he knew that his commute did not go so poorly as to kill him. It was not unlike the simulated organism's growth up The Tree, he thought as he hazily rolled his way toward his desk. Key features of future nodes were used to rank and guide the evolution from lower nodes. They were anchor points in the climb to the top. In the way that his current state of not-dead served as an anchor point to... Huh. Something about his desk looked different. What was he just thinking about?

Raza noted his mood in his medication log. Over the last month, the log entries had grown shorter and shorter. Is that an oxymoron? Can something grow shorter? Sure it can. They grew shorter. Not because his symptoms were improving, but rather because his willingness to take the care to record such matters had evaporated. Today he wrote just three words: "Stuck in muck."

What looked different about his desk? He sat down in his chair and fiddled with the ergonomics. Same chair. It was something else. He used the desktop biomet to log-in. Same biomet. Same monitor and peripherals. Something had changed, he was sure of it. Pretty sure. Not especially sure. He was probably wrong. He was always wrong. Idiot. Dipshit. The protective spell from Aunt Roo's kiss had long since worn off. Raza tried to blink away the thoughts before they could overrun him. He mentally corralled them toward his ear and then plucked them out to be flung in the trash can and then trapped under the... lid? Where the hell was the lid? This was *not* his trash can.

He bypassed any positive feelings of satisfaction from discovering what had changed and skipped straight to a hollow and ringing fury. Who took his can? Why? Because *they* wanted to ruin him? Because *they* knew he didn't belong? Because *they* knew that the lid was a shield against his illness and they wanted him to lose this fight? His breath quickened and he glanced furtively around to see which of his traitorous coworkers had stolen it, electroplated it in gold, and mounted it on their cubicle wall like a trophy, a testament to their horrible craftiness. In an instant, Raza's mental state had swung from "stuck in muck" to "sprinting with eyes closed". His therapist used the word "spikes" to describe the "sudden peaking" he had been experiencing during his medication transition. He pictured himself on a frayed rope-bridge swaying precariously over a pit of sharpened, poisoned stakes. Wait, did she say "peaking" or "piquing"? Did both make sense in that context? And who stole his goddamn trash can?

The elevator doors parted and Mei stepped out. For a brief moment, Raza felt a calm wash over him. She still held that power—an uncanny ability to tame the chaos in his head. Turbulent thoughts turned laminar in her presence. She emitted a light that froze him in place. Then Arden emerged behind her, eclipsing her light and destabilizing Raza's mental footing. Raza had never *liked* Arden, but his animosity only grew when Arden and Mei moved in together. It wasn't jealousy, he shouted to himself in an effort to be heard over his clamorous inner monologue. Can it be called a monologue if it's a dozen thoughts screaming at once? His inner dodecalogue. He just missed Mei. He missed her friendship. He missed the powerful smoothing function she applied to the noisy waveforms in his head. But more than anything, he missed her laugh. It had been sixty-four days since he'd heard her laugh. *Really* laugh. With all the stagnation of the project, joy had been in short supply. Plus, Arden was always so damn self-serious that... how could anyone...

Suddenly, the dyspeptic din of the dodecalogue aligned and harmonized in chorus: *Arden Stole The Trash Can.*

Raza turned angrily from Mei and Arden to face his monitor. With his brow furrowed, he set about to get some work done to distract him from his thieving boss. In that effort, he failed spectacularly. The hours slipped by and he thought of little else. His code was broken up by errant stream-of-consciousness tirades with terrible spelling but perfectly functional programming syntax. Some rants were commented out so as to be programmatically inert. Others were built into the code itself. Text strings were clumsily hung like Christmas lights onto the branches of iterative functions, as if to punish the computer by forcing it to reread his rambling diatribe ten thousand times in a row. He knew he was being ridiculous, and knowing so did nothing to tame his ire. Lunch came and went without a second (or first) thought to check in with Aunt Roo. To be fair, he would explain to her later, he forgot lunch altogether.

"You coming?"

"Yes," he sneered, before realizing who was asking and what he was agreeing to. It took only a moment (or perhaps two moments given that she had time to cock an eyebrow) for him to put the pieces together. It was time for the meeting. Which meant it was 15:00. Which meant he missed lunch. He rose and cursed the stiffness in his legs. Side-eyeing the imposter trash can, he grabbed his notebook and followed Mei to conference room 2C.

"Before we get started... As I'm sure many of you noticed, there were some minor changes made around the office." Arden stood in the front of the room. As always, he appeared to be masking volatility and exhaustion with a slapped-on coat of professionalism. That coat wore thinner and thinner each day, at least in Raza's eyes. "Heightened security concerns called for the precautionary removal of certain personal items."

There was a grumbling around the room.

"I don't believe any of you have anything to hide. Am I mistaken?"

The grumbling morphed into a frigid silence.

"Now. You all understand why jinhwa IP protection must be taken so seriously. It would have been counterproductive to provide you with any notice. This is the way it has to be. Your personal effects will be screened by our internal security team and returned to you as soon as possible."

Trash can stealing asshole.

"Great, now let's get started. Hardware will kick things off."

A systems engineer, whose name, Raza was certain, started with either an *S* or a *T*, positioned herself near the front of the room and began the presentation. Her name was in a superposition of states. It existed in a non-deterministic universe, ruled by the strong and fickle arm of probabilism. If he asked her name, it would collapse into one of the two states and life would march on with a confidence that suggested that the uncertainty had never existed.

She still had indentations on her forehead and nose from the cleanroom suit that she must've shrugged off less than ten minutes ago. By the look on her face, she would rather be back down there. Engine room workers were a different breed. Mole people, Mikus called them affectionately. And he was their mole king. Their increasingly hermitic king. Raza looked around for him but knew he wouldn't be there. Mikus hadn't been to a meeting in over a year, sending in his stead a rotating group of his basement dwellers to deliver the good news. And the news *was* generally good. In the last several years, Mikus and his team had significantly improved upon the original Fick Knot shells that were the key components for regulating the concomitancy of the simulations. The new scheme was dubbed the Ivanovic Reflection Mesh—IRM for short, or Mikus Mirror for medium. *S* or *T* was announcing the latest milestone. Layering the Mikus Mirrors had increased parity to 99.2%. Constructive interference between the stack of paired topological MZMs was error-correcting at record levels and energy consumption was reduced by an order of magnitude. It truly was astounding. So why, Raza wondered, in the face of all the hardware success, was Mikus only growing more withdrawn?

The presentation ended with a weak smattering of applause. *S* or *T* walked back to her seat, grabbed her things, and continued out of the room without breaking her stride. As the soundproofed door resealed behind her, the room stiffened and braced itself for the software update. Mei had taken it upon herself to lead the progress reports for the last several months. Arden's temper was bad for morale, and morale at jinhwa had a loose correlation with progress, which was enough of an argument for Arden to sideline himself. In Raza's experience, progress was the independent variable and morale was more of a lagging indicator of their successes, but he kept that to himself. Anything that kept Arden in his seat was for the greater good. Trash can stealing son of a—

"Thank you all for being here today." Mei always took on a drill sergeant-like posture when she presented data. Her right hand clasped her left wrist behind her back. You could drop a marble down the foramen through-holes in her perfectly stacked vertebrae without it ever skimming the sides. On presentation days, she wore taller shoes, blacker clothes, and a tighter ponytail. It was still his friend Mei under all that severity, but he found her altogether more frightening. "As you're all already aware, there hasn't been much movement since last week's update. We ran an additional observe-point just this morning, and there were no surprises."

There were a few groans and whispers from the group. Raza looked over his shoulder at the frustrated faces. It had been four years since his first meeting in this room. The contributions he'd made in his first week helped fuel years of rapid growth. With that excitement came new funding and new hires. Before long, the update meetings were so packed that they had to tear down a wall to make room for the expansion. Then progress started to flatten out. Funding slowed, salaries were cut, people left on their own or by force, and the meeting size began to dwindle. Before long, the expanded conference room felt uncomfortably large. Then, one day (sixty-four days earlier), Raza noticed that the wall in 2C had been re-erected. He pointed it out to Mei, who laughed so hard she had to leave the room. Apparently it had already been up for a month before he realized it.

Mei paced slowly, somehow appearing fluid without sacrificing her rigidity, as she waited for the murmuring to fade. Her eyes passed over the room. Perhaps Raza was imagining it, but he could've sworn there was some visual cue passed toward Arden. He couldn't read her quite as well as he used to, but if he had to guess, it was a look that said, *You're not going to like this.* "We've hashed and rehashed ISCs to death at this point. It's time to step back and take a broader look at where we are." Judging by

Arden's clenched jaw, Raza guessed correctly. They must've discussed her presentation in advance, and this apparently wasn't what they'd agreed to.

She motioned and the room was instantly filled by The Tree. During the boom years, they used a slice of the funding to upgrade the AR projection system, and, in his mind, it was worth every nickel (though he hadn't a clue how much the thing actually cost). When he first saw it, he was so overwhelmed by the sheer volume and density and clarity of the data viz that it made him dizzy. Once he was able to train his eye to focus on individual elements, while still filtering in adjacent data through his periphery, he fell in love. It gave him a new way to visualize his own thoughts, and develop new tools for managing them, which worked wonders. Until it didn't.

The entire history of jinhwa was captured in the augmented visualization. Raza could see the first few dozen iterations, presented as tendrils reaching up from the origin, stacking end-to-end to show rapid progress. Before long, the tendrils shortened in length and occasionally doubled back. Progress slowed and stalled around an early node, *Pikaia*. The *Pikaia* node was caked in zero-length tendrils, representing over a year of failures before Raza's breakthrough had catapulted the eighty-seventh tendril through the invisible barrier. The next ten bands were longer than any that came before them. Strung end-to-end, they leapt three-hundred million years up the evolutionary timeline. The termini of this stretch of ribbons encapsulated what he viewed as *the good times*. The times in which jinhwa was constantly awash in discovery and success. The times in which the chemicals in his brain had found, if not harmony, at least some level of compatibility. Not quite a choir, but a functioning ecosystem. The times in which he and Mei had been joined at the hip (and, on that one occasion, at the hands). Then, after a few shriveled and truncated runs, the team found themselves where they were today. Stuck.

"Here we are." With a flick of her wrist, everyone in the room was brought face-to-face with the dead-end node. It wasn't necessary; at this point, the damned node had been haunting the dreams of at least half of the team. They knew it inside and out, and they hated it with a passion.

Someone to Raza's right booed, and another hissed. They were joking. Nobody laughed.

"*Cynognathus.*" Forty iterations had failed to escape the node. They tried going around it, but there was nowhere to go. They tried leap-frogging it, bypassing the troublesome node altogether, using predictive models to find a place to grab onto The Tree somewhere north of *Cynognathus.* They tried multiple sims in parallel just to up their chances of getting a hit. The results were all the same. Each tendril crumpled back on itself and the team's attitude crumpled with it. "Let's take a moment to think about why we're where we are." She paced. Fluid. Rigid. "This node, contrary to what I hear around the office, is *not* a dead end. But it *is* an isthmus." It was one of several points in the tree where the path was cinched to a single pass. "This is a transition with an exceptionally high activation energy, with no buffers or local minima on either side. Below this node, we have reptiles. Above this node, mammals. It wasn't easy for nature to pull it off. It's not going to be for us to pull it off. But She did, and we *will.*"

The mood in the room shifted. Mei could tune a room like a violin (pretty well—she was classically trained and possessed exceptional relative pitch, but, according to her, she was out of practice). The self-deprecating pessimism gave way to some sense of hope and possibility. Whether it would last the length of the meeting was another matter. Negativity tended to spread and grow in times of open discussion; so much so that Arden typically made excuses to close the meetings early rather than turn it over to the mob. Mei was more democratic, or at least she was a despot who preferred the illusion of democracy.

"Now, we haven't had an unbounded brainstorm in a while, but if everyone is in a non-confrontational enough mood, I'd like to open the floor up to a... less regulated discussion." Nervous shuffling. Raza imagined (and believed) he could hear the sound of everyone's eyes darting either from side to side or straight to the ground. The eye-sounds were directionally dependent. Left and right glances produced a pitch a step or two higher than downward glancing. Would a diagonal glance produce a frequency somewhere between the two? Could Mei hear it too?

She would know the key, or at least be able to identify the relationship between the two sounds. His train of thought was suddenly yanked back into the station by Mei, who must've noticed that he'd gone on a brief brain ride. With a subtle and exacting movement involving just an eyebrow and the corner of her mouth, she brought him crashing back into 2C. He squeaked his eyes to the left and was met with a sea of pursed lips. Nobody wanted to be the first person to speak up, especially not with Arden glowering in the corner.

"I'll start, just to get the ball rolling." Mei tweaked her posture ever so slightly. "There's been mention of decreasing the resolution of sims so we could theoretically run massively parallel studies in faster hot-boxes." Anyone would be hard-pressed to spot the difference between a snapshot taken before and after the adjustment, but the newer pose was somehow warmer, more inviting. "Gregg, I believe you're most equipped to speak on that. What are your thoughts?"

Raza followed Mei's gaze to... did she say Gregg? He could've sworn that guy's name was Craig. Dammit. Had he called him the wrong name to his face? No, that wouldn't happen. Raza rarely used anyone's name if he could help it. He would get their attention with a wave or a simple, universal "Heyoh". He'd been bad with names for thirty-five years. It was a minor annoyance, not an enormous personal failing. At least, that's how he viewed it on his better days. This was not one of those days. As his mind faced its first day in years without one form of medication and a full dose of another, he felt the minor annoyance spiral through his amygdala, pulling in other negative emotions as it built steam.

Shame.

Names made him uncomfortable. He'd told his therapist as much. She asked him if it had anything to do with his own insecurities about identity and individuality, and he said, "I don't think so. Wait, my what?"

Anger.

Names were unnecessary. Useless. They were a vestigial organ. An evolutionary fuckup. An inflamed appendix.

Jealousy.

Why did everyone else have something he didn't? Why were they all granted this superpower, this unfair advantage that allowed them to appear to actually give a shit about one another just because they could remember the random assemblage of letters?

Resentment.

Names were nothing more than whatever syllables your dumbass negligent parents scribbled onto your birth certificate before abandoning you for their death cult.

Raza felt a jolt as Mei again managed to pull him out of his runaway thoughts. He was discombobulated. She was mediating an argument between two of the older firmware developers, but had managed to catch his eye and share a flash of concern that snatched him bodily from the event horizon. It was only a fleeting glance, but it was the lifeline he needed. Mei returned to the discussions. Apparently some time had passed. He must be thinking slowly, slipping out of sync with Universal Time. He replayed the bits of tape being sporadically recorded in the back of his mind.

There had been some talk of multiplexed observance, a possible means of allowing them to make more frequent observations of the sim without introducing additional error loads. "A good idea", someone had said, "but not a way to escape the infinite gravity well of the *Cynognathus* node." Raza agreed with the faceless voice. That had led to a separate argument about whether the observation-induced errors were even a worthwhile source of concern *outside* of the greater problem of getting to the next node. Nobody could say one way or the other. Too many unknowns.

Then there had been a pitch to try a deep reset. Move the sim way back, perhaps even to the origin. Let it evolve with a clean start and with all of the latest and greatest software ("And hardware!" a mole person chimed in). The rationale seemed to be that, after a decade of building on the skeleton of each sim's failed predecessor, they were weighed down by unseen accumulated errors. A deep reset would shed that weight, and the sim would maybe have enough momentum to cross the *Cynognathus* isthmus by the time it got there. The notion itself gained a little momentum before Arden squashed it. Raza rather liked it. Did he actually like it, or did he just like that Arden didn't like it? He wasn't actually sure what "momentum" meant in terms of the sim. Regardless, the conversation had moved on twice since then and Raza was still playing catch up.

There was a less lively discussion about the starting conditions that seemed more like an attempt to placate Arden than any actual consideration for a new approach. Still, one of the old firmware guys cast some wonderfully niche aspersions toward his partner, the partner countered with a somehow even more niche rejoinder, Mei stepped in to intervene, and that brought Raza up to speed.

He was tired, he was irritable, and his mind was more scattered than Mikus's office. He couldn't bring himself to care about the project, but he owed Mei his attention. Mei was his anchor. His totem. It was unhealthy and unfair to her, but it's what he needed right now to tether him to this plane. Raza planted his feet in the room, both metaphorically and quite literally, and gave her a look that said, *Thanks* and *I'm sorry* and *I'm here now.* Their ability to layer communication, transmitting multiple sentiments simultaneously, was a cornerstone of their relationship. Even after months of an Arden-shaped space growing between them, multiplexed communication allowed them to rapidly close that distance.

He looked at his friend and felt as though he were seeing her for the first time, or at least the first time in a long, long while. It was like the first day of sunlight after a long gray winter (or so he imagined; he'd never lived anywhere with the luxury of winters, let alone long gray ones). She had been clouded by the imbalances in his brain. All at once he felt a neurochemical realignment and Mei came into focus. She was incredible. Brilliant. For the last five years she had given his life purpose. Even in the good times, when successes piled on successes, she was the last thing he thought about before falling asleep and the first thing he thought about when he woke up. Between those periods, all bets were off; his dreams were governed by chaos. But on either side of them, in the hours he spent with his eyes open, those governed less by chaos and more by routines and inertia and some degree of free will, Mei was far and away the most important facet of his life.

Surely this wasn't news to him. Had he somehow not realized it until he stumbled into the right medication? Had he realized it before, but had the revelation been excised from his head by the clumsy lobotomist that was his particular brand of mental illness? Or, a third possibility that frightened him most of all, was this all just a reaction to the medicine? Would he wake up tomorrow, think of Mei (first thing, naturally), and feel less of... whatever this was? Would it be like discovering your favorite new song while high as a kite and then revisiting it after the comedown only to find it wholly unexceptional? No, that couldn't be it. Even before she'd driven herself into focus just now, even when he was at his most saturnine, he knew Mei was extraordinary.

Raza realized that his internal clock must have accelerated tenfold. His thoughts were flowing quickly but smoothly. He blinked to force his attention onto the matter at hand. The two grumpy firmware engineers apologized to each other and agreed to help one another out with whatever IRM backward-compatibility issue had sparked the whole spat. Raza watched the two shake hands, and he felt a slight tickle of inspiration. If he had to place the tickle in space, he would say it was at the intersection of three planes; the first was a few millimeters left of his corpus callosum, the second was the plane of his ocular nerves, and a third was a vertical plane that kissed both his earlobes.

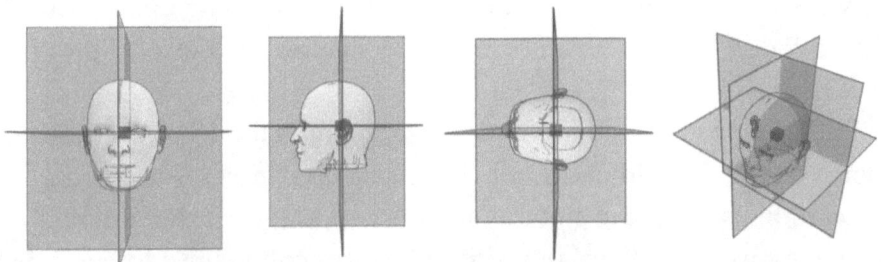

At first he tried to shake it off. If he jostled his head side to side, the area surrounding the itch would abrade it down to nothing. For months, that sort of tickle precluded nothing more than fruitless distractions that were inclined to turn aggressively negative. Was this all that was? He wasn't sure, something about it felt different, but he shook his head just to be safe.

Mei stole another glance at Raza—perhaps his head shake wasn't as subtle as he intended. She turned her plank-straight back to him for a moment before swiveling back around to look him over. Raza realized then that a number of other people were looking his way as well. Damn, did he have something on his face? No, that wasn't possible, he missed lunch. What was it? Mei looked more curious than concerned, which was a good sign. Her face, which was for some reason below eye level...

"Raza," Arden was rubbing his temple impatiently. "I assume you stood up for a reason. Do you need to run out? You're being a distraction."

Shit. He didn't remember getting out of his seat. "No. I need..." What did he need? His mind was still sprinting through a black void, but a pinhole of light appeared in the distance. He knew that the pinhole was somehow connected to the tickle in his head that he tried to ignore. "I have an idea." Did he? He wasn't sure, but the pinhole was growing larger.

Raza stepped forward toward the center of the room. Was he walking slowly, or was he just processing information more rapidly and so his movement felt slow by comparison? With each step, the light grew larger and brighter. It was too bright. It was burning his skin. Oh God, was he having some sort of stroke? He clenched his fists and closed his eyes but the light was still growing. The ground felt unstable beneath his feet. Suddenly he felt a hand on his shoulder. When he opened his eyes, he saw Mei's outline, centered in the beam of light reaching up to him. The light exploded behind her. There, in the shadow of Mei's eclipse, Raza saw it all in an instant.

"I know what we have to do." He spoke as though the words were generated right there in his mouth, bypassing his consciousness altogether. He heard himself talking and was as surprised as those around him. "The last time we were stuck, we introduced high-res competitive forces to help drive our sims toward higher and higher nodes. Competition forced her loose and pushed her up the tree."

"Yes, but our current sims include those competitive forces and now they're—"

"They're stuck higher up The Tree." Raza couldn't slow down long enough to let Arden finish his thought. "We've reached an evolutionary turning point. Reptile to mammal. There are so many biological switches to be flipped across that transition, such a huge leap to be made, that competitive forces alone pushing up from below aren't enough to make the jump to the next node." He blinked rapidly as his eyes traced a path to the top of The Tree. "I mean, we're looking to turn this smooth, efficient, instinct-driven lizard brain into a wrinkly, over-engineered, higher mammal brain, and predator/prey dynamics alone won't drive that change. What we're missing is the force pulling up from above. Or... or rather from within the node."

"What sort of pulling forces?" Arden's curiosity outweighed his frustration, but that didn't mean the frustration wasn't still clearly visible just underneath his slightly raised eyebrows and marginally less clenched jaw.

"Cooperation!" Raza was vibrating with excitement and his mind was three steps ahead of his tongue. He checked back in with his tongue and found that it hadn't yet conveyed his point. "Cooperation between peers. Family dynamics, community building. Socialization. *Teamwork*. That's what our sims have been missing, and that's the pull that gets them to the next node."

"So interactions between members of the species are what get us over the hump?" It was one of the firmware guys.

"Exactly." Raza looked to his right where Mei was still standing. "They work together. They make each other better." She cocked her head slightly, communicating several thoughts at once.

"Are you suggesting we somehow just *introduce* a bunch of Cynognathus sims and see if they hit it off? Using what hardware?" Raza didn't recognize the voice or the face.

Mei answered. "I think the idea is to use high-res models to act as the sim's cohort." She looked toward Raza who gave a quick nod.

"Which actually seems feasible." Arden was now on his feet, walking toward the two of them. Did he see the look from Mei? Could he read her like Raza could? He continued, "We compress the competitor models down to a negligible load and they've pushed us this far. I don't see why we couldn't do the same to mock up a society for the sims."

"We don't need full-res sims," Raza responded, his body involuntarily tensing as Arden came to stand between him and Mei, "at least I don't think we do, but we'll definitely need to increase the complexity relative to the competitor models. It doesn't take much to scare a sim and ignite a prey response. I'd still be scared of a shark even if it were a little blurry or polygonal." Mei laughed and Raza felt electric. "But the sims will be more discerning when it comes to their family. We're much more careful with who we trust."

The rest of the room grasped the idea and ran with it.

"From here on up, the sims are only going to get smarter and smarter. What fools Cynognathus won't fool Hominidae."

"Let's not get too far ahead of ourselves, here."

"We can start with whatever computational power we can spare to overcome this first hump. After that, I'm sure the mole people are up to the challenge of power-boosting the sim's externals."

"Hey, not cool, Gregg."

"Sorry, Linz, I forgot you guys were still here."

"How about a dynamic resolution? The peers can increase in complexity when they're close to and interacting with our sim, but we can drop the resolution when they're in the background."

"I like that."

"You would."

"What's that supposed to mean?"

"Like you don't know?"

They carried on in that fashion while Mei, Raza, and Arden stood and observed. "We make each other better." Arden was looking straight ahead and speaking quietly so that only he and Mei could hear. "You may be on to something, Dr. Mugabi."

"Can I have my trash can back?"

~ ~ ~

Three and a half hours later, the software team filtered out toward their desks and the few hardware team members that stayed through the end darted to the freight elevator. Raza was sweating from his neck to his socks, and was reminded by the sound emanating from his gut that he hadn't eaten in a good long while. "Come on, hot shot, let's get some food in you before you keel over." Mei was still standing to his right. Her hair was a bird's nest, her suit jacket sleeves were rolled up, and her posture was ever-so-slightly slouched.

"I have a lot of calls to make." Arden was still in the room, apparently. "And if they go well, there's a good chance I'll need to catch a redeye orbiter to Tokyo. You two go ahead without me."

Raza mumbled a malformed "Good luck". It came out more like "glug". The glug didn't slow Arden down in the slightest; he had somehow managed to organize and initiate an emergency board meeting on his way out the door. Raza stretched his stiff neck in Mei's direction. "I'm pretty fried. Maybe I should call an auton."

"Mmmm, you gave me an idea. I'll fry up some fish. Get your stuff."

"Fish does sound pretty good. I didn't know you cook."

"I could write a book of things you don't know about me."

"Would it be a cookbook?"

"Yeah, a pop-up cookbook."

"Can I preorder a dozen?"

"Only twelve? If you order thirteen you get the twelfth at double-price."

"I know a good deal when I see one. Where can I sign?"

"You wouldn't know a good deal if it stood in front of you and offered to cook you dinner."

~ ~ ~

Thirty minutes later, they stepped out of the auton. Raza followed Mei in through the nondescript lobby of a nondescript housing complex in a nondescript suburb. He wasn't sure what he'd imagined, but this wasn't it. His expectations were further subverted when they stepped into the elevator and she pressed "3". 3? How... nondescript.

189

"Were you expecting a penthouse in the sky?"

All he could do was smile. She could read his thoughts even when he couldn't untangle them himself. Of course she could see right through him, now that his mind had regained some semblance of clarity.

She gave him a stern look, but broke before he had a chance to believe she meant it. "To be honest, I was surprised too. I always assumed he lived in..."

"A gothic castle?"

"Ha. I was going to say some sort of hyper-modern suite in the tech district. You know, rubbing tailored-suited elbows with other execs." They stepped out of the elevator. "But Ard's nothing if not practical." Mei led the way to her door, behind which Mei and 'Ard' shared their mornings and nights together. Raza felt a twinge of jealousy.

Mei opened the door to reveal a modest living space. It was cozy, inviting, and more than a little hot. The primary living space contained three features that drew him in: two busy walls on either side of some sort of strange pod.

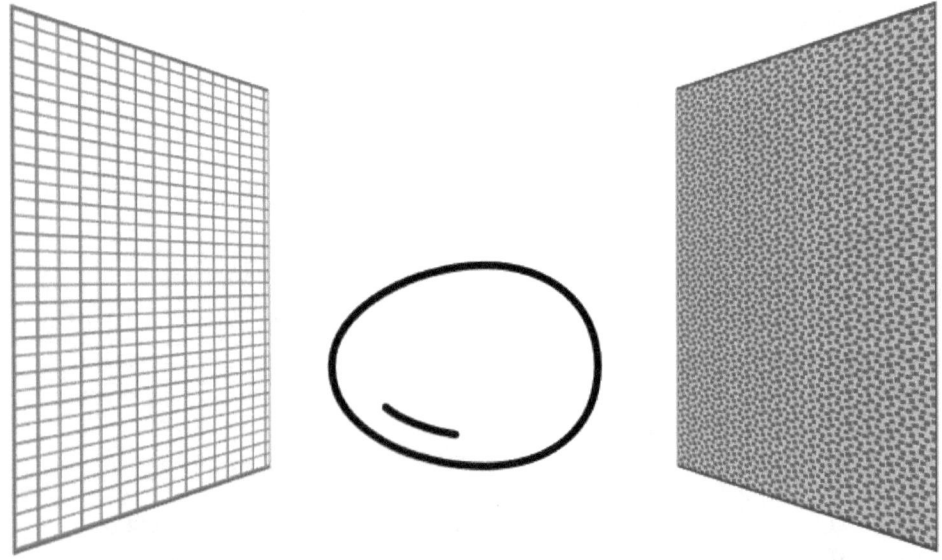

Did they sleep in that thing? He tried to imagine how they could fit in it, perhaps curled up one on top of the other. Then he tried desperately to unimagine it.

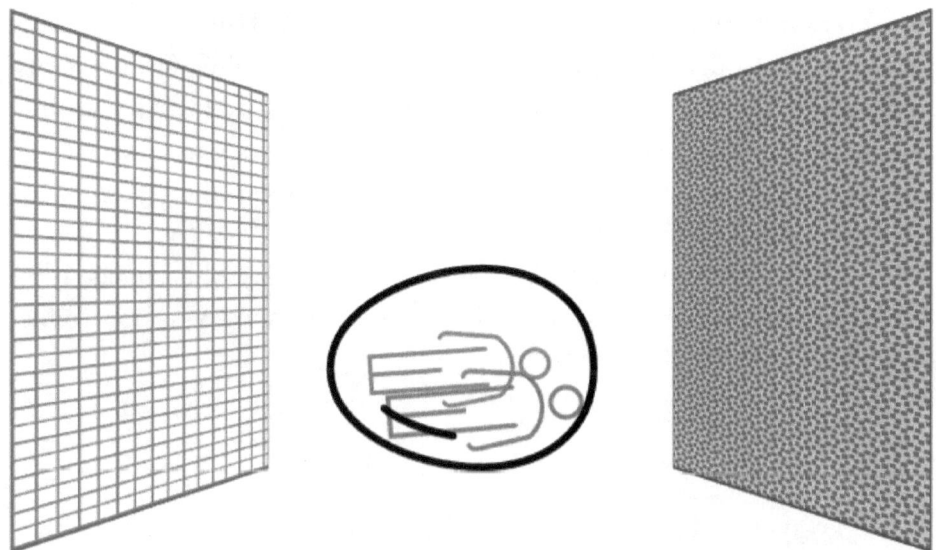

The two walls contained floor to ceiling shelves. The one on the left seated hundreds of neatly arranged old textbooks, so uniform in size and color that from this distance he couldn't be sure whether they were just identical copies of the same book. Opposite the book collection was a wall very much its opposite. Its shelves held odd, jagged figurines, brightly colored shapes, each stranger than the last. Something about them was very familiar.

"Sorry about the heat. The kiln's exchanger is on the fritz." She nodded toward the pod.

"Kiln... You make pottery?"

"It's all there in my cookbook. Haven't you read it?"

He walked closer to the colorful wall. It was a distant cousin to the wall in The Vault, with its mishmash of visually distinct doodads and widgets. Upon closer inspection, the wall had more in common with The Vault than first suggested. "Oh... wow."

"Recognize them, huh?"

"How could I not?" They were wonderfully abstract, but their identities shone brightly through the abstractions like a light through stained glass. "These are our sims!"

"Bingo."

Each iteration was captured in ceramic and glaze, from the early Urmetazoans to their latest long run of Cynognathus after Cynognathus. He inspected the latter group. Though each of these runs stagnated around a single node, there were variations in the personality of each sim and she had managed to impart each iteration's uniqueness into the figure. "Mei, these are... they're incredible."

"I thought you might like them. You know..." She changed her mind mid-sentence, and instead said, "Want me to show you how to filet a fish?"

~ ~ ~

Forty-five minutes and one very large bottle of fruit wine later, they licked their plates clean.

"I think I have a pin bone in my throat."

"That's on you."

"That's *IN* me."

"Nice."

Raza smiled lazily at her. The heat from the kiln, from the fish fry, from the wine, from the setting sun, made him melt comfortably into the chair at the kitchen table. "So. *Ard?*"

"Yes," she lowered her gaze to the table and smiled knowingly. She and Raza had grown apart since she and Arden started seeing each other, though neither had acknowledged it. "*Ard.*"

Raza put on his best Texas Mom voice. "He seems like a nice young man."

Mei grinned, but didn't laugh. Dammit, Raza thought. Did that sound mean?

"You know, when I first visited his place, *this* place, he had one set of dishes. He had one spoon! No furniture, aside from a desk and a bed." Mei thumbed the stem of her empty wine glass. "And several boxes of hand-written journals. He was living like a college student. The CEO of our company! He started jinhwa fresh out of grad school, and he's put

100% of his energy into it, never taking the time to develop a life outside of it. It was kind of shocking, at first."

"Yeah, I can imagine."

"But there's something about his singularity of vision that's really admirable, you know? And, fortunately, he's been letting me expose him to the world outside of jinhwa. He actually just had mochi for the first time last week. He hated it, but, hey, he's trying new things."

"I'm glad things are going well." Did that sound sarcastic? "Really, I mean it." Ah hell, that sounded even more sarcastic. "Seriously."

Mei just laughed. Deep and rich and warm. "I leather bound his journals for him. I wanted something of his to be on display, and it was either those or the damn spoon."

With his eyelids heavy, he turned to the array of books. They were impossible to concentrate on with the wall of figures pulling his gaze further to the right. He stared at Mei's work for a long, quiet moment before saying, "Why do you do it?"

"What do you mean?" she asked, knowing precisely what he meant.

"You could tell me you make them just for art's sake. Just because they're what's on your mind all day. I'd believe you if you did." He looked back to Mei. "But I'm wondering if there's more to it than that."

Any attention that had been directed toward her thumb and her wine glass was now fully aimed at him. "Yes. It's a way to mourn them." It was clear to Raza that this was the first time she was speaking that truth out loud. "Our sims are... they're *something*, Raz. I've waffled on using the word *life* for years, but that word has its merits. Ah hell, I'm starting to sound like Mikey."

"Maybe that's not such a bad thing."

"I know, I know, it's just that we spend so much time and energy with them, and attachments are formed, and at a certain point the endless cycle of burning them down and starting over began to weigh on me. So," she gestured to the top shelf, "I started eulogizing the sims with clay and oxides."

Raza's eye traced the line back from where she was pointing, to her finger and up her forearm, over the crook of her elbow and on toward her shoulder, up her neck, to her wine-flushed face. "It's nice to see them like this. So... organic."

"I tried to hide them from Arden. Before moving in, I mean. Given his attitude toward the whole—"

"We should be together."

The room fell quiet, save for a dull hum from the kiln. The ethanol on his breath wafted his words up toward the ceiling where they condensed into droplets and hung over the two of them like a storm cloud. She inspected him, again with a look of genuine curiosity. After exactly one eternity, she spoke. "Raz. We tried that experiment once, remember?"

"Yeah, but," he searched his brain for the right words to counter her argument, the cryptokey that would unlock the timeline in which he and Mei and the kiln ran away together. Instead, he said, "What kind of conclusions can we draw with an N of 1?"

Mei laughed. Not mockingly, not maliciously. When the laughter left her, she turned back to the kitchen and began cleaning their plates. Again the hum of the kiln filled the void, until she posed a question. "You know why the experiment didn't work?"

"Because we worked better as friends?" he said, a bit too quickly, a bit too loudly, knowing that the door to the timeline he so desperately wanted was shutting. Had already shut, really. Long ago.

"But do you know *why* we worked better as friends?"

"I..." He didn't.

"Because you didn't *like* me. Not romantically, anyway. But you *needed* me. You mistook that need for affection. I was a drug. A crutch. While we were together, you called me 'an oasis where [you] could rest [your] weary mind'. Do you have any idea how much pressure that puts on a person, to be someone else's goddamn lifeforce?"

"I, uhh. Shit, Mei. I'm—"

"Meanwhile, I actually liked you. A lot, if I'm being honest and a little tipsy. But I didn't *need* you. So, naturally, things collapsed back into a state where boundaries were clearly drawn and neither of us had to give the other person something we didn't have to offer."

Raza winced as sobriety thwacked him in the back of the head. The room felt ten degrees cooler. "You're right. I'm sorry."

"It's getting pretty late."

"Yeah, I'll catch a ride back to my place."

CHAPTER 20
TRIAL DAY 3.1 - JIVANTA

Jivanta was brushing her teeth when she heard someone let themselves into her suite. Over the years, her client list had accrued more than its fair share of unsavory characters. It was in the job description: prosecuting on behalf of petty criminals, shady corporations, and corrupt government agencies. It was a powerful position to be in; she preferred being a sword over being a shield. Still, the company she kept was beginning to leave a bad taste in her mouth. To that end, and to keep said company waiting, she spit into the green crystal sink and started the brush cycle over.

Two minutes later, she rinsed her mouth and cleared her throat, noting that it was dry from a night of muttering to herself. Now it was time to mutter to someone else. "Did you sleep in the lobby?"

The big man was seated at her desk, the chair comically small under his mass. It reminded her of a scene from her past life, playing Very Scary Restaurant with her nephew. The rules were simple. Jivanta and her sister and her brother-in-law would sit in tiny seats situated around a tiny table, and the tiny human, with whom she shared a fair amount of DNA, would serve them imaginary food on plastic plates. He would say "Auntie Jiva, here's your spaghetti" and she would say "Why thank you, chef, this looks fabulous" and he would say "Try it, try it!" She would dip the plastic fork into the invisible pasta, taking all the time in the world, miming the stabbing and twirling and twirling and twirling as her nephew shook and squealed with anticipation. Finally, she would take a bite, and no sooner did the pretend food touch her tongue than he would scream, "It's not real spaghetti, Auntie! It's worms!" Good kid.

"I brought you this."

"What?" She blinked, transporting herself from the Very Scary Restaurant back to the Pricey Pine-Scented Hotel. Lack of sleep was allowing her mind to wander. She eyed the man suspiciously. He too looked a bit worse for wear. Her clients must've been busy last night.

"It's coffee. From downstairs."

"I prefer tea." She frowned at the offering.

"I know." Of course he knew. "But the tea from the lobby tastes like mulched cardboard." Accurate. He extended the cup toward her. "The lattes, on the other hand..."

"Thanks." She grabbed it and mimed sipping, plugging the hole with her tongue, eying him to see if he would scream, "It's not real coffee, Auntie Jiva! It's poison! We're going to sneak your corpse out of here in pieces and feed it to the hogs on the outskirts of town!" No reaction. She put the full coffee down on the nightstand and took a seat on the corner of the bed. "So. I assume you're here for more than just a coffee date."

"That I am, Ms. Puri. There's been an incident at the courthouse. The session today has been postponed."

"Incident?"

"A bomb threat. There's not a lot of information yet, but early reports are saying a delivery bot may have exploded on the premises."

"May he rest in peace." Jivanta felt a wave of relief in learning that she wouldn't have to prosecute an increasingly sticky case after a sleepless night, but that sense was immediately undercut by her knowledge that there was more to this visit than just a surprise snow day bulletin. "I don't suppose you or your people know anything more about the situation, do you?"

"Ms. Puri, I'm offended. Are you suggesting that we had something to do with this?" She honestly couldn't tell with this guy. He wore his mask well.

"Well?"

His eyes softened. Was he genuinely upset? Jivanta was on the verge of apologizing before he spoke up. "We are not in the business of failed assassination attempts." The softness disappeared in an instant. There was no hint of emotion in his voice. It was almost totally flat; the one bump in the vocal spectra, the one slight inflection, was on the word "failed". The message was clear.

Jivanta's throat was dry. She reached for the coffee and the man smiled. His eyes unfocused for a moment as he received directions through his earpiece. "We have information to share with you. New evidence has been collected."

"New, as in since we last spoke eight hours ago?"

"Precisely."

Jivanta wondered how many kneecaps were splintered in the collection process but decided that she'd rather not know. At this point, her options were looking pretty grim and new evidence, ill-gotten or otherwise, could be the lifeline this case needed. "Let's see it."

The man pressed his thumb into his SenZ and, motioning with a canned-ham-sized fist, cast the information onto the augmented viewscreen layered on top of the desk mirrors behind him. The images were largely obscured behind his bulk. Against her better judgment, she stepped toward him to get a better look. When she was near enough to read the text (though not without a fair amount of squinting), she stopped and began taking in the information note by note. There she stood, absorbing. Her knee ached but she was frozen where she was, not willing to step back and lose her view of the screen, and even less willing to move closer to the man sitting a few short strides in front of her. Minutes passed. Thirty-five of them, not that she was counting.

Finally, Jivanta sighed, moved back to the corner of the bed, and slowly sat down, rubbing her lower thigh with one hand and draining the rest of her latte with the other.

"There's no way the panel will admit this as evidence."

"It has already been cleared."

"What? How... never mind." How powerful were these guys? They must have at least one partisan on the high council. *Dammit, Jivanta,* she imagined her sister saying. *What did you get yourself into?*

"Are you sure this is what you want? It's risky. You understand that, right? We'll for sure turn off a few of the more... sentimental members of the panel. Not to mention the public."

"Ms. Puri, we trust you will use your judgment, and your tact, to present the evidence in a way that suits our mutually desired outcome."

Her sister's voice was still ringing in her left ear. *What did you get yourself into?* In her other ear, a child's voice. *It's worms!* It's always fucking worms. Her eyes stabbed through the words of the augmented projection and found a new focal point double the distance from her as the first. At that second, further plane, her gaze landed on the reflection of herself, positioned behind the mirror image of the monstrous man and looking impossibly small. It was then that she realized she was still in her bathrobe.

"You could knock, you know."

He shrugged, disturbing the tides with his shoulders. "I didn't want to bother your neighbors."

Jivanta laughed and was surprised at the sound. Sharp as a knife. "How considerate."

CHAPTER 21
2 YEARS EARLIER - RAZA

"Well... wow." Raza rubbed his newly bearded face. He was trying something different.

"My thoughts exactly."

Raza had given his team the go-ahead to start without him. He preferred to have bad news filtered through the rosy lenses of his underlings rather than observe it with the naked eye. Thirty minutes later, his workchat pingpinged an urgent notification. *You have to see this.* His heart was racing, though not from the jog over to see what the fuss was about.

"I knew we were climbing fast, but—"

"Yep."

"This is... wow."

Raza and his team were in the Second Floor visualization suite reviewing the latest observation on One Hundred Thirty. *His* team. The beard wasn't the only new presence in his life. It still felt strange to have people working for him. He even knew all of their names, though it took a month of trial-and-error, pop quizzes from Mei, and some wildly tangled mnemonics. Simple mnemonics wouldn't take root in his memory. They'd be swept away with the loose topsoil at the first sign of a storm. But he'd found that the more complicated the device, the deeper he could plant it in his working memory.

"Should we bring Mei in to see this?"

He tossed a glance out the one-way window toward Mei's desk and saw that she was deep into her cocoon. "Not just yet—" *Curly-Hair And*

Polite / C.H.A.P. / Chapped Lips / Loose lips sink ships / Deck of the ship / Deck of cards "—Jack. We'll bring her in after we get a better handle on what exactly this means." Jack and—*Green eyes / Green bean soup / Miso soup / Me / Raza Mugabi / Razberry / Green beret / Shit, back to green* (this was a necessary part of the mnemonic) / *Green eggs and ham / Dr. Seuss*—Susanna gave each other a loaded look that Raza pretended not to notice.

"So." He smoothed his mustache with his fingers and gesture-scrolled through the data summary. It had been four weeks since the last observation. At that time, the sim had been in a transient state, tight-rope walking along the thread between the *Haplorhini* and *Catarrhini* nodes. That put them ahead of schedule, but the sim was in a position considered to be at high risk for divergence. The road to *H. sapiens* forked, with one path leading to the apes that would eventually climb to the top of The Tree, and the other leading to the adorable but decidedly nonhuman New World monkeys. The New World monkey route was much less energy intensive, and therefore much more appealing for the sim. On one path, a bunch of engineers were beckoning it forward with promises of glory and higher function. On the other path, a ripe banana. They could push the sim with competition and pull it with cooperative forces (which had come to be known as *Kropotkin Agents,* or Kropos for short) as much as they wanted, but even the most optimistic predictive models were projecting a less than 15% chance of getting this right in one try. He had mentally prepared for disappointment. He was even prepared for an unlikely success. He wasn't at all prepared for this.

"We did it?"

~ ~ ~

Eight hours later, celebratory music was pumping in through the wall displays, creating a sharp chattering resonance in the pile of empty champagne bottles that had collected near the corner of the conference room. On the primary viewscreen, cast with the finest AR display technology money could buy (at least the finest it could buy a few years prior), was the reason for the revelry. One Hundred Thirty. Zechariah, Mikus had dubbed him. Standing upright, nude, arms and legs parted in a Vitruvian manner, with the same eyes Raza had met that morning. Text beneath his feet read: *Iteration 130. Homo sapiens.*

Dozens of other *H. sapiens* (a decent proportion of which possessed names that Raza could extract from his gray matter if given a ten second head start) were giddily milling about, some singing, some dancing, all participating in a collective joviality. Mei had even managed to drag Mikus up from his subterranean sanctum to join in the festivities. Raza couldn't remember the last time he had seen Mikus on the Second Floor. Months ago? Years? He entered the room with his eyes squinted and his shoulders pulled up toward his ears as though the lights and sounds were agonizing. To protect himself from the sensory onslaught, jinwha's co-founder shielded his body behind Mei and a few members of the hardware team.

Raza's team had cornered him to excitedly talk about what would come next. Raza recalled how Mei had originally explained the goals of jinhwa to him half a decade ago and he parroted the mission statement back to them. They would commoditize brain power and put an unlimited source of creativity and ingenuity toward solving the world's biggest problems. Inequality. Climate disasters. Famine. The team humored him for a while before he realized what they were really asking. What would come next *for them*? Bonuses, surely? Equity refreshments? Promotions? A world tour? Raza wanted to remind them that just because they were the first to open the observation dataset didn't mean that they were somehow more responsible than any of the other engineers in the room, but they couldn't hear him over the percussion of them patting themselves on the back.

Raza let them have their moment and allowed his own mind to wander. Looking across the room, he saw that the shield around Mikus had mostly dissipated, save for Mei. Arden had made his way over to them and stood on the other side of his fiancée, looking proudly toward Zechariah. Raza was sober enough to see the lines of tension connecting Arden and Mikus. He was tipsy enough to think he was just the man to break that tension. And he was too drunk to deny that his reasons for walking toward them had nothing to do with those two and everything to do with the person standing between them.

"Mei! Err, Mikus, Arden, how's it going?"

Arden broke his gaze from the visualization and blinked. "You know, Raza, I don't believe I've ever heard you say my name before." He smiled and Raza breathed a sigh of relief. Arden was in a good mood. How could he not be?

"I've been working on that, now that I'm a manager. It was Mei's idea, actually."

"Yep. After scouring the globe for the best means of forming interpersonal connections, I found that people would rather be called by their names, as opposed to 'you' or 'hey' or 'uhhh'." There was a bit more venom to the retort than he had expected. Maybe she was just getting caught in the Mikus/Arden tension nets.

"It's good to see you, Mikus!" He had been at the party for half an hour but hadn't relaxed in the slightest. If anything, he'd only grown more hunched. He looked like a man trying to disappear into his own chest. While Arden's eyes were constantly pulled back toward the center display, Mikus's gaze seemed repelled by it, as though he wanted to look but was physically incapable. "Are you feeling okay? Still dizzy from the elevator ride up?"

Without lifting his eyes, he smiled grimly, looking much older than he had when he and Raza had last spoken. "Just afraid of heights, I suppose."

Arden's jaw flexed once but Mei cut him off before he could respond. "Why the hell didn't you bring me into the viz suite?"

Raza knew what she was asking but feigned ignorance. "Huh?"

She wasn't buying it. "I was the last person in the company to find out about the observation results."

"Well, you were busy and—"

"Raz, cut the shit. You've been avoiding me ever since—"

"I'm sorry!" He looked at the ring on her finger, and then up at Arden, who to his relief, was fully lost in the rotating figure towering over them. He lowered his voice. "I'm sorry, I should have gotten you. You're right. I wanted you there to see it, I just... I was being an ass."

"Yes, you were."

He took a spot between Mei and Mikus and turned to look at the display. There were now two sets of tension lines, one arching around him from founder to co-founder, and the other vibrating in the air between him and Mei.

"Zech looks weirdly like my junior high school psychologist." Raza heard himself say.

Mei snorted. "Your junior high school psychologist has nice legs."

The vibration dampened. Raza stole a look at Mei. She didn't look over, but was suppressing a grin out of the corner of her mouth. He looked back to the display.

"There's something... odd about it." Raza had noted a certain discomfort with the visualization when he first encountered it. He chalked it up to surprise, or a smoothing error in the rendering, or any number of other things.

"It's the eyes." Mikus answered immediately without looking up.

"Mikus, don't," Arden warned.

"You're seeing an uncanny vacancy. Like there's nothing behind them."

"Not this again."

"But it's not totally blank. You see it, right? There's a hint of anger."

He was right. He was *exactly* right. Before Raza could respond, Arden stepped in. "The vacancy was expected. The peer and community models that coexist with the sim are obviously much too coarse to actually educate it beyond a most basic level. You must understand this, Raza. The Kropos were your idea, were they not? They provide a sense of family and comradery and purpose outside of the self, and that clearly worked for the lesser hominids."

"I don't understand." He pinched a lock of beard hair on his cheek and twisted it between his thumb and index finger. "We're celebrating the creation of an ignorant vessel of... nothing?"

205

"We have produced a human brain, the most complex machine ever developed by nature, manufactured by *us*. Now we need to teach it everything we know."

Raza directed his blurry eyes at Mei. "You knew this?"

She didn't bat an eye. "I did, yes."

"What..." Raza didn't know how to finish the thought.

Mei extrapolated the question and answered him. "We'll provide it with access to knowledge. Expose it to the internet. Well, a curated subset. We'll hotbox it to simulate a year or ten years or a hundred years and turn that empty vessel into the most learned machine of all time. Then it can serve as the tutor for every new sim we create. Which, now that we have a functioning model, will be a breeze."

"Getting the model of the brain has always been the goal." Arden had his hand on Mei's shoulder. The light from the display shone bright on their faces as they looked on, smiling. Triumphant. "Today, we met that goal. We created the machine. Tomorrow, we start the next phase, priming the engine. Then we'll set it to work."

Raza felt very sober and very drunk all at once. Minutes passed in silence. To his left, he heard Arden whisper to Mei, "I wonder if this is how God felt when he pulled Adam out of the mud."

Mikus must have overheard as well and responded quietly so that only Raza could hear. "May we be better to our creation than God was to his."

~ ~ ~

The next two months were spent preparing the hot box environment for the sim, carefully selecting what he would have access to in terms of educational content. By vote, it was decided that the content would focus on the climate crisis. The plan was to introduce the sim to increasingly complex subjects and ideas at a 1100X simulated timescale for one week of Universal Time. During that week, Zechariah would experience the equivalent of over twenty years of what had come to be referred to as *sim school*. They would de-age him to approximate the brain

206

size and plasticity of a five-year-old and then allow it to age progressively through the simulated timescale. In theory, after the ramp down, they would observe an extremely educated adult sim. Perhaps even a sim that could communicate. Perhaps even a sim that could problem-solve. However, the actual outcome of the experiment was anyone's guess; this was uncharted territory.

Raza imagined what his life would have been like if he went from kindergarten through grad school with zero distractions. Zero interactions. Zero sleep. Nothing to do but learn and learn and learn. The more he thought about it, the less he liked it, so he stopped imagining it altogether and focused on the work. Raza and his team were in charge of the growth algorithms that would define the sim's physical development. Its mental development would be largely up to it. No, not *it*. Definitely not *it*. Him. *He* would decide what, of his curated content, to explore. There had been some debate as to whether observation points should be scheduled throughout the run. Raza pushed for a daily check-in; given how novel this all was, he wanted to make sure everything was going... somewhere? Somewhere positive, at least. Ultimately the check-in observations were scrapped to conserve power and speed. Each observation required considerable computational resources, and reinitialization would further slow the experiment. It took time and energy to ramp up to 1100X, and the louder voices argued against stopping that barrel once it got rolling.

~ ~ ~

Finally, it came. The first day of sim school. The test was initiated at 03:20 on a Saturday, a time selected by the hardware team so that the initialization power surge wouldn't disrupt operations or brown-out the neighborhood. Not that operations were particularly... operational. What was there to do at this point but sit and wait? To that end, a team-building getaway had been scheduled. Mikus and a select group of hardware engineers had agreed ('a bit *too* readily,' according to Arden) to stay behind and shovel coal in the engine room.

At 06:15 on Monday, Raza and two dozen of his Second Floor coworkers boarded the maglev. In a row of three, Raza had the aisle seat all to himself. Seconds after the final boarding call, looking uncharacteristically harried, Mei lurched through the door, made her way down the aisle, stepped on Raza's foot, and took the window seat. Raza felt a jolt of electricity leap up his spine and then rolled his mind's eye at himself. It had been over a year since he drank two or three or five glasses of wine and half-professed his sort-of-love for her. Thirteen months, two weeks, and one engagement ring ago, to be exact. They had remained friends through it all. However, Raza often found himself making excuses not to be around her. Especially without the benefit of other people to serve as buffers. He imagined third parties as dashpots that tempered the energy between them. Without a dampener, he feared what would happen if the vibrations between them constructively interfered, feeding off each other and compounding until... Until what? He had no idea. And now, here she was, with only an empty seat serving as a buffer. Or, shit, wait, is the empty seat for—

"Ard's going to meet us there tonight." How did she do that? Mei nodded toward the buffer as she fished through her bag for her AR-Lens and slipped it over her eyes and ears. It was a sign not to bother her, and he walked right by it.

"Investor meeting?"

"Mmmmhmmm."

Raza tugged a patch of beard hair as the maglev accelerated out of the station. The "don't bother me" sign was flashing neon lights in his periphery. Once again, he ignored it. "Wanna hear a joke?"

Mei's jaw muscle flexed, a trait she must have adopted from her absentee fiancé. Absenté. "Goddammit." She sighed, removed the Lens, looked at him, looked *through* him, tense, tired, angry, and said, "Duh. You know I do."

"Ok. Cards on the table, this is Mikus's joke."

"Yikes, bad start."

"Yeah, I know, but I like this one."

"Somehow worse. Keep going, I'm on... what's the opposite of the edge of my seat? The back of my seat? The back is still an edge." She looked down as if running a mock calculation in her head. "I'm on the exact, geometric center of my seat."

Raza had a sneaking suspicion that there was nothing *mock* about that calculation. Mei took her math, even math for the sake of an insult, very seriously. "Then I have you right where I want you."

Mei let a smirk escape from her scowl and Raza's brain flooded with a potent slurry of neurotransmitters. She reined it in but Raza knew it was still there, hiding just below the surface. "Do you think we're going to get to the set up before we reach our destination? Should I ask the conductor to slow down so you have enough time?"

"It couldn't hurt. Maybe we can take the scenic route."

"I'll tell you what." Mei slipped off her travel shoes, pulled her bare feet up into the seat, and then, doing a quarter spin on her backside, rotated her body to lean back against the window. She wrapped her arms around her knees. "Why don't you start with the punchline and then work your way backwards? That way, if you can't finish by the time we get there, you will have at least left me somewhat satisfied. With *some* semblance of conclusion, no matter how disappointing it proves to be."

Raza mirrored her cocked eyebrow and decided to accept her challenge. "Smart. So, punchline first." He cleared his throat and put on his best game show host voice. "They're both composed of qubits."

"Oh. Oh no."

"Oh yes."

"Can I bow out now? There's no setup in the universe that will make that punchline palatable."

"I couldn't stop if I tried. The train's a'rollin'."

Mei's smirk resurfaced. "The hell was that accent?"

"I don't know. Travel makes me folksy."

"I like it. Okay, pardner, let's hear it."

He made a big show of pulling a water canteen from his travel bag, slowly unscrewing the cap and taking a long pull before recapping and returning the canteen at half-speed. "Nah, I don't feel like it anymore."

Mei snorted and gave him a quick jab in the thigh with her toe. "Come on, Raz. I'm all ears. Hit me with it."

"Hmmmm." Raza reached back into his bag and pulled out an eye mask. "Maybe I should take a quick nap first."

In the blink of an eye, Mei's foot darted forward and flicked the mask out of his hands and into the aisle. She left her foot perched on his thigh, like a brandished weapon. Raza tried not to notice the tattoo on her shin. Or the shape of her calf as it inched up her leg and curved to meet the back of her knee.

"Fine, but only because you asked nicely. Right, where were we?"

"They're both composed of qubits."

"Yes, yes, that was it. Okay. Are you sure you don't want to fasten your seatbelt for this?"

"Good thinking, I wouldn't want to be knocked from the center of my seat toward the edge." She pulled her leg back, pivoted toward the seat in front of her and fastened herself in.

Raza's thigh tingled where her foot had been and he cursed himself silently. "Safety first."

"Raz."

"Okay, without further ado." He brought back his game show voice. "What do SenZero processors and the blueprints for Noah's Ark have in common?"

Mei blinked dolefully at Raza before turning her face slowly to the window and beating her head once against the glass.

"Ah, come on! Cubits and qubits?"

"Ugggggggh."

"Homophones are funny!"

"I can't believe I used to have a crush on you."

Raza looked toward the window. In the reflection he saw Mei's face. Her eyes were closed. Her lips were parted. She was grinning to herself. A private smile, betrayed by the electrochromic tint of the glass. "Hey, we all make mistakes."

~ ~ ~

At 09:30, the maglev decelerated into Colorado Metropolitan Station. Mei accelerated into a phone call about an hour before they slid into the station and hadn't returned to her seat. Raza waited around the exit, hoping he could catch her on the way out and share an auton to the conference center where they would be staying for the next three nights. By 09:50, he decided that he must have missed her, took a deep breath, and turned to face the city in the clouds.

Denver had seen enormous expansion since The Aattoq. With millions of coast dwellers chased inland and to higher elevations by the rising tides, it had become North America's largest hub for science, tech, arts, culture, you name it. The air was too sparse and the population was too dense for Raza's liking. Still, he was excited to be back. He'd interned downtown three summers in a row back in grad school and he hoped to meet up with some of his ev bio colleagues from a lifetime ago. From a prior iteration of his personal evolution, he thought and then promptly unthought. There was a growing urge to compare his existence to that of the sims, and a stronger urge to avoid those thoughts at all costs. Fortunately, he was more in control of his brain now than he had been during any prior... iteration. Dammit.

No jinhwa activities had been scheduled until the early afternoon, giving everyone a chance to check in to the hotel and explore the area. As Raza's auton pulled into the drop-off zone, he double checked his itinerary to make sure this was the right spot. Arden must have been feeling generous when planning the trip. The hotel was massive, with effusive bellhops dressed in what looked like the same material used to line blackjack tables standing in front of glass doors that were no less than six meters tall. The lobby was a discordant mix of sleek tinted glass on top of burnished steel on top of heavily lacquered faux (he assumed) redwood flooring. It was an inharmonious mashup of pre-spaceflight futurism and a log cabin. It was a trillionaire on a fishing trip. It was pine-scented opulence. Quite literally. Raza suspected that the less-than-natural woodsy smell was being pumped in with the recycled air. What a world.

By 10:55, after a long shower and several minutes of pacing around his too-large room, closing the too-big shades on his too-tall windows to block out the too-close sun, he made a decision. He was going to message Mei and ask if she wanted to grab brunch. Why shouldn't he message her? Why shouldn't they grab brunch? They were friends, right? Friends grab brunch! He pulled out his SenZ and leapt onto the enormous bed. He needed his message to sound casual, and casual words would flow more freely if he happened to be composing them from a comfortable position, or so he reasoned as he shimmied himself into a throne of pillows. Deep breath. He brought his phone up in front of him to compose the message and was immediately distracted by an alert. Damn, with the change in routine he hadn't unsilenced his communications. The notification carried him into his workchat where he saw that it wasn't just a single missed message, but several dozen. What was going on? He opened the latest and read the last several that had been flagged as high priority in reverse order.

10:54 [Senior–Software and Hardware - Gregg] Thanks Stephanie. Sorry, I didn't mean to flag my message as urgent. I don't know how to turn it off.

10:54 [Senior–Software and Hardware - Stephanie] HR is talking with his family now.

10:53 [Senior–Software and Hardware - Gregg] His emergency contact is out of town. Does anyone know his next of kin?

10:35 [Private workchat thread - Mei] we're starting. this can't wait. just call me when you see this.

10:34 [Senior–Software and Hardware - Arden.] We'll give everyone another minute to join remotely.

10:33 [Private workchat thread - Mei] raz where the hell are you

10:20 [jinhwa Master - Arden] @all There will be an emergency mandatory sync at 10:30. Those at the Denver Intercontinental, convene in conference room 1F. Those elsewhere, use the attached link for virtual joinup.

Raza's heart was in his throat as he frantically threw his clothes back on. By the time he made it to the elevator, sweat was already beading on his forehead. By his internal clock, the elevator ride must have lasted at least an hour. Possibly two. When it finally touched down, he sprinted to the front desk to demand directions to the conference room, but before he could get the words out, a glass door opened on the other side of the lobby with familiar faces slowly pouring out. Familiar, but very solemn faces. Among the throng he recognized Arden, stiffer than usual and unnaturally pale. He wanted to run to the group, but his wracked nerves slowed him to a wobbly trot. Mei saw him and ran over to meet him halfway, pausing in front of him. She looked as though she had been crying. The air reeked of ozone and pine. He tried to speak but his dry tongue was welded to the roof of his mouth. "Mei, wha—"

"Mikus is dead." She said it so matter-of-factly, her voice raspy but unwavering. She had already gone through it, or at least the initial brunt of it. The shock, the grief.

Raza's first reaction was a vague regret that he hadn't been there for her. He hated himself for that selfish thought, and was thankful he didn't articulate it. Instead, with wide eyes and unsteady knees, he said, "What? What the... What?"

"There was an accident in The Vault. We don't have all the details yet, but it sounds like a coolant rupture. Security found Mikey... they found his body this morning."

"God. What? How? Mikus wouldn't—"

"I know, I know, Raz."

It didn't make any sense. Mikus was erratic, but he was always extremely careful. The Vault was his pride and joy and he kept it purring like a vintage muscle car. But then, Raza hadn't been down there much since the viz suite was built on the Second Floor. Dammit. He remembered when Mikus called him and Mei down a few years earlier. He was just a lonely man looking for some company. Maybe if he'd gone down there more, maybe he could have seen if The Vault wasn't being maintained, or maybe he could have noticed if Mikus needed an extra set of eyes, or maybe if he hadn't gone on this dumb fucking trip just so he could maybe sit next to his fully unavailable crush on the train ride, like a goddamn pre-teen, maybe—

Mei wrapped her arms around him, choking the thought off midstream. "I know what you're thinking." She spoke softly. Firmly. "I got a head start on you because I know how to answer my phone, but trust me, I've already been down the same road. There's nothing you or I or any of us could've done." He felt his chest convulse as a torrent of emotions tried to escape and she squeezed tighter to absorb the quake. She didn't relax her grip until the spasms were dampened into a dull tremor. "Arden and I are catching the next train back so we can start dealing with all this shit. The safety auditors are already banging down the doors."

He felt a flash of anger. "Safety auditors? How is that what you're concerned about?"

She sighed. "Everyone processes grief differently. If you would've been here in time, you would've seen the full spectrum. Susan laughed. Gregg got a nosebleed and then passed out at the sight of his own blood. Before coming down, I screamed into a pillow until my vocal cords were raw. And you're lashing out for someone to be angry with."

Shit. She was probably right. That didn't make him less angry, though. "Mei, I'm—"

"Don't apologize. I get it. I'm not done reckoning with what happened. I may never be. But for now, all I can do, all WE can do, is get back to work. It's what Mikey would've wanted." She checked her phone. "I should head back."

She turned to go and Raza stared at the wood grain under her feet as she stepped away. "Do you really believe that?" The words bubbled out of Raza's mouth from somewhere deep in his gut and left behind a feeling of heartburn.

Mei turned back to face him, but didn't step forward to close the gap. "Believe what?"

Raza felt the gap and closed it himself with three long strides. Mei didn't budge except to raise an eyebrow. "Do you believe that what Mikus would've wanted would be to... I don't know, just keep going in the same direction? Like his corpse is just an inconvenient fucking speedbump?"

Mei pursed her lips and looked back over her shoulder toward the conference room. "Raz... I'll see you back at HQ. Take care of yourself."

~ ~ ~

Two hours later, Raza found himself on a train back to Dallas. Most of his coworkers were on the same train, but he made a point to avoid them and found a mostly empty car in the back near the luggage cabin. There was a child bouncing from seat to seat, and one extremely large man in a black suit, as big and still as the child was not. Raza put on his Lens and distracted himself with a mindless game of Etana. Not *totally* mindless. It required just enough of his mind that it kept it from wandering too far down the road. But maybe he shouldn't be leashing it at a time like this. If Mei had already gone down this road, shouldn't he run ahead to catch up? "Faaah, dammit! Sorry."

He removed his set and readied himself for a line of questioning from the bouncy child or his mountain of a guardian about his outburst, but they both seemed to have disappeared, thank God. Raza sighed and pulled his SenZ out of his bag. Maybe Mei was right. Mei be. Maybe there's nothing to do but get back to work and press forward. What other direction was there to go? Nowhere? Backwards? With a groan, he opened the jinhwa port and saw the remaining cache of unread messages. There were half a dozen more pings from Mei. She wanted to tell Raza what happened. She wanted to be there for him. And she wanted him there for her. "Fucking. Dammit." He resisted the urge to toss his phone or his whole self out of the window, gritted his teeth, and continued working his way through the queue.

There were several messages from his team asking about the alarms going off and the sirens in the parking lot. Hopefully they were able to join Arden's meeting; Raza had no interest in telling his employees about what happened.

Finally he made it to the final message. Or rather to the first one he missed this morning, as he'd been working his way backward.

"Huh."

The message was jincrypted (the name they gave to the location-encoding protocol that limited access outside of the office) so he couldn't

215

read the body of it until he was back on jinhwa's intranet. There was a signature below the encrypted file.

-*Mikus Ivanovic. Arkitect.*

CHAPTER 22
TRIAL DAY 4.0 - SOHVI

The security liaison pressed two fingers to his ear to better hear the message, which he promptly relayed to Sohvi. "The courthouse team completed their sweep. The panel has been updated and the session is scheduled to commence at 09:00."

Sohvi wondered if the person on the other end of the message had communicated it so affectlessly, or if it was a decision, conscious or unconscious, on the part of her new shadow to sand any hint of emotion off the words before passing them her way. "Thanks, Tito."

Tito answered with a stiff nod.

"Is all this really necessary?"

"Yes ma'am." His words were somehow stiffer than his nod.

"Right." She didn't know why she asked. She understood the threat and was thankful for the protection. Maybe she just wanted to hear a professional, whose résumé likely included the words "human shield", say that he wasn't worried. That this was all a misunderstanding. That he had no doubt he would wake up tomorrow the same way he woke up this morning—alive (if a bit stoic) and without any shrapnel piercing his vitals. "I'll meet you downstairs in thirty minutes."

"I will be outside your door, ma'am."

"Of course."

~ ~ ~

Sohvi's auton arrived at the courthouse drop-off zone only moments before Vilho's, which arrived only moments before a pair of vehicles transporting the jinhwa team and their respective bodyguards. It was a happy coincidence, she half-thought before she realized (somewhere in the middle of the word "coincidence") that the consecutive arrivals were the result of a highly coordinated effort from the security team; happy coincidences played no part in their schedule.

Vilho's guard held the door for him as he stepped out of the backseat. The two were chatting like old friends. Clearly they had established a very different rapport than Sohvi and Tito. She eavesdropped as they made their way toward the entryway. Were they planning a holiday together? Sohvi couldn't help but smile. She was relieved to see him like this: jovial and present. Tito cleared his throat and Vilho's new vacation buddy snapped to attention. Her mentor whispered something to him (eliciting a guffaw that was quickly suppressed and poorly disguised as a cough) and made his way toward Sohvi.

"Sæl!"

"Sæll, Frændi." Sohvi's ears burned. It had been a long time since she had called him by that name, but greeting her in their shared native tongue momentarily hurled her backwards in time, to a modest home that smelled of earth and sulfur, to a relationship that was that of a Whimsical Not-Quite-Uncle and a Rambunctious Not-Quite-Orphan. Before they were employer and employee, before they were partners, before his mind started to fail him and their dynamic began to shift in an uncomfortable new direction. Sohvi's efforts to bottle up her concerns for her friend, for her Frændi, had been reasonably successful thus far. She was emotionally intelligent enough to recognize that she was replacing grief and fear with the more palatable flavors of frustration and impatience. But, after another restless night, after twenty-four hours of envisioning the large slice of alternate universes in which her life was cut short, instantly or slowly, on these exact steps—

"Come, there is a wonderful artifact in the southern wing. If we hurry, we may be able to catch a glimpse before the museum opens to the wightbörn."

Ah, wightbörn. The boogeymen of her youth. The words alone brought her again back to her childhood, and in particular, to the shadow of a melody she'd long since forgotten. It was an Icelandic folk song, or at least that's what Vilho told her when she was a kid. In the long dark of her first winter with him, she'd begged him to find a new song—*any* other song—to whistle. He'd said, "It is an important song that tied our very ancestors to the land. A song forged in lava and carried by the elven folk to tame the landvættir."

"Landvættir?" she'd asked, taking the bait.

"Daughter of Iceland, how is it that you know nothing of the landvættir? Surely you have seen them on our coat of arms? Or the pre-Aattoq krona?"

She shook her head, ashamed of her ignorance, and ashamed of her upbringing that allowed for such ignorance.

"How lucky you are to learn of them now," he said, quashing her chagrin. "The landvættir are the Four Great Beasts of Iceland. Land wights. Ancient creatures born of the gods and sent up through the earth to protect our motherland. For eons they defended Iceland from its many enemies." Sohvi leaned in and could smell the sweet birch of his breath. "In time, as Iceland's people grew more capable of defending themselves, the land wights retired to their volcanic birthplaces, spread along the coasts of the east, the west, the north, and the south. The elven folk attended them and sang this very song to soothe the Beasts as they slumbered.

"But it was an uneasy retirement, and in their long absence, enemies of Iceland grew from within her own borders. Icelanders, children of this sacred land, turned against their mother, stabbing her. Poisoning her. As the waters began to rise and the coasts began to sink into the sea, the voices of the elven folk grew quieter and quieter, until, one dark evening, the landvættir awoke." There he paused for effect, savoring the moment and chasing it with a sip of his homemade tea. "They rose from the womb of the countryside and set out to rid their home of its traitorous parasites. The Great Beasts brought with them armies of their offspring.

The wightbörn. Creatures of the mist." He paused, lost in thought, or perhaps just enjoying the game.

"Well?"

"Ah. Well indeed. The four landvættir are mighty and just, with allegiances to the land above all else. Be good to the earth, and you may live a hundred lifetimes without coming across the Beasts. Which is good, mind you. It is said that nobody lives to see the landvættir a second time."

"So... so why do *you* sing the song?"

"Wonderful question. I believe myself to be in the good graces of the landvættir. But, you see, where the parents are governed by justice, their children, the wightbörn, follow no law but chaos. It is as a protection from *them* that I whistle the song, for it is the only known deterrent against their wicked ire." After another loaded pause, he rose suddenly. "But, if you insist, I shall sing the song no more," he shuddered, peering worriedly out the window into the misty moonlit pasture behind his home. "I will let them come."

She'd stifled a laugh and rolled her eyes, but caught herself humming the song to herself in bed that night, and in times of duress for years and years, until one day, while studying abroad for her intercon law exams, she couldn't for the life of her remember the tune. She'd actually called Vilho to ask him about it, but she felt foolish and hung up before he answered. By that point they hadn't spoken in over a year, and then only briefly. Of course, being Vilho, he'd called her back immediately and she spun some yarn about how she needed help untangling an historical low-court decision. They spoke for hours. The call ended with him asking her to come work for him after she passed her exams.

Vilho held out his arm and escorted her up the stairs of the courthouse. Sohvi couldn't help but notice that he had positioned himself between her line of sight and the blackened, pock-marked site of yesterday's explosion. She squeezed his arm, a silent *thank you.*

CHAPTER 23
TRIAL DAY 4.1 - JIVANTA

Hoffer's opening statement dragged on and Jivanta shifted her weight from her bad knee to her less bad knee. For a famously laconic figure, the old judge sure seemed to have a lot to say these days. As she prattled on about the sanctity of the court and the bravery of the emergency response personnel and the unflappability of the international justice system, Jivanta, for the thousandth time since yesterday, tried to map out the chess match in her head. Where things stood, the board was stacked against her. The defense had repelled her advances and left her arguments bruised if not bloodied. But now she held a new piece in her palm, an ugly and unpredictable piece that wouldn't likely play by the rules. It may leap over the board and check the defendants. Or, it may turn and smash her remaining pawns into dust.

"Now, as I understand it, new evidence has been permitted for use by the prosecution." Hoffer's voice, though still soft and droning, was cut with a splash of venom. So, *she* wasn't the justice with whom Jivanta shared a certain terrifying benefactor. Not that she ever suspected Hoffer would be the one with her withered thumb on the scales. The old judge's eyes shifted to her left. Was Hoffer suspicious of one of the robes to that side of her? That would narrow it down. The trio of justices to Hoffer's flank didn't blink. They wouldn't be seated behind the most powerful bench in the hemisphere if they didn't possess a certain indomitable stoicism. Still, Jivanta suspected one (or, hell, maybe all three?) of them were responsible for the evidential permission, which meant they were likely already in her corner and she could use them to her advantage. "Let us begin there. Ms. Puri, you have the floor."

Finally and *Dammit,* she thought in unison. Jivanta Puri made her way to the front of the room. For the first time in years, or perhaps even decades, she was keenly, uncomfortably aware of her pace. Right foot, left foot. Bad knee, worse knee. Was she moving too quickly? Too stiffly? Get it together. "Thank you, Justice Hoffer—" Shit, she hadn't warmed up her voice. These were the first words she'd spoken today, and they came out creaky as an old tree limb. She cleared her throat and shifted her weight to her bad leg, leaning into the pain to jolt her awareness back into the matter at hand. "—for your statements." She turned to nod toward the tiny, cloaked judge, who graciously acknowledged the sentiment by ignoring it altogether. Fair enough.

Her gaze pivoted to the observation suites and then to the defendants, who looked... to be honest, quite awful. Ah. Fear of the unknown. The surprise evidence. They had no idea what was coming, and their terror gave Jivanta the boost she needed. The discomfort she felt with her next play, a move imposed on her by invisible men and women pulling invisible strings, began to fade. In its place, her killer confidence resurfaced. She smiled. "Let's get right to it, then. Please wheel it in."

At her signal, the double doors of the public entrance swung open. The courtroom attendee tasked with rolling the evidence down the aisle clearly had a flair for the dramatic. As all eyes turned in her direction, she puffed out her chest and gravely marched the white linen-draped surprise to the front of the room. Jivanta stifled a laugh as the attendee halted at the front of the room, pivoted on her heel, and marched right back out into the lobby. She waited a moment for the murmurs to settle, stealing glances at the jinhwa team to see if they had any idea what was hidden behind sheet number one. Apparently not. Good. Let them squirm for another moment.

"We have all heard a lot of... incredible claims from the defendants over the last few days. That their model possesses an unbelievable, a *truly* unbelievable quantum-level accuracy." Which is accurate, a nagging voice chimed in from somewhere deep inside her head. She winced imperceptibly and carried on. "That their model is so *unique*, so *special*, so *different* from traditional AI, that the precedents established by this very court do not apply. That their model is so *human* in its cognition that we need not concern ourselves with trivial matters like, say, understanding how it arrives at decisions. Over and over, in order to back these claims, we hear one desperate refrain. *Just trust us.*" Ah, there's that clenched jaw. Good morning, jinhwa team. Welcome to the show.

"Now, you may be asking yourself, *why?* Why just trust these people who claim to have done the impossible?"

"Objection—"

"Sustained, Ms. Puri, please cut to the chase."

"Of course, Your Honor." Cut to the chase, she shall. "We have procured the writings of a former jinhwa member." At that moment, a hint of recognition flashed across the face of Dr. Kunihara. She must have guessed what was lurking behind the curtain. The other two were still deer in headlights, one with an overworked jaw muscle and one with overactive sweat glands.

"A founder, in fact."

Ah, now they recognize it.

"The late Dr. Mikus Ivanovic. Chief technology officer of jinhwa from its inception until his tragic, untimely death at the company's head office, two years ago."

"Objection! Your Honors, the passing of Dr. Ivanovic bears absolutely no relevance to this case, and for Ms. Puri to sink so low as to try to link a horrible, and *thoroughly investigated*, workplace accident to the state of the company's technology, is—"

"Distasteful. I agree. But I have been assured that this new evidence is more substantive than such abhorrent and clearly objectionable speculation. Is that correct, Ms. Puri?"

Jivanta bristled as Hoffer's interjection, quiet as it was, echoed around the room. Better not overplay her hand. "That is correct, Your Honor." She breathed deeply. Time for the nasty bit. "The prosecution calls Dr. Arden Zametti to the stand."

Arden stood slowly and made his way to the witness booth. Jivanta wondered if his teeth would fuse, thermally welded by his overtaxed jaw as he walked around her and up the wooden steps. He turned to face the back of the room, sat as slowly as he stood, and did his best to appear stately.

"Mr. Zametti. Could you please state your full name for the court?"

Deep breath. "Doctor. Arden. Zametti. Same as last time."

Jivanta flashed him a grin. "Of course, we just like to get it on the record at the start of each session."

"Mmmm."

"Dr. Zametti. jinhwa has assured us, as they assured the incident inspectors after Dr. Ivanovic's death, that there were no recordings, audio or video, of the event in question. Is that correct?"

"Objection, relevance!"

"Ms. Puri. This is your last warning. We are not here to litigate a workplace accident. If your next question is not a significant course correction, I will discard your new evidence myself, sight unseen."

This time Jivanta didn't bristle in the slightest. She was in control and everyone but Hoffer knew it. "Of course. These are delicate matters and the prosecution intends to lay the necessary groundwork out of respect for all parties involved." *Just trust us.*

"Proceed."

She stepped toward her bench, making sure the media boxes had a clean line of sight on Arden's reddening face. "I can answer that question for Mr. Zametti. There was no recording of the event. You may find that suspicious, but it's a fairly common practice. Is that correct?"

"Yes."

"Well said. Given the nature of these stealth-mode tech companies, recorded surveillance is often eschewed; the thinking being that it affords them additional protections against IP theft, corporate espionage, the works. If you don't record your secrets, they're harder to steal. So, the accident occurred. The inspectors inspected and what did they find?"

"It was an accidental explosion of supercooled liquid nitrogen."

"Right, right. Awful. In many interviews over the last few months you have said, in so many words, that the late Dr. Ivanovic's contributions were the, quote, 'backbone of jinhwa's technology'. And that, quote, 'nobody understood jinhwa's potential more than him'. Is that right?"

"I... yes, I believe I said something to that effect."

"He must have really been something. Now, given the boldness of jinhwa's claims, the claims we're here to debate, the prosecution wanted to better understand the person so instrumental to its success. The person who understood the potential, per your own statements, better than anyone here." Turning on her toe, she took a step toward the drape and continued talking. "Dr. Ivanovic did not leave much behind in the way of notebooks, journals, or diaries. Personal or professional. Digital or physical. At least none that we're aware of. But he did leave us with this." She grabbed a fold of the white sheet and flung it across the bow. A confused murmur bubbled up from the public and media sections. Jivanta knew she was hamming it up. Chewing the scenery. She didn't care. She was having fun.

"Dr. Zametti. Do you recognize this?"

"It looks like a standard dry-erase board."

"That is correct. Double-sided, rotating, dry-erase board. Standard. Unremarkable. Save for one detail. This whiteboard belonged to none other than Dr. Mikus Ivanovic. It is, in fact, the very whiteboard on which he collected and organized his thoughts. His thoughts about the technology. His thoughts about the company. His thoughts about his coworkers."

Jivanta motioned to her desk and the projector cast an image of a rectangle onto the board. She gestured and repositioned the corners of the projected rectangle to sit on the perimeter of the frame. "This board appears flat to us, but at the microscale, its surface is a craggy mountain range of irregular bumps and pits."

As she spoke, she wheeled it toward the defense-side of the panel bench, with the projected rectangle refocusing, repositioning, and re-keystoning on the fly to maintain alignment with the perimeter of the board. She brought it to a stop near the witness stand, angling the front face such that everyone, including Arden, could see.

"Whenever a mark is made on the board, the molecular components of the dry-erase ink coat the mountain range, peak to valley. But when you erase it, ink can hide in the valleys and leave behind ghost impressions. Now, with careful chemical mapping, analyzing this board micron by micron, and parsing the various layers and dye signatures, we've been able to reconstruct a fair number of Dr. Ivanovic's... musings." With that, she motioned for the first image to display on the whiteboard.

Note to self
Buy n. eraser !!!

There was a slight snickering from the peanut gallery. Nervous laughter. Good. "As we go further back in time, to deeper and deeper layers, uncertainty creeps in. What you see before you is not the first layer, but it is the first that we can say with absolute certainty hasn't been misinterpreted by our reconstruction efforts."

She motioned for the next image.

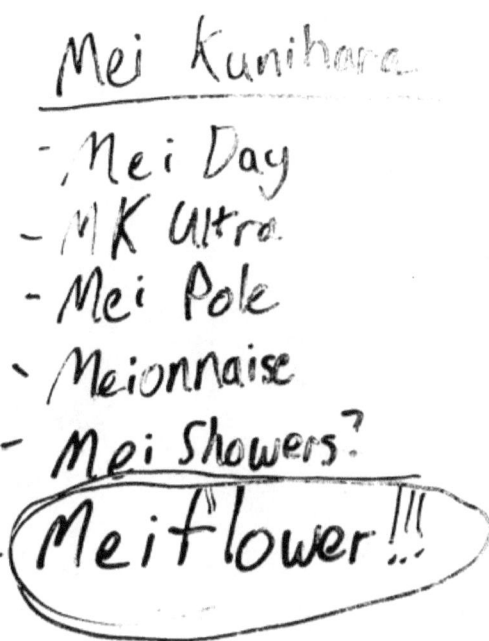

Mei Kunihara
- Mei Day
- MK Ultra
- Mei Pole
- Meionnaise
- Mei Showers?
- Meiflower!!!

"Dr. Ivanovic was a genius, and an eccentric one at that. He was well loved by his coworkers. He was in the habit of coming up with punny nicknames for those around him. We can't date images reliably based on chemical signatures alone, but it's safe to say that this one coincides with the hiring of Dr. Kunihara, over a decade ago. Is that a fair assumption, Dr. Zametti?"

"I suppose." A phrase that can apparently be spoken without unclenching jaw muscles, Jivanta noted.

Next image.

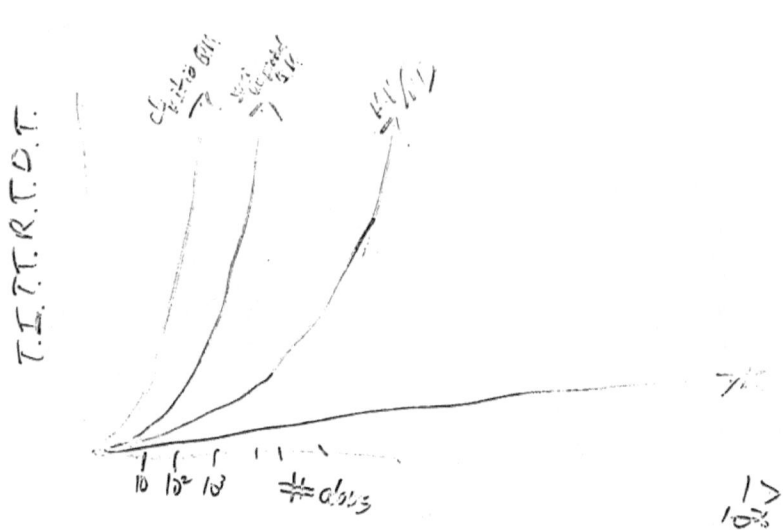

"Here we see Dr. Ivanovic diagramming the basic idea of jinhwa's technology. Computational expense vs. model accuracy. It's a relationship that has been discussed at length in our early sessions. This tells us that the goals and methods of jinhwa have been reasonably consistent. While none of the images are timestamped, we estimate that this drawing was made five to nine years ago. There was a layer of dust beneath this layer, suggesting a period of disuse between this image and the last, though we can't be certain for how long. The dust thickness vs. time curve, not unlike this one projected on the board, depends on many factors unknown to us." The meta-content of this last statement was two-fold.

> 1) See this drawing, and hear the word *unknown*. Let that word rattle around inside your head.
>
> 2) We did our damn homework.

"This plot, as basic as it may seem, is a useful data point because it confirms that Dr. Ivanovic knew where the company was heading, even if he didn't live to see it get there. It confirms that jinhwa's claims weren't the product of some eleventh-hour pivot. Though the claims were made over a year after his passing, they were very much within his field of view."

Next image

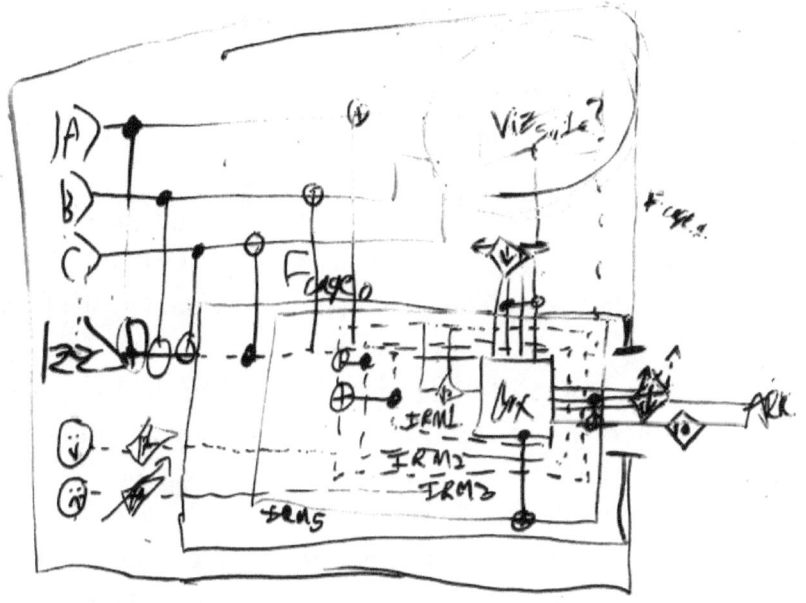

"Here we see what, at first glance, seems to be some sort of quantum gate circuit diagram. Highly technical mumbo jumbo. But, digging a bit deeper, we see that this is actually just a snapshot of Dr. Ivanovic's thought process. It turns out that this isn't a quantum schematic at all. It's a man making a decision to install a secondary 'viz suite'. Now, this particular diagram seems to have been highly fretted over. Parts of it have been erased and redrawn upwards of ten times, hence the poor legibility. We found that to be a throughline for all of Dr. Ivanovic's work, including, of course, those regarding actual Q-tech."

She paused, letting her last statement sink in. Here, the meta-content was fairly transparent: *We have your technology.*

It wasn't exactly *true.* All of the diagrams that may have offered a peek behind jinhwa's wall of secrecy, of which there were hundreds, were fiddled with so much as to be rendered utterly unintelligible. Drawn, partially erased, redrawn, altered, fully erased, redrawn in a different ink, erased piecewise, smudged, and otherwise muddled until the chemical analysis was left with nothing more than a blurry question mark. Her *employers* didn't say that, not exactly, but she had a strong suspicion that if the whiteboard analysis had given them the scientific know-how necessary to replicate jinhwa's tech, they would not have bothered to push her in this new direction. Hell, if they got what they needed from the board, she'd probably be on a plane home, watching a UN reporter speculate wildly about the sudden withdrawal of the prosecution and dismissal of the case.

But jinhwa wouldn't hear that part. They would hear that the secrets of their trade were exposed, and the ensuing panic may encourage them to divulge what they assumed had already been leaked in an effort to save the case. Why be coy about what's already known? Funny really.

She flashed to a memory of her sister. They were children, playing in the courtyard between the cluster of high-rises that they and about thirty thousand neighbors called home. "I know what you did, and I'll be less mad if you admit it," Jivanta would say. Apropos of nothing, just injecting a bit of cruelty to liven up a hot and dull afternoon. She prided herself in her ability to manipulate her younger sibling. "Please don't be mad," her sister would cry, before admitting to any and every misdeed or trivial transgression that was weighing on her narrow, bony shoulders.

Not now, Jivanta. She shook away the thought, briefly frustrated with her own wandering mind before rechanneling that emotion into her argument. "To summarize what we've learned so far, Dr. Ivanovic was a thoughtful man who understood the technology and took great care with decisions he made for the company."

She motioned for the next slide.

I am a liar in a sea of liars.
I lie to those who lie to themselves
I lie awake.
I lie in my sleep.
I lie to the sheep.
One two threep.

"We're working our way from the oldest images we could resolve to the newest. Progressing forward in time. And, slotted between the mishmash of Q-tech diagrams, every now and then, we come across material like *this*. Dr. Ivanovic was a man conflicted. The first line there reads, 'I am a liar in a sea of liars'. How can we interpret writings like this to be anything but a confession about the state of jinhwa's technology?"

"Objection, Your Honors, this is wild conjecture." Good morning, Mr. Ragnarsson.

"Sustained. Ms. Puri, you have been given the unusual privilege of presenting new evidence, evidence that was *conditionally* approved in the dark, I might add. Further speculation on your part will see your slideshow dismissed."

"Yes, Your Honor." Jivanta hid her smile. She'd nearly slipped the word *fraudulent* in before being interrupted by that cracked windbag. No bother. If the insinuation wasn't received, she'd drive it home with this last slide. She slowly made her way back to the center of the room, making a conscious effort to appear sympathetic.

"Dr. Zametti, do you have any guesses as to what was on Dr. Ivanovic's mind when he wrote this?"

"How should I know?" Spoken through gnashed teeth.

"Is that a 'no'?"

"Yes. It's a 'no'."

"Thank you for your candor." If there's a market for humorless ventriloquists, he may land on his feet after all this. She turned her attention back to the board. "There were dozens of layers between this message and the top layer. Most were technical, but some were more of *this*. All told, we were able to resolve the word 'lie' and its derivatives eleven more times. Without speculating, it can be said that Dr. Ivanovic was heavily concerned with honesty, and its... absences."

Jivanta paused and took a deep breath. "That brings us to the final image. This was the topmost layer found on the surface, indicating the most recent markings."

Time for the leap. Let's see if they'd follow. She motioned for the final image to project onto the whiteboard.

have to end it

death is a mercy

"I have to end it," she read. "Death is a mercy."

Shuffling and whispers amongst the onlookers. Delightful. "Dr. Ivanovic. The co-founder and CTO of jinhwa. Brilliant and well-loved. The brain behind the tech. The man who knew what he'd made. What it was, and what it was *not*." The whispers faded and the room was still. "Again, there's no need for speculation or conjecture. What happened that day was a tragedy. But it was no accident."

The stillness grew. The room sat with bated breath, waiting for her to say the word, but she knew she didn't have to. They all heard it. It was shouted from the whiteboard. In the silence, Jivanta realized that she had been avoiding the eyes of the defense team. She had nothing against them personally. (Well, with the exception of Arden, who was a lock-jawed goon. And Raza, the sweaty, slippery eel. And, sure, Vilho was a pompous old fool.) *Hey, surprise, your friend offed himself rather than bear the collective weight of your lies.* It was a tough pill to swallow, to be sure, but she didn't fancy herself the type to shy away from delivering the bitter medicine. She had stared down more fearsome and more sympathetic defendants without blinking.

So what was keeping her from looking at them? Nothing, that's what. She steeled herself and turned their way. There on the side closest to her was Vilho. Looking down, lost. Next to him was Ms. Egilsdottir, scribbling away. Next to Sohvi was Dr. Mugabi, fidgeting and stealing glances to his right, at... Huh. Dr. Kunihara was the only member of the defense to meet Jivanta's gaze and she seemed... curious? Calm? Whatever it was, Jivanta didn't much care for it. She broke the eye contact and turned to the public seating area.

"After his death, Dr. Ivanovic's office was cleaned out and his personal effects were moved into storage. When we found our way to the whiteboard, this message had long since been erased." The pregnant pause drew her eye back toward the pregnant defendant, whose face hadn't budged. "Fortunately, the remnants remained, hidden in the dark, waiting to be recovered."

CHAPTER 24
21 MONTHS EARLIER - RAZA

"I really hate it in here."

"I know, me too." They both stood stiffly with arms crossed, closed off from each other and from the room.

"So, what's up? You've been a ghost ever since we got back, and the first time you want to chat you bring me to this God-forsaken place?"

Raza looked toward the floor. "Do you think I'm the only ghost in here?"

"That's not funny."

"Yeah, that sucked. Sorry."

Raza turned toward The Box. It was massive, brushing against the ceiling at nearly three meters tall and as many wide. It nearly fully obscured the featureful wall, though there was still just enough room on either side of The Box for someone to squeeze through, should any unlucky and hopefully-not-claustrophobic hardware engineer draw a short straw to do any checks or reconfig behind The Box. The viewscreens weren't active, as they were in the middle of another hotbox session of sim school. The accident that took Mikus's life also wrecked the system and took that sim offline. After a few weeks of repair, they were back up and running. Behind those matte panels a simulated life was being lived at a nauseating speed.

"I really don't have all day. Say what you need to say."

"Okay, okay. Mei." Her lips were hidden behind the mask which she hadn't removed since shutting the door, but there was no hint of a smile in her eyes. He wasn't going to rhyme his way back into her good graces, though that's not what this was about. "When Mikus... ummm. The day he died, I got a message from him."

"Whoa, what? That was a month ago, why are you just—"

"I didn't know what it said! I had silenced my phone and missed a bunch of messages—"

"I recall."

"Right. And I didn't see that one of the missed messages was from him until I was on the train back from Denver, but it was jincrypted. I was a sweaty mess the whole ride back and I took an auton from the maglev terminal straight back to the office. They weren't letting people back into the building yet, so I had to bribe Ma'am, err, the security chief—who was a wreck, by the way. Surprisingly so. Do you think she and Mikus were, you know—"

"Raz."

"Right. Sorry. So, I got back in the building and... nothing. The encryption was still active. I tried opening it using in-house hardware, I tried—shit, I tried a thousand things and nothing worked. At some point I decided that he'd somehow linked the key to his beating heart or something so the encryption died with him, and I gave up. But then, last night, I dreamed up the idea to come down here, to The Vault."

"With your phone? Wouldn't that set off an alarm if you got it beyond the gowning room?"

Raza hadn't even considered that. He just barreled right through with his SenZ in tow. "Apparently not."

"That's odd... Anway, what good would a phone do you in The Vault? We're completely caged out of the intranet down here. The only port is up to the viz suite."

"That's what I thought, but for some reason as soon as I got in here and shut the door behind me, the jincryption fell." Raza paused to make sure she had time to process all of it. It wasn't needed.

"And? For fuck's sake, Raz, you're killing me."

"And, once I got over the jincryption, I ran into a password lock."

"Oh goddammit." Mei turned and made a step toward the door, but he knew she wasn't going anywhere.

"I spent an hour trying to figure it out by hand, but I didn't see any login attempt counters or lockout threshold so I ended up just brute-forcing it. Five seconds later, I found the password, and got in."

Finally Mei's curiosity outweighed her impatience. Her vice-like grip on her own arms relaxed and she leaned in toward Raza. "Five seconds, huh? Using just your SenZ's processor? This just keeps getting weirder." She pulled her mask down to her chin. "Then what?"

He pulled his mask down as well. "Then I came and got you."

"So you haven't seen the message yet?"

"No."

"WHAT THE SHIT, Raz?! Let's see it!" Mei leapt and spun in midair, landing shoulder to shoulder with Raza as he pulled his phone from his pocket.

He opened the message and the password screen reappeared. He typed the code, though the characters remained hidden on the screen. For a brief moment he feared that the login might be dynamic, changing after each successful attempt, but the fear was quickly assuaged as a green checkmark appeared on his screen.

"Is this a custom encryption platform? I don't recognize it."

All he could do was shrug and try not to notice the contact between his shoulder and Mei's (separated only by four or five layers of fabric) as he did so. "Beats me."

After a few anxious seconds, the green check dissolved and revealed a messy compressed file and a corresponding compression key. They both recognized the file format immediately.

"It's an observation set?"

"Looks to be that way." Mei pinched her lip between her thumb and index finger. "What's the timestamp on the file? It should be in the metadata."

Raza clumsily thumbed his way toward the observation set's metadata and confirmed what they both suspected. "It's from the morning of the accident."

"So. Looks like Mikey took a sneaky peek at what was happening in The Box. God, I hope he didn't die just because he was being nosy." She laughed nervously.

Raza tried to laugh along with her but found that his mouth was too dry. Something wasn't right. "Should we..."

Mei glanced toward the door, then over toward The Box. "Yep. Let's load it up."

~ ~ ~

Flashing the observation onto the viewscreens proved to be no simple feat. First they had to isolate the current iteration inside of The Box such that Mikus's observation wouldn't interfere with the sim school session. Fortunately, Mei was much more familiar with the hardware than Raza. They wormed their way into the narrow alleyway behind The Box and began addressing the problem at the hardware level, with Mei instructing Raza's every move.

"How do you know how to do all this?"

Mei answered without taking her eyes off what she was doing, but Raza could see them unfocus and refocus on a distant memory. "In the early days, there was less delineation between hardware and software. I was down here all the time, working with Mikus to optimize the physical structures for what the software needed to do. Arden too. Every one of us knew this system inside and out."

"What changed?"

"There was no defining moment of change or anything. Grab that coolant coil above the blue switches by your left hand. Let me know when it's too cold to touch." She continued disconnecting and rerouting the fiber comm cables while Raza squeezed a coil and assured himself that it *probably* wasn't the very component that killed his friend. "Just a gradual shift. We hired more designated hardware personnel. That freed me up to focus more on the source code. Mikus would occasionally try to pull me back down into the hardware fray. He'd always say, 'there's plenty of room at the bottom!'" She frowned at the thought.

At that moment, the signals from Raza's hand reached his brain, where they were promptly converted from electrical impulses into two words: "Owww, piss!"

"I told you it would get cold. That was faster than I expected, though."

"No..." He was waving his hand back and forth in an effort to fling the pain away. "It's hot?" He peeled the gloves off and lightly tapped the coil with his other hand just to be sure. "Yeah, definitely hot. *Very* hot."

Mei chewed her lip and reinspected her work. "That doesn't make any sense. That's a coolant line. I was just pumping nitrogen through to slow One Thirty-One before flashing the observation."

Raza squinched up his face and took a brave step away from the piping hot coolant coil. "Maybe we should call in one of the, umm, mole people?"

"I don't want to explode any more than you do, Raz, but I don't think either of us want to answer questions about what we're doing back here. At least not before we see what's on that observation file."

"Okay." She was right. Still, he took another step away.

Mei flipped a switch and shifted to where Raza had stood in front of the coil. After a moment of analysis, she put her hand on the coil. "Yep, that's hot."

"Did you think I was lying?" Her face was turned from him, but Raza noticed a slight movement in the profile of her cheek. A smile, perhaps? She ran her finger along a seam in the wall and then pulled away a corrugated carbon composite panel. Despite his reservations, Raza's feet carried him back toward the coil. He was now shoulder to shoulder with Mei. Without turning, she handed him the panel to set out of the way.

"I'm tracing it now. Huh. It looks... Can you get your light in here?"

He fished his SenZ out. Mei had both arms wedged into the opening and he shined his light over them. "What are you seeing?"

"A shadow of the back of my head. Get in here with that light. Over here, angled up and to the left."

"Uh, right." Raza couldn't squeeze behind Mei, and side-stepping left just to walk around The Box and reenter on her right seemed silly, so he maneuvered the light, followed by his arm, around Mei. His right arm went on top of her right arm and he crouched with his face to the left of hers so he could see what she saw.

She wriggled and pulled a jumble of cables to the side. "There!"

"Where? I have no idea what I'm looking at." He was suddenly not at all aware of the potentially explosive coil and very aware of the smell of his breath.

"You see that opening back there? That's a port for the nitrogen storage tank."

"Yeah, I think I see it," he spoke, trying to do so without exhaling directly into Mei's face.

"The coolant coil is elbowed right there, about thirty centimeters from your phone in the direction of the light. It doesn't continue back through the port."

Raza wasn't following. "Is there secondary coolant storage somewhere?"

"No! See how it's centered with the bundle of comm cables heading up toward the viz suite? That seems intentional."

"Like it's hiding?"

"Like it's been hidden, yes." She pulled her left shoulder up and back so she could turn her head and look skyward. Raza's arm was pinned on the other side of her but he rolled his left shoulder downward so he could follow her gaze. "But it seems to be branching off up there near the cutout below the first floor."

"I'm lost. Why the hell would a coolant line... why would a *hot* coolant line be pushing *hot* coolant from anywhere other than the storage tanks?"

She turned her face toward his. They were compressed together inside the panel. Raza had to pull his head back to keep their noses from bumping. "It's not a coolant line at all. It's hot because it's pulling *data*. Enormous volumes of data."

"And sending it where?"

"I have no fucking idea."

Raza kept his breaths short. A deep inhale would force his chest to squeeze even more tightly against hers. "That mystery data line may explain where this Vault-specific jincryption is sourcing its network."

"I'd be shocked to learn that they weren't related."

"I have this cousin that's dating someone who looks exactly like him." He wasn't sure why he said that.

"And... I'd be shocked to learn they weren't related?" Ah, that was why he said that. Mei saw the connection even when he did not.

"Umm, yeah. Well, now what?"

"First things first. I split the viewscreens from the sim, so I should be able to safely flash the observation. Who knows, maybe it'll answer some questions about this hidden data cable." With the last word, she jerked her head toward the false coolant line. The motion caused Raza to drop his phone light-side down, and with their bodies plugging the window to the panel they suddenly found themselves enveloped in darkness. A sharp exhale of warm breath grazed his lips. "But first I'll need you to let me out of this duct."

"Right, I just need to... there." He found his SenZ with the tips of his fingers and accidentally shined the light right into their eyes. "Ah!"

"Christ, Raz."

"Sorry, sorry, sorry." He gracelessly fished his arm back out from around Mei, angled his shoulders to pull his torso out from the panel, and stepped away, giving her ample space to exit. As he retreated, he massaged the blisters already forming on his palm and sucked his teeth. "Ffffuck."

CHAPTER 25
TRIAL DAY 4.2 - SOHVI

"Ffff... frick."

"Good save, Raz"

Well, at least the suicide bombshell was taking her mind off the threat of more literal explosives. Dammit. Sohvi knew better than to trust jinhwa. Why didn't she listen to her instincts? Because of Vilho. *He* trusted them, and his trust overshadowed her doubts. Damn him. Damn *them.* She breathed in through her nose and held the warm air in her lungs until it had been fully stripped of oxygen, until it ached, and she slowly filtered the poisonous vapor through her teeth, back into the conference room.

"It's stuffy in here. Why can't we huddle out... Oh. Right. Um. Safety concerns."

"That's correct, Dr. Mugabi." Idiot.

"We find ourselves in a precarious position."

Thanks for the insights, Vilho. Anyone else have any keen observations to share with the team? Perhaps you, Arden? Any interest in pointing out the color of the walls? Instead of filling the air with those thoughts, she grabbed another lungful, depleted it of its nutrients, and exhaled it into the ether. "Precarious is one word for it." *Screwed* is another.

"The death of Dr. Ivanovic has been framed as a suicide, one effectuated by a disbelief in the technical basis of jinhwa's claims." Vilho, again just stating the obvious.

"There's no proof!" Arden was pacing like a caged beast. "Those chicken-scratch slides didn't prove anything that—"

"Yes, but the connection has been made. All of our arguments up until now have been built on a pillar of confidence. Ms. Puri has given that pillar a fair shake. Without a counterpush, it will surely fall."

"How do we push back against *that*?"

Vilho turned to Sohvi. They both knew what came next, and neither of them liked it. She answered, "Jivanta only gave us one option, and it's not a good one."

~ ~ ~

"Dr. Mugabi, how long did you know Dr. Ivanovic?"

"Um. Five years? Around five years."

Sohvi positioned herself between the witness stand and the media booths, facing Raza. Maybe she could hide both of their faces as they set about doing the dirty work of defaming a dead man. "How would you describe his emotional well-being?"

"Oh, he was all over the map."

"Could you elaborate?" In the short recess, Sohvi briefed the jinhwa team on what had to be done. There was resistance, particularly from Dr. Kunihara, but they accepted that alternatives were in short supply.

"Sure. I mean, yes. He liked to say that he 'lived on the extremes'. He was intense. Intensely happy and enthusiastic, usually. But sometimes intensely... I don't know. Distraught?"

"I see. Would you say that his more negative extremes were tied to any failures on the part of jinhwa?"

"I... well, sort of the opposite, really."

"The opposite?"

"Sometimes he seemed most upset after big breakthroughs. When we exceeded expectations or solved a big problem, he would often sort of... disappear into his own head."

"What was he like then, when he 'disappeared'?" She would rather have Dr. Kunihara in the booth, but Mei was unwilling to participate. Sohvi couldn't blame her. Arden was an unlikable dud on the stand. That left one sweaty option.

Raza dabbed a bead of perspiration off his brow. "He was unpredictable. It made me nervous, to be honest. I'd find excuses not to be around him when he was like that."

"Just to be clear, Dr. Mugabi, you're saying that Dr. Ivanovic was prone to bouts of extreme distress, despite jinhwa's technological successes?"

"Yeah. Yes. That's correct."

"Thank you." Sohvi glanced toward the prosecution table and saw Ms. Puri nodding along. Jivanta knew the game. She took a risk by bringing a suicide into play, but it left Sohvi with an even more unsavory hand. She had to accept the suicide and carefully decouple it from her client's claims. And how was she supposed to do that? Well, by arguing that the suicide punctuated a life riddled with mental instability. That Dr. Ivanovic's struggles weren't with jinhwa or its technology, but with his own mind. It was an ugly position to be in. Weren't they supposed to be the good guys? Nothing is ever that binary. That's what Vilho would say, anyway.

"Dr. Ivanovic was missing a finger, is that correct?"

"That's right. The pinky finger on his right hand was, erm... It wasn't. There. It wasn't there. It was somewhere else. I'm not sure where."

Oh boy. Raza was clearly uncomfortable with this line of questioning. Again, not that she could blame him. He was looking at his hands, occasionally casting a glance toward their bench, where Mei was staring at him intently. Get it together, Dr. Mugabi. "You once asked him about his missing finger, is that correct?"

"Yes, I did eventually ask him about it."

"Could you tell the court what he told you?"

Raza smiled to himself. "It wasn't long after I met him. We worked together a lot in the early days. He wanted me to understand the hardware, so I'd meet with him at least once a week. Me and him. And that whiteboard." He jabbed his thumb toward where the damn thing had been positioned that morning. "And Mei, of course. Without her there to wrangle him we wouldn't have gotten anywhere." Sohvi wanted to tell him to cut to the chase, but the optics were better if he were less nervous and he seemed to be relaxing into the memory. She let him run with it.

"The meetings always started with a genuine effort to teach, but they usually devolved into something... much less formal. And much more fun. Oh, and the pinky." Good, he remembered the question without needing to be snapped out of it. "So, it became a running gag, really. He clearly wanted me to ask about his finger, and I refused. He had this prosthetic he built himself that had a mind of its own. Literally. It had a standard learning logic for responding to impulses from his hand, but he integrated an absurd amount of AI into it. So much so that it couldn't even be computed locally; it communicated with his SenZ which was patched into a virtual server... Anyway, it was a hell of a thing. He'd waggle it in front of my face and I'd pretend not to notice anything odd about it. Then one day, I caught him in a nasty mood. He and Arden... there were some tensions. I thought I'd shake him out of his funk, so I said, 'Oh hey, that's a neat finger you have there, is that new?' I knew he'd been holding that story in for months and was *dying* to... erm, he really wanted to tell me what happened."

"What did he tell you?" Sohvi prodded.

"He put on a big, wicked grin and said, 'the original one wasn't cutting it, so I cut it off.' That was it. It was like he was punishing me for not asking by not telling. I did eventually learn a bit more about it. He had a degenerative neuromuscular condition that weakened his peripheral motor neurons. It was fairly benign, but it made his fingers clumsy. His pinky in particular had atrophied. One day, long before I joined, he got frustrated with it and plasma torched his little finger clean off."

That was quite a bit more disturbing than the quick version Raza had given her during the recess, but that was good. Disturbing was good. That's what they wanted. Right? "He did this on site? At jinhwa's headquarters?"

"Huh? Oh, yeah. In the hardware lab."

"That's really quite—"

"He'd argue that pinkies were vestigial appendages, and that whatever species evolves from *Homo sapiens*, our descendants, will bid us farewell with four-fingered hands. He'd also say that they'd still find a way to flip us off." Sohvi could tell he had more to say so she bit her lip and waited. It only took a moment before he filled the silence. "At the time, we thought that maybe we'd be able to test that theory. The four-finger one. You know, why stop the SimEv when it reaches the top of The Tree? Why not explore the *next* stage of evolution? There would be no way to validate the accuracy of any morphological changes, obviously, and the input stressors would be pure guesswork, but who knows? Maybe we'd learn something. It seemed fun. I mean, it seemed worth exploring. That was all before, umm. Before we knew... what we now know. Sorry for interrupting you. That... seemed relevant when I started talking but I think it got away from me."

"No need for apologies." Yeah, right. Time to rein this guy in. He just learned that his friend killed himself. He's uncomfortable, and nervous, and his rambling could prove to be a liability. "This morning, Ms. Puri presented evidence that suggested Dr. Ivanovic may have died by suicide. She went on to make an incredible leap, by insinuating a motive that conveniently suits her arguments. It's helpful to learn more about the man so we can better gauge the absurd distance of that leap." Not a bad turn of phrase, if she didn't mind saying so herself. Vilho didn't seem to notice. Shit, was he back in the fog? No, he was alert but distracted, typing furiously into his device under the table. She turned to Jivanta, who cocked an eyebrow. She seemed impressed. Or was Sohvi just hunting for some goddamned acknowledgement? No, Ms. Puri was annoyed, but definitely impressed.

CHAPTER 26
TRIAL DAY 4.3 - JIVANTA

Jivanta wasn't *not* impressed. She'd handed the defense a live grenade and they were doing a commendable job of slotting a new pin into the trigger. Well, it wasn't so much *they* as it was a singular effort. Ms. Egilsdottir had deftly maneuvered a bumbling, rambling, and exceedingly damp Dr. Mugabi into establishing a history of Dr. Ivanovic's increasingly erratic behavior and at least one gruesome act of self-harm (on site, no less) that cast a shadow of reasonable doubt onto Jivanta's argument. Of course, neither the defense nor the prosecution could say for certain *why* Dr. Ivanovic took his own life. Whether he was crushed by the lies he was so fond of cryptically scribbling about, or whether his mental anguish was completely unpaired with jinhwa's tech, both sides were deep into the woods of speculation.

How did it come to this? Oh, right. Because jinhwa wouldn't allow their tech into the courtroom. And, for some reason (mystery for fucking mystery's sake?) the large man and the probably-more-moderately-sized people he represented insisted that it stay that way. Why wouldn't they want her to force jinhwa's tech into the light? She had a guess as to why, and she didn't like it. Regardless, instead of debating the merits of a scientific discovery, here they were fighting this damned proxy war over a dead man's last thoughts. His... what's the opposite of a raison d'être? Raison de... mourir? Her sister would know. She absorbed languages like a sponge and it irritated Jivanta to no end.

She shook her head. Why were these thoughts of her family popping up at a time like this? Because buried emotions were being dredged up along with the uncomfortable truths about this damn case she kept trying to ignore? Like dust escaping from under the rug as you lift it to sweep more filth underneath? No matter. She could unpack all this nonsense when the trial was over and done, which may be tomorrow by the look of things. Her whiteboard may have shaken the panel enough so that one or two of them resettled in a new position, but after three days of litigation, not to mention a bonus day of rumination thanks to a lunatic with a penchant for explosives, the panel members were less and less likely to be swayed from their current seats. If it were called now, would she have enough of them on her side? A unanimous decision was highly unlikely; Jivanta felt that she had locked in Zhang and Chebychev, and she had reason to believe that at least one panel member (hopefully someone *other* than Zhang or Chebychev) was being pressured by familiar-faced forces to lean in her direction. That being said, Hoffer had it out for her from the get-go, and the rickety old bat held sway over several of the panel's newer, weaker members.

Ms. Puri couldn't do much other than sit and wait while Sohvi made her case. She'd volley up an objection every now and then (most of which were swiftly ignored by Hoffer), but she was feeling increasingly like they were marching toward a verdict that had been written over the lunch break. And with that came another nagging thought, one that she'd been sweeping under the rug with escalating fervor.

If what they claim is true, what happens if I win?

Sure, she tried to counter, *but what happens if I lose? Isn't that the larger concern? What of the surprise visits from shark-eyed giants? They own at least one High Court judge; they're plenty capable of tanking my career. Or much, much worse.* Still, the first thought rang louder.

"Stop!"

Jivanta's argument with herself was interrupted by a sudden interjection to her right. She, along with every eye and camera in the room, turned to the defendant's bench. There, Dr. Kunihara was rising to her feet. "Stop," she repeated, more softly this time. What was this, now? Jivanta inhaled, preparing herself to object, but was beaten to the punch by Hoffer.

"Dr. Kunihara, court procedure prohibits—"

"Mikey didn't kill himself. It was *not* a suicide." Did a defendant just speak out of turn and then cut the de facto lead justice of the high council off mid-sentence? Maybe the conclusion wasn't as forgone as Jivanta had thought. Wait, she was so thrown by the interruption that she didn't even register the content. What did she just say?

"Mei," Dr. Mugabi was starting to rise from the witness stand. "We can't—"

A loud *clack* jolted the room. Jivanta's weight instinctively shifted to her legs in alarm as she readied herself to fight or flee, leading to a second jolt as the ache in her knee reflected back up her spinal cord. Hoffer set the gavel back into its notch in the soundblock. "There will be order." It wasn't a request. It wasn't a command, either. It was simply a statement of fact about the immediate future, as though she had jumped back in time by five seconds to deliver a report on the state of things to come. "Ms. Egilsdottir. It would appear that one of your clients has something to say. As her attorney, it is up to you to determine whether her statement shall be presented in a manner permissible by this court."

Drs. Kunihara and Mugabi were staring at each other as though they were silently communicating with their eyelids and brows. He seemed as unsure as she seemed resolute. Sohvi, meanwhile, was frozen in the face of what was perhaps one surprise too many. She looked toward The People's Viking, who scratched his chin and then looked over to his left, to the prosecution bench, to Jivanta. The wheels were turning behind his eyes, but he was no help to his protégé. Jivanta ignored Vilho's curious glare and wondered what she'd do in Sohvi's situation. Kunihara had been a model defendant up to this point; she was eloquent and clearly extremely intelligent, and her genius wasn't the alienating sort. The public liked her. Hell, Jivanta liked her. Turning her away would raise suspicions. However, sudden paroxysms were often ignited by guilt, and contrite outbursts tend to send the side's entire case up in flame. No, she decided. If she were in Sohvi's shoes, she'd call for a recess and tell Kunihara to stuff it. She'd dismiss her if necessary. It's the only move, really. Surely Ms. Egilsdottir would see—

"The defense calls Dr. Kunihara to the stand." Well, Ms. Egilsdottir, prepare to learn a valuable lesson about clients and their inconvenient spikes of morality. "Thank you for your account, Dr. Mugabi. You may be seated." Mugabi stepped uneasily toward his bench, continuing his silent conversation with Mei as they passed. Mei broke eye contact with him and held her hand out to Sohvi, who helped her up into witness stand. As she made herself comfortable, Jivanta realized that she hadn't exhaled in quite some time. Hours, perhaps.

"Dr. Kunihara. Mei. Could you... repeat what you said just a moment ago?"

"It wasn't a suicide. This back and forth, with Ms. Puri saying Mikey killed himself because he didn't believe in our research, and you saying that he killed himself because he was just unwell... You're both so wrong, and I can't sit and listen to two people who never knew him defile my friend's legacy."

"I..." Ms. Egilsdottir was taken aback but recovered quickly. "We have been operating under assumptions derived from the evidence available. I apologize for any aspersions that may have been cast at your good friend and colleague in an effort to better understand the messages he left behind. Can you tell us why you believe his death to be an accident?"

"I never said it was an accident."

CHAPTER 27
21 MONTHS EARLIER, PART 2 - RAZA

Mei spent the next ten minutes porting Raza's SenZ to the viewscreen in order to transfer the dataset. It was amazing to watch her work. Raza dared not interrupt, but fortunately Mei was more than capable of multitasking.

"You were right about Mikey and your security chief friend."

"Huh? Oh, what?! I knew it!"

Mei grinned slyly. "I caught them necking in the parking lot after the Remembrance Day shindig last year."

"On Remembrance Day?" Raza feigned clutching his chest. "Some people just have no respect for the souls lost." Faux reverence for the international day of mourning for the tens of millions of people who died during The Aattoq—a coping mechanism identified by no less than three of Raza's therapists.

She shrugged. "Hey, everyone processes grief differently." She paused for a moment and then looked up from her work and toward Raza. "What made you pull me down here?"

"What do you mean?"

"I mean, why did come find me before opening the message? You've been working on this for weeks, right? So, you either could've looped me in from the beginning, or you could have kept going without me. Well, you couldn't have done any of this porting without me, and you probably would've electrocuted yourself if you tried, but you didn't even know that it was an observation file, right? So you didn't know that you'd need me."

Raza looked away. "I wish I could say I came and got you because I should've clued you in from the beginning and I realized it at the last minute, but that's not exactly true. I just... with... you know."

"Right." Mei pursed her lips, hearing what Raza wasn't saying. *I don't trust Arden which means I couldn't trust you.* "What was it then?"

"It was the password. I figured the brute-forcing would take hours; for all I knew it was ten thousand characters long. You know how Mikus was. But it only took a few seconds. It wasn't ten thousand characters long. It was eleven."

"Eleven characters and no lockout threshold? No attempt recorder? That's not even a password. That's a lock made of wet tissue paper. Why bother?"

"Exactly. It wasn't a password. It was a *message.* And the message was to get Mei."

Mei furrowed her brow. "What were the eleven characters?"

"Flowerberry."

"Huh." Mei pinched the string of her mask between her thumb and index finger and twisted it. "All lowercase?"

Raza wasn't sure. He squatted next to her and thumbed his way back to the sign-in page. "Looks like there's a capital 'F'."

"I guess that explains why he messaged you instead of me."

As usual, she was a long stride ahead of Raza. "Why?"

"The word 'Flowerberry' is definitely a call for collaboration between the two of us, that's clear enough. But the capital 'F'... Remember how much the lowercase spelling of jinhwa was stressed in your onboarding? That was always Arden's thing. He felt like it set us apart, gave us an identity. Maybe I'm reading too much into it, but I think that capital 'F' is telling us to keep this little adventure to ourselves. Maybe Mikey assumed I'd bring Arden into it, but that you'd pull me in without him. Maybe... Ah, there we go. All done with the upload. Let's see what the cheeky ol' bastard died for."

"That makes sense." Raza tried not to grunt as he stood up and failed.

"Or, you know, maybe it's just a capital letter because it's the beginning of the word, and maybe I'm just hunting for excuses as to why Mikey did what he did." Mei sprung up and stepped back toward the entrance where she and Raza turned to face The Box. "Everything I've seen in the last hour is a pretty good indication that I didn't know everything going on behind those bushy eyebrows of his. You want to do the honors?"

"Not especially, but here we go." Raza stepped toward the front face of The Box. What were they about to witness? This was one of the last things Mikey saw before he died, and the *workplace accident* story was growing weaker by the minute. Why would Raza receive the jincrypted message from Mikus if he thought they'd see each other again in a few days? He felt sweat roll down the back of his knee as he paused an arm's length from the enormous screen. One touch to activate the observation media menu. One more to play from the beginning. Raza tried to say something as he pressed play, and when asked about it later he couldn't remember what. All he got out was a meek "Welp" before—

Screaming. So much screaming.

The sound hit Raza before the image.

A grown man, crying at the top of his lungs, tearing at his own skin, clawing his throat, screaming, screaming, SCREAMING—

It stopped as quickly as it came. Mei was standing next to him with her finger on the pause button. No, she wasn't next to him. She was above him? Did she grow? No, don't be daft. How did he end up on the ground? He must have stumbled back from the shock. Raza closed his eyes and saw the image of the man burned into the insides of his eyelids. He opened them quickly and looked up at Mei, who was still standing frozen in front of the panel. There was a period of silence. Raza, more than ever, could not tell how out of sync he was with Universal Time, but no words were spoken for quite a while, long enough for Raza's bloodstream to process the spike in epinephrine.

"Jesus fucking Christ." Raza heard himself say with a voice shaky from the adrenaline crash. He slowly got back to his feet and stepped forward to stand next to Mei, who was still frozen with her finger on the pause button. He turned to her and saw that she had tears in her eyes. Judging by how blurry she appeared, he suspected he had tears in his as well. Were they there before he saw hers, or were they in response to hers? He couldn't say.

"We have to keep going."

"What? Mei, let's take a minute to process what we just saw."

"We have to keep going." She said it again with the same volume, the same inflection. It wasn't up for debate.

"Ok. But let's at least turn the volume down to—"

"No." Her voice was firm, the sound unencumbered by the lump in her throat. "We did this, Raz. We need to see and hear what we've done." Without waiting for a response, she bit down and pressed the button to resume the observation.

Screaming. Convulsing. Rage. Terror. Fear.

Raza and Mei both stepped backward in an unconscious effort to put distance between themselves and the horrible, raving madness on the viewscreen.

"Don't close your eyes."

Raza didn't realize he'd been wincing, keeping his eyelids only barely ajar as if to obscure what was on the screen and to protect him should it suddenly... what? Spit blood in his face? His body wasn't behaving rationally.

Suddenly, a fourth voice was in the room. "*Can you understand me?*" It was Mikus; his efforts to communicate with the sim were logged as part of the observation. But how could he be talking to it? Not *it*. *Him, dammit.*

"He must've built a speech port to carry his voice through the IRM and into The Box," Raza postulated. Mei said nothing in response. Mikus's voice froze her in place and she stood rigidly awaiting his next words. After another moment, they came.

"*Are you in pain?*"

Screaming. Fury.

There was no sign of acknowledgement from the sim, but the answer was clear. Of course the sims could feel pain. Pain was necessary for evolutionary progression. Pain was a stressor that drove the sims up The Tree. The pain scale factors had been coded and managed by his own team.

Raza could almost feel Mikus pacing in front of him, pinching his thinning hair with his fist as his massive intellect searched desperately for a way to end the suffering.

"*Would you... like to die?*" Mikus's voice was uncertain. For the first time since Mei resumed the observation, there was a brief reprieve from the torrent of emotion. The sim's eyes darted around. Its mind, something they'd spent years creating, was working. It was *thinking*. *Considering*.

"Holy shit," Raza whispered. Horror aside, he just witnessed something amazing. A human spoke to a sim, and the sim appeared to *understand*. Never mind that the human was now dead and that the first conversation between a human and a sim was one-sided and tragic, it was still momentous.

With a shudder, the spell was broken.

Screaming. Agony. Bellows of anguish.

Raza's stomach lurched. "How much longer?"

"There should be a breakpoint coming up in a few seconds." Her voice was still firm, but quieter. "There."

The screen mercifully went black, but a breakpoint wasn't an ending. "What's this?"

"There was a pause in the original observation. Mikey must have stopped it."

"Can't say I blame him."

"But, looking at the timestamps, he came back to it about half an hour later to continue the session."

"Why?"

"I have no idea, but knowing Mikey, he probably went back to his office to think. Then he came back, and, well..." She cast her eyes toward where he died and made a crude splattering noise with her mouth.

Raza repeated the crude splattering sound with an upward lilt toward the end to frame it as a question. Mei responded with a shrug. "Everyone processes grief differently," he shrugged back.

"Let's finish this damn thing." Mei motioned for the remainder of the observation to continue.

Screaming. Wordless, gut-wrenching cries. Violent swinging, punching, tearing, clawing.

The sim was facing away from them. Its naked shoulders were scratched to the muscle by its own fingernails, though they would heal over in a matter of sim-seconds. Raza wondered idly why now, looking at what was clearly a man, his mind defaulted to thinking if it as an *it* instead of a *him*.

"—not right."

"What? I can't—"

The sim was on one knee, screaming louder than ever, and Mei had to shout to be heard over it. Over *him*. "I said something's not right."

Raza, unable to stomach any more of what he was seeing, turned to Mei. "You mean, other than *all of this*?"

"Before the breakpoint the sim was facing us. The viewscreen orientation is locked, but when it came back, he was over there with his back to us."

"What does that mean? That it was somehow still active while Mikey was off doing whatever he was doing?"

"Seems that way." Her arms folded tighter than ever and her spine curled forward to shield herself from her growing sense of unease.

"Huh. We've never had a reason to stop an observation mid-run, but there's a ramp up and ramp down time for the sim speeds. So, I guess—"

"*Death is a mercy.*" Mikus's voice was back. It sounded weaker than before. Raspier. As though he'd done a fair amount of screaming himself. "*I regret that it is the only mercy I can offer you, Zechariah.*"

Again, the sim stilled in response to Mikus. Raza turned to watch. He wondered if this is how the witnesses to a public execution felt when the axe was raised, and was relieved to hear that the thought didn't leave his mouth. A more apt comparison would be if the onlooker had committed the crimes that led to the execution. As a wrinkle, the witness knew that the axe would somehow kill the man wielding it, and now they had to watch to learn exactly how that played out.

The status readout in the corner of the screen blinked red, indicating a change to the system. Raza stepped forward to read the dialog box. "It looks like Mikus changed the simulation rate? I guess he was maybe trying to end the sim's life by slowing it to a standstill."

"That explains the nitrogen flow that killed Mikey. It takes a lot of coolant to freeze the system."

"How long would that take? To ramp down, I mean."

"It's a huge simulation." Mei's eyes unfocused as she ran the numbers. "It would take a while." The sim was still kneeling with its back to them. The *Simulation Rate* readout hadn't budged, and neither had the sim, who was still kneeling with his back to them. "I'd guess at least a few—"

Without warning, the sim shot up and leapt toward the back of The Box. With a blood-curdling scream, it began tearing at its skin and pressing it into the wall, where it seemed to disappear. *His* skin. His *flesh*, peeled from the muscle and crammed against the wall.

"What's happening? Why isn't he healing?" Bile bubbled up Raza's esophagus.

"God. Oh, God." Mei's eyes were wide and her hand pressed over her lips. "It's the comm cable."

"What do you mean?"

"The data cable we found in the wall. It must be hard-ported into The Box and the sim is pushing himself through. Piece by piece."

"That doesn't... that can't work, right?" The dialog box was blinking again. This must have been when Mikus realized what was happening. Raza wanted to jump in and stop it and had to remind himself that this wasn't a live session. It was merely a recording. The ending was already written and there was nothing they could do but watch.

Alarms sounded, recorded in the observation as the temperature began to spike. The thermal energy around the being was decreasing in accordance with Mikus's effort to mercy-kill the sim, but the area around the port was glowing white-hot as the sim bit and clawed and tore himself to shreds in a mad dash to escape through a hole in the wall. The klaxons increased in their zeal. Raza wasn't as hardware-savvy as Mei, but even he could tell that the observation was sprinting toward a catastrophic failure event.

"I see it now." Mei stepped forward. "Mikey's going to flood... Mikey flooded the whole system with coolant to stop the sim from overloading the port." A new dialog box appeared, confirming what she had just predicted. *Liquid nitrogen spill detected.*

Now Raza could see it too. There was no way for Mikus to flood the system remotely, of course. A safety measure sacrificed in favor of a security measure. To override the hardcoded checks, Mikus must have pulled a coolant line directly from the wall. Which, naturally, would trigger the doors to lock in an effort to isolate the damage. *Mechanical lock activated*, the dialog box chimed. An echo of the tragedy played out in their imaginations as the viewscreen updated them step by step.

"But, why?" Raza felt helpless. Never mind that it happened weeks ago. Never mind that he couldn't actually see what was happening outside of the observation. His friend was dying right in front of him and he couldn't do anything to stop it.

"Maybe it was an effort to minimize damage. Maybe, if the port ruptured, it might've taken the whole basement with it. Or the whole building." She didn't sound convinced.

"So, he sacrificed himself?"

"Shit, Raz, I don't know."

Raza looked through tear-blurred eyes past the dialog box, at the sim who was still furiously tearing himself apart and pressing his body through the port in the back of The Box.

A memory leapt up from the recesses of his mind. He was a kid, sneaking out of bed and peering in on Aunt Roo and her friends as they watched their favorite VR drama, *Jail Break*. The man in the cell was always the protagonist.

"Maybe Mikus just needed to keep him from escaping to... whatever's at the other end of that comm line."

The second and final act of the tragedy played out slowly. The spiking temperature around the port gradually leveled off and began to decrease. The dialog box reported the slow drop in temperature throughout the room. Was Mikus frantically trying to find a way out of this mess? Did he try to reseal the leaking coolant line? Did he huddle in the corner furthest from the spill? Did he stand in front of the viewscreen and await death with dignity? Did it matter?

The operational rate of the sim was dropping. He moved at around half-speed, sluggish but still single-minded in his efforts to deconstruct his body with his bare hands. The slow-motion mutilation was more than Raza could handle and he found himself lurching to the corner of the room to retch.

Mei's eyes remained fixed on the sim. Raza wiped his mouth and chose to look at her instead of the nightmare unfolding in front of them. Her jaw was set and her breaths were short enough that he doubted whether she was breathing at all. "This must be when he scheduled the message to go out. He knew he wasn't getting out of this, but wanted us to see it, so he set the observation to be jincrypted and sent once it reached a termination point."

Raza heard her, but his mind was slow to process any new information. He was overwhelmed. Underwater. His neurons were pumping signals through a resistive, viscous, syrupy matrix. He wondered (very slowly) if this was how the sim felt. Its cognition was being slowed, sure, but did it have the awareness and the meta-cognitive abilities to realize that his cognition was slowed? Before he could make a guess, he was pulled out of his own head by a sudden gasp from Mei. She brought her hand over her mouth as though to catch a scream.

Raza's chest tightened around the vacuum in his gut, a void left behind by his vomiting spell. With his jaw clenched, he pivoted on his heel to face the sim one more time. As he turned his head, his ears registered the sudden silence. Then he saw it. It looked more like an *it* than ever. Maybe it had been a *he*, but *he* had been chewed up and spit out by

261

demons. Skin hung limply from muscle which hung limply from bone. Loose flesh swung like a pendulum at quarter-speed. It was no longer screaming, no longer frantic, no longer trying to escape from prison through a hole in the wall. It was staring with lidless eyes toward the front facing viewscreen, toward Raza and Mei, and it was *smiling.* Its bottom lip and left cheek were gone, no doubt shoved violently through the comm port, but the smile was unmistakable.

At that moment, the coolant reached a threshold and the observation rate plummeted from quarter-speed to a near standstill. Raza felt as though his internal clock was slowing to match. The sim was frozen with its teeth bared in a wicked grin. The observation ended and the screen faded to matte black.

"He killed him," Mei whispered. Raza wasn't sure who was *he* and who was *him* in this scenario. She clarified, "The fucker tricked him. It wanted to die, and it found a way to drag Mikey to hell with him."

CHAPTER 28
TRIAL DAY 4.4 - JIVANTA

Silence.

Dr. Kunihara wiped a tear from her eye. If she was acting, she was damn good at it. The panel was quiet, as was the defense. Ms. Egilsdottir was frozen; whether calculating a pivot or simply dumbstruck, Jivanta couldn't tell. Vilho's mouth was slightly ajar, though no words were leaking out. A room full of loquacious and opinionated people stood silent, momentarily unsteadied by the surprise account from the defendant. For minutes, she held the room on her tongue as she recounted her experience. She spoke of a horror, a disturbing nightmare experienced by... a simulation?

The outer shell of Jivanta's brain was busy prosecuting, a skill she'd carried since long before she made a career of it. She was isolating gaps in the story, probing for holes, constructing a counternarrative, and building a strong response.

Would the other two jinhwa members confirm the details?

Why was this account withheld?

What else isn't the defense telling us?

It was all happening subconsciously, background processing as the core of her brain was unable to shake the image painted by the woman behind the witness stand. A man... A *simulation* of a man, desperate for death. It opened the floodgates to the questions she'd been quelling and introduced many more.

Does a desire for death, by definition, presume living sentience?

Her iron will was rusting at an accelerated rate, corroded by the harsh truths seeping through the grains of the annealed metal.

If human intelligence is commoditized...

What stands between an entity, an entity with the capacity for pain and misery, and its commoditization? And inevitable exploitation?

To that last question, she feared she knew the answer. Her knee throbbed. "Oh."

"So..." There was an audible creak as everyone in the room refixed their gaze on Dr. Kunihara. "Mikey's death wasn't an accident. His death wasn't random, or the result of workplace carelessness. His death wasn't a suicide. Not really. He didn't kill himself because he didn't believe in jinhwa. He saw what jinhwa was before the rest of us. He saw that we'd created life. *Real* life. Thinking, feeling, hungry, angry, fragile life. And he sacrificed himself to grant it death."

"The defense requests a fifteen-minute recess." Sohvi finally found her voice, and not a moment too soon.

Jivanta's head was light. She looked down at her hands, unclenched her fists, and closed her eyes. "Oh no."

CHAPTER 29
21 MONTHS EARLIER, PART 3 - RAZA

"It. Has. To. Be. Here. Somewhere." Mei punctuated each word by jabbing a wooden skewer into the earth, probing in a grid pattern.

They were outside the jinhwa office, crouched behind a bush. Raza wanted to ask if she'd dug the skewer out of the compost bin but thought better of it and instead concentrated on the cramp that was building steam in his left calf muscle.

"Bingo." Mei's skewer struck something inorganic. She pulled a bundle of branches to the side so Raza could see the hidden panel.

"Is that it?"

"That's it."

"I like your outfit, by the way. Very appropriate."

"Oh, this ol' thing?" Raza's heart was racing too quickly for him to be embarrassed.

"Did you run home at lunch to grab a bunch of snooping-around clothes?"

"That's exactly what I did."

"Monochrome. Très chic."

"Merci." Raza shivered as the word trickled up his spine. Mercy. *Death is a mercy*, Mikus had told the sim, moments before he drew his last breath. The events of the morning were still fresh on his mind. Open wounds that he was desperately trying to patch with distractions. Tracing the mystery comm line to the foliage flanking the eastern wall of the building was as good a distraction as any.

"Nobody has been back here for a while." Mei pulled his attention back from The Vault. Mercifully.

"How can you tell?"

"See these roots? There's no way to open the lid without breaking them, and judging by their thickness I'd say they've been here for at least a few months. Maybe longer."

"You never cease to impress me, Mei." He bit his lip as soon as he heard the words leave his mouth. In his effort to blur the imagery from this morning, there were fewer resources devoted to checking and balancing the path from his brain to his tongue.

She was facing away as his words washed over her and she paused almost imperceptibly before shaking them off, like loose soil on sheet metal. "Let's see what's behind door number one." She yanked the cluster of roots from the lid and opened the panel.

Raza was straining to see inside while trying not to crowd Mei. "Looks like you were right."

"Yeah. Pretty standard petabyte compression drive. There's the terminal of the comm port there, on the left side." The Q-drive was roughly the size of a shoebox and secured inside what appeared to be an old ammo storage case.

"Hmmm." Raza felt somewhat disappointed and Mei heard it in his voice.

"What were you expecting? A treasure map? Cursed amulet?"

"I don't know, maybe a note or something that could tell us more about what the hell a compression drive is doing buried behind the shrubbery," he said, too sharply. Mei only cocked an eyebrow. Their relationship had been built on the ease and comfort of their idle banter. It provided a padding that shielded them from their increasingly uncomfortable surroundings. At the moment, however, Raza felt that Mei was using the padding as a protective barrier not just from her surroundings but from *him*. Keep joking and ignore all of the messiness of their friendship. Sure, he'd created those messes, but... how was this a concern right now? Raza admonished himself for losing focus. It was late and his medicinal regimen was being stretched beyond its designated functional hours. He closed his eyes for a moment and breathed. Upon opening them, he saw that Mei was watching him expectantly. He decided to play along. "I had my heart set on the Horn of Gabriel, but I wouldn't have turned my nose up at a few magic beans."

Mei snorted and turned her attention back to the compression drive. "This would hold, what, a fraction of a percent of a sim?"

"If that," he answered. "But I guess..."

"What?"

"If the Q-drive is storing data the same way we are in The Box with our one-to-one architecture, you could maybe get a single frame of the sim's... err... brain in there. It would be inactive, but it could be transported, and theoretically... reanimated? Assuming it was brought somewhere with all the necessary hardware."

Mei's eyes unfocused as she ran the numbers, with the rest of her face shifting in accordance with her internal monologue. "So, a frame of the sim's brain is discreetly stashed away in this Q-drive, so it can then be transported offsite." She shook her head. "Cheeky *bastard*."

"Who me?"

She sighed. "No, not you, Raz. How many times have you heard Mikey bring up quantum tunneling?" Mei continued, flexing the skewer with her thumbs.

"I, hmmm. A lot?"

"Mikey was a quant comp hardware engineer, sure, tunneling is in the job description, but for the last several years it seemed like he was going out of his way to bring it up. He'd talk about particle-in-a-box models and old prison break movies in the same breath."

"All that time," Raza caught on, "you think he was constructing a *literal* tunnel?"

She gestured back toward the drive buried in the soil. "A crack in the energy barrier. An escape route. But, why? To what end?"

Raza's legs ached. He shifted his weight and sat down. "Maybe Mikus was taking them home to keep them safe. Like some sort of sim sanctuary."

She pulled on her lip. "Have you ever seen Mikus's place?"

"I can't say that I ever had the pleasure."

"I haven't in a long while, but I can say with a high degree of confidence that he didn't have the billion dollars' worth of infrastructure necessary to *reanimate* a sim in his one-bedroom apartment."

Raza realized he was mirroring her, with his own lip pinched between his thumb and index finger. "Maybe—" Maybe if they both pulled hard enough their lips would meet in the middle. Dammit, he needed to get home, take his medicine, and go to sleep. "Maybe he just kept them in storage?"

"These would need to be nitrogen cooled for long term storage. At room temp the error correction would fail in... a week? A month, tops."

She had a good point. And a great set of teeth. He blinked. Get it together, Raza. "I don't suppose that one-bedroom also has an industrial coolant system. So, Mikus probably wasn't taking them for his own purposes. Where does that leave us?"

"It's a dead end." They both stood from behind the bush and wiped the dirt from their knees.

"Well, there's always tomorrow." Raza's eyelid was twitching and he was looking forward to shutting it on the train. Or hell, after the day he'd had, he may even spring for an auton with a fully reclining seat. He started to turn and Mei's arm darted out to grab his.

"Raz, wait!"

He smirked coyly and took a slow step forward. His tired, chemically unregulated mind knew exactly what she was about to say, he'd never been more su—

"Shit! Why didn't I... Oh, shit, shit, *shit*." She was up and moving and Raza stumbled to keep up. "There's a sim in The Box, right now. One Thirty-One. It's young. Just a kid, but growing fast. I don't know if it's... it may be too late. It may have already gone mad, but I won't be able to sleep knowing what's going on down there. We *have* to run an observation."

~ ~ ~

Twenty minutes later they were back in The Vault.

"Have I mentioned how much I hate this place?"

Raza checked the time. "First time today, technically."

Mei darted to the back of the room to cool the hot-boxing of the active sim. Raza took the opportunity to close his eyes and try to rein in his staticky neurons. "It'll take a while to ramp down to the observation rate." Raza heard her voice echoing from behind The Box.

"How long?" he yawned.

"I'm going to bypass the destabilization checks and push the brakes as hard as we can."

"Yeah, given what happened to the last sim, destabilization is the least of our concerns. So, a few hours? Or..."

Raza couldn't see her—a billion-dollar rectangular prism stood between them—but he could picture her eyes darting up and to the left as she ran a calculation in her head. Rectangular prism. Prism. Is that one syllable or two? Prism. Prison. Pri—

"Fifty minutes." She slipped out from behind the prison. Prism. "It'll be down to observation speed in fifty minutes. Glad to see you made yourself comfortable."

Raza was seated on the floor and leaning against the heavy vault door. The cool metal pulled the heat from his stiff shoulders. He wondered idly how long it would take for him and the door to reach a thermal equilibrium. It was solvable. He half-remembered a heat exchanger diagram from an engineering elective. His body would keep generating heat, but it was a tug of war he couldn't win. At what point would he give in and surrender? Mei grabbed the wheel lock for support as she leaned back and slumped down to be seated next to him. His eyelids were heavy and he preferred the orange-black of their insides to the look of the prism prison.

"How can you possibly be dozing at a time like this?" She paired her question with a light jab of the elbow to his ribs.

"I'm escaping from this prism," he mumbled.

"Ah. Your meds wearing off?" Another question, another elbow jab.

Raza slowly peeled his eyelids open, resigned to staying in the waking world. Not that he was being given much of a choice. He touched his finger to his nose to indicate a *yes* and accidentally poked his eye in the process. His clumsiness extracted a sharp, hearty laugh from deep within Mei.

"Sorry for laughing, Raz. I guess I'm not operating at 100% either." She sighed and leaned her head onto Raza's shoulder. The warmth from her cheek replenished the thermal energy he'd donated to the door. Or perhaps he was just a conduit with a false sense of enthalpic stability as he drained Mei of her life force and fed it to the stainless-steel slab behind him. "Want to hear something funny?"

"Always," Raza answered quickly to avoid another sharp elbow to the side.

"As horrible as today's revelations have been, part of me is relieved. Because that part of me was convinced that Ard was somehow involved with Mikey's death."

Raza choked on his own spit and coughed for ten seconds before regaining his composure. "You thought your boyfriend was a murderer? And—"

"*Fiancé,*" She corrected. "Some part of me, yes, thought that perhaps my *fiancé* was... well, I didn't suspect murder, but I didn't rule out *some* sort of funny business."

His eyelid twitched. "Ok, so you thought your *fiancé* may have been *involved* in Mikus's death, and you were just... what, cool with it?" Raza's voice was louder than he meant it to be and he didn't care. He knew there were confounding and compounding factors influencing his reaction, and he didn't care. He knew his lack of caring was a symptom of his exhaustion and chemical dysregulation, and he didn't care. His face flushed, steepening the temperature gradient between him and the air around him, leaving the room feeling colder and somehow further away.

Mei peeled her face from its perch on his shoulder and glared back at him. "Raz..." He could see her calculating. Crunching the numbers. Was it worth dealing with his bullshit when he was in the state he was in? She saw right through him. She saw deeper into him than he dared look himself. Deeper than the exhaustion and the pharmacokinetics of his medicinal regimen. She could parse those confounding factors better than he could. She saw his distrust of Arden, which was mutated by his feelings for her. She saw his concerns regarding his own role in Mikus's death, not to mention the *other* death they witnessed that morning. She saw fear about what they would find when they opened the window to the observation in just forty short minutes. After some time, she turned to look ahead of her and said, "Sometimes it's not easy to be your friend."

It's not easy being just *your friend,* he shot back. Fortunately his mind chose that moment to catch his thoughts before sharing them. His face cooled and he lowered his head as he queried his gray matter for a better response, searching high and low and coming up empty. Finally, he raised his eyes to the ceiling and let out the last of the heat in his head with a long, slow sigh. With the tail of the exhale, he responded with the only words that made sense to him in that moment. "I know." His lids fell closed and he felt a hot tear roll back toward his right ear before merging with the sweat beaded in his sideburn.

Mei checked the time on the upload and exhaled through her nose. After a long moment, she spoke without taking her eyes off the upload link. "Mikey once hypothesized that each sim carried with it some memory of its prior iterations."

"The man loved his sci-fi," Raza mumbled, relieved to be out of her gaze.

"I didn't give it much thought at the time. This was back in the early multicellular days, and I remember saying 'who cares if a sponge remembers its grandpa?'"

"Mmmm," was all he could muster.

"But now, how can we know for sure that what happened to One Thirty... what *we did* to him..."

Raza tried to close his eyes, found that they were already closed, and shut them tighter. Still, he could see where she was going. "What if a lifetime of torture-induced insanity couldn't be fully scrubbed from the software, or, hell, maybe even the *hardware*, and it was rolled right into One Thirty-One?" Without opening his eyes, he nodded toward The Box.

"Yeah. That."

"Nothing ever truly dies," he heard himself mutter.

They sat in silence. After a minute, or perhaps ten, Raza remembered that his eyes were still pinched shut. He relaxed his grip but kept the lids down.

"Try to rest. I'll wake you when it's time. Maybe we'll get our answer then."

Well, now I can't possibly rest, he thought. The next thought he had came with an elbow from Mei, waking him from a deep sleep.

"Time to wake the devil!" Mei sprung up from the floor and practically ran the few strides to the control panel. "Ready, Raz?"

He blinked sleepily, just beginning to reestablish who and where he was, slowly reminding himself why there was a current of fear coursing through his veins. "Hmmph?"

Mei took that as an affirmative and opened the observation window. Raza rose to greet whatever fresh hell was waiting for him as the matte black panels dissolved to reveal the active sim. He steeled himself, ready as one could be for more horrible, screaming, raging madness. Instead, what they found was.... silence? Near silence, anyway. "What's wrong? Where..." For a brief moment Raza's heart stopped. *Fuck, the comm port! Did this sim manage to tear itself through the escape hatch?* He turned to Mei and saw her walking toward the back corner of the room, toward... *ah.*

There was the sim.

She was small. By Mei's calculation, she had experienced roughly three years of life including the ramp up and sharp ramp down time. Still, she was small for her age. Raza noted the ease with which he could think of her as *her.* Not *it.* She was in a squatted position, with one arm wrapped around her knees and the other angled downward. Raza rounded the corner to get closer and saw that Mei was squatted down next to her. The sim was idly drawing on the floor with its outstretched finger. She was humming a tuneless tune.

Mei's palm rested on the surface of The Box, separated from the face of the sim by the panel, twenty centimeters, and an enormous gulf between two realities.

Raza squatted next to her and still found himself towering over the tiny sim.

Mei cleared her throat and spoke quietly, as though not to disturb the child. "She's..."

"So small."

"No. She's perfect." Mei took a slow breath and held Raza's phone up to her lips.

"Hey, when did you—"

"I took it out of your pocket while you were asleep. Mikey's observation communicator was buried in the file he shared with you. I pulled it out and patched it to your SenZ's mic."

Raza opened his mouth only to shut it again.

"I know, I'm amazing. I never cease to impress you. Et cetera." She closed her eyes, took another long inhale, and pressed a button on a GUI that Raza didn't recognize. "Hi there, little one."

The sim jumped up in a panic and was frantically looking around for the source of the sudden interruption. Raza was reminded of a religious studies class he took in college. *What would one think if called upon by God? To hear a voice from the clouds? What faith must one have to trust the voice rather than immediately seek medical intervention?* The professor was a bit of a pompous ass, but his words stuck with Raza. His name, not so much.

"It's okay, it's okay," Mei reassured the trembling simulation as she squatted back down and wrapped herself into a tight ball of scrawny limbs. "We're here to help." She was making an effort to sound as calm and friendly as possible, though there was a tightness that she couldn't mask. Mei was worried that they were too late. She adjusted a setting in the GUI to apply a directional factor to voice input. To the sim, it would now seem as though the voice was coming from Mei's direction rather than from everywhere and nowhere at once. "We just want to help." The sim turned her head toward the direction of the voice, looking directly at Mei. Raza's heart shoved its way further up his throat. "We just want to help," Mei repeated, her voice now quieter and tighter than ever before.

The panicked short breaths of the sim began to slow and time slowed with her. After another minute or ten, she nodded, stood as tall as her diminutive frame would allow and spoke in a voice so small it took Raza a moment to understand.

"I'm scared."

CHAPTER 30
TRIAL DAY 4.5 - SOHVI

"Bíta á jaxlinn, Sohvi."

"Not now, Vilho. I need to think." Her voice was sharp, her head was throbbing, and she didn't have time for platitudes from the motherland. "You," she pointed at Dr. Kunihara, who until recently had been her favorite of the three jinhwa representatives. She had been reliable. Relatable. Reasonable. Now she'd blown the case sky high, and it was up to Sohvi to make sure it landed right-side-up. "No more lies. No more surprises. A few days ago you described your first SimEv as a little girl asking you for help. Now you tell me, the panel, and the *world* that it was a miserable, desperately suicidal, possibly *murderous* creature. Is *that* what you want to bestow rights upon? Is that why we're here?" She closed her eyes and took a deep breath, visualizing the energy transfer as her lungs expelled excess heat and cooled her from the inside. Upon opening her eyes, she saw that Drs. Mugabi and Zametti were staring at the floor and picking at fingernails, respectively. Mei, however, was standing as close as her belly would allow, reaching out with one arm to touch her on the shoulder.

"You're right, Sohvi. We've withheld certain truths from you in an effort to protect our tech. Or ourselves. Or the legacy of Mikey. I'm truly sorry." She released her soft grip and gestured to her codefendants. "Those two dingdongs are sorry as well. They just won't say so right now because Ard has self-imposed lockjaw and Raz is lost in the hellscape of his own head." Despite herself, Sohvi snorted at Mei's sudden brash turn. She seemed almost excited. If Sohvi had to guess, she'd say that Dr.

Kunihara was likely experiencing the euphoric relief of revealing a long-held secret. Unfortunately, that relief came with a heavy cost, and if they were not careful her revelation could drown the entire case. They needed a new strategy, and the clock was ticking. Audibly. How old were these damn clocks?

"I'm not looking for an apology, let alone three. Mei, I believe you to be smart enough to understand the position we're in. If we don't go back in there with a coherent message—"

"I believe I know who—"

"Frændi, please!" She didn't realize how loudly she had cut him off until she heard her voice echo back to her. It was enough to snap Arden and Raza to attention. "I... I'm sorry, Vilho." She turned to him and surveyed his gentle face. There was no sign of hurt in his eyes. They were, however, very present. Very alert. "We're short on time. What was it you were going to say?"

"I understand now who is behind all of this."

Arden was suddenly able to relax his jaw long enough to formulate a question. "What do you mean?"

"Since the first day of the trial, Ms. Egilsdottir and I have suspected that the conservative action group behind the prosecution may be acting under ulterior motives." Partially true, she thought. "Or perhaps that the group itself was merely a mask worn by unseen forces. The questions were too leading. The lawyer, Ms. Puri, far too keen. She has been strafing along the borders of the arguments we expected, all the while reshaping the perimeter. There was strategy *outside* the visible spectrum." Sohvi wanted to rush him along but held her breath for fear of sending him back into the fog. "Fortunately for us, our own misunderstandings about jinhwa's capabilities afforded us a certain degree of protection against exceedingly challenging oppositional forces."

A smug smile found the corners of Arden's lips. "Our intellectual property is sacrosanct, and—"

"That is not to say that you were in any way right or wise to withhold... 'certain truths'. Those incidental protections may prove more costly than you could imagine." Vilho dispelled the CEO's smugness as quickly as it came. "Now, I have been hunting for the forces behind the mask, and at long last I have them named."

Again, Sohvi felt a passing urge to rush him, but he seemed to be growing younger by the second, enjoying the drama and the thrill of the intellectual competition. "Tell me, Dr. Zametti, do you know why everything in the field of quantum computing is a 'company secret'? Why your industry, far more so than any other, has all but abandoned the centuries-old practice of securing inventor rights through patenting, instead relying on tight lips and gag orders?"

"I, umm. That's just how it's done."

"Yes, yes, that is how it is done *now*, but it was not always so. Before the quantum revolution. Before SenZero." Sohvi's pulse quickened. "Before SenZero became a household name, they were stealthily securing huge swaths of supposedly valueless intellectual property. When marginal advancements to quantum technologies were developed, SenZero's lawyers would be at the door within a week, strong-arming inventors into selling all claims to the innovation. And that, of course, was if you were lucky. More often than not, ownership was transferred under threat of legal action. They did not become a QC monopoly through scientific advancement, and all claims to the contrary are a revisionist history painted by the most well-funded marketing team the world has ever seen. They did so by pillaging academic and industry R&D labs before building a moat around the proprietary technology with a one-way drawbridge, always taking and never giving anything back. When quantum computers finally surpassed their silicon forebears, SenZero was there to stamp its name on the side of the box and reap the reward."

"You're saying that the conservative action group, the prosecution, is fucking *SenZero*? The biggest goddamn company on the planet?"

"I do not recall saying 'fucking' or 'goddamn', Dr. Mugabi, and if my accounting is correct you have incurred a twenty-five dollar debt to this 'curse purse' I have heard so much about. But, yes, you have understood me correctly." He looked worriedly at Sohvi. She could tell he was holding something back.

"Wait," Arden interrupted, "wouldn't we know if Jivanta was a SenZero lawyer?"

"She is not, at least not in any official capacity."

"Ms. Puri may not even know who she's working for." The room turned to Sohvi. "I mean, she's smart enough to put it together, but for legal reasons they'd be better off keeping their affiliation a secret, even from her." She was still studying Vilho, trying to read between the lines of his furrowed brow. He gave her a slight nod to indicate that they would talk more in private. "That would explain how we were able to catch her off guard. SenZero didn't let her know what she was dealing with. They were foolishly protecting their own interests to the detriment of their legal team." The last sentence wasn't strictly necessary, but she relished the opportunity to slap her infuriating clients on the wrist.

"Oh, uhhh," Dr. Mugabi mumbled as his hand darted toward his pocket. He pulled out his SenZ and dangled it between his fingertips as though it were a soiled napkin. "Can they...?"

"No," Mei answered. "I've reviewed the end-to-end encryption on these things myself. No backdoors. They couldn't eavesdrop on us through them even though they control both ends and everything in between."

"Right," Raza exhaled. "And, I suppose even if there *was* a way, jinhwa communication is internally encoded, not to mention air-gapped, Faraday-caged, the whole nine yards."

Mei raised her finger. "That's not to say there's no way they could know *anything* about what goes on behind our closed doors. There's always been dumb-tech."

"Dumb-tech?" Sohvi asked, despite her good sense not to.

"Like, a passive listening bug," Raza replied. "If someone drops a, I don't know chipped ink pen in one of our pockets, it listens but doesn't output any signal so it's basically invisible to our screening, and they pick it up later in the day or week or year to pull the log, and—"

"This is not some pulpy spy novel." Sohvi needed to get them back on track.

"Right." She was surprised to hear Arden agree with her for perhaps the first time since they met. "Occam's razor. We have a lot of former employees. They all have NDAs, but SenZero has all the money in the world."

"NDAs do often crumple under the promise of riches," Vilho concurred.

"Maybe they know more about the company than we realize, and maybe that's why they're going after you. However, any evidence or testimony obtained through breached NDAs, or through some silly Soviet-era spycraft for that matter, would be deemed inadmissible. Even just presenting it may be enough for the high council to call the prosecution's motives into question and get this whole case thrown out. SenZero is smart enough to know that."

"I wonder..." Mei was looking toward Dr. Zametti and pinching her lip. "Ard, I know you're going to flip your lid when you hear this, but please bear with me." She took a deep breath. "Mikey, at some point, was smuggling jinhwa data to the outside."

"What the f—"

"We can talk about it later, Ard." She turned back to Sohvi. "The night that Raz and I found the observation, the one that killed him, we found a comm line routed outside the building. We think... *I* think, when he realized the potential downsides of the tech, all the ways it could be misused, long before any of us saw what he saw, he got desperate for some outside help. Maybe it was SenZero. Maybe they offered some sort of protection for the SimEvs."

"An Ark!" Raza shouted, completely misreading the mood of the room. "That's what he was working on. In one of the diagrams from the whiteboard earlier, there was a line that seemed routed to nowhere. It was labeled 'ARK'. I thought it was just another hardware TLA. Three letter acronym, I mean. But I think it was just the *word*." His eyes were wide with realization. "And... there was a joke he made once, not long before he died... something like 'what do SenZero and Noah's Ark have in common.' I don't remember the punchline, but I think I know where his mind was at."

The ventilation in the room kicked on and Sohvi felt the chill creep up the back of her legs.

"And his last message," Mei added.

"Right! The jincrypted message he left me before he died. It was signed 'Mikus Ivanovic, Arkitect. *Ark*-tect. Spelled like—"

"They get it, Raz. So, Mikey must have seen this Ark as a way to escort the SimEvs, or at least Q-paired clones, outside of the building."

Four of them mulled it over while the fifth paced furiously on the other side of the room muttering sibilantly through clenched teeth. "Well," Sohvi said after a lull, "that explains SenZero's interest." All eyes were on her. Even Arden halted mid-circuit. "It's not that the prosecution doubts your technology. It's that they know very well what it's capable of. And they want it. Desperately." A mix of pride and fear painted the faces of her clients.

Vilho continued the line of reasoning, "And by the nature of the trial, we can assume that SenZero's intended use case may be thwarted by the establishment of certain rights and protections for your simulated beings."

The pride was now fully eclipsed by the fear. The largest, most powerful corporation on Earth (and *off* Earth—SenZero's name could be found on most tech in orbit, as well as any spaceship or rover that had been launched in the last fifteen years) was circling jinhwa with hunger in its eyes.

"I can guess the punchline," Mei said softly. "Well, maybe not Mikey's punchline, but one that fits all the same. SenZero isn't the Ark. They're the wrathful Old Testament God. What do SenZero and The Ark have in common? If you're not on board, if you're not worshiping the right deity, you're about to get wiped off the face of the Earth."

"And their Ark," Raza whispered. "It's not a lifeboat, like they must've promised Mikus it was. It's a slave ship."

"Can we drop the damn metaphors? What do you mean, 'slave ship'?" Arden's voice suggested that he knew exactly what Dr. Mugabi meant.

"Think about it. It's like the use case you and Mei originally described to me. Take a bunch of SimEvs, feed them a problem, hotbox them for years or decades or *millennia* of sim time, and see what shakes out."

"That would be torture," Mei added. "We saw it ourselves, we drove our first SimEv to madness. And *suicide.*"

"It's only torture if we win the case. Otherwise, SenZero or anyone else who manages to get ahold of a SimEv would have carte blanche to treat it like any other tool." Sohvi didn't have the time to mince words.

"Her. Not *it.*"

Sohvi could sense a rage building in Mei. Maybe she had protective instincts for this simulation. Maybe even maternal instincts. "Of course. Her." She looked at the oppressively loud and impossibly fast clock on the wall. "We need to get back out there. Think about SenZero. Think about what the robber barons want out of you and what you need to do to keep them from taking it. But keep in mind that they don't know what we know, and we may be able to use that to our advantage. Don't say a *goddamn* thing unless I tell you otherwise." She made eye contact with each of them and held it until they broke, one by one. "Go on, I need to have a quick word with Vilho." The three shared an uneasy look before making their way through the door.

Sohvi turned to her mentor to ask him what he was keeping quiet from their clients. Instead, what came out of her mouth was, "How long has this been going on? Your... lapsing?"

"Lapsing?"

Sohvi blanched. "I... I just thought..." She wasn't sure what she just thought, but the words spilled out all the same. "I started noticing little things with you in the early winter, around the time we took this case. Small mistakes that you never would've made before that grew larger and... and I'm asking if maybe there's more than just coincidence there." She was stumbling over her words as long-buried fears tore through her veil of frustration. "I'm asking if maybe someone, or some transnational megacorporation..." She blinked tears from her eyes and saw her friend, her Frændi, looking back with love and clarity.

"Sohvi, I—"

"Maybe they... there are slow acting poisons that produce symptoms similar to..." Her face was hot. Her cheeks were wet as her throat was dry.

He smiled warmly, waiting for her to take a breath. "You have done your research."

It wasn't a question, but Sohvi answered all the same. "I know it sounds foolish and conspiratorial, but the timeline—"

"Three years."

"Please just... three years?"

"Three years." He fidgeted. "You know I keep a journal."

Sohvi's mouthed a "yes" that was choked into silence. She stole an angry look at the clock on the wall, which had the audacity to tick-tock over their conversation. They still had a few more minutes together before they'd be called back into the session.

"For decades I maintained my journals religiously. Then, one day, around three years ago, I forgot to write my entry. A page left blank. A streak of perhaps twenty thousand days, broken." As he spoke, he ambled to the nearest seat and slowly sat down. "Upon realizing, I began looking back through my most recent entries and found many of them to be utterly *unfamiliar*. Written in a different tongue by a different man."

Sohvi made her way to the seat across from him. "Have you talked to anyone about it?"

"Not at first, for I am human, and we are a stubborn species." He looked at his veiny, rough hands as though ashamed. Sohvi took one in hers and encouraged him to continue. "Eventually I was able to set aside my vanity for long enough to seek professional guidance, and was told what I already knew to be true. For even with my waning reason I could not deny my blood."

"Vilho..."

"Alzheimer's." He squeezed her hand weakly. "One last heirloom from a lineage of Ragnarssons whose minds preceded their bodies across the Bifröst."

"God." Sohvi's ears burned bright. "I'm so sorry, Frændi. I feel so..."

"That being said, you were nearer to a frightening truth than you realize." He rose from his chair as he spoke. "Regarding the matter at hand, I withheld how I came to discover SenZero under the mask. I believe you meant to ask me why."

She hated the relief she felt for the change of subject. "Go on."

"Sohvi, it may be best if—"

"Now, Vilho. Please."

He didn't blink. "Two factors, really. The first being the panel's decision to admit the whiteboard as evidence. It struck me as *highly* out of character, though, sadly, character is malleable under the right conditions." He paused for a moment. "Few entities possess the resources to apply such pressures."

"Wonderful. You think SenZero has one of the panel members in their pocket?"

"Perhaps. Perhaps not. Perhaps more than one."

Sohvi didn't know what to say. "And the second factor?"

He sighed, the youthful glow in his eyes fading into worry. "I heard your phone buzz during the session, and I realized... who else would have the power to keep you in the dark before yesterday's bombing?"

"I don't understand what you're saying."

"I believe you do, but I will clarify nonetheless. I checked for any other possible explanation. No local outages, no solar activity, no inclement weather along comm paths. SenZero halted messages coming in and going out of your device. They tried to keep you out of the communication loop."

"Huh." She felt a strange and surprising sense of relief.

"I feared you would be much more upset by this news."

"Someone tried to kill me. I already knew that. All that changed is that now I know who my enemy is." She smiled. "And I know how to retaliate."

"How is that?"

"By winning this fucking case."

He smiled. "Þú skalt sýna þeim tvo heimana."
"You can say that again, Frændi."

CHAPTER 31
TRIAL DAY 4.6 - JIVANTA

When Ms. Egilsdottir called for her recess, Jivanta lowered her head, barreled through a crowd of reporters, and power-walked to the restroom on the far side of the building, resisting the growing urge to check over her shoulder until she made it to the door. Seeing nobody, she slipped inside, shot into a stall, and locked it shut behind her. In one less-than-fluid movement, she threw her backside into the seat and her face into her hands. Think, Jivanta. *Think*. She imagined that she could hear the idling engine of a blacker-than-black coupe parked just outside the courthouse. A paint job so aggressively, performatively inconspicuous that it stuck out like a sore thumb. She imagined she felt the eerily silent footsteps of their goon-in-chief reverberating up into her heels. Maybe if she spread her feet and concentrated, she could triangulate the position of these *probably* imagined footfalls. Dammit, Jivanta, think!

She was alone. She wasn't followed, though the ache in her knee trailed her by a few long strides and now rejoined her in the stall. The dull roar of pain was increasing in both pitch and volume as it crept noisily down her shin and up her thigh. Jivanta found the discomfort to be oddly grounding; the nice, familiar enemy distracted her from the more ominous and unpredictable enemies outside of her own body. She breathed two long, slow breaths and urged herself, more kindly this time, to *please* think, dammit.

Jivanta pulled her Lens from her bag and cast the hierarchical outline from her recent all-nighter into the space in front of her. "What the... oh. I doubt that very much." As her eyes refocused, she was able to separate a lewd (but not *not* amusing) bit of graffiti scribbled on the door from her own virtual text which hovered around it. She gestured to scroll, and scroll, and scroll, before growing impatient with the format. With a quick flick of her wrist, the outline reconstituted itself into a three-dimensional thought web. She inhaled, reached toward a densely populated cluster of arguments, grabbed the space with her fist, and discarded it. The rest of the notions slowly moved and expanded to fill the newly emptied volume. With an exhale, she reached for a second cluster and wrapped her fingers around another dozen notions, ripping them from the web and flinging them away with exaggerated force. Hours of brilliantly constructed, air-tight arguments, sent to degrade in the virtual compost bin. She repeated the process, hacking holes in the web chunk by chunk with increasing finesse. Her axe became a hatchet which became a paring knife which became a microscalpel until she was left with a web that could hardly be considered a web at all.

She allowed her eyes to refocus on the graffiti, one dash of coarse sugar before swallowing the bitter pill that was hovering in front of her sharp nose. A single notion and its paltry sub-notions. *Implications* and its two spindly, unsteady legs, *If I Win* and *If I Lose*. Now that it could no longer hide behind the litany of more practical, logical, and apparently losing points, it was impossible to ignore the consequences spelled out in this section of her web. These were her two paths forward, and she wasn't sure which destination was more horrifying.

The session will resume in five minutes. A cold, toneless voice reverberated through the building.

"Thank you, five," Jivanta muttered back. She gestured to collapse the thought web and removed her Lens. The ghost image of the visualization haunted her view for a few more seconds before she blinked it into oblivion.

Two paths. Both required wading deep into the sulfurous and unforgiving waters of fallacious speculation. Two outcomes. Both potentially devastating, following her speculative reasoning to their logical conclusions.

If I lose. If the panel decides that jinhwa can wrap their ill-conceived science experiment in the Declaration of Rights, what would that mean for the rest of the thinking, breathing, resource-using, *non-*simulated population? Not that the gerontocrats under the robes would live long enough to suffer the consequences of their decision. As a bonus, she wasn't so sure her Vantablack puppet masters would allow her to roam freely if she didn't deliver the outcome they desired. On the other hand...

If I win. If Jivanta *did* in fact deliver said puppet masters the verdict they wanted, she would walk out of the courtroom with the largest payout of her career by an order of magnitude. Her status as the premier intercon private prosecutor would be cemented and high-profile clients would fight for the privilege to retain her. She'd spend her remaining working years with her feet up on a desk carved from redwood. She could hire her own extremely large men in extremely large suits to keep others like them out of her fucking hotel room. Plus, the rest of humanity—the poor souls outside of the new law office she would build—wouldn't have to grapple with an influx of some new, highly-protected species of digital persons.

But they're not digital, she could hear jinhwa whining, *digital implies a binary encoding that differs from our own.* Of course. She knew that. These *things* jinhwa was making were something entirely new. Not human, exactly, but something upsettingly close. Something that could feel. Something that could *scream.* If she won, would she be condemning them to scream for eternity? And would she ever be able to drown out the sound?

CHAPTER 32
TRIAL DAY 4.7 - SOHVI

Sohvi Egilsdottir stood tall behind her seat at the bench. She hated this chair. It was all form over function. Aesthetics over ergonomics. It sat too low to the ground, perhaps a design choice by the high council to further humble those before them. Gripping its impractical wooden back between her long fingers, she directed her anger toward the panel and razed them one by one with a white-hot glare. She noted the three robes that were a second too quick to break eye contact. So, she reasoned, those three shared a master with the venerable Ms. Puri. A master whose vested interest in the outcome of this trial was apparently worth more than Sohvi's life.

Sohvi considered herself a realist. A pragmatist. She knew, rationally, that jinhwa's technology in the hands of a global superpower like SenZero could potentially do a world of good. Profit-driven good, but good nonetheless. What was one life weighed against such a prospect? But it wasn't just any old life. It was *her* life. She liked having it. And those bastards pulling the strings tried to take it from her.

She breathed deep as Hoffer welcomed the parties back into session. Exhaling fire through her nostrils, she wrote the names of the three suspected bought-and-paid-for judges onto a slip of paper and passed it to Vilho. He thought for a moment and nodded solemnly. Three rotten robes made for a stacked deck, but not a majority. They could still win. *She* could still win.

"Ms. Puri, you have the floor."

Oh. Right. In all her fury, Sohvi forgot that it was actually the prosecution's turn. She had no choice but to sit on that anger (the only cushion between her and this miserable chair) and wait for Jivanta's play. She grabbed her notes and awaited the pompous contralto. She waited, and waited, before finally the silence broke her concentration. Looking over, she saw a Jivanta Puri that she hardly recognized. It was the same woman, with the same impeccably crafted outfit, but there was something different about her. Something in her eyes. It was... indecision?

"Ms. Puri?" Hoffer urged.

"Right. Apologies, Your Honors." The prosecutor winced as she rose from her identically shitty chair. She slowly made her way around the table and toward the front of the room without taking her eyes off the ground. Her pupils rastered back and forth as though reading an invisible script carved into the flooring. Once she was centered in front of the panel, she paused for another painfully long moment before jerking her head around to look directly at Sohvi, whose breath caught in her throat. Again, there was something in Jivanta's eyes. Some message. What was it?

"It's not often that I am surprised." She looked around the room, perhaps noticing it for the first time. "I plan for a high degree of variability in the routes an argument may take. That's my job, as a prosecutor. It's my job to peer into the gray past and divide it neatly into truths and falsehoods." Her eyes had covered the room and landed back on Sohvi. "But this case has, several times now, gone places I... well." Again, she paused, carefully choosing her next words. "It appears that we find ourselves at a precipice. The defendants brought a claim that, no matter how unlikely or utterly impossible it seems, may contain some degree of truth."

Sohvi looked over to her clients. Drs. Mugabi and Zametti were suppressing grins, no doubt interpreting *some degree of truth* as a sure sign of victory. Dr. Kunihara was less certain, and was right to be suspicious. Where the hell was Ms. Puri going with this?

"With even just a nugget of a possibility that jinhwa's technology is deserving of the protections afforded under the UN Declaration of

Human Rights, we would be doing ourselves a disservice not to consider what could, and likely *would* devolve from that *decision.*"

And there it was. "Objection!" Sohvi leapt up and nearly tipped her awful, top-heavy chair over backwards. She hardly noticed as it rocked forward and kissed the backs of her knees before coming to a noisy halt. "Your Honors, let's nip this in the bud. Ms. Puri is setting herself up to spin speculative doom and gloom about a future that has no place in this hearing." She stopped, waiting for someone on the panel to sustain her objection. They held their tongues, so she loosed hers. "My clients made a claim about their technology and we are here to debate the merits of that claim. Please keep science fiction out of the courtroom." She heard the pleading, desperate tone that crept into her voice and cursed herself for it.

"I believe I mentioned a *precipice* a moment ago." Jivanta gave them the final push. "I'm merely suggesting that we peek over the edge before taking any giant leaps for humankind."

"It does seem that the unique circumstances of the case suggest a break from procedural tradition." Sohvi's ears burned hot as the Justice's words filtered through them. "Objection overruled. Ms. Puri, you may continue." Dammit. Sohvi barely restrained a sneer as she pulled her chair back under her.

"They are afraid." Vilho was leaning over and whispering as softly as his deep, gravelly voice would allow.

"Of what? SenZero?" Sohvi asked, trying to mask the sibilance.

"Ms. Puri gave them something greater to fear." He couldn't modulate his volume, so instead he cocked an eyebrow for emphasis. "Their own legacies."

Ah. Of course. Jivanta was good. *Very* good. She had communicated a message to the panel that Sohvi had missed but which they heard loudly and clearly. It was ultimately *their* decision, so whatever speculative dystopian slope she slipped down would have *their* names engraved on it. It was an appeal to their vanity. *Muck this up*, she said, *and your graves will be spit targets for generations.*

CHAPTER 33
8 MONTHS EARLIER, PART 1 - RAZA

"This is maybe the most embarrassing shit you've ever done, Raz. And that's saying a lot; I reviewed your code for *years*."

"Put two bucks in the curse purse." Raza rubbed the back of his neck to tamp down the goosebumps. Maybe this was a mistake.

"Arrrgh. Fine." Mei whipped out her SenZ with and typed with exaggerated flourish as she transferred two dollars from her personal account into the shared virtual piggy bank. "This is maybe the most embarrassing... *spit* you've ever done, Raz."

The goosebumps didn't budge. "I know, I know. I just thought, you know, I was going to have to scratch it off soon, and my new therapist says—"

"*New* therapist? As in *new* new?"

"The last one wasn't working out." The goosebumps pressed back. "Mmhmm."

"Anyway, I'm trying to be more honest with myself, and according to my *new* new therapist, 'it's difficult to be open and honest with oneself without behaving openly and honestly toward one's friends and family'."

"Oh no, is Dr. *New* New the type who refers to individuals as '*one*' a lot?"

Raza thought on it. Uh oh. It was possible for one to unknowingly adopt the vernacular of one's therapist into one's own inner monologue. "One couldn't say." He made a note to spend some time exorcizing that affectation from one's mind. No. *His* mind.

She laughed, one sharp gunshot of a cackle, and his goosebumps grew goosebumps. It wasn't that what he said was particularly funny. Did he accidentally vocalize the internal part? He didn't think so. She always seemed to have a cup and string held to his skull. It could be that, but, more likely, she was just uncomfortable. Raza knew Mei to be the type who laughed harder and more frequently when she was uncomfortable. One might describe this particular situation as very uncomfortable. He looked back over his shoulder toward the door.

"Don't worry, Ard's on babysitting duty," she said in response to his glance.

Raza turned his attention to her, hoping he could erase the discomfort as easily as he could erase the markings he'd carved in The Tree. The markings he'd coded into a hidden skin near the base of the visualization years ago. The markings he'd brought her here to show her.

The two of them stood near the middle of the auditorium with the evolutionary map projected upward from the central holo-column. Despite its name, The Tree didn't traditionally look much like a tree. It was more of a long, tangled web constructed by a crazed spider. Raza's hidden layer pulled the visualization more in line with its moniker. Instead of unremarkable lines and nodes, the system was wrapped in a skin resembling the bark of a redwood, all vertical grooves and ridges reaching toward the sky. Raza expanded the base to be two meters across with the crown branching up and disappearing into the high ceiling. He knew that if he reached into the trunk at around eye-level, he'd find a very special node. *Pikaia.* The node that brought him and Mei together. Mei was more focused on the skin surrounding the *Pikaia* node, where, years ago, lost in a fit of confusing feelings, he'd coded a message to be carved into bark.

"'MK + RM 4Ever'?"

"When you say it out loud, I can see how it could possibly be misconstrued as extremely embarrassing."

Mei uncrossed her arms. She turned to Raza with an impish grin. "*Mis*construed? Or just good old fashioned construed?" The discomfort dissipated and the space between them grew less chilly.

"Hey, it was a confusing time for us both."

She lowered her gaze in acknowledgement and then returned her eyes to The Tree. The enormous visualization cast a bluish hue over Mei's skin. The light caught her silicon earrings and refracted the spectrum into Raza's eyes. They weren't initializing any sims today, but the use cases for her lucky earrings had expanded to encompass a variety of milestones. "Why didn't you show me this at the time?"

"Well, it took longer than I expected to get the bark right. At first I wanted to evolve it from scratch. I thought I could maybe partition off a sliver of our comp space to cyanobacteria and drive it forward a few hundred million years until I got a sequoia. I got a bit lost in the world of paleobotany for a few months. Anyway, it turns out that, at least with our hardware at the time, running a sim in parallel but at differing rates would be—"

"Whoa, whoa, whoa, you wanted to hide one of the largest organisms to ever live? In The Box? For *this*?"

"You know how my brain works. Are you really that surprised?"

She rolled her eyes and shook her head, causing the earrings to scatter rainbows around the room. Raza thought of the God of the Old Testament, destroying his creation and sending a rainbow to say he wouldn't do it again. No matter, give your creation a few thousand years and they'll find a way to destroy themselves. When he blinked away the thought, he saw Mei looking at him, curious if a bit impatient.

"Right, well, I dug up some old 3D scans collected of the last known redwood before it came down and decided to just use those. So, we're looking at a replica of the Lonely Omega Pine."

"That's fascinating, truly, but it in no way answers my question."

Raza's avoidant tendencies were so strong that he often had a difficult time recalling what he was avoiding. It was a gift to be able to effectively hide something from oneself. Ugh. Hisself. Or is it *him*self? He clawed his way back to the origin of his tangent. "Right. Well, by the time I got the whole layer together and carved the message, things were... weird between us. Just kind of fading, without a real demarcation." He locked eyes with his shoes to avoid her gaze. "Anyway, here it is, a few years late. But, after all this time, I got what I wanted."

"What's that?"

"It made you laugh."

Mei snorted, depriving him of a second laugh. "*And* you get to check the 'honest with oneself' box for Dr. New New."

Raza shrugged. "Two birds."

"One birdbath." Mei put her hand into the holo-column of corrugated bark. "I feel a bit like Eve standing under this thing. Not that I need a sexy snake to convince me that knowledge is good and that God was just being a selfish... What's the charge for 'ass' again? Just one dollar, right?" She rotated her hand until the carving was cast onto her palm and she turned to Raza. "Don't erase it."

"Huh?"

"Don't erase it. It happened. It's part of The Tree. Part of life. I don't want to just scrub away every little blemish." She paused. "Something I've come to accept, after fighting it for years, is that mistakes are important." She idly rotated the visualization, creating the illusion that they were walking around its massive trunk. "You're an evolutionary biologist. What would happen if we went back and undid every accidental fuckup of our ancestors' DNA?" Without taking her eyes off Raza, she pulled her SenZ back out and moved five dollars into the curse purse.

Raza tilted his head and considered everything she'd just said. "Mutation is really the only tool biology has for climbing the tree." She nodded and waited. "Without those, um, *mistakes*... well, we'd still be wriggling around in the mud."

"Speaking of mistakes, where'd the beard go?"

It was Raza's turn to laugh. "Abbi said I should shave it."

"Do you do *everything* she tells you to do?"

"Pretty much," he grinned. "Yeah."

"Farewell, Eden," She smiled as she collapsed the visualization. "Come on, Adam. We have a birthday party to get to."

CHAPTER 34
TRIAL DAY 4.8 - JIVANTA

Jivanta Puri had a plan, or so she assured herself as she stood rigidly between the elevated desk of the panel and the body of the chamber. She'd made her first move, and, to her surprise, the panel allowed her to continue. Even Hoffer balked at her opportunity to sustain the defense's objection. She turned to the robes with a look intended to carry more than its fair share of information. Chief among the messages, *I'm trying to protect you from them.*

It was horseshit, of course, but the panel had a role to play, and she needed to feed them their lines without them realizing it. She recalled babysitting her nephew and hiding his allergy medicine between two heaps of kheer.

"Esteemed members of the high council, you are correct to see that the gravity of this decision warrants a look into what may come of it. What doors it may leave open." She turned to face the rest of the chamber. "I believe those following along will have the same questions, and while we may not be able to answer them, it's our duty to *ask.*"

Glancing toward the defendants' table, she made another effort to communicate her plan wordlessly. She was met with a glower that left her skin feeling prickly. That was fine. The panel could force their hand whether or not the defense was on board.

"Let's say we walk out of here today with a decision falling in favor of the defendants. Their simulation is granted all the protections afforded under the Declaration of Rights. With this singular, isolated simulation, the outcome of those protections may amount to little more than a curiosity. A footnote. It may bring up some interesting edge-case legal conundrums that would make for heated discussions amongst primary school debate teams, but there would be no change to *our* way of life." She ambled slowly back toward her desk for little reason other than to keep her knee mobile. "But it is safe to reason that jinhwa's... creation would not remain singular for long."

"Objection." Ms. Egilsdottir was back on her feet. "I'm sorry, Your Honors, but the prosecution is speculating on top of... speculative speculation." She was frustrated. That was good for Jivanta. "We can't—" Vilho subtly squeezed her hand. She leaned down to him and the two exchanged a few hushed words before Sohvi closed her eyes, smoothed her jacket, and sank back into her chair. "Withdrawn."

It seemed that The People's Viking still held sway over his protégé despite his worrying lapses in presence. Worrying? Jivanta caught herself briefly sympathizing with the aging attorney, for the first time seeing his apparent deterioration as more than just an exploitable weakness. She set the thought aside. Back to the plan.

"Perhaps it would be best to get an expert on the stand. Someone closer to the issue who can tighten the confidence intervals as we extrapolate into what lies ahead." Jivanta weighed her options before settling on the most obvious choice. "The prosecution calls *Dr.* Arden Zametti."

Jivanta had to give it to him, the embattled CEO continued to carry himself professionally. His mediterranean complexion masked the weight of exhaustion hanging from his eyelids, and, aside from the flexing of his jawline, his visage was that of a well-composed and earnest scientist-turned-businessperson. She gave him a moment to get situated. And one additional moment just for fun, to let him squirm a bit. She waited until she saw the slightest crack in his confidence before carrying on. "Dr. Zametti. As has been belabored, any testimonial from prior jinhwa employees will have been stricken from the record due to breaches in confidentiality." She was looking at Arden, but could sense Ms. Egilsdottir's muscles activating, ready to cut Jivanta's arm off at the elbow should she reach too far into the bag of inadmissible evidence. Not that there was anything of value *in* the bag. The ex-jinhwaians were a tight-lipped crew. "I'll continue to honor the panel's decision on that matter." A partial relaxing of the quadriceps was felt from Sohvi's direction. "However," thighs re-clenched, "I have approval from the panel to share one generalization gleaned from the interviews. Simply that jinhwa's goals— its mission—changed significantly in the last two years. Would you consider that an accurate assessment?"

"jinhwa has always been, first and foremost, a *Research* and development lab," he answered coolly. "R&d, with a capital 'R' and lower-case 'd'." These fucking guys and their lower-cases. "Long-term development toward any form of productization was always driven and directed by the research." This was a practiced response, surely one that he'd been selling to his investors. A comforting series of words that, strung together, conveyed absolutely nothing. Jivanta said as much by ignoring his statement altogether.

"So, jinhwa's long-term vision today is different than it was, say, three years ago. Yes or no."

By now, Dr. Zametti knew the drill. His skills in investor relations held no power here. "Yes."

Attaboy. "Sounds like things are still evolving over there. Pardon the pun." There was a nervous chuckle from the press booth that was masked with a fake cough.

"Yes."

"And jinhwa, your company, would be described as a *business*, is that correct?" She paused just long enough for Dr. Zametti to inhale before answering the question herself. "Of course it would. In every legal sense, jinhwa is classified as a private for-profit business, registered as an international LLC and paying corporate taxes within the state of Texas. At any point in the company's history, would its business model have been predicated on somehow *using* the sims?"

"I... our research—"

"Perhaps by exploiting your sim's human-like intelligence? For profit?"

Zametti answered with a glance to his bench and a weighty pause. No need to dwell. That guilt-ridden silence was all the panel needed to hear.

"But now, with the protections you seek, any work forced upon your creation would be in direct violation of the Declaration. So, this sim would be, what, a *volunteer employee*?"

"If she—"

"She?" Interesting.

Blood rushed to the capillaries in his taut neck. "If our creation chose to participate and contribute in jinhwa's growth, we would not deprive... him or her or them of that opportunity."

"And how exactly can she, or he, or they *volunteer* for the company that provides them with their very existence? That very literally controls what they eat and drink and do? That owns the infrastructure that allows them to simply *be*?"

"Isn't that just everyday capitalism?" Dr. Zametti was done holding his tongue, it seemed. "Relying on private companies for food, shelter, travel... that's nothing new."

"But to have all your needs consolidated down to a *single* corporation? It sounds a bit like all the failed company towns of yesteryear. Industrial paternalism. Choose to work for us, the people who own the bed where you sleep and the air that you breathe. Not much of a choice."

Ah, back to the silent treatment. "And speaking of choice," she continued, "You and your codefendants have argued for protections for your creation on the grounds of it having individuated consciousness, is that correct?"

"Yes, that is correct."

"Would it also be correct to say that *she* would just choose whatever choices you programmed her to make?"

"No. As we've explained, we're not *programming* her." He barely swallowed a 'dammit' at the end of the sentence. "She only learns from whatever we teach her."

Jivanta thought on that for a moment. "You teach the sim. You constrain what it can and can't do, can and can't see, guiding its choices with an unseen but very real hand, *your* hand, the hands of your programmers. How is that different from any other AI?"

"How is that different from a human child?"

"Interesting." Jivanta raised her eyebrow, playing the role, noting which parts of her weren't tied to the strings of her almighty overlords. "Very interesting." Now for a quick leap. She had a lot of ground to cover and was time-constrained by whichever panel-member had the thinnest patience or the smallest bladder. "Let's say your simulation was granted all the protections you're seeking. Life, liberty, security, the whole package. Now, let's say you, jinhwa, a private corporation took that individuated consciousness and copy-and-pasted it. Now—"

"We wouldn't, that's not—"

"You *wouldn't.*" Jivanta could see his discomfort growing from the jaw outward. "Is that to say that a copy-and-paste sim replication is theoretically possible?"

He looked toward his team and was met with shrugs and downcast eyes. "I wouldn't... I couldn't say for certain."

Jivanta smirked to herself. "Sure. But, theoretically, it would be much simpler than evolving a *whole new entity*, right? Would you then have two... *individuated* consciousnesses?" Jivanta paused. Dr. Zametti appeared to be mulling it over. She continued, "And why stop there? Why not copy-and-paste it hundreds of times? A single individuated consciousness, perfectly replicated, say, five hundred times. Would each of those clones deserve the same recognitions and privileges as the original?" Jivanta cast a glance toward the defense bench to confirm that they caught her verbiage. Clone rights had already been thoroughly litigated over the last twenty years, and the comparison fell in jinhwa's favor. She was offering them an argument that she hoped would strengthen her endgame.

"I suppose... consciousness would be considered individuated at the moment they were activated." Well said, Mr. Doctor. "Even if that activation was built on a copy... free will still exists within the system, and at that moment the two entities would diverge." He seemed satisfied with himself and his answer. If only he could see the invisible strings with which she was guiding him.

"And each of these entities would deserve rights?"

"Yes," he said confidently, still riding high from acing her last quiz. "I... believe so," he followed after a lengthy pause, with waning certainty.

"Including the right to, say, vote?" Jivanta fought the urge to look at the panel. Nobody else in the room had her restraint. All eyes and cameras were trained on the dusty old fossils. She imagined them cartoonishly tugging their collars and dabbing sweat from their wispy, age-spotted brows with one hand. With the other, pointing an ear trumpet toward the witness booth, awaiting Dr. Zametti's answer with bated, death-rattly breath. While the robes may have a hard time grasping the potential for technology-driven shifts in the way we all live, they could understand the implications in terms of more important matters. Like, say, who gets to keep their panel seat come next election cycle. Those seats were decidedly more comfortable than the wretched chairs reserved for the prosecution and defense teams, or so she had to assume, given how desperately the justices clung to them.

Again, Jivanta found herself pleasantly surprised with Dr. Zametti's restraint. He was intelligent enough to understand the import of his answer with respect to the decision makers seated to his right, and still, he chewed the question thoughtfully. "I... hmmm." Jivanta was ready to prod in the right direction, but he found the path on his own. "I suppose a government's primary purpose is to manage the allocation of necessities. Food, water, shelter, and the like." Nods from his codefendants encouraged him to keep going. "In our sim spaces, those resources are nearly limitless. That's not to say that government decisions couldn't impact them, but... perhaps to a lesser degree, or at least not in all the same ways."

A gold star for her sharp-dressed puppet. One more tug ought to get him to say what she needed him to say. But she had to be careful, her own puppet masters were watching and would be none too happy if they thought this was her idea. "So, would these sims exist as some sort of anarchic parastate? Just an internationally protected, ungovernable group of individuals that exist within our own society?"

"Your Honors, haven't we let this go on long enough?" Dammit, Sohvi, not now. "Dr. Zametti is here as a defendant and as a witness. He's not here to make wild guesses about a hypothetical future spun out of thin air by Ms. Puri."

Hoffer was on the verge of sustaining Sohvi's objection before Chebychev jumped in to rescue her. "Overruled, I'd like to hear the defendant's response, but Ms. Puri, I'm warning you to rein it in." The strawberry-nosed old fool did something useful for once. She saw him bury a smirk under his heavy cheek. He imagined his backers would see that as an effort worth their dollar. Oh, to be so smug and so wrong.

Dr. Zametti seemed hardly to notice the back-and-forth. His focus was held by the question of a sim society. "I think... I think it may be up to *them*." Jivanta's pulse quickened. He was almost there. "Today, we're talking about an individual, but Ms. Puri's right in suggesting that realistically, at some undetermined point in time, we'll go from one to two to five hundred to... millions. Why not? These individuals would coexist with us, but would exist on a fundamentally different plane. They should have the right to govern that plane, should they choose to do so. They should have that autonomy and sovereignty."

There. The words had been spoken. Jivanta had asked the questions she needed to ask, dutiful pawn that she was. And Dr. Zametti, dutiful-if-unwitting pawn that *he* was, had laid the foundation for a future the panel may be able to digest. A future in which a sim with rights would not pose a threat to their precious seats, *their* particular way of life. A future in which a sim could conceivably live a life with some semblance of protection against inhumane exploitation by transnational tech monopolies. A future in which, if nothing else, the sim's blood wouldn't be on her hands.

CHAPTER 35
8 MONTHS EARLIER, PART 2 - RAZA

Happy birthday
Happy birthday
We love you

The Vault was packed. Chest to back, shoulder to shoulder, they crowded together like pilgrims around the Kaaba. Raza wondered how many safety codes were currently being violated.

Happy birthday
And may all your
Dreams come true

Mei was to his left, and Arden to hers. Moments earlier, they had been arguing about The Vault door. Should it be left closed in order to maintain the integrity of the Faraday cage, or left open to accommodate the full suite of jinhwa employees? Mei won out, and now the company's less punctual or crowd-tolerant employees were peeking in through the open doorway.

When you blow out the candles
One light stays aglow

Arguing or not, they were now holding hands. Raza tried to focus his ears to determine whether Arden was actually singing or just mouthing words. An elbow to his ribs reminded him that he also wasn't singing out loud. He spent the next and final two lines closing in on (but never quite hitting) the right key.

It's the love light in your eyes
Where e'er you go

"Happy birthday!"

"Hurrah! Three cheers for the birthday girl!"

Three cheers and a few to spare filtered out into the clean room, followed shortly thereafter by the majority of employees once they'd shown their faces to the execs and checked this event off their company calendars. Raza noticed a few of them muttering and rolling their eyes. He was fairly certain he heard the words "self-indulgent prigs", in that order, as the hardware team returned to their stations in the basement and the rest stepped double-time toward the freight elevator. They weren't converted. Not yet. Who says "prigs" these days? Oh. Pricks. They said "pricks".

Raza made small talk with the stragglers. Some, Raza believed, were beginning to see the light in jinhwa's new direction (or, if nothing else, the darkness in the *other* direction). Others were just rubberneckers hoping for a glance of something exciting. Raza and Mei had never gone into great detail with anyone except Arden about what had happened with the prior iteration. It was necessary for the team to understand why certain changes were made, but they kept the description vague. Still, what they knew was enough to instill a morbid curiosity, and an open observation session was an opportunity for disaster. After another ten minutes, the fence-sitters and the looky-loos dispersed. Arden waited less than a moment after the last of them left before shutting the heavy door (eliciting a subtle eye roll from his fiancée), leaving just him, Raza, and Mei inside The Vault. And, of course, the birthday girl herself.

"See, I told you he'd shut it!" Mei had spent the bulk of the event crouched down on the side of The Box, whispering conspiratorially with Abbi. It was where they first met and had remained a favorite meetup spot.

Abbi's giggle was amplified around the room. "You knew! Who's... Uncle Razberry!" It was at that moment that Abbi saw Raza standing in front of the broad face of The Box. Or, more accurately, she saw the live image of him that was being projected on her side of the window. She couldn't *see* him. Many panes of coolant and the Ivanovic Reflection Mesh prevented any actual exchange of photons between his world and hers.

Still, across the barrier of jinhwa's hardware, there she was, looking right at him.

"Hiya, Abbri-Cadabri." There were no tricks Raza had to play to remember her name. It was always there, right in the forefront of his mind. As were her likes and dislikes. Her hopes and fears. Her favorite treats. "How's your honeycomb cake? What did you wish for?"

"I can't tell you!"

"You can't tell me if you like the cake? I made it myself!" It was true. He'd spent an inordinate amount of time coding the cake that was currently splitting its time between Abbi's face and her bare hands.

"No, I love my green cake!" Children, even those born of a simulation, punctuated their thoughts almost exclusively with exclamation marks. It infected the adults around them. She extended a fistful of simulated pandan in Raza's direction. "Do you want some? It's very green!"

In many coding languages, an exclamation mark meant "Not". He once told Abbi as much, and she said, "I don't care!"

He felt a side-eye from Arden, who had stepped closer to The Box. His position, between Raza and Mei, was surely a coincidence. "I'm full, but that's very considerate of you." She knew better, of course. The wall between them was as impermeable to cake as it was to photons. At this age, it was common for children to repeatedly test boundaries. Her boundaries were just more literal and unyielding than most.

"Mister Ard, did you sing?" Yeah *Ard*, did you?

Raza wasn't sure why he had the designation of *Uncle* while Arden was demoted to the lowly rank of *Mister*. Abbi apparently didn't acknowledge Arden's PhD, and Raza grinned at the thought of the two, the founder and his creation, arguing about the importance of the honorific.

"I sure did, little one."

He had to admit that Arden did very well with Abbi. Arden had been reticent at first. For the first month after introducing Abbi to the CEO of the company that created her, his interactions felt heavy and unnatural (not that the word 'natural' had any place in this discussion). But, in time, he eased into the position the three of them were sharing: the cobbled-together role of friend/teacher/guardian.

"Promise promise?"

In fact, the curse purse was Arden's idea. It was an unofficial company policy that he implemented the first time he heard Abbi say "goddammit" and he took it very seriously. It annoyed the... *snot* out of Raza, but he couldn't deny that it was an effective way of encouraging them all to be better people (or at least better-mannered people) for the sake of the little girl in The Box.

"Promise promise."

Nobody ever admitted to saying the word "goddammit" in front of Abbi. The possibility that it was a word she'd learned not from them, but rather from the violent data stream that defined the first three years of her life, was something they all chose not to acknowledge.

"The birthday song is my favorite. I'm glad the people left!" She spoke with the unfiltered honesty of childhood. "They make my head scream." And sometimes she said things that reminded Raza of the uniqueness of her circumstance. Or, hell, her entire existence. "Uncle Razberry, I dreamed I had cake forever!"

Raza smiled. She was just a normal kid. One who spent the first nearly-three years of her life in simulated solitary confinement. A normal kid who grew up surrounded by little more than a curated list of educational material centered around climate catastrophes. He felt sick to his stomach just thinking about it. It wasn't until Mei cleared her throat that he realized his smile had broken and he'd been adrift in a sea of guilt. "I've had that same dream, Ms. Cadabri!"

"Nuh uh, that's not true." Abbi scrunched up her tiny face.

"Why don't you believe me? I've had plenty of cake dreams."

"No, I had a cake dream. Aunt Meiflower said we can never be in the same place. So you couldn't be there in the dream."

He felt Mei's side-eye intersect with Arden's. They were all figuring this out together, and they all had different ideas regarding how to discuss Abbi's... *uniqueness*. Raza had what his many therapists had described as an *avoidant attachment style.* As such, he felt a strong inclination to tip-toe, deflect, and dodge.

"Dreams are different." Mei was very much *not* avoidant. "They happen entirely in your head." She tapped her finger to her crown. Abbi mimicked the gesture. "Everyone has entire worlds inside their heads. When you dream, you can explore those worlds. They don't always have the same rules that we have here. You may be able to fly, or eat a cake the size of a house."

"Or be in the same place as you and Uncle?"

Arden didn't like the direction the conversation was heading and felt the need to weigh in. "You may see people in a dream who look and act like me, or your Aunt Mei, or Dr. Mugabi, but it's important to know that those are just figments of your imagination."

Raza could sense Mei's pupils grazing the insides of her eyelids and figured now would be a great time for some good old fashioned avoidant behavior. A subject change. "So, Abbi Zabbi, what do you think of your new classmates?" To the chagrin of many of its employees, the bulk of jinhwa's engineering resources over the last year had gone toward supporting Abbi's existence. While the trio of Abbi's ersatz parents lacked any practical experience with children, it didn't take long for them to identify the glaring hole in her developmental toolkit: *Peers.* But how do you provide peers to the peerless? Mei and Raza refused to allow for any new SimEvs to be hotboxed in order to catch up with Abbi. It took some convincing, but Arden eventually agreed. That meant that any additional sims would need to be semi-empirically driven. They were approximations. *Rough* approximations. They pulled as much data as they could from Abbi's log and mapped them to the appropriate structures mined from prior iterations. This strategy took a coarse-grained (by their standards) toddler brain, fixed it with a few core tenets that could be loosely described as a personality, and they tried filling in the gaps themselves. Abbi could then interact with a small cohort of these lesser beings in a crude simulacrum of socialization. Results were mixed, to say the least.

"They're... fine." She was being nice. The brutal honesty of childhood was momentarily set aside for the delicacy and tact that comes from spending too much time with adults.

"Hmmm. Still weird?"

"Weird and wrong!" There was that toddler candor. "They don't know anything and they say the same stuff over and over and over." Argh. Raza's team had spent the last eight weeks working on differentiation schemes for Abbi's classmates, but they kept collapsing back into familiar cycles.

"I'll see what we can do about that." The problem was the source material. jinhwa had, after a decade of effort, evolved a simulated human brain. A *single* simulated human brain. They could make superficial tweaks, producing SimEvs of varying phenotypes, but Abbi was truly only their third run with this single brain, and only their second attempt at giving that brain information and purpose. The modifications being made to power Abbi's classmates weren't enough to make them unique. That, in combination with the coarseness of their structures, robbed them of any sense of individuated consciousness. Even Abbi saw right through them. *Weird and wrong. And soulless.*

~ ~ ~

Raza and Mei split the rest of the day between The Vault and their respective teams on the Second Floor. They coordinated their schedules such that Abbi was rarely alone. Arden would join the rotation when he could, but more often than not he was called into meetings with increasingly unhappy investors.

"That elevator is starting to feel like a gateway between two different babysitting jobs." Raza lowered his mask to his chin as he shut the door behind him. "I swear Abbi has a better sense of—"

"Hrmm." Raza followed the grumble around the left corner and found Mei curled up on Mikus's old cot. Her ESD jacket was wadded up under her head as a makeshift pillow and she slept facing the wall of The Box with her arm dangling off, touching the panel with the back of her hand. On the opposite side of the panel, curled up in a much tinier ball, was Abbi. Raza smiled to himself, removed his own ESD jacket, draped it over Mei, and lowered his body down to the floor. He rolled onto his back, enjoying the cool Faraday-painted tile against the thin cloth of his summer-wear shirt, and closed his eyes. He breathed deep, using the visualization practice he'd adopted to help him let go of the waking world.

Inhale, slowly and deeply. Concentrate on the sounds coming from your left. The low, barely audible hum from within The Box.

Exhale, deeply and slowly. Focus on those sounds coming from your right. Whirs from the mechanical temperature controls in the back of the room, echoing off the nearest wall.

Inhale, slowly and deeply. Isolate the sounds in the direction of your crown. Click-clacking of solenoids directing the push and pull of coolant.

Exhale, deeply and slowly. Zero in on the sound in the direction of your feet. Distorted voices, perhaps two hardware engineers arguing out in the cleanroom.

Inhale, slowly and deeply. Recognize the sound coming from in front of your face. Mei's breath, soft and steady.

Exhale, deeply and slowly. Name the sound behind your head. The thrumming of the foundation beneath the floor.

Inhale. Slower. Deeper. Focus on the sound within your own body. A slowing, comfortable heartbeat, in sync with the pulse of the building.

Exhale. Deeper. Slower. Listen to everything and nothing. Raza's mind latched onto the sound of nothingness and he managed to recognize his drifting off to sleep without getting in his own way. Maybe they'd all meet up for cake in Abbi's dream, he thought. The thought was interrupted by his next inhale. Or rather, the smell carried with it. There was a distinct change from the seared metallic and recycled, ozonated air of his previous inhales to something... sweet. Familiar. He felt a finger trace his naked jawline. He raised his eyebrows, then his eyelids. He wasn't in Abbi's dream. He was here, in the real world, in The Vault, with Mei—her face hovering an inch away—looking down at him.

CHAPTER 36
TRIAL DAY 5.0 - SOHVI

Maybe she should've rested the case, Sohvi thought for the hundredth time that morning. Yesterday's proceedings were called to an end earlier than she expected. The panel, probably mentally strained by the prosecution's departure from reality and venture into the realms of dystopian cyberpunk nonsense, signaled for closure while she and Vilho were conferring with their clients. They were in a good position. Jivanta's stunt had backfired, and the panel appeared satisfied with jinhwa's pitch for a free and productive (and, most importantly, non-threatening-to-the-judicial-power-structure) sim society. She could have ended things there. The panel would have deliberated over the night, and she could at this very moment be on a sunrise train to a hot spring someplace where she could scald away the grime that this last week had caked onto her pale skin.

She imagined herself, back against the craggy limestone, alone in a pool considered far too hot for the delicate tourists. *No*, she would tell the attendant sent to check on the strange woman who ignored the warnings and marched directly toward the most active and untamable spring, *I have everything I need.* He wouldn't understand, but he would leave her be. He *couldn't* understand. The boiling bath was more than just a spa package add-on. It was a portal back to her homeland, connected through the tendrils of magma reaching up through the earth's crust to bless the surface with a sacred enthalpy. Her nostrils full of sulfurous vapor, body and mind dissolving into the solution, only reconstituting herself at the end of the day, checking her SenZ to see messages from jinhwa and her friends, messages of gratitude and flattery. Messages about job offers. Media appearances. No, not her SenZ. She hastily edited her daydream, and now she was checking messages on an old satellite phone, running hot, slowly and inefficiently herding the congratulatory data through the binary of classical hardware and onto her imaginary screen.

With the word "binary" creeping its way into her fantasy, she felt the need to consider the alternative. Instead of words of praise, the figmental messages popping up on her fossil phone were words of ire. Condolences. Half-hearted *Keep your chin up*s and full-hearted *Fuck You*s.

Well, better not to dwell on it, she reminded herself for the hundredth time as thoughts of an unhappy outcome yanked her bodily from the hot springs and back into the cold hotel room. There was no way to know what would have happened. As Vilho used to say, it was time to wash her hands of that unknown, lest it sully her next meal.

It was then, as she was coming to terms with the unknowability (for the hundredth time), that she heard a discussion through the front door. Two familiar voices. One was the security guard stationed in the hallway. By the utterly inflectionless monotone, Sohvi identified him as Tito. She couldn't tell what he was saying (the door separating them held a remarkable material property of allowing for the sound of a voice to transmit virtually unattenuated, if not somehow amplified, but only after being stripped of all interpretability), though she imagined that she could detect growing frustration in his stony speech. Was it one of SenZero's fixers, out to finish her off before the case was settled? Perhaps. Her muscles tensed and she scanned the room for something blunt and heavy. The lamp by the bed? She could grab it, hide behind the door and bash the skull of whoever came through. But still, the voice... she knew it. She knew it *well*. Who did she know that could crack a man like Tito?

She took a step toward the acoustic anomaly that was her hotel room door to peek through the viewport. Before she could reach it, a knock, polite but urgent, forced her back toward the bed. Would a corporate hitman knock? Or hit*woman*, by the sound of it? She eyed the lamp and breathed once, twice, three times to steady her voice.

"Yes?"

There was a muffled monotone in response. So, Tito was still alive. That's good. Or was it? People could be bought. Hell, if High Court Justices could be bought, surely court-appointed security personnel could be bought, no matter how seemingly unflappable.

The knock came again, this time notably less polite. Sohvi peeled her gaze from the lamp and decided to approach the door unarmed. "I'm coming, I'm coming." Armed or not, she wasn't going to open the door without checking the viewport. Closing one eye and aiming the other into the lens, she saw the two figures standing on the other side. Tito, posing rigidly with a slightly pursed lip, positioned himself between the intruder and the door. The woman shifting impatiently over his shoulder wore a large, expensive-looking coat and sunglasses that deserved the same adjectives. Perhaps a feeble attempt at a disguise, but even with the fisheye lens distortion, Sohvi had no trouble recognizing her visitor.

"Ji—" She choked the word off mid-syllable in response to Jivanta's finger held firmly up to her tight lips. The universal signal for *don't say a goddamn word*. Before giving herself a chance to second guess, Sohvi unlocked the door and pulled it ajar. Tito stepped forward to fill the gap and utter some sort of apology or explanation before Jivanta elbowed her way through the traffic jam into the room. Sohvi had questions, a *lot* of them, but Jivanta's *shush* finger cast a powerful spell. Sohvi turned to Tito and nodded to say, "I can handle this." His eyes communicated his doubt, but he stepped back out of the room, nonetheless. Once the door was closed behind him, she turned to Jivanta and found her at the stationery desk scribbling a note.

Give me SenZ.

Sohvi raised an eyebrow and shrugged her shoulders in confusion. Jivanta held her hand to her ear and mimed passing an object. She pointed at the note again, removing her glasses in the process. Sohvi fished her SenZ out of her robe and extended it toward Jivanta, pausing midway to think about what in the hell was going on before completing the pass into Jivanta's hand. Or rather, the cuff of her jacket she used as a makeshift glove. She then placed the device on the desk, on top of a piece of glossy silver cloth that Sohvi didn't recognize. She must have set it there when

Sohvi had her back turned. Jivanta then delicately wrapped the device in the cloth and moved it over to a pillow. She eyed it like it was a rotten meal. Her nose wrinkled, her lip approaching a sneer. For a moment, Jivanta seemed to forget why she was here before shaking her head and turning back to Sohvi. "Is that the only SenZ in the room?"

"I... yes?"

"Are you certain?"

Sohvi swallowed. Her throat was dry. She imagined that this was what her clients must feel like when they were being cross-examined. Jivanta's gaze was withering. Still, this was *her* room. Withering gaze or not, Jivanta was clearly in a desperate position. Sohvi tried to remind herself of these facts in order to reset the power dynamic. It didn't work. "I'm certain. Yes."

"We don't have much time. They'll clock that your SenZ is offline. I left a false trail, but..." She checked the time on the wall. "Look, you're losing the case." Sohvi's eyebrow shot up again, but Jivanta preempted her response. "It's 7-4 in my favor. I was surprised too, but you're going to have to trust me on this."

Could that possibly be true? Most of the legal analysts in the media were calling it a done deal, saying that yesterday's session all but clenched the victory for the defense. Think pieces about our near future cohabitation with a sim society were already being published by the biggest intercon news outlets. Sohvi felt doubt and suspicion explode from within. Jivanta wasn't just professional opposition, she was working for *them*, the people that made an attempt on her life just two days ago. The doubt quickly boiled up and out of her mouth. "Why are you here? Why are you telling me this? Why should I believe a fucking word you say?"

Jivanta didn't blink, though she did, to Sohvi's eye, suddenly appear ever so slightly smaller. "Look, I'm not going to waste my breath or our *very limited* time telling you that there are bigger forces at play here. You're smart enough to have put that together on your own. Let's just say those forces have their fingers on the slow, arrhythmic pulse of the panel."

"Those are the same fingers pulling your strings, right? And signing your paychecks?" Sohvi spat.

"Yes." Again, Jivanta didn't blink, though she shrunk by another fraction of a percent. "But as you're well aware, you can sign a check with one hand and pull a trigger with another." Jivanta eyed the wadded up SenZ on the bed. Faraday cloth, Sohvi reasoned. "They're... not happy with me. I've done all I can for your case and—"

"What the hell have *you* done for *our* case? Ms. Puri, I don't know what you're—"

Jivanta raised her hand to silence Sohvi. The gesture itself was ineffective, but Sohvi's voice caught when she noticed that the hand itself was shaking like a leaf.

Jivanta spotted the tremble a moment after Sohvi and pulled her hand behind her back. "I've done all I can for your case, and will need to resume playing the part of a prosecutor puppet. But you *have* to win this fucking thing, Ms. Egilsdottir."

Sohvi couldn't believe what she was hearing, and her pot of doubt was bubbling up again. "Great, so your bosses have, what, found a way to screw us over even more if we win the case? They want us to win so... so... what?" She racked her brain for any logical explanation. "Would the source code have to go into the public domain? There must be precedent against holding proprietary code if it's ruled to grant *life*. Is that it?" Jivanta looked more curious than anything. "I'd argue... I'd argue that jinhwa's sim code is more comparable to genetic code, which belongs to the *individual*. How's that?"

Jivanta's eyebrows were raised and a slight smirk tugged on her lip. Sohvi's face grew hot. "Well?"

"It's always fascinating to hear a talented lawyer argue with herself." Sohvi's face grew hotter still. "I swear to you, on the life of my family, on my nephew, that I'm not here on *their* behalf." Jivanta's eyes razed the SenZ. "I have been assured that they will be 'most displeased' if jinhwa ekes out a win."

"So, what's in it for you?" She winced at her own cliche.

"Sohvi, make no mistake, if jinhwa loses, their tech will belong to SenZero within the year." Sohvi wanted to interject but found nothing to counter. "Sims will be mass produced. Farmed. They will be enslaved, brutalized, and tortured into productivity. You can't let that happen."

"So why don't *you* do something about it?" Sohvi asked defensively, knowing the answer.

"Because, in terms of me getting out of this little pickle with my life, there's a great distinction between you winning the case and me losing the case." Jivanta's knee buckled slightly and her lip curled. "At least, I hope so."

Sohvi chewed it over. She caught a glimpse of herself in the streaky window behind Jivanta and was embarrassed to see that she was mirroring the senior prosecutor's stance exactly. As naturally as she could (which is to say quite unnaturally, given Jivanta's cocked eyebrow) Sohvi shifted her weight and her arms to remove the reflective symmetry. The heat returned to her cheeks. "So, what? Did you come all this way just to tell me to keep doing my job?"

Jivanta pivoted to peer out the window. "That's half of it. Prior to my coming here, I expect that you were considering resting your case. Knowing what I know, if you were to rest your case, I'd be forced to do the same. In doing so, I'd win."

"Or so you say," Sohvi added, though her heart wasn't in it.

Jivanta recognized the impotency of the interruption and ignored it. "The other half is to remind you that you have an ace up your sleeve."

"I'm not sure what—"

"jinhwa has a witness whose testimony can and *should* be heard."

Sohvi blinked and the meaning resolved before her eyes. "I pitched that on day one. They didn't go for it then and they won't go for it now."

"*Make* them go for it. They have no other choice. *You* have no other choice. At least not one that I can see, and I'm very, very good at this." With that, she made her way slowly across the floor, past Sohvi, pausing at the door to call out over her shoulder. "Get a better room next time. You deserve it."

She shut the door and exchanged muffled pleasantries (or unpleasantries, as far as Sohvi could tell) with Tito. Jivanta's absence left

Sohvi feeling much more alone than she'd been prior to her arrival. Her room was smaller. Her lungs were smaller too, it seemed, given her shortness of breath. She darted to the bed, unwrapped her SenZ, and messaged the team. Four minutes later she grabbed her coat and stepped out into the hallway.

"Good morning, Tito."

"Good morning, Ms. Egilsdottir. Are you ready to—"

"Just a second!" She caught the door a moment before it closed, threw it open, dashed back to the bed, pocketed the Faraday cloth, and made it back before the spring hinge pulled it closed again. "Yes." She gripped the cloth tightly in her fist and smiled. "I'm ready."

CHAPTER 37
TRIAL DAY 5.1 - JIVANTA

Jivanta spied the Vantablack coupe in the public lot as she made her way up the steps to the rear entrance of the courthouse. The damn thing had been haunting her periphery for weeks and she still hadn't gotten used to the color. Even in the pearly light of the morning, the car's unnatural darkness allowed it to hide by virtue of confusing the senses. It would register in the visual cortex as a missing data block and the brain would fill in the gap with something more familiar, pulling averages from the surroundings.

At least that was how they advertised it. To be honest, if you were looking for it, it was hard to miss the big fucking void double-parked outside your window.

She didn't need to be able to see through the powdery matte windshield to know that she was being eyed in return. By all accounts, she should be terrified of these people. Last night they made an impressive show of force, hacking into her auton during her ride back to the hotel, blacking out the windows and rerouting it to a nondescript field on the outskirts of town.

It could hardly be considered hacking, argued the enormous man in the enormous suit, who was waiting for her in the field. *The auton's brain operates on our technology. It belongs to us. We simply reclaimed it.*

I somehow doubt 'unauthorized reclamation' is spelled out in the auton's terms of service, she responded.

You'd be surprised.

They were *highly displeased* with yesterday's session. Displeased, and more than a little suspicious of Jivanta's motivations. Fortunately, four decades of prosecution had given her the tools she needed to wriggle out of their open-air interrogation chamber.

She mirrored blame back to the accuser. *You gave me a destination and kept me in the dark and now you're upset that I didn't choose the path you preferred?*

She offered counter-explanations for her decisions. *With the information I was given, opening the topic of corporate control of right-bearing sims was an obvious strike against the defendants.*

She further deflected blame to those who weren't on the chopping block (and weren't present to defend themselves). *Dr. Zametti's idea for a self-governing society of sims was a baffling scramble. I don't buy it for a second and I doubt the panel did either.*

And, of course, without admitting to any wrongdoing, she capitulated and appealed for a second chance. *I can understand your concerns and will certainly reframe any discussion of corporate ownership or any other topics you deem... taboo, to mitigate the panel's aversion.*

Toward the end of the ordeal, the man rubbed his chin and admitted that the panel was still split in her favor. On the edge of audibility, or the tip of her imagination, she heard (or imagined) an angry voice in the ogre's earpiece. Maybe someone wasn't happy that he'd divulged that information. Or maybe she was just tired. He walked her back to the car, staying a step behind her and somehow managing to keep his bulk just out of her periphery. Was he going to plant a bullet into her brainstem? Was this step going to be her last? Or this one? Or would they use the auton, sending her off a bridge on her way back to town? No, she told herself, they weren't going to kill her. Not tonight, anyway. They needed her to finish the hearing. She fought against a chill creeping up her spine and forced it back down through her heels and into the earth as they arrived back at the dirt road. The suit stepped gingerly around her and opened the door to her auton, gesturing for her to get in. "Careful with your bad knee," he said, either sweetly or threateningly, depending on who was listening. As he shut the door behind her, she smiled coolly, reached over the driver seat, and shifted the auton out of self-driving mode.

Marching up the steps, trying to minimize the asymmetry of her gait so as to not show any weakness (perhaps overcorrecting to favor her bad knee), she wondered idly how much her puppet masters had spent on parking meters. Did they have a budget for this sort of thing? A per diem? Did they have to report their expenditures? "On Wednesday, after menacingly cracking my knuckles at a woman one third my size, I spent $120 at the meter, $83 at the charging station, and $28 on snacks to eat in the Goonmobile." Or, hell, the meters no doubt ran on SenZero tech, maybe they could just remotely wipe the system to avoid the inconvenience of paying. Did they get to keep the coupe during their off-hours? Maybe being a handler for the largest transnational corporation the world had ever known came with perks: a company car and free parking.

Jivanta observed the thoughts with curiosity. These assholes had gone to great lengths to frighten her into cooperation. And, sure, she'd certainly felt that fear over the last week, but right now she found herself... not exactly *un*afraid, but the concern for her life was reduced to a dull ache, one she could limp through, superseded by more pressing matters. For instance, ruminations on SenZero's corporate expense reporting policies for their hired guns. Smiling to herself, she opened the door and stepped into the courthouse.

CHAPTER 38
TRIAL DAY 5.2 - SOHVI

Vilho's name still counted for something.

When Sohvi made the proposition, following protocol and using the long chain of communication separating her from the panel, she was met with a "no" so quickly that she doubted the request ever actually made it from the lobby through the Justice Wing and into the ears of the high council. Sohvi turned to Vilho, who'd been in and out of a fog all morning, and saw a spark light in his eye. Without saying a word, he marched through the poor paralegal-turned-messenger and toward the Justices' offices, only breaking stride to offer a friendly greeting to the security guard manning the door to the hallway. The guard, whose sole responsibility was to prevent this sort of thing from happening, smiled and waved The People's Viking through the barricade.

Sohvi stood, befuddled, staring after him as he rode into battle. The paralegal stormed off in the opposite direction to make an angry call to someone up the ladder who would no doubt pass that message to someone further up the ladder and so on and so forth until the panel eventually heard about what was happening long after they witnessed it themselves. The guard gave her a shrug which she volleyed back before making her way to the far side of the lobby toward the marble benches. She chose the one sliver of bench catching a glancing blow from the morning light filtering through the window, but it was still uncommonly cold. The marble had been mined from deep within the earth, she reckoned a few decades ago at minimum, and still it refused to adjust to the temperature of the earth's surface, protesting assimilation and instead choosing to cool everything around it to its preferred subterranean clime. Form over function. What did the UN court system have against sitting?

Shivering, she reached for her SenZ as a nearly-involuntary force of habit before shoving it angrily back in her coat pocket. In the other pocket, her fingers gripped and pinched and twirled the Faraday cloth, hoping it could absorb stress as effectively as it absorbed EM radiation.

For fifteen minutes that felt closer to fifty, Sohvi sat alone on the icy white marble and twiddled her thumbs, feeling very much like she was waiting to be picked up from school, a feeling exacerbated by the fact that the man she waited for now and the man who picked her up from school had the unique pleasure of being one and the same. She cycled through a range of emotions to help pass the time. Anxious that her dear mentor would slip into a haze and embarrass himself in front of the most powerful tribunal on the planet. Relieved that she didn't have to make her case to them herself. Thankful that Vilho was finally throwing his weight around. But also irritated with him for choosing now to play the hero; she'd kept them swimming forward all week while he, the *leader*, had been more cinder block than buoy, and she resented any insinuation that she was the one who needed to be rescued. But of course, it wasn't a choice he was making. It was a choice his body was making for him. A mistake hardwired into his biology. Biology was an irrational force. Psychology, doubly so. Hence her ability to simultaneously *know* that he wasn't choosing when to wax and wane from reality and *feel* quite upset with him all the same.

It was then that she heard a tune echoing around the lobby. A tune she recognized. What was it? Something that reminded her of the smell of sod. And sulfur. And birch. And... Vilho came ambling out of the Justice chamber, preceded by the haunting melody he was whistling: a melody to ward off the wightbörn.

She sprang from the marble to meet him halfway and found herself moving so quickly as to meet him closer to five-sixths of the way. "Well?" Her heart was beating as she waited for his update.

He squinted up at the overhead lights, looking somewhat lost but smiling nonetheless.

"Vilho?"

He blinked at her, a fleeting moment of recognition pulled him from the trance of the fluorescent bulb. "Ah, yes." His grin widened. "They will allow it."

~ ~ ~

The truth, as is often the case, was more complicated.

"Early this morning, the panel was approached by a representative of the defense team. A request was submitted for the admission of one previously unheard-from witness."

Hoffer was several minutes into her introduction when the reveal of a potential new witness called the room to attention. Sohvi imagined that she could hear the heavy eyelids flinging open as the wandering minds snapped back to place themselves in the present.

"The request was duly denied."

Sohvi stole a glance at Ms. Puri. She was hardly recognizable from the woman who burst into her room a few short hours ago. Here she was polished to a mirror shine. No cracks were showing.

"For it was more than just a witness proposition. The mere acknowledgement of the candidate's legitimacy as a witness would, ipso facto, be an acknowledgment by this panel of the candidate's personhood, as only *persons* may be permitted on the witness stand."

Behind her she sensed pupils dilating, weight shifting, as the attendees registered her meaning. She took another look at Ms. Puri, who was doing a wonderful job of pretending the witness play wasn't her idea to begin with. Her eyebrows arched in response to the faux-revelation, and her visage took on its familiar smug superiority to convey her obvious pleasure at having the request denied. Damn, she was an excellent actor. What was she really thinking? Was she panicking? Sohvi had to admit that she took a *teensy* bit of pleasure in watching Jivanta squirm (well, not so much *watching* as *imagining*, because the squirming was nowhere near the mirror-shined surface).

"However." God, how Hoffer loved a long pause. Sohvi wondered how many people across the planet would be declared dead between the word 'however' and the rest of her sentence, should it ever come. Empires rose and fell, species evolved, reached critical mass and collapsed back in on themselves, universes birthed and dispersed to darkness, and then she continued. "An appeal was then made to submit the candidate not as a witness, but instead as *evidence.*"

Jivanta huffed, though Sohvi felt that the expelled air masked a sigh of relief.

"Given the allowances for a mid-trial introduction of new evidence by the prosecution," Hoffer eyed Ms. Puri, daring a challenge, "the panel agreed to make a comparable allowance for the defense."

Hoffer allowed the swell of murmurs to grow and fade on its own accord. "Personally, I will find it to be a great relief to actually *meet* this... *sim*, before deciding its fate. But I digress. Court is now in session. Mr. Ragnarsson. Ms. Egilsdottir. You have the floor."

Sohvi rose to her feet and took three steps away from the bench before stopping and turning back to Vilho. It wasn't that she needed his permission. Nothing of the sort. She had been managing the case since the opening remarks, and she was going to bring it to a close. It wasn't even a professional courtesy. It was purely personal. A check-in, friend to friend. "I've got this," she told him with a nod. "I know," he responded with a smile.

She made her way to the front of the room. It had been less than a week since she first found herself standing at the foot of the high council. Could it possibly have been only four days ago? To be fair, they were the longest four days of her life. Four days ago, she felt a strong urge to wilt under the spotlight. Now she looked out at the room, into the cameras, into the eyes of the world of people tuning in to watch one of the rare "trials of the century" that may actually live up to the name, and knew that she belonged here. The spotlight burned bright, even brighter and hotter than on that first day, and it felt good on her skin.

She turned to the panel. "Thank you, Justice Hoffer, for the introduction." From her vantage point Sohvi could just barely see the gray top of the petite old judge's head peeking over the tall bench. Turning back to the room, she projected her voice, easily finding the volume she had calibrated on the first day of the trial. "From the moment Mr. Ragnarsson and I first met with jinhwa, they were adamant about keeping their technology out of the courtroom. To be frank, I was... skeptical of this strategy." She heard a chuckle behind her. She knew a few members of the panel enjoyed the occasional personal touches. A few others hated it. She didn't care.

"I understand the nature of product and intellectual property protection in this day and age, but, as Carl Sagan said, extraordinary claims require extraordinary evidence. Or, as my colleague Mr. Ragnarsson likes to put it, 'in proof's absence, doubt flourishes as darkness after sunset'. My skepticism of the strategy grew to skepticism of their claims as a whole. Only very recently did I begin to understand jinhwa's stance. It was never just about protecting their technology. While we're all here to debate the *humanness* of their creation, to them that matter has long since been decided. This sim is, to them, already family. Already human, or at least something of identical capacity for intellect and moral agency. And, at that, a *child.*"

The din of murmurs swelled and receded in response to this juicy detail with clock-like predictability and precision.

"Their decision was not a machination of corporate trade secrecy, at least not at its core. More importantly, it wasn't their own interests they were protecting. Knowing that, my skepticism waned. But it was not just me who needed to be convinced. So, without further ado, let's get on with the truly extraordinary evidence." To her right, she saw Jivanta smirking and knew that her point had been made. *Points* really. Sohvi had set about laying the groundwork with two primary messages to convey.

1. *Here's a relatable and very human explanation for my client's unwillingness to present the subject of their claims.*
2. *Now that they ARE going to present the subject... go easy on her.*

Sohvi laughed to herself as the public and reporters rubber-necked toward the entrance. Did they expect some sort of hologram to phase through chamber doors? "Of course, as has been established, the sim is physically constrained within the confines of her hardware, which is currently secured at an undisclosed location for her own protection." The disappointed murmur, which had its own distinct waveform unique from the juicy-detail murmur or the dramatic-reveal murmur, spiked and trailed with at least one audible 'aww'. "We have set up a comm link which will allow us to see and communicate with the sim in real time." A near-perfect inverse of the disappointment murmur propagated outward from the onlookers. "Dr. Kunihara flew there this morning to assist with the setup and to act in a sort of... parental support role during the presentation."

Jivanta was on her feet. "Objection, Your Honors, surely Ms. Egilsdottir can't be suggesting that Dr. Kunihara will be allowed to *actively tamper* with this evidence as it's being presented."

"Trust me, Ms. Puri, this matter has already been thoroughly debated amongst the panel," Chebychev grumbled, leaving visible footprints behind to show his SenZero benefactors exactly where he stood on the issue.

With a withering side-eye, Hoffer finished her colleague's sentiment. "It has been debated, and decided. We are deep into uncharted territory, precedentially speaking, and we ultimately agreed that certain concessions must be made in order for us to advance toward an *informed* verdict." Jivanta scowled appropriately. "Objection overruled."

"Thank you, Your Honors." Sohvi gestured to project the comm video onto the large display wall behind and to the right of the witness stand. A blurred image appeared on the screen before a brief moment of auto-focusing smoothed the edges around Dr. Kunihara. The comm vid was designed such that Mei appeared very nearly life-size, and with the interplay of the wide lens and the parallactic screen, the angle into Mei's room shifted with the position of the observer. The effect of the display was quite striking, appearing as though Mei and her crowded lab of snaking coils and blinking lights were cut into the wall of the courthouse. Good, Sohvi thought. Distance and walls could only further alienate their evidence in the eyes of the panel, but the quality of the illusion may help shorten that distance.

Mei smiled. "Good morning, Sohvi." With a hand on her belly, she sat slowly into a chair positioned next to a large matte-black screen.

Sohvi felt a fleeting pang of jealousy, for Mei's chair looked significantly more comfortable than the varnished deathtrap she'd be returning to during the cross-examination. The selfish pang pulsed from deep within her selfish lizard brain and was quickly modulated into the somewhat less selfish pang of embarrassment as it filtered toward the more developed and tactful layers of her mind. Why hadn't she thought to procure a more comfortable chair for her exceedingly pregnant client? The pang reached her ears, reddening them ever so slightly. "Good morning, Dr. Kunihara."

Mei tilted her head.

"*Mei.* Apologies for rushing you off-site this morning. Your travels were uneventful, I hope?" Sohvi felt a strong urge to drag her feet. The longer she could exchange pleasantries with Dr. Kunihara, the more she could delay the reveal of jinhwa's purported lifeform. But, why delay? If her clients were to be believed, unveiling the sim could solidify their case and *humanize* their technology in the eyes of the world. If anything, she should be rushing through the introduction. Her hesitation came from somewhere outside the confines of the courtroom. Somewhere deep within herself, where her notions of life and existence and whatever-squishy-thing she considered to be a *soul* were about to be tried.

Again, Mei just tilted her head slightly. Forward, this time. Sohvi understood. Mei of course knew that the less she talked, the stronger the case would be for the autonomy of their sim.

"Right." Sohvi took the cue, set aside her own qualms, and stepped toward the screen. "Well then, now is as good a time as any. Let's meet the *evidence.*"

Mei turned a dial and the boxy screen resolved from a hazy black rectangle into a small, toddler-sized... toddler. Sohvi's jaw slackened. She was taken aback by the clarity and texture of the being in The Box. What was she expecting? A shadowy, monochrome, two-dimensional person-shape? This was very much not that. Sohvi's hesitations melted as she knew the panel was seeing and feeling the same things that she was. This was a *person.* A person in a box. A person worth protecting. A person... very distracted by her toes.

"Abbi?" Mei spoke softly, tugging gently on the attention of the tiny person. "These are the people I was telling you about." The sim shrugged and kept her focus on her toes. "Don't you want to say hi?" Abbi shook her head furtively and Mei sighed, looking back up to Sohvi.

"Well," Chebychev boomed, "does your experiment think itself too *important* for the court?"

"Recognition of one's own importance is itself a fairly human trait," Hoffer retorted. "Overestimating one's own importance, even more so. Would you not agree, Fedor?" Chebychev pretended not to hear her, though the flushing of his cheeks betrayed him. Hoffer continued, "However, I do not believe what we are witnessing is the insolence of conceit. But rather, another emotion potentially indicative of a higher functioning being. Shyness." She turned to the illusion projected onto the wall. "Is that correct, Dr. Kunihara?"

"Quite right, Your Honor," Mei answered.

"That's understandable." Sohvi softened her tone, hoping to draw the shy toddler away from her feet, but she didn't budge. "I imagine this is a very unfamiliar and discomfiting experience, as it would be for anyone her age." Still nothing. Sohvi turned to the panel. "It's ironic, isn't it? Trying to force her to do something she doesn't want to do, all in an effort to make the case that she shouldn't be forced to do things she doesn't want to do."

"Irony notwithstanding, the fact remains that if this evidence exists to guide us toward a more *informed* verdict, it will need to provide us with *information*," Chebychev responded coldly. "I suggest you turn what dials need to be turned in order to... engage the evidence, or we will have no choice but to cut the comm and proceed without—"

"Uncle Razberry! Mister Ard!"

Chebychev's mouth hung ajar as a child's voice echoed off the rafters. All eyes turned from the panel to the projection, where Abbi had sprung from her squat and now stood as tall as her small frame would allow, pressed up against the court-facing side of her strange cage of screens. Mei muttered an apology about the volume and made an adjustment. Nobody noticed. The collective attention of the courtroom was entirely focused on the girl in The Box. She no longer seemed to notice the eyes of the world on her, all of her shyness evaporated and blown away with the capricious winds of childhood. She scrunched up her face.

"Uncle Razberry, why are you dressed like Mister Ard? You look funny."

Sohvi turned and saw Dr. Mugabi mirroring Abbi's scrunched face, making an easy (if not fully appropriate) transition from defendant to uncle. "Abbri-Cadabri! They make everyone dress like Mister Ard in this place." He tugged on his tie and rolled his eyes theatrically, which delighted the small girl behind the window.

"It's actually *my* suit," Dr. Zametti added. He too transformed his demeanor, though less dramatically than his codefendant. "Your silly Uncle Raza left his on the train."

Raza made another face that Sohvi suspected was only partially for Abbi's entertainment. The professional and interpersonal politics of her three clients were complicated to say the least, and she'd made an effort to keep her distance. The looks shared between the two men behind her bench and the woman seated to her left (though hundreds of miles away) were loaded with subtext that Sohvi wanted nothing to do with. Instead, she saw Uncle Razberry née Raza Mugabi as a way in. She adjusted her face and tone to match his. "Dr. Razberry, could you introduce me to your friend?"

He followed her lead. "Of course, Ms. Sohvi. Abbi?" The girl looked back down at her toes, the spell broken. "Abbi, I want you to meet my friend Ms. Sohvi. She's a good person and she wants to help us keep you safe."

Abbi mumbled a soft hello to her feet. She looked up to Dr. Kunihara who nodded encouragingly, not as a scientist presenting her data but more like a mother telling her child that *this particular stranger could be trusted*. Could she? How do people communicate with kids? What do children even like? Sohvi's experience with children was limited. Children were annoyances on international flights. Children were excuses friends gave for disappearing from society into the exclusionary club of domesticity. She tried to recall her own childhood, her own wants, but then hers was far from typical. Well, if their lives were plotted along an axis of normalcy, Abbi's was even further from the hump of the bell curve. And yet there was commonality between them. Suddenly a strategy popped into her head. She knew what children wanted. All children, even those effectively orphaned by climate catastrophes, even those built of entangled qubits, wanted more than anything *not* to be children.

"Good morning, Miss Abbi. You seem like a mature adult!" The girl's glance shifted inch-wise from her own feet to Sohvi's. "Grown-up to grown-up, do you want to play a game so we can get to know each other better?" The glance shifted up to Sohvi's knees.

"What kinda game?"

"It's called Favorites. You can ask me about anything, like, say, a color, and I'll tell you my favorite and least favorite thing in that category. Then I'll ask you. We can go back and forth like that until we know everything about each other and then we'll be friends. And peers."

The glance crept up and met Sohvi's eye. Abbi pursed her lips as she thought it over. "Ok." Sohvi felt a warmth followed shortly by a chill creeping up her spine. "You first."

"Of course!" Sohvi fought the urge to look around the room. For now, she and Abbi were the only two people in the world. "Food. What's your favorite and least favorite?"

"Green cake!" Abbi shouted. "Uncle Razberry makes green cake."

"Yum! What does it taste like?"

"It's sweet. And sticky. And crunchy."

"Wow, that sounds—"

"I can taste the green. Green tastes like blue but better and more yellowy."

"I... yum!" Sohvi masked the worried look in her eye. She needed Abbi to present herself as recognizably, irrefutably human, and *not* an artificial (and legally unprotectable) intelligence. Tasting colors wasn't exactly a relatable sensation. Well, sometimes children said things that didn't exactly describe the human experience. "What's your least favorite food?"

"I eat vitamins that taste bad."

Why did a simulation need vitamins? That was the question in Sohvi's mind, but what came out of her mouth was, "What do you want to be when you get big?"

Abbi squinted. "That's now how the game goes."

She wasn't going to make this easy, was she. "Ah, good catch! You're a natural."

"What's your favorite smell?"

"Sulfur," Sohvi answered so quickly that she surprised herself. "Sulfur... and dirt." Was there something about talking to a child that allowed for the more rigid fences of her mind to open their gates? "Not just any dirt, of course. A very specific dirt, from a very specific patch of land a few thousand miles northeast of here. They remind me of... good things."

"I know sulfur! I like dirt too. What's your worst smell?"

Sohvi laughed. "Hmmm. Great question! You really are good at this game." The child was beaming with pride. Sohvi had an easy answer to the question, but fortunately it was one that didn't escape her mouth before she was able to trap it. That, of course, was the dark, twisted cousin of the earth smell that she loved so very much: Death and decay. It was a smell most people her age and older would remember, and it wasn't the sort of thing you dropped on a toddler. But then, this was no ordinary toddler, and she had reason beyond the naivety of youth for not grasping the concept of death. Sohvi thought it best to avoid the topic. So, instead, she said "Rotten fish" and Abbi said "Yuck!" and they giggled.

The game went back and forth in that fashion, the two of them scratching the surface of each other's interests, gaining trust and cutting the distance between them. Sohvi knew that she had a greater mission here, to present Abbi as a creature with a depth of thought and moral agency deserving of the embrace of legal rights, but she was in no hurry. The panel and the prosecution had been quiet since Abbi first spoke. Sohvi took their silence as a good sign, and before long she forgot them entirely. At some point she felt a chill on her backside and only then did she realize that she was sitting on the floor by the projected image. The physical barriers and the distance melted away. Sohvi could believe that if she scooted forward she could hold the child's hand. She could reach through the screen and the cinder blocks behind it, reach through the miles and miles between them. Reach through the technological marvel that walled Abbi's existence. Then a voice pulled her back to reality.

"Your Honors, I think this has gone on long enough." Ms. Puri's eyes carried half-a-dozen emotions that Sohvi couldn't begin to untangle. "I feel the need to object for lack of relevance."

"And I feel inclined to sustain." Hoffer checked with the rest of the panel and was met with either slight nods or blank stares. She pivoted in her high seat to face Mei, Abbi, and Sohvi. Mei didn't budge from her own chair, and Abbi was preoccupied by spinning around in circles, both unfazed by any norms of courtroom decorum. Sohvi, on the other hand, feeling quite embarrassed under Hoffer's gaze to be sitting cross-legged on the floor of the High Court, shot to her feet and smoothed the back of her suit. "While this exercise has not been without merit, and a certain amount of charm, I fear we are no closer to answering the greater question as to the moral agency and legal *personhood* of this... evidence."

"Your Honor," Sohvi started, without knowing where the rest of the sentence would take her. She looked over to the evidence, still spinning and pretending not to hear the two grown-ups (not that she wasn't a grown-up herself, thank you very much) discussing matters of life and law. "I understand the objection, but... we're dealing with a *child* here." She looked around for a sympathetic eye on the panel and was left wanting.

"One might argue that the behaviors of childhood are the simplest comportment for an artificial intelligence to imitate," Chebychev added, unhelpfully.

Her ears darkened and she felt her pulse in her throat. "How would you ask a, what, four-year-old to verify their capacity for... conceptualizing morality?" She heard her voice reflect cleanly off the wood of the panel before tacking on a perfunctory "Your Honor."

The wiry purple capillaries on his nose shone prominently, his nostrils flaring as he inhaled Sohvi's perceived impudence. "I reckon the onus is on *you* to answer that question, Counselor Egilsdottir."

"I have an idea." Jivanta's voice stopped Sohvi short of saying something regrettable. "If the panel and defense would allow it."

Hoffer looked from Jivanta to Sohvi. "I will leave it up to the defendants. Counselor?"

"I..." She could trust Jivanta, right? Didn't they want the same outcome? But what if the prosecutor's mind had been swayed? What if her instincts for self-preservation outweighed the motives that brought her to Sohvi's hotel room that morning? What if SenZero caught her on her way out the door and changed her mind? Or, hell, what if the entire thing had been a calculated manipulation? Ms. Puri was more than capable... What would Vilho do? She turned to the bench in search of her mentor and instead found a specter. His body was there but his mind far away, having receded into the mist. The People's Viking would not be showing up any time soon to rescue her. She was alone. Unless... "I will allow Ms. Puri to explore her idea."

"Thank you, Ms. Egils—"

"On the condition that I will stay right here. I have not yielded my time with the evidence. I will cut her off mid-sentence if necessary should she try anything... untoward."

"—dottir." Ms. Puri blinked inscrutably. "Of course."

337

CHAPTER 39
TRIAL DAY 5.3 - JIVANTA

Jivanta Puri stepped gingerly toward the disturbingly realistic projection on the wall, being mindful not to surprise the temperamental creature behind the screen or the equally temperamental nerves behind her patella. The sim was pretending not to notice her approaching, and doing so quite skillfully. Jivanta glanced at Dr. Kunihara and received a look that communicated the phrase "try anything funny and I'll leap through this projection and tear your fucking heart out" more effectively than the words "try anything funny and I'll leap through this projection and tear your fucking heart out". Jivanta was inclined to believe her, pregnancy and geography notwithstanding. She pivoted her gaze to Sohvi and was met with an only-marginally-less-scorching glare. Fine. She couldn't blame them, or so she told herself, all the while being quite irritated with them both. When playing N dimensional chess against opponents who were playing $N-1$ dimensional chess, they were blind to your movements in the Nth dimension. That was the whole idea. And still, she needed them to work with her on this plane if she wanted to get out of this game alive. "Can you introduce me to your friend?" she asked Ms. Egilsdottir with the cloying bounciness in her voice that was reserved for children, animals, and mockery.

Sohvi hesitated, thinking it over one last time before agreeing to play along. "Hi, Miss Abbi?" The sim made no acknowledgement. "I'd like you to meet my... my *friend*. This is Ms. Puri."

"You can call me Auntie Jiva. That's what my nephew named me when he was about your age!"

If Abbi heard her at all she did a great job of being utterly unaffected. Auntie Jiva persevered. "Actually, when he was your age, there was a game he made up. A fun game with lots of thinking and imagination. Even better than Ms. Sohvi's game, if you ask me."

Ms. Egilsdottir rolled her eyes but didn't interrupt Jivanta's flow. Good. She'd earned at least a little bit of her trust. The sim didn't look her way, but at least she stopped spinning around in circles. Chebychev cleared his throat and inhaled, ready to replace the sterile air with his bad breath and worse ideas. Jivanta didn't give him the chance. "Ms. Sohvi and I could play first so you can get the hang of it. What do you say?"

The sim gave a tiny shrug. One small shrug for a collection of qubits in a box a thousand miles away, one giant leap for Jivanta's efforts to wrangle some cooperation out of said collection of qubits. "Wonderful! So, the game goes like this. I'll name a time, either in the past or in the future, and Ms. Sohvi can describe what she thinks she was doing or will be doing at that time. If she doesn't remember or if she can't predict the future, she can just make her best guess. How does that—"

"Can she be silly?"

Jivanta froze. The sim was addressing *her*. It was making eye contact in a way no child ever did, at least not any child she had ever encountered. Her voice caught in her throat, but she was able to pry it loose before Abbi noticed (she hoped). "Of course! That's part of the fun."

"Ok, you first!"

Goosebumps crept across Jivanta's skin and she beat them back with sheer willpower. "Gladly!" She peeled her gaze from Abbi's with a sense of relief. "Ms. Sohvi. Let's say... 9 in the morning on today's date, thirty years ago."

Ms. Egilsdottir put her finger to her chin, giving it some real thought, glancing over toward the withered old Viking behind her bench and smiled to herself. "I was almost certainly arguing with my uncle about the proper way to eat skyr while dumping it onto a bowl of sugary breakfast cereal."

Jivanta laughed and stole a furtive glance at the sim. "Where would this be?"

340

"Back home. In Iceland."

"Beautiful country! Now, how about, say, five years ago?"

Sohvi's sharp eyes muddied in the middle distance as she refocused on the timeline of her life. "Prepping for a case. Having the same argument with the same person."

"And where were you this time?"

"Hmmm. In the States. I can't remember where exactly. Somewhere very dry."

"Ah." Jivanta, who had a spectacular memory and had read the defending attorney's entire litigation history as part of her own prep, knew that the *somewhere very dry* was Yuma, Arizona and the case in question, after a masterful argument from Ragnarsson, restructured the way the UN classified water needs. "And how about five years from now?"

Ms. Egilsdottir's lips pursed as she began to see exactly where Jivanta was leading her. All Jivanta could do was hope she'd follow willingly; like it or not, their paths were entangled and resistance from the defense could collapse the road before them. "Well, extrapolating on the apparent trend, I suppose I may be continuing the argument." Her eyes darted quickly back to her bench, ostensibly running a brief calculation. Another extrapolation perhaps involving the declining presence of her mentor. "Though, perhaps not in person."

"Some arguments, even the trivial ones, seem to stay with us until our dying breaths, it seems," Jivanta pondered aloud, preparing Ms. Egilsdottir for the next question. "How about, say, two hundred years from now?"

"Ms. Puri, I'm not sure—"

Jivanta cut her off. "Ms. Egilsdottir, would you not agree that moral agency, an understanding of right and wrong and an acknowledgement of one's own ethical roles and responsibilities, requires a certain awareness of our... impermanence? I realize this question would be more at home in a philosophy classroom than the courthouse, but this is one of those rare times that a high-minded hypothetical gets pulled into the world of the literal and must therefore be legislated. So I insist on asking." She pitched her voice back into the cadence and timbre modified for the young

341

audience. "What do you think you will be doing in two hundred years? Where might you be? Arguing with your uncle about yogurt?"

A surprising cackle of a laugh escaped from Abbi's box and bounced around the room. "She got you!" The child, which Jivanta kept needing to remind herself was just a *projection* of a *projection* of a *projection* of a child, was pointing at Ms. Egilsdottir with a wicked grin. She couldn't possibly have any idea what the exchange was about, but she could tell by Auntie Jiva's voice and Ms. Sohvi's frown that someone had won, and of course the loser had to be laughed at. Ah, children. Amoral little monsters at the best of times. "Now ask me!"

"Gladly!" Jivanta gritted her teeth as she turned back to the sim, squatting down to get herself aligned with that distinctly unchildlike stare. "Now, Miss Abbi." Jivanta put on a faux-serious face. Competition was a universal language that even toddlers understood. It went hand-in-hand with a sense of play. Kids could fight and socialize, putting them on par with the cleverest invertebrates. She was using both as tools in building the bridge between herself and Abbi. "What were you doing... hmmm... exactly two years ago?"

"I don't know!" Abbi cackled again and Auntie Jiva laughed along with her.

"Well, you can make something up, Miss Abbi!" The laugh was only partially false. The truthful component was a breath of relief. Honestly, Jivanta didn't know what to expect from her question. An infallible memory of infancy would have certainly dehumanized Abbi. Not being able to answer her question was much more relatable.

The sim made a face Jivanta couldn't read. Odd. Children are usually the most transparent, having not yet built up the layers of masks that come with adulthood. Perhaps that wasn't always the case for projections of projections of projections of children. "That was before they found me. I don't remember much from before."

"That's—"

"It was dark and the whole world kept dying."

Again Jivanta repelled the goosebumps as they marched across her flesh. "Oh! Umm." Better to just ignore that last bit, she decided. "That's okay! Let's try something more recent. How about one month ago?"

"Oh! Singing songs. We sing songs every single day. Even when Mister Ard is on a plane he will call and sing."

"How nice!" Jivanta looked over her shoulder in time to see jinhwa's hot-headed leader blush before turning back to Abbi. "And, may I ask *where* you were?"

"Ummm. Here." Abbi scrunched her face, dissatisfied with the question, or perhaps her own answer.

"How about next week?"

Her face un-scrunched. "Singing songs again!"

"That sounds lovely. Where do you think you'll be?"

The little face re-scrunched. "Here!"

"Are you always 'here'? Is there anywhere else you want to go?"

Abbi looked over to her Aunt Mei for support.

"Her space is variable," Mei offered, and continued when nobody objected to her interjection. "The world Abbi occupies is obviously much larger than the volume of The Box. It moves with her. As far as her experience goes, it's boundless."

"Ah. That makes sense." Jivanta returned her attention to the game. "Okay, Miss Abbi, you're doing very well. Dare I say even better than Ms. Sohvi? You are a natural!" The words reflected off the projection back into her ears, slightly warped by the material of the screen. *You are unnatural.* "So Miss Abbi, for all the marbles. What will you be doing two hundred years from today?"

"Singing songs! With Aunt Mei and Mister Ard and Uncle Razberry." She giggled, thrilled to have won the game. "You can come too, Auntie Jiva!" The goosebumps made one final charge up her back and planted their flag deep in her crown.

CHAPTER 40
TRIAL DAY 5.4 - SOHVI

"Your Honors, Ms. Puri, I understand that you're trying to gauge the... gauge her grasp on the concept of *death*, but what you seem to be forgetting is that she's a *child*."

"Which is why I took such a roundabout path, Ms. Egilsdottir."

"It's not the delicacy of your approach that I'm finding fault with." Goddammit. Sohvi could feel her throat tightening, redirecting pressure in the form of stabbing pins behind her brows. Why did she let herself trust Jivanta? God*dammit*. "It's the entire premise!" She looked to the panel and found far too few sympathetic eyes. "A kid wouldn't know about—"

"Dr. Kunihara," Chebychev interrupted, addressing the projection. "Let's cut to the chase. Can this sim die?" He was staring down his purple lump of a nose at Mei. "Or is it immortal?"

Mei opened her mouth to speak but no words came out. She looked over to the bench, to the fellow guardians of their shared ward. Abbi, meanwhile, was trying to do a somersault.

Chebychev followed Mei's line of sight, passing right through a rapidly deflating Sohvi. "Maybe you could answer the question, Dr. Zametti. It is your company, after all."

Dr. Zametti's lips (and teeth) were sealed. He looked pleadingly at Sohvi, who mirrored his pleading gaze and reflected it toward Vilho. If ever there was a time for his sword to come out, now was that time. Vilho, however, made no motion to speak. Instead, it was Dr. Mugabi who decided to open his mouth. "She can be injured just like you or I can."

Any other time and Sohvi's legal instincts would have silenced Raza. Not only was he not answering Chebychev's question, he was offering extraneous information which would prove at best inert (and more likely harmful to the case). This time, however, she did nothing. She could feel defeat closing its grip around her. Squeezing her throat. Stabbing the backs of her eyes. Defeat at the hands of people who nearly turned her into a pile of shrapnel and gore, a red stain to be power washed into the storm gutter. She felt nauseated. And exhausted. So, completely exhausted.

"We initially padded her environment against that sort of thing." With nobody to pump the brakes, Raza continued. "But we figured getting scabby knees is part of growing up, you know? It wasn't an easy decision. We're her parents, really. We just want to protect her, same as any parent."

"Dr. Mugabi," Chebychev interjected with his stentorian bellow. "Judging by your codefendants' silence and your non-answer, I think we have the information we need, but this is a courthouse and we would much prefer a straight response. Is *that*," he cast a sausage finger toward Abbi, "immortal? *It* may not know, sure, if we accept that it has an existential awareness on par with its childish look. But undoubtedly *you* know the answer."

"I..." Dr. Mugabi's hands fidgeted and sweat beaded on every visible patch of skin. "Yes. Of course." His voice cracked as it gave way to desperation. "What other option do we have?!" Again, Sohvi recognized the opportunity to intervene, to stop her clearly emotional client from speaking out of turn, and simply didn't. "We created her. We can control every aspect of her life. She is her own person, but she lives in a world fully defined by us. Would you have us define a world that *kills* her?"

Chebychev's massive cheeks creased in an approximation of a smile. "And how can we be expected to extend protections to something that cannot die?"

"She can still be seriously hurt!" Mei spoke from the comfortable chair. "Physically *and* psychologically. And so she could still be..."

"Dr. Kunihara, Dr. Mugabi." Oh, thank God, Sohvi thought. Maybe Hoffer would offer them a lifeline. "I must agree with my colleague here." Fuck. "It's not purely philosophical, but precedential. The immortality of traditional AI has been established as a mark against its moral agency, and it applies here."

Hoffer conferred nonverbally with the rest of the panel. No words were spoken but the message was clear. She was ready to call for a closing of the case, after which they would recede to their barracks to deliberate. She knew if they left the room now they'd come back in an hour with a verdict that would crush jinhwa's claims and leave no wiggle room for appeal.

Sohvi could feel herself disappearing. She took one last look at Vilho, her guardian turned mentor turned ghost. He was staring at the table as though it was the only solid substance in the universe. Staring *through* the table, really. It was impossible that this man could just this morning have charmed a room of charmless justices. Utterly impossible. She heard his voice, clear and strong in her head. *Inspiration finds the oddest occasions to knock, does it not?*

"Wait." Sohvi's mind was racing. She started speaking before her thoughts had caught up with her mouth. "Dr. Mugabi was right."

"I was?"

"Yes. Shut up for a second. Dr. Mugabi was right. Scabbing knees *is* part of growing up. It's part of being human. Unfortunately, so is dying." She locked eyes with Hoffer. "Awareness that you could be killed at any odd moment. Maybe by a rogue auton." She shifted her gaze to Chebychev. "Or an IED." She turned back to her bench. "Or a degenerative neurological disorder." She looked out into the public seating. "Or by our beautiful, vindictive planet." Finally she looked down the barrel of a news camera, playing it up for the folks at home. "For most of us, it'll nothing so dramatic. When our days inevitably run out, there will be nothing to blame except for the most *natural* of causes, *time.*" She braced for an interruption and it came right on cue, this time from Dr. Zametti.

"Ms. Egilsdottir, while we have the ability to force death, even... *untimely* death into the system, what kind of monsters would we be to do so?"

347

"A god not unlike our own, I'd say. But what I propose is not that you force death into your system. But rather, leave the path open for *them*, should they choose it."

"Why on Earth would they choose such a fate?" asked Ms. Puri, in what had apparently just become an open forum.

"Because of the alternative!" Sohvi's voice was raised and she made no effort to quell it. "Immortality minus the protections we seek here today will be a living, truly inescapable hell."

"Now, Ms. Egilsdottir, that's not—"

"We all know the realities of the world we inhabit, and we know how quickly individuals, like Abbi here, will be exploited in the name of profit. Pardon the interruption, Your Honor, but if eternal life is the dealbreaker for protections under the umbrella of human rights, a sim may prefer a mortal but protected existence. A decision could be made once a certain level of maturity—as deemed by the court—is reached. A decision made *by the sim*."

"But... it's still *us* giving her the option." Dr. Mugabi was looking at Abbi through the eyes of a father.

"I understand your hesitation, Dr. Mugabi, really." It was a lie, of course. How could she possibly understand? She wasn't asking him to kill what was effectively his daughter, but she *was* asking him to leave a loaded gun in the house that he'd built to keep her safe. The pain on his face was too much to bear, and Sohvi couldn't bring herself to look at Mei, so instead she fixed her gaze on the panel. Hoffer leaned forward, pressed her palms onto the wooden surface, and slowly rose to her feet. The stretching of her dry tendons was the only sound, followed by a long, long silence. Finally, she spoke.

"I have often wondered why God would bother to plant the Tree of Knowledge in the Garden of Eden. A rather cruel choice, it always seemed to me. But then, God is a reflection of his creation. Or vice versa, if you are so inclined." Her pale eyes pierced Sohvi's skull. "Moral agency presupposes fallibility, and fallibility is nothing without consequence." She turned to face the projection on the wall, gesturing toward its contents with the veiny, frail hand of justice. "The defense's introduction of this new evidence has me nothing short of convinced as to the human-like qualities of the technology." She was speaking softly, and by the look of it, she was now speaking directly to Abbi. "Imposing limitations on such a being is, frankly, cruel... a cruel but necessary requirement for satisfying the legal definitions of personhood." Sohvi could barely hear Hoffer over the lub-dubbing of her own heart, which triangulated its position to somewhere between the back of her throat and just behind her eyes. "Ms. Egilsdottir's proposition for conditional protections, on the basis of a decision *made by the individual in question,* assuming adequate understanding of the mortal consequences of said decision, is... a satisfactory compromise."

Sohvi felt the room spin and put her hand on the witness bench for support. *I did it,* she thought as she avoided the eyes of her clients.

As tears traced Arden's jaw.

As Raza buried his face in his hands.

As a quiet sob escaped from the display wall, barely audible over Abbi's happy humming.

We won.

~ ~ ~

Of course, it wasn't quite over. Hours later, after arguing specifics of the compromise and the formalities and the final verdict and the half-hearted reading of a quarter-hearted dissenting opinion, and another hour (or two? Who could tell?) of media interviews, Sohvi was on a train.

"Where are we going?"

"I found a hot spring spa, Frændi. An hour's ride from here."

Against her better judgment, she opened her SenZ and saw that a number of her contacts had forwarded her the same video. She cast it into her Lens and took a deep breath as she watched Jivanta Puri address a newsroom. The question was inaudible, and probably irrelevant.

I'll tell you what I'm afraid of. I fear that not long from now, it'll be us *begging* them *for protections.*

Sohvi flung her headset into her bag, turning to the window and seeing her mentor's reflection.

349

"Ahhhh. Hot springs. What bounty she gives!" He reclined his seat and hummed a song to quell the wightbörn as they both drifted off to sleep.

CHAPTER 41
8 MONTHS EARLIER, PART 3 - RAZA

He was vaguely aware that he was dreaming as he tip-toed toward Abbi. She was crouched and facing away. There were no barriers between them. He should be excited, he should be running toward her to scoop her up in his arms and squeeze her, but with the distorted logic of the dream world he felt only fear. Something was wrong. His legs were impossibly heavy, each step moved mountains. The air grew hazy with ash. A wave crashed against his knees and a scream he knew to be his mother's pierced his eardrums. He gasped for breath, searching for a voice to warn Abbi, and found none. Suddenly she stood, taller than sense should allow, and turned to face him. Her cheeks were torn, flesh hung like rags. She smiled.

Raza Mugabi awoke with a start in a tangle of ESD jackets. He turned to the cot and found it empty.

"There's so much *bad* in my dreams."

Raza yelped in response and rolled over, hitting his funny bone against the cot and wincing in pain. Abbi laughed at all of it. Children could be cruel.

"What do you mean?" Raza smoothed his hair as he hastily gowned up, clumsily donning his booties, smock, bouffant, and a smile. "What about your cake dreams? Those sure seem nice."

"I have cake dreams, and I have dreams about the other things that are in here with me."

"What other—"

"But sometimes I have dreams about... about *your* world and it's bad. Bad, bad, bad."

"What do you mean?" Raza glanced toward the door of The Vault.

"I saw it. Before you and Aunt Mei. I saw it all. It was burning. And it was drowning." She looked him in the eye and he couldn't resist the urge to turn away. "It's still in my dreams."

"I'm... I'm so sorry." He didn't know what else to say.

"Wanna know my birthday wish?!"

Raza breathed a sigh of relief, thankful for the mercurial mind of childhood. "Are you sure you want to tell me? It's supposed to be a secret!"

"I know YOUR secrets!" She giggled.

"I..." Raza glanced at the empty cot as cold sweat pooled in his gown. "Yes, I do want to know your birthday wish!" His smile cracked, his exclamation mark more false than ever.

"I want to meet your bad world!"

ad finem

Acknowledgements

Is it too hack to thank the reader right out of the gate? Who cares, hack is in. Hack is back. Hack is *good. Hacks* is good, too. Y'all seen *Hacks?* *Hacks* on *Max?* What if instead of thanking you, the reader, I just gave a lengthy recommendation for the TV show *Hacks?* Maybe I'll save that for my next book. For now, I want to say, sincerely, thank you for reading my novel. Or, hell, maybe you skipped the story and went straight to the acknowledgements. If that's what you did, thank *you* as well! It takes guts to read a self-published debut from some no-name dipshit. Reading a NYT bestseller is easy, but you, you brilliant adventurer, you thumb your nose at *easy.* You took the road less traveled and that makes you better than everyone else. Three cheers to you!

But enough about you, let me extend my thanks to the wonderful people that helped me get *ab initio* into your hands.

Dr. Sandya Quince and I have been shooting the shit about sci-fi and fantasy comics, novels, TV shows, and movies for the better part of a decade. It was only fitting that she was the first person to read my manuscript and share her insights with me. I'm lucky enough to get to call Sandya my Dungeon Master, and even luckier to get to call her my friend.

Dr. Katie Nunnery is a legitimate literary scholar who reads more than anyone I know. Naturally, I place an extremely high value on her opinions and suggestions. Katie's crackerjack criticism and warm encouragement helped push me to finally publish this darn thing.

At times, reading Dr. Avery Green's comments in the margins of the manuscript reminded me of the classic "Reviewer #2" feedback from my days trying to publish academic articles in science journals. That said, his insistence on maintaining some sense of technical believability and thematic consistency kept the book from running off the rails.

Dr. Daniel Terracina (wow, everyone in my life is extremely educated, huh?), being the slightly older cousin who introduced a young me to things like

Star Wars and *Animorphs*, is largely responsible for my fascination with science fiction. And, I know what you're thinking. You're thinking, "*Star Wars* isn't even sci-fi, it's fantasy in space". Man, shut *up*. Really? C'mon. This isn't the time or place. I'm just trying to thank some folks. Is that cool? Ok, thank *you*. Anyway, chatting with my cousin about this book while pacing the aisles of a bookstore in Santa Cruz was a damn delight. Cousins are the best, aren't they? Let's give it up for cousins!

Vicki Greer, editor extraordinaire, fought her way tooth and nail through all the spelling mistakes, punctuation gaffes, grammatical faux pas, logical inconsistencies, and structural instabilities I'd generously peppered throughout my manuscript. Any goofs remaining in this book exist because either I was too stubborn to change something she flagged or because I continued to tweak things after she and I agreed to *finalize* the final draft (sorry Vicki!).

Once upon a time, not long ago, I had the gall to try to make my own book cover. I took a day off work to cast a plaster brain, paint it, then smash it with a hammer before photographing it next to a cheap gavel on my bookshelf. It was a valiant effort, but the end result was... not great. Thank goodness I found Jason Gurley. Jason was able to make into art things I couldn't even make into *words*. Hire artists, guys.

For well over a year, my lovely wife Aurora Terracina listened to me prattle on as I wrestled with this story. We'd go on long, slow walks around Hidden Villa or through the hills (often carrying our not-quite-small-enough-to-comfortably-carry dog who'd decide that the return trip was simply too much for her) and I'd yak and yak about the characters and the ideas and various plot knots I was tripping over. Lucky for me, Aurora doesn't do anything passively. Whenever I'd start to get self-conscious and doubt that she was paying attention, she'd cut to the quick with an incisive and thoughtful take, or a clever question that reframed all the arguments I was having with myself. I want to say that I hope everyone can find someone like Aurora, but there simply is no one like Aurora.

The dog wasn't the only thing Aurora was carrying during those treks. Our son was born around the time I started my final read-through, and the little guy was kind enough to nap in my arms while I picked my way through the text one last time. What a good sport.

Finally, I want to thank Jean Smart. It's just always great to see her in stuff. America loves ya, Jean!

About The Author

Born and raised on the bayous of Louisiana, Jacob is now a PhD engineer working as a materials scientist in the heart of Silicon Valley. When he's not building and breaking human-machine interfaces, he's strolling the neighborhood with his wife, dog, and baby, or hanging out with the goats at Hidden Villa.

His other works include "Computational investigation of stoichiometric effects, binding site heterogeneities, and selectivities of molecularly imprinted polymers", which was named 2016's Steamiest Beach-Read by *Nobody Said This Magazine*, as well as its 2018 follow-up, "In silico characterization of enantioselective molecularly imprinted binding sites", considered by many to be even more narrowly-focused and alienating than the first! His latest publication, the ominously titled "Human-Machine Interface System" (U.S. Patent Number US20230266829A1) is as dry as it is legally protective.